Through Three

Red Binding –
Jan Minkowski

Praise for
The True Story of Hansel and Gretel

"A provocative transformation of the classic fairy tale into a haunting survival story . . . darkly enchanting. . . . No reader who picks up this inspiring novel will put it down until the final pages." —*Publishers Weekly*

"It's the scariest of all fairy tales, and it's retold here with gripping realism. . . . The Grimms' story is always there like a dark shadow intensifying the drama as the searing narrative transforms the old archetypes." —*Booklist*

"Purely imaginative . . . The witch Hansel and Gretel find in the woods is a marvelously drawn old crone . . . who takes them in and shelters them. . . . [Murphy's] characters speak to us with terrible prescience." —*The New York Times Book Review*

"Filled with the breathtaking, sometimes death-defying contortions of war." —*Los Angeles Times*

"Unusually gripping . . . Lyrical, haunting, unforget-table." —*Kirkus Reviews* (starred review)

"A page-turner as well as a moving testament to the human will to do good and survive despite all odds. Highly recommended." —*Library Journal*

Typhoon – Joseph Conrad – next yr.

Louise Murphy was born in Bowling Green, Kentucky. She is the author of the novel *The Sea Within* and a book for children, *My Garden*, and the recipient of a Writers Digest Award for formal poetry. Her poetry has been published in *Sojourners*, *Commonweal*, *Bitter Oleander*, and other journals. She lives in northern California.

The True Story of
Hansel and Gretel

Louise Murphy

PENGUIN BOOKS

PENGUIN BOOKS

Published by the Penguin Group

Penguin Group (USA) Inc., 375 Hudson Street, New York, New York 10014, U.S.A.

Penguin Group (Canada), 90 Eglinton Avenue East, Suite 700, Toronto,
Ontario, Canada M4P 2Y3 (a division of Pearson Penguin Canada Inc.)

Penguin Books Ltd, 80 Strand, London WC2R 0RL, England

Penguin Ireland, 25 St Stephen's Green, Dublin 2, Ireland (a division of Penguin Books Ltd)

Penguin Group (Australia), 250 Camberwell Road, Camberwell, Victoria 3124,
Australia (a division of Pearson Australia Group Pty Ltd)

Penguin Books India Pvt Ltd, 11 Community Centre, Panchsheel Park,
New Delhi – 110 017, India

Penguin Group (NZ), 67 Apollo Drive, Rosedale, North Shore 0632, New Zealand
(a division of Pearson New Zealand Ltd)

Penguin Books (South Africa) (Pty) Ltd, 24 Sturdee Avenue, Rosebank,
Johannesburg 2196, South Africa

Penguin Books Ltd, Registered Offices: 80 Strand, London WC2R 0RL, England

First published in Penguin Books 2003

30 29 28 27 26 25 24 23

Copyright © Louise Murphy, 2003

PUBLISHER'S NOTE
In this novel Louise Murphy uses the art of fiction to cast new light on
the horrifying facts of the Holocaust.

LIBRARY OF CONGRESS CATALOGING IN PUBLICATION DATA
Murphy, Louise, 1943–
    The true story of Hansel and Gretel / Louise Murphy.
        p.   cm.
    ISBN 978-0-14-200307-7
        1. Holocaust, Jewish (1939–1945)—Fiction.   2. World War, 1939–1945—Fiction.
    3. Brothers and sisters—Fiction.   4. Jewish families—Fiction.   5. Children—Fiction.
    I. Title.
    PS3563.U7446T78   2003
    813' 54—dc21   2003045976

Printed in the United States of America
Set in Filosofia
Designed by Ginger Legato

For Christopher,
   artist, friend, and son,
   and because we grew up together

Contents

The True Story of
Hansel and Gretel

The Witch

Caught between green earth and blue sky, only truth kept me sane, but now lies disturb my peace. The story has been told over and over by liars and it must be retold. Do not struggle when the hook of a word pulls you into the air of truth and you cannot breathe.

For a little while, I ask this of you.

Come with me.

Once Upon a Time

"You've no choice. Look back."

"No." The man looked over his shoulder and saw the lights of another motorcycle—two—no—three motorcycles following them. He couldn't go faster on the dirt road. The ruts were frozen and the machine would tip into a ditch. The dark forest imprisoned the road. He could smell snow coming.

The children in the sidecar stared into the night, eyes slitted against the wind. The girl's hair wrapped around her head like a scarf and was the only covering that protected her thin throat. The boy was rolled low into the metal egg, his curly head dark in the moonlight, so thin he took almost no space at all.

The woman squeezed the man's sides until he grunted.

It was unfair. He adapted. He became like everyone else. College in France. Work as an engineer. New knowledge for new times and new people. Rejecting the sidelocks of his father. Leaving the study of dead laws and old men swaying in the temple. His friends had been Christian Poles, and none of them had been religious either.

But the world of intellectual talk and scientific study exploded. He fled from western Poland not in an airplane, defying the old laws of gravity, but crawling along in a peasant's cart pulled by a spavined horse bought with all the silver spoons his wife owned.

Her silver had protected them from being in the city when the Nazis arrived, but it did not protect them from the bombs. He buried his wife beside the road after the strafing, when she lay with her beautiful torso facing the sky, dress torn, nipples like dead eyes, unblinking.

A quick learner, he survived the Russians by being a mechanic for them. He survived the Bialystok ghetto by being a mechanic for the Nazis. He had remarried this woman who now clutched his sides until he couldn't breathe. He had gotten all of them out of the ghetto before the August deportations, hiding the children in tires strapped to the back of a truck, cutting their stepmother's hair and giving her men's clothes, passing through the barbed-wire fences as mechanics and hiding in a grease pit. Knowing that the trains were loading the other Jews. Hearing the screams and shots all night. Hearing them when he was awake. Hearing them in his dreams when he slept. He would not look over his shoulder again. The pursuing Nazis would be closer and he couldn't bear much more.

"Your children will be dead if they catch us." The woman clung tighter. "They'll shoot us beside the road."

"No." He howled it, the shouted word giving him back for a moment his life that was lost in the whispering years of submission and hiding. "Someone could take pity on them. The girl is eleven, old enough to be useful. They may have luck."

The girl in the sidecar looked back, her bony shoulder rising, blue eyes almost white in the moonlight. Three lights. It was almost over. She wrapped her arm tighter around her seven-year-old brother. She saw his throat move and knew what he was doing. She had taught him how.

He had saved his spit for over an hour. She had told him to think of biting into a lemon to make the spit flow, but he couldn't remember lemons. He thought of vinegar. His spit spurted and he had extra juice at the end of the swallow. A mouthful of spit swallowed slowly was almost like drinking soup. Hot soup with potatoes mashed in it. He felt his stomach contract and willed it to stop aching.

"We have to hide the motorcycle and run into the forest." The woman would not shut up.

"With the children," the father shouted.

The boy listened. The Stepmother would get her way. She wasn't their real mother.

"They'll bring dogs. The children will slow us. Leave the children, and we'll all have a chance."

The father hated her with such a surge of his blood that he almost stopped the motorcycle so he could choke her. Beat her. He clung to the anger as long as he could because it squeezed the truth out, but the feeling seeped away and he concentrated on the road. He needed a curve, a hill, something to block the view so he could put the children down.

"It isn't deep enough," he said of the first curve. When he didn't slow for the third, she gripped his sides again and howled like a dog.

The father braked on the fourth curve and leapt off. He grabbed the girl and wrenched her from the sidecar. The boy staggered when he was set on the road.

"Go," he whispered. "Go into the woods. Run."

The woman sat with her head down, but she called out to them. "Hide until the other motorcycles are past. Then find someone. Find a farmer who will feed you."

The girl shook her head. "They'll report us. If they don't, the Nazis will kill them."

Her stepmother looked back. She had to end it.

"You don't look Jewish. You're blond. Your brother—" She stopped and stared behind at the machines coming toward them. What was, was. "Don't let him take his pants down in front of anyone. They'll see he's circumcised. Do you hear me?"

"Our names?" The girl clung to the sidecar.

"Never say them. You don't have Jewish names anymore."

"Who are we?" The boy smiled. It was interesting. He wouldn't be himself.

"Any name. Any name that's—" the stepmother paused and she couldn't think of Polish names. Her mind was blank. She knew it was hunger. Six hundred calories a day for two years—on the good days, on the days when there was something left to sell. Sometimes she went blank.

The boy took his sister's hand and moved toward the woods. "Who are we?" he called back.

The Stepmother moaned and slapped her face viciously. The man got on the motorcycle and they moved off slowly so the wheels wouldn't catch in the ruts.

Slamming her fist against her head, their Stepmother shook loose an old memory.

"Hansel and Gretel," she screamed over her shoulder at the children who were now almost hidden in the trees. "You are Hansel and Gretel. Remember."

The man couldn't look back. He gunned the engine and moved away from that place. The two adults had become the lure that would lead the hunters away from the children. The gas would last for another ten miles. Their motorcycle could stay ahead with the weight of the children gone. The Nazis mustn't know that anyone had been left behind.

Hansel and Gretel

The children stood near the trees and looked after their father and stepmother until the three motorcycles following droned louder.

"Quick." The girl helped her brother climb over a log and push through the piles of crackling leaves.

They moved back into the darkness between the trees. The boy stared up and saw only a few stars. Clouds obscured the moon, and as the two children staggered through the deep layers of leaves, stiff-legged from being folded into the sidecar, they heard an owl call nearly over their heads. The boy almost cried out, but remembered the need to be silent, and bit his lip so hard it left a half-moon line of red when he unfastened his teeth.

"Lie down." His sister pushed him into the leaves and lay beside him.

Their voices would not have been heard over the roar of the motorcycles that came slowly but steadily down the rutted road. One in front. Two behind in perfect formation. Precision even at midnight on a dirt road while chasing subhumans in eastern Poland.

The boy lifted his head above the leaves and watched. He stared admiringly at the clean uniforms, the smooth metal bowl of helmet. The three motorcycles swept past, and the child marked down in his mind the way the Nazis sat perfectly straight and weren't afraid of being seen.

The noise of the engines grew fainter until there was complete silence. The girl felt panic rising. The silence was unlike the constant moaning and screams in the ghetto. Too many people in such little space. Always someone dying or losing their last rag of dignity and howling for food or fighting or weeping. It had never been silent for so much as a second.

She felt the tears run down her cheeks, and her brother watched her with interest.

"You're crying?"

"Everyone's gone."

"They didn't see us. I was quiet."

She nodded. "You were good—" She paused. The new name. It took a moment. "Hansel."

"What's your name?"

"Gretel."

"Maybe I'm Gretel."

"Gretel is a girl's name."

"All right. I'm Hansel." He smiled. He was not himself anymore. He was not the little Jew who hid in the grease pit. He wondered if he could change his stomach to a stomach full of food. He tried to imagine it but couldn't.

"We can't lie here. They could come back. They could have dogs."

"Wait a minute, Gretel."

She didn't flinch when she heard her new name, but her lips quivered for a second. She felt herself wanting to relax so she could cry again, but there wasn't time. "Come on."

He followed her back into deeper darkness, walking with one bony fist smaller than a windfall apple pushed deep into his gut to stop the pain. The brush was thinning, and the enormous height of the trees rose over their heads in a canopy which allowed only moss and low plants to grow underneath.

They had gone only a few steps when he stopped, holding her back like an anchor. She turned and waited. She knew his nature. It was impossible to move him until he was ready.

He was making a great decision. He had some in his pocket, but it would mean breaking the most sacred law. You never touched the last piece of bread until everything had been done. The swallowing of spit. The fist in the gut. Forcing yourself to feel the stomach pain as if it belonged to someone else standing beside you. Father had taught him how to do these things.

Only when the pain gave up could you touch the last piece of bread. Gretel said it was the law. You had to eat it slowly, not gobble it. It was how they did it. He didn't know why.

He took the piece of bread out and measured it with his eyes. His father had stolen it from a pile that had been forgotten in the burning and killing. Like all the ghetto bread, there was a dark mark where the metal rods that pressed into the bread while it baked left lines. There had to be lines on the bread so it could be divided evenly.

Both children leaned toward the bread until their noses almost touched the hard lump. They stared at it with the gaze of connoisseurs. It was slightly larger than the piece that Hansel usually managed to save.

He looked at Gretel appraisingly. She might forbid it, but it was his right. No one could take it from you. Even if they were sick or starving or hungrier than you. The Stepmother had taught them. Your bread was your bread.

He pinched off a tiny piece and deliberately let his fingers open so the bread fell to the leaves under their feet.

Gretel's eyes widened. The hunger tore through her, and her hand twitched but she did not grab the bread from Hansel. He picked off another piece and threw it back toward the road.

"Why?" Her mouth grew wetter as she thought of going back, finding the breadcrumb, holding it in her mouth.

"If we leave bread, they can find us. Later." He began walking into the dark and every ten steps he dropped another crumb.

"The leaves will cover it up."

"Stepmother can find a crumb on the street, in the middle of bodies thrown out in the morning. She'll smell it."

Gretel nodded. The Stepmother always found crumbs, pressed them into a flat pancake with water, and divided it meticulously among the four of them. It was true.

"She'll find the bread."

Gretel couldn't really believe it. It would be too hard to find in the leaves. The Stepmother was used to concrete pavement where crumbs lay naked. But the law was the law. It was his bread. No one else could eat it, and if he chose to waste it, she guessed it was his right, although no person had ever done that as long as she could remember.

There were memories. Far back. Food on a table. A hand pulling off a piece of bread carelessly, without measuring. Candles. The bread—challah—the word stuck in her mind. She savored the sound—it reminded her of someone—not her mother—

A man. White hair and beard. She could shut her eyes and see him smiling down at her, and he was saying something—asking her to do something.

The memory was gone. It bothered her. She had lost so many memories during the ghetto.

Forcing her mind, she saw the curtains again and felt the warmth of summer air moving the cloth like mist over the window. Then she quite deliberately shut the door in her mind. It wasn't good to think of things that were too far off, and now it was the first day of November. Warmth was too far in the future.

She turned and plunged past the trunks of trees that became larger as the children moved deeper. Her hair rose on the back of her neck. They were bigger than any trees she had ever seen. They weren't like the spindly, friendly, little trees in the gardens by the Bialy Lake in the city. Those were trees that men had planted, little umbrellas of trees, in pleasing patterns following the paths.

Gretel touched the bark of a tree, and as she did the owl hooted again, deeper in the forest now. "Listen, Hansel."

They stood and stared ahead into the gloom. Had the trees been in full leaf, the darkness under the canopy would have been absolute, but only the scudding clouds blocked the moonlight fitfully.

"The owl is leading us," he said. "Listen."

They waited, breathing shallowly, and heard the call, mournful as the voice of the mad cantor who had stood calling on the corner of Pilnesky Street under their window.

Gretel smiled. "We'll go that way."

Hansel nodded, only partly attentive, his whole body tense with the work of giving up his bread, crumb by crumb.

They walked on for a long time, and the way did not get more difficult. The ground was soft at times, but their slight weight made only dents. They came to a stream and both knelt and drank the icy water.

"We ought to wade in it so if there are dogs they can't sniff us." Hansel held only one crumb now, and he did not want to eat it. It wouldn't be perfect if he did. He thought of the soldiers riding in formation, so clean, so unafraid.

"You do it too." He cut the crumb with his thumbnail and gave one part to her. Gretel took it carefully, ignoring the hunger in herself so she could behave with dignity.

"It's still my bread." He picked the other piece out from under his nail. He had to do it quickly or he would put it in his mouth. "You have to do what I say."

"All right."

"Like this." He threw it hard and it went into the flowing water of the stream. She threw her bread too, and they stood watching the water.

"They do that, some people," she said, an old story she had heard coming back to her.

"Do what?"

"Throw bread on the water."

"Why?"

"It carries their sins away."

"What are sins?"

"Bad things you do."

Hansel thought about it. "How much bread did they throw?"

"Maybe a whole marked piece."

"From the end to the mark?" He couldn't believe it.

"I don't know. We can't walk in the water, Hansel. It's too cold, and we'd get sick."

"The dogs will smell us." The sound of barking always made him have to pee.

"No dogs. We'd hear them."

She was so tired, and she knew he was too, but they had to find someone. A farmer who had a lot of food. If they didn't they'd die. But if the farmer was too afraid of death, then he would report them.

"I have to pee. Wait." He pulled down his pants.

"No." She grabbed him. "Not even in front of me. You have to go behind a tree."

He pulled his pants up and began to walk around a tree. "It's dark."

"Shut up. You can't let anyone see it."

"You've seen it before." He pushed hard to finish and go back to her.

"You can't pee in front of anyone. Not ever again."

"Why did they do it?"

"Do what?"

"Why did they make my penis this way?"

"Because they had to. They didn't know it'd be like this."

She couldn't walk much farther. They followed the owl's call until another owl began to call off to their right, and then a third owl answered on the left. It was too confusing.

"There aren't any farmers in the forest," she told him. "We have to go to sleep and then find a farm tomorrow, when we get to the end of the trees."

"How long will that take?"

She stared ahead. The moon was covered with dense clouds now and the air smelled of snow. She knew it wasn't safe to go to sleep when it was so cold, but she walked on until there was a small clearing in the middle of circling trees. The sky was dark and high up.

"Help me." She kicked leaves into a pile in the middle of the clearing. He got on all fours and pushed leaves, sneezing from the dust. When the pile was large enough for her, she got on all fours with him.

"Now we're like little rabbits. We'll make a hole in the leaves and sleep under them."

"Rabbits live under the ground. Uncle—"

"Don't say any names."

"I didn't say it." He was nearly in tears.

"Just don't. Come on. Crawl in the leaves. It'll make us warmer."

It was harder to crawl in than she thought it would be. The leaves moved away from them and fell off, but finally she lay beside him and pulled as many leaves over them as she could, covering even their heads.

"Roll over." She wrapped herself around him, and his back and her stomach grew a little warmer where they were pressed together. "Now go to sleep."

He was cold, but everyone was cold for part of the year. It was how things were. He fell asleep quickly and his fist, pressed again into his gut, relaxed and softened.

She felt him relax under her arm, and then she fell asleep too, but not before she heard it. At first she thought it was the owls, but the sound was too great for the wings of owls. Then she thought it was the wind in the trees, but that wasn't it either.

It went on until she was too tired to wonder and fell asleep, with the sound of great wings over them, beating, cracking the air, the sound continuing as the sky darkened and the first dust of snow fell onto the wings of the angels and through the moving sinew and muscle and feather onto the pile of leaves which covered the children.

Magda

Hansel woke first, but he couldn't bear to move. He was terribly cold, but the air outside the leaves was colder. He wasn't hungry now and smiled at the feel of his stomach with no pain in it.

Gretel stirred and the leaves moved. A leaf with a few flakes of snow on its brown surface fell beside Hansel's face and he stuck his tongue out and touched the white crystals.

"Snow."

Gretel was awake instantly when she heard his voice.

"Shut up!"

He lay, ashamed. He had spoken aloud.

They curled under the leaves, nearly frozen, and listened, but there was no sound. Even the birds had left the forest. Not a footstep, not a crack of a twig.

Gretel pushed a few leaves away and stared out at the floor of the forest. It was covered with a dust of snow. She craned her neck and examined the whole surface of the clearing. Not a single footprint marking the snow. They were alone.

Unless someone hid behind the trees. She shut her eyes. It was different in the country. It was harder to hide. It was bigger.

"I'll get up first. If anything happens, just lie still." Her mouth barely moved near his ear.

She rolled to the side and pulled up on her knees and then stood stiffly. Nothing. No shouts of "Raus! Raus!" or the bark of a dog or the thump of a blow.

"It's all right. Get up—" She hesitated and was frightened for a second. "Hansel," she said, remembering. "We have to practice our names."

"What's our last name?"

"It doesn't matter." Her face twisted with worry. He was right. They'd need a last name.

He stood and brushed the leaves off. His face was very pale and he looked hopefully at her. "When will we find a farmer?"

"Soon. Maybe."

"I'm not hungry now." He smiled at her, but she didn't smile back. There were no hunger pains in her own body, and she knew what it meant. Ransacking her pockets for a crumb, no matter how small or dirty, she felt the panic rising again. Just a tiny crumb swallowed could bring the hunger raging back. There was nothing in her pockets.

"Come on. We have to go fast now." She knew they had to get food before night. "The dogs might come."

He would go faster if he thought about the dogs, and they had to get out of the forest. Stealing food could take time, and stealing was safer than asking. They moved at a trot through the trees and she wondered how you stole food from farmers. She had seen pictures of farms in a book, but she couldn't remember if farmers had refrigerators or kept the food outside in their barns.

They had a refrigerator once. When she was little and lived in a city somewhere else. Two men carried it up the back stairs into the kitchen. She remembered the maid shrieking when she opened it up and felt the cold air coming out.

The sun was only a glare through the clouds and the cold didn't get any better. Gretel could tell it was midmorning by the silver disk of sun in the sky when she glimpsed it through tree limbs.

"Can we whisper, Gretel?"

She looked around. It was silent except for the sound of their feet and their breathing.

"Only whisper." She leaned toward him so her voice didn't have to rise.

"I'm thirsty." His whisper was loud, but she was glad he had thirst.

They had come a long way. The forest was bigger than Bialy Park, maybe bigger than Bialystok itself. The forest might not ever end but just keep going east until they were in Byelorussia. She remembered the map on the wall of their room in the ghetto. She had watched her father tear it out of a book and hang it up. He had been able to save only three books.

"A mathematics book and an atlas. We will study logical thought and the world. Not everything is Poland and Germany. And one book of fairy tales, for you, daughter."

Then he pointed. "This is Poland. This is Germany. But the rest of it, look now, the rest of it is the world."

Her father taught them ever since she could remember. Math lessons and geography. And the third book that lay in the corner of the room where she slept on a mat with her brother.

There had been a lot of books on the cart. The cart. Going down the road, and the blankets piled up, and her sitting on top—until the airplanes. For a second the airplanes hung in the blue sky of her mind like silver wasps, and then the door in her mind shut and they were gone.

"Look." Hansel had stopped so abruptly that she nearly knocked him over. "Look at that."

Beyond them she heard the sound of water, another stream. Ahead she saw a group of particularly large trees, she didn't know what kind they were, and in the middle of the trees was a tiny house—not a house—sort of a shed—like the one where Uncle—she shook her head to stop the name from coming into her mind—where someone kept his gardening tools.

Smoke came from the pipe that stuck out of the roof at an angle, but it wasn't the smoke that Hansel was staring at. Before she could stop him, he ran through the trees and reached toward the side of the hut. She wanted to call out, but knew it was too late. She could have helped him if he had waited, but he couldn't wait, and she knew that too.

He stood on tiptoe and tore at a piece of dark bread that had been pressed over a metal spike sunk in the wood of the hut. Hansel couldn't reach it and, afraid he would call to her, Gretel sprung across the clearing and pulled the bread off the spike.

"Mine!" He remembered to whisper, but his tone was fierce.

Gretel gave it to him, grabbed his arm, and was pulling him toward the forest when she saw the woman. She was very old, white hair hanging down past her shoulders, her eyes so dark they only showed as holes in the wrinkled skin of her face. She wasn't much taller than Gretel herself.

Gretel pulled Hansel around, and the jerk made him drop the bread.

"No," he screamed, and she knew it didn't matter. The woman had seen them.

Gretel was running with him, struggling as he tried to go back and get the bread, the two of them in a tangle of feet, and then she fell, dragging him on top of her. The woman was near them, but Gretel didn't dare look at her.

And then Gretel heard the laugh. Husky at first, then clear and ringing through the air. It made Gretel stop struggling with Hansel, and he crawled back to where the lump of hard bread lay on the ground.

Gretel stared at the dirt under her head. The woman had laughed, but sometimes they laughed before they killed people. She waited for the pressure of the gun against her neck and imagined how the bullet would tear through the bone of her skull and blow the whitish brain tissue out through her forehead. She knew the flesh would spill out of her skull and cover the ground like a dropped pudding, but the bullet didn't come.

Looking up, the girl saw the woman coming into the clearing, dressed in dark clothes, ragged like everyone was, a bucket of water in each hand.

"If you want to eat my bread, you have to carry these pails, boy."

"No." Hansel was gnawing on the bread, ignoring the gray of mold on one corner.

"You won't work?"

Hansel shook his head. Gretel knew his mind was too connected with the bread to understand. Hansel never said anything to people while he ate except "No."

"I'll carry them." She held out her arms. They were thin but she'd prove they were strong.

The woman wasn't listening to her. "The boy could almost be one of the Rom."

"His name is Hansel. I'm Gretel." She didn't know what the Rom were, but it was better not to be anything.

The woman wore a piece of blanket cut to make a shawl. Under that were several sweaters, the color of dirt, then some sort of dress. Over the skirt of the dress she had layered a woolen skirt that dragged in the dirt, heavy with mud on the bottom. Gretel stared at the woman's clothes, but it was all right. There was no lump of a gun, no stick or whip under her clothes. None that the girl could see.

Stretching out her hand, the woman lifted a strand of Gretel's silvery hair, moving closer until Gretel could smell a musty odor. Suddenly the woman took Gretel's face in her hands and imprisoned it with hard fingers. Gretel stared into the black eyes with her blue ones and hoped the woman wouldn't twist her neck and break it. There was nothing to do. The woman held her too tightly.

"But you're not of the Rom."

"No," Gretel whispered.

"And you have such nice, sturdy, German names."

Gretel willed herself to stare in the woman's eyes but her eyeballs twitched like a horse's.

The woman dropped her hands and nodded. "And where are your adults?"

"We're looking for farmers." Hansel had finished the bread and was drinking with his hand out of a bucket.

"Where are your parents?" The woman looked at Gretel. "Hiding back there? Waiting to come out and kill me for my bread?"

Gretel couldn't think of an answer. She stared at the hut and saw another piece of bread and then another on the boards. "Why do you put bread on your house?"

"The birds feed on it."

"That's wasteful." Gretel frowned at her.

"Wasting a little shows you believe in tomorrow."

Gretel knew then that the woman was one of those who had lost her mind. "Bread is important."

"Bread is more than that, little girl with eyes that flinch. Bread is your luck. If you throw it away, you throw your luck away."

Hansel looked up from the bucket. His face crumpled.

"But you throw your bread away. You tack it up for the birds."

"I give it. Giving isn't throwing."

Hansel's face crumpled more. He began to make those breathy sounds that were so hard to stop once he had begun.

"I threw the breadcrumbs on the dirt, Gretel."

"Don't be stupid." She dragged him to his feet and slapped his face. It was what the Stepmother did to stop the sound. "She's crazy. Like the old man under our window. You remember?"

The sounds stopped and he nodded. "But I threw the bread-crumbs—"

"It doesn't matter."

The woman turned her dark eyes to the boy. "You threw your bread away?"

Hansel nodded.

"Then we'll try to make it right again. You have to pay me."

"We don't have any money."

The woman walked to him and looked at his coat. She reached out and with a quick jerk took one of the metal buttons in her fingers and tore it from the material. Before Gretel could protest, the button was tucked into the bosom of the woman's dress.

"Now." She walked to the trees and searched the ground, picked up a long stick, and came back to the children. Gretel stepped in front of her brother.

Ignoring her, the woman drew a circle through the dusting of snow, a groove into the dirt around the two children. She left the circle unconnected until she had stepped inside and then connected the two lines to close it.

"Hold the stick." She held it out and Hansel put his hand on it. Gretel put her hand over his.

"Protected by the closed circle, this child with moonlight hair and the other, the child who is almost of the Rom, will have their luck back."

She muttered something in a language that wasn't Polish or German or Yiddish. Then she fell silent, and the three of them stood close until the woman laughed and walked to the buckets. Still holding the stick, the two children watched her.

"Who are the Rom?" Hansel asked.

"Gypsies. But there are none left now. They killed them first. They were gone before they started on the rest." She picked up the buckets and grunted from the weight.

Gretel stepped forward.

"No!" The woman nearly spilled the water. "Don't step on the line."

Gretel drew back and waited while the woman walked around the circle whispering and rubbing at the dirt, until Gretel's footprint marring the circle, and the circle itself, were obliterated.

"Will Gretel have bad luck?" Hansel asked.

"The wheel moves on, and we move with it." The woman stared into the forest as if she were listening for someone.

"Who are you?" Gretel asked.

"I am Magda. Magda the Witch they call me in the village." She picked up the buckets, swung open the door of the hut with a twist of her foot, and went inside.

The Forest

The motorcycle whined in complaint and they nearly skidded off the road on every curve. His wife didn't cry out but clung to him with eyes shut. Soon they would have to stop and run. She made her mind still and saved her strength.

"The next curve," he shouted into the wind. She squeezed his sides to show that she heard. It came upon them in an instant, a curve topped heavily by trees. But then he was unsure. Perhaps it should be less impenetrable so they could run. The Nazis would have dogs with them—now or later—they always brought in the dogs.

He couldn't think about the boy. Or the girl. There were no children now. "They died in the Bialystok ghetto," he muttered, rehearsing.

The engine sputtered. The gas was gone. It was going to be here. "Get off."

She leapt from the machine and he managed to ride it into a ditch. Holding the throttle open, he walked the machine into the brush and let it drop. As the engine cut off with a last jagged cough, the silence of the forest was around them. The Nazis' machines were a distant hum. He stood and couldn't move.

"Quick!" She grabbed his hand and pulled him through the brush.

He knew that if he put his hand on her chest he would feel her heart nearly pushing through the bone. They ran.

He knew she had held the dogs in her mind all along. He took her hand, but the thought of the children came to him. He sobbed and staggered.

"Not now." She led the way, moving as fast as possible through brush until they were deep enough so the trees around them had been standing for hundreds, maybe thousands of years. These giants were too tall and leafy in summer to allow much to grow under them.

They trotted steadily through the trees, stumbling occasionally when the moon was hidden behind the clouds. He ran into low branches and ignored the whip against his skin. Once he saw her face looking back at him, and she had blood oozing from a cut over her eye. She did not cry out ever, and he was glad. He had no comfort to offer her.

They came to a creek. He threw himself down to drink, and took water into his mouth. I have to drink, he thought, but the water gushed out from between his lips. He couldn't swallow.

She drank deeply, great gulping mouthfuls. Then she pulled off her boots and the socks layered under them. She had lovely, strong feet.

"We'll walk in the creek. It'll throw the dogs off."

He sat and watched her feet, white against the black moss on the bank.

She wished she could hold him, but there wasn't time. She had to break through his shock. Leaning forward, she punched him in the chest to make him move.

They waded for a long time. She kept looking for a place to leave the creek. Her feet were numb from the cold water, and it didn't hurt as much when she slipped and hit her toes.

Then she saw the long slope of stone. She nodded toward it, and hoped he understood. He said nothing, so she grabbed his hand and pulled him toward the shelf of rock. It hung over the water, and she wasn't able to push him up.

Bending double she braced her hands against the rocks on the creek bottom. Her face was close to the running water. "Step up," she ordered.

She thought he would say he was too heavy, but he did as she ordered. His weight, all bone and stringy muscle, made her gasp as she tried to lock her knees and keep her back high.

Then he was up. She stretched out her arms, and he pulled her onto the rock overhang. Her bones struck against it as if there was no flesh, no shirt and pants and coat protecting her.

"Put on your shoes," she whispered. The leather might have less scent than bare feet.

They walked, leaping from stone to stone until it was inevitable. They were walking again on the leaves of the forest. She looked up. The smell of snow was sharp in the air, the coldness making the red warmth of her lungs ache.

"It's going to snow."

He didn't answer, but she was becoming more confident. It might be possible. The dogs would have trouble tracking through snow.

"Why would they bother coming back tomorrow?" he asked. "We're only two people." He couldn't help going on with his ideas. "Why did they bother tracking down Mr. Samuels, who was nearly dead and hiding in the sewage tank? Why did they shoot the boy who sold saccharine candy on the corner of Lipsky Street? Why did they beat my mother and father and brother to death? Why've they done any of it?"

She felt the rage coming up in her body. Why had they lifted her baby and smashed his head against the terrace wall? She didn't say this aloud. She had told him about her family, her husband dead during the first days of the invasion, but not about the baby. She would have told him, but she couldn't make her mouth say the child's name.

"Fuck why." He had to stop talking.

They moved onward. He hoped they weren't going in a circle, and when they came to another creek, he worried that they had doubled back on themselves.

"It's all right," she said. "I don't think it's the same one."

He had never been in the forest at night.

"Did you walk in the forests—before?"

She smiled. "Not this far east. This forest has never been logged. Never. I wandered in the smaller forests in the west."

She had told him about it. The big house. The servants. The fields of grain moving like an ocean around the house. Lying in the fields in summer with the straw smell of grain around her. Looking up into the sky and watching the wind move the heavy heads of the wheat, bending them until she would pull one off and chew it. And going by cart with the peasants to watch the logging. The trees falling with shrieks as real as human screams.

It would have been wonderful to sit down and think for an hour about the past, but there was no way to think about the good parts without having her mind drift to the terrible things.

"We have to rest," he said.

"No. We'll keep moving until dawn and then sleep. We can't move safely by daylight."

So they kept walking, breaking into a stumbling jog when the brush was thin. They had to rest more often than she liked. They were too starved to move steadily.

He felt the air grow even colder and the snow began to sift down on their heads. Large flakes. She smiled at him, and he was almost able to smile back at her. The silence was total and unnerving.

And then it was dawn. The light went from black darkness to gray like velvet against his eyes and faded to silver with no touch of pink. It was snowing hard now, and soon they would stop and try to find a place to sleep.

She was almost happy. No sound of dogs all night. They might not find the motorcycle in the brush until the next day. If they waited too long, the machine would be covered by snow.

They both heard the click of the pistol being cocked before they saw the man. He was ahead of them and had stepped out from behind a tree. He had a pistol in his hand and a rifle strapped to his back.

She heard her husband catch his breath in a sob, and turned to see his face. His features were twisted and frozen in a grimace of pain. She took his hand and squeezed it.

"City Jews!" The man with the pistol spit on the ground as he said it. "Useless, fucking, city Jews."

"I grew up in the country—" she began.

"Do you have a gun? Do you have bullets? Do you have a tank that you just happened to capture?"

The husband and wife stood silent.

"No winter clothes. No guns."

"We waded in the water." She was getting angry. "They can't follow us."

"At least there aren't any brats. I wouldn't be talking now if there had been brats." The man spat again.

"The children are dead," the husband said.

"Thank God. You think I should help you? You're walking corpses."

"We're not dead." Her body held too much cold and pain to be dead.

"The Nazis don't have to kill you now. Winter is the Nazi in this forest. If I let you go, you'll lead them right to us."

The woman was filled with rage again. He was right. They had no guns. But he had a gun.

The man with the pistol leaned against a tree and pulled from his coat pocket a cigarette, which he smelled delicately and then placed between his lips and lit. The smell of tobacco was like food entering her body. Then he walked to her, put the gun against her head, felt her breasts and hips and ran his hands in her coat pockets and between her legs. The husband moved to protect her, but the woman knew it was nothing. The man didn't touch her with any interest.

Then he ran his hands over her husband with the same intent and smiled. "Not even a carving knife. And I should just leave you? Let you walk on? What happens when they catch you? When they say to you, 'We won't kill you if you show us where you saw the partisan. Lead us to the spot and you can live.'"

"I wouldn't tell. Never."

"What about him?" He looked at her husband, and she knew it was true. Her husband would not watch her being killed and maimed just to save this man with a pistol.

"He wouldn't tell," she lied.

He drew on the cigarette again and then lightly ground out the glowing tip against the tree. He put the unfinished cigarette in a leather bag, tenderly, like a woman places her pearls in a silk case, and shook his head.

"We'll see what the others say. But don't get hopeful. You're useless."

They walked in front of him, going as he ordered. With the sun a silver ball behind the clouds, she could get her bearings enough to tell that they were circling. We nearly walked over them, she thought, and shivered. It would have been death to surprise these people.

"Who are you?" she asked.

He didn't answer, and then she saw it in front of her. Her eyes could barely differentiate the structures from the forest floor. Bark roofs covering holes dug in the dirt. Burrows. Like the holes where foxes hide when the hounds chase them.

The other men were around them now. She counted six, seven.

"Who are you?" she asked.

"What does it matter?" A man moved close to her, and she knew from his scarred forehead and cheeks that the Nazis had branded him with a hot iron as a Russian prisoner of war. His Polish was almost unaccented.

"The NSZ, the AK, the AL, the Greens—who the hell cares? The Nazis wouldn't care. We could be Jews like you."

"Then help us," her husband said. "In God's name."

"God packed up and left Poland in 1939."

There was another man lying on the ground beyond the roofs of the dens. He was tied and moved only his eyes. His face was swollen as if he had been beaten, but she didn't see that at first. It was the uniform that held her eyes. It was black and silver—the colors of Hell—although she didn't know if she believed in Hell. But the Christians did, and there were times when she hoped they were right. She could stand everything if only they were right about Hell.

She waited for an opportunity while the Russian talked to her husband.

"They died in the ghetto. Typhoid. Last winter. We have no children. None. We—"

She snatched the pistol from the hand of the man who had caught them and bolted toward the Nazi who lay on the ground. She didn't hear the shouts. She put the gun to the head of the soldier and looked back at the men.

"He's a Nazi?"

"Yes. We caught him raping a girl in the woods yesterday." The Russian smiled.

She didn't hear anything he said after the word yes. The explosion of the gun filled her ears and she knew joy. One gone. And she had done it. She hadn't fired a gun since before the war, and she'd never fired at a man.

They were all screaming at her, and she stood holding the gun limply by her side. She was smiling. Her body was warm all over and bile rose into her mouth. She coughed and spit.

Murder is warm and it's bitter, she thought. She had hunted deer with her father, but she'd never killed a human before.

"Crazy bitch!"

"Now what?"

Her husband was crying.

The Russian looked at the woman and smiled. "Bury the bastard. Deep. Strip him. She can have the coat and pants. She earned them. We've got his gun and his cigarettes. That was all he was good for."

"And then?"

The Russian looked at the woman and the crying man. "She can stay if she can keep up."

"A woman can't keep up."

"This one will. She could be useful. People don't suspect a woman. They feel sorry for her, or want to fuck her. She can stay but not the man."

She walked to the Russian and put the gun against his gut. She leaned into the gun so he would feel it.

"Both of us."

He looked into her eyes. "I'd call you She Wolf, but I don't like wolves."

She stood with the gun pushing into him. He saw in her eyes that she would never be charmed by anything he could say. He sighed.

"You have to be sensible. He's too weak."

She thought about this, and no one moved. Then her husband spoke.

"I have a motorcycle. It has no gas, but it runs well."

They stared at him, and he went on more quickly. "I'm an engineer. I can fix anything. Make anything run. You'll need me."

"We don't have machines," the Russian said.

Her husband smiled for the first time since they had gotten on the motorcycle. "One hundred thousand Germans surrendered at Stalingrad. When the Russians come they'll have trucks, tanks. We'll get machines later, and I'll make them run."

"You're an optimist. I like that. Optimism can keep you warm."

"Or get you killed," murmured one of the other men.

"It'll have to be Russian trucks. Hitler didn't send oil for our winter. All the German gears have frozen solid." The Russian smiled.

"Why didn't they send the right oil for winter?" Her husband was interested. It was a simple mechanic's problem.

"They thought they'd be in Moscow by October of 1941. They figured that by first snow, the Russians would be supplying their oil. They didn't know the Russians."

The men laughed, but it wasn't a long laugh.

"They should have asked the Poles about the Russians," said one man, and the laugh was louder this time, but with the same sad edge to it.

The Russian was not offended. He nodded. "He can stay. He's the Mechanik." He gave the word the Polish pronunciation. "We may need him, God willing."

She kept the gun in the Russian's belly for a second so he could see that she would never waver, never, and he understood. She lowered the gun.

"But do you have guts? She showed us. Now it's your turn."

There was a muttering of approval.

"Where is this motorcycle?"

"Back there. In a ditch beside the road. Under some brush."

"Then you have to go back and find it. Walk it up the road. Keep walking until you reach the first dirt track turning into the forest. Turn off on the track and walk until we find you."

She stared at them. "No."

"I'll get it, darling. Don't worry."

"He needs food. He'll get lost. He'll—"

"You get the motorcycle and bring it back. Then you're one of us, Mechanik."

She watched her husband turn and walk into the trees. He began a staggering lope, trying to move faster than his strength would allow. He was weak because he always gave his food up to his children when she wasn't watching. She knew he was hurrying to try to find them. She knew it. For a moment she hated those children.

The Russian was pleased. They would either acquire a motorcycle and a mechanic or the man would be killed. If he was killed, it was a sign that he hadn't been able to survive and they were right to test him first. Of course, if he was tortured, the man might tell where he had come from—where in the woods he had last seen the partisans. But that would also expose the woman. He wouldn't want to do that. It could be dealt with. They would move fast. He began to unfasten his pants. "Piss now. Shit if you can." The men began to unfasten their pants.

"You too."

"You do this next to where you live?" She was scornful. She knew all about hiding excrement. They had hidden their shit for months so the Nazis wouldn't find them.

"We don't sleep here. We just want to leave our stink so if they bring dogs they'll think they've found our camp."

"We don't live this nice," said a younger man whose ears stuck out from his head and had reddened with the cold. His round face was very young. "Not nearly this nice."

The men laughed. "Listen to Lydka. He's right."

The woman smiled. The boy's nickname, Lydka, suited him. He moved restlessly, with the springy walk of a young calf.

She squatted and pulled aside her pants so the piss wouldn't wet her. The men paid no attention. Her mind went to her husband, alone and running through the woods, back toward the hunters and dogs. There was nothing she could do for him now. She thought of the black and silver of the uniform splattered with red blood. She thought of the dead German, and she was happy for the first time in four years.

Brother and Sister

Heavy snow had begun to fall. Gretel and Hansel sat watching Magda's hut for nearly an hour. Every few minutes they stood and jumped up and down to get warm and knock off the snow.

"Take a piece of bread. She won't know."

"We can't make her angry. Wait, Hansel."

Another hour went by. The door opened and Magda came out, ignoring the children and walking past them to the woods. She moved slowly, her back bowed with arthritis.

"We can help." Hansel moved after her.

"It won't do you any good. I can't help you." Magda talked without turning. Occasionally she leaned over and picked up a piece of wood. "There've been others. I couldn't take care of them either. Walk a mile toward the sun. There's a village. I can't keep you."

Hansel dropped Gretel's hand and began to pick up wood. He filled his arms, grunting with the effort, and Gretel picked up wood until she was breathing hard. They had walked for too long, and Hansel was giving a little moan with each exhalation.

When they returned to the clearing, Magda went into the hut, and Hansel walked in behind her without knocking or begging. He just walked inside and Gretel followed. They put the wood on top of a pile near the huge stove that filled half the side of the hut.

"Come on, Gretel."

They climbed on top of the sleeping platform and sat on the blankets laid out on the shelf above the great oven. Hansel had never seen such an enormous stove in anyone's house. It was like the stove that bakers used. The warmth almost made the boy laugh, but he was too intent on disappearing from the witch's mind so they could sit and be warm.

Magda sat opposite them on the only chair, a wooden rocker with no cushion or comfort to it. The thump of her rocking and the moaning exhalation of the boy were the only sounds.

We will sit and maybe the war will stop, Gretel thought. Someone will come and tell us that it's over, and we'll find Father, and go home, and live in our house, and it will be summer. She drooped into sleep.

The door to the hut opened.

"What's this? What can you be thinking?" An old man stared at the children. "You have to get rid of them."

"You kill them. I'm too tired. You're the priest." Magda kept on rocking.

"For God's sake, don't be crazy." He was thin and white-haired with piercing eyes.

Hansel stared at the man. He had seen priests on the street. This man didn't wear the things that priests wore. He had on woolen pants and rough boots like a peasant. His coat was ragged at the cuffs and missing two buttons.

"Go report me to your friend, the Major. That fine man." Magda spit on the floor.

The priest pulled a stool from under the table and sat. His head was lower than Magda's. He did not look at the children.

"You only survived by accident, Magda."

"And you also."

He was silent for a moment. "The fire in Warsaw—the birth records destroyed—was good luck. Your grandmother was whoever we said she was."

"My grandmother was one of the Rom. She never tried to steal land and kill people."

"They hate Gypsies more than Jews."

"She helped everyone."

"She was a thief. She killed babies. She spent six years in prison."

"She sent unborn babies back to God when no one would love them in this world. She only stole from those who were stupid and fat.

The villagers would have helped her if they had been as Christian as they bragged. She saved them from their greed."

Hansel felt himself falling asleep. He had to stay awake. If they didn't get food soon, he wouldn't care about eating, and when the caring was gone, death would come.

"I got you clean papers! All the money and trouble! And now you'll be killed when they find these children. Give them one crust of bread, and you'll die."

"We ate some bread." Hansel spoke and his voice woke Gretel. "The witch didn't want it. It was for the birds."

"No one comes here." Magda rocked rhythmically. "Everyone stays away. Who's to know?" She smiled at the man and he winced.

"Children talk. They'll make noise, and run, and play games. Children are the worst. They have no sense. They forget." The man was sweating.

"I don't care anymore."

"You cared when you came running to me in a panic for false papers. And what about Nelka? She's pregnant."

"Why do you talk to me about her? Everyone knows who should be taking care of her."

The man was silent and stared at the floor. Hansel forced himself to stay awake.

"If you keep these Jews, they'll kill her too. Pregnant or not. You'll both be put on the trains or shot right here."

"You should know. You should know about the shooting in the forest."

"I didn't shoot anyone," he shouted. "I never killed anyone."

The shouting made Gretel come completely awake, and she stared at Magda, willing her to look back. Magda lifted her eyes and looked into the blue eyes of the child.

"We can stay inside. We can be quiet. There must be a way," Gretel said.

"All the ways are over." The priest didn't look at the girl.

Magda shook her head. "Stalingrad held fast. One hundred thousand Germans captured."

"Sent to Siberia like the Poles. God help them."

"God damn them." Magda stopped rocking.

They sat until Gretel felt the tears coming. She choked them back. Weak people weren't good for anything. Crying twice in two days. She had to stop.

"It will end, Piotr. I see it coming."

"And you can be here when it does. Think. You can sit here and wait for the end."

"Someone in the village could tell about Grandmother."

"But they haven't so far. No one has told. Even Jedrik, who pointed out the Jews for a sack of potatoes, is afraid to point out the priest. The village would kill Jedrik if he turned me in and I died, but I can't save you if you keep these Jews."

How does he know we're Jews? Gretel thought. They always seemed to know. It wasn't their accent. She and Hansel spoke good Polish. No one had used Yiddish in their home. Father had hated it when she repeated a Yiddish word heard from others.

"My children will be citizens of the world," her father always said. "They will speak perfect Polish. Perfect German. Then English and French when they are older."

Gretel put her arm around Hansel. She remembered her father arguing with someone—someone who wanted them to learn Yiddish—but how did everyone always know about the Jewishness? What could it be?

"The girl is blond."

"The boy has dark eyes. Curly dark hair." He shook his head. "And he must be circumcised."

The priest stepped to the sleeping platform. Rolling Hansel over, he fumbled with the boy's pants. Before the man could lower them, Gretel fell on his arm and bit him. He shrieked and shook her off like a dog.

"You can't look at him." Gretel was screaming.

Magda didn't move.

"He's circumcised. I told you. How the hell do you hide that?"

Magda was silent for a minute and then she smiled. "My great-niece. The crazy one. Our sister's granddaughter."

"You haven't seen her in years. She's probably dead."

"She was always crazy. Joined any group that would have her."

"So?" He rubbed his arm and glared at Gretel.

"So we will say that she joined the Karaites."

He stood silent and then his jaw dropped. He understood.

"She joined the Karaites while she was pregnant and they told her to have the boy circumcised because the Karaites believe that should be done even though they are Christian. She was such a fool. Of course she did it. She'd do whatever anyone said. She was mixed up with the Karaites and had the boy."

"So you'll explain the circumcision by claiming he was with the Karaites? Half the Jews in Poland must be claiming this. And why aren't the children with their crazy mother now?"

"Because she was sent into Germany to work on a farm. She used to work on that farm near Warsaw. Do you remember? And she couldn't take the children so she sent them to me."

"And if she turns up in the village?"

"Who will travel east with the Russian wolves creeping down on us? Everyone with a brain will go west."

"She never had a brain. It would be like her to arrive now."

"And you only need identity cards for children over eleven. The boy looks no more than six. She looks about ten."

"But they would need—" He stared at her and she smiled, amused at his panic.

"You could get them."

"I won't."

"Two baptismal certificates. Zbigniew would take a picture of them standing in their communion outfits. Pictures of the little Karaites getting ready to eat God."

"I'm sitting the war out in this backwater. I can't take any more chances."

"And you helped shovel the dirt when they shot the mayor and the Jews."

"What good would my death have done?"

"All your damn holiness. All your life. And an illegitimate daughter, and now a pregnant granddaughter, and you vowing celibacy."

"Half the village is dead. Sent to Germany as slaves. Sent to Russia to build roads in Siberia. Shot. Starved. Forced to enlist in the Russian army. They'll shoot the whole village if they find these children hidden with you."

"We won't hide them. We'll treat it all as natural. You have the connections. Get me peroxide. I'll dye the boy's hair. Get the baptismal certificates. We'll apply for food coupons."

"You'll kill the whole village for those two?"

"What has the village ever done for me?"

"They've kept silent about your grandmother."

"They sent her to prison after she spent years cleaning up their embarrassing mistakes."

He stood and stared at Magda. She stared back, and Gretel shut her eyes and prayed. Let the woman win.

"You want me dead," he said.

"Why not pretend to be a Christian?"

"Don't use God as a weapon against my life. I have a duty to abstain from suicide."

"Your whole life has been a suicide."

"Go to Hell."

"This is Hell. God couldn't invent anything worse. The Nazis have exceeded the imagination of God."

"Blasphemer."

"If you won't do it as a priest, I demand that you do it on the head of our dead mother."

"Don't drag her into this. She was dead before it started."

"She took you and abandoned me and my sister. She left us with my grandmother because I wasn't beautiful enough. She dumped us and never looked back and took her golden boy. Her blond, beautiful, clever, good, pious little altar boy with her. And then you abandoned her."

"Enough."

"She came back to me, and used up all I had with sickness."

"She died."

"On her miserable head, I demand that you do this. Get the certificates."

"Why punish me now?"

"Because it amuses me. You and your going to Rome. The boy genius. You're a trapped rat with all the other stinking rats now."

He was silent, and sweat ran down his face.

"Do this, brother, or I'll march these children in and leave them in your church. I'll say you hid them there, and they'll burn the church to the ground with you and the children and everyone else inside."

"You don't care about these Jews."

"That's none of your business. Go and do your duty. Tell Zbigniew to bring his camera."

"He has no film."

"He has film to take pictures of documents and make identity papers for those with enough money. He can spare an inch of film to help me. Remind him of his clerk. She could have embarrassed him badly before the war. She was a Jew and she carried his half-Jew child until I helped her."

The man ran his hand through his hair. His eyes rolled like a horse hearing the airplanes coming back over the fields. The whites of his eyes showed for a second.

"I couldn't help you with our mother. When she was sick I was in Rome. We'll be killed for this."

Magda looked at the two children. The boy was nearly dead. The girl was forcing herself to stay awake in the warmth of the hut. Only a gray light came through the one window, but the girl's hair shone like moonlight.

"Our grandmother would have fed them."

"Those were different times."

"Besides, I need help. I can hardly get wood. The girl is strong enough. The boy is tough. I'll survive the winter with them to help me."

"It may be impossible."

"Do it."

He left the hut and Magda sat very still for long minutes. She began to rock finally and looked up at the girl.

"Can you make soup?"

"Yes." Gretel had never made soup, but she had seen it made.

"I'll show you where the food is hidden outside, and you can begin."

Gretel climbed down and the two of them, the girl walking now only by will alone, and the old woman nearly bent double, went into the snow, leaving the boy asleep and dreaming on the platform.

Nelka

The woman's hair made Hansel remember a jar of honey, the comb dark gold and the liquid honey lighter gold around it. He knew she wasn't fat. She had a baby inside.

The woman turned and saw the boy. She stared at the child, her skin glowing in the watery light of winter, her cheekbones like wings, full lips curving into a smile. Hansel felt a smile pulled out of him in return. The woman went into the hut and the door closed behind her.

"Someone's come."

"Hide," Gretel whispered and scuttled between the trees like a squirrel in the snow.

"She's all right."

"How do you know?"

"Her hair looks like honey."

"Gretel? Hansel? Come inside." Magda called from the hut.

Gretel moved behind a tree, but Hansel ran to the door and went in.

"I'm Nelka, Magda's great-niece, Hansel, so we are related now."

He had never seen anyone so beautiful. It wasn't just the color of her hair. It was that she looked happy. And her eyes weren't afraid. They looked Hansel full in his face.

She isn't scared, Hansel thought, and she wasn't angry either. Everyone was afraid except the Germans, and they were angry.

"How did you know my name?"

"A bird told me."

Magda snorted. "A bird called Telek. Telek knows everything that happens."

The woman laughed. "Telek travels all over the woods to gather firewood and snare rabbits."

"Telek is in love with you. You ought to take him on."

"I'm married."

"A Polish husband in Russia is a dead husband."

There was silence in the hut, and Hansel didn't hear the door open and Gretel creep in.

"Hello, Gretel. I'm Nelka. I'm your cousin now."

Gretel stood and thought. "Magda is your aunt?"

"Great-aunt. Yes."

"Enough of this fine family feeling." Magda began to smooth the blankets on the sleeping platform. "Bragging about it, almost."

"Magda's brother is the priest. Priests don't have children." Gretel stared at Magda.

"Did you drag yourself out here to discuss the family tree, child?"

"I came to see what you're up to, dirty old woman."

Hansel took Magda's hand. "She isn't that dirty."

"Too dirty for me and everyone else, and so are you. We're going to get the big tin tub and fill it with water and wash all of you in it."

"All at once?"

Nelka laughed. "Come on, Hansel, let's ask Telek to bring water for us."

"No one's out there." Gretel knew she would have seen him.

"If Nelka is here, then Telek is here, poor fool." Magda shook her head.

Opening the door Nelka called, "Telek, can you help us?"

"The power of this girl," Magda sighed.

Telek stepped from behind a tree. Gretel's mouth fell open. He had not been there before. She would have sworn it.

"We need water. We need a fire to heat it. These children are filthy. Please."

He nodded and walked back toward the creek and became lost in the trees. His clothes were the color of bark and dead leaves. His hair was blond but dirty-colored like leaves too. He was strong looking, but he moved so softly that he seemed smaller than he was.

"How does he do that?" Hansel asked.

"He spent most of his life living in the forest."

"You should marry him, girl," Magda said. "He'd keep you safe. And I don't need to wash. I'll get the grippe and die if I get wet."

"First Magda, and then the children. Then we'll do the walls and blankets."

"You can't wet the blankets. They'll freeze."

"We'll pass them over the fire and drive the lice out. You know the children are crawling."

Nelka grabbed Hansel and handily lifted his shirt. "Look." She pointed to the red bites of lice made worse by his scratching.

"Set the tub on the floor, Telek."

Gretel saw how Telek looked at Nelka. As if none of them existed except her. His face was bony like a fox's, and when he turned to glance at Gretel, his eyes were chips of light blue. His eyes were the only color about him, and he turned them away quickly when Gretel stared.

The children were sent outside to help gather wood for the fire while Magda bathed. They piled up wood as fast as they could carry it, and when Nelka called them inside, Magda sat on the sleeping platform, wrapped in a blanket, her hair neatly braided.

Nelka turned to Hansel, beginning to undress him, but Hansel struggled, and turned so his pants would stay around his bony hips.

"Magda will die if she has to feed all your lice."

"Nobody can see me," Hansel shrieked.

"Don't be shy. I'm your cousin now."

Hansel hesitated and Nelka stripped him with a few twists of her hands.

"Aren't you scared of me and Gretel?"

"If I was scared all the time, I'd get constipated. It wouldn't be good for the baby."

Hansel thought about this as he lowered himself into the tub. Then he couldn't think about anything. It was too wonderful. The warmth of it. He dipped his face in and made little muffled snorts.

First Nelka rubbed kerosene in his hair. It stung and burned and he shrieked. Nelka laughed and kept rubbing it in. Then he had to sit and wait while it killed the lice, and Nelka scrubbed him all over with the soap until he thought the whole top layer of his skin was going to be rubbed off. But Hansel didn't care about the burning because by then, Nelka had won him over.

"Nelka," he crooned after she had scrubbed the kerosene out of his hair. He pushed his wet head against her bosom. "You can live with us and wash me everyday."

"And who would take care of the baby that's coming if I have to fuss with you, my Lord?"

"Gretel and Magda can take care of the baby."

"Out. You're done." Nelka plucked him from the water.

"More." He struggled free of the blanket and tried to leap back in the tub. "I can feel my heart, Magda. Thumpa-thumpa-thumpa."

"Nelka, you'll have another one following you. Telek will have to drown him like a kitten."

The water was changed again, and Gretel was washed as thoroughly as Hansel until finally all three of them were sitting in smoky blankets on the sleeping platform.

"We'll heat your clothes in a pan and drive out the rest of the lice."

Nelka patted Magda on the head like she was a child, and Gretel saw that Magda liked it. The three of them sat in a row while their clothes were heated and then they dressed one by one.

"Now the rest of this pig sty."

Telek had been bringing wood and water and carrying steaming buckets until he sweated. He had taken his coat off, and Gretel saw his muscles under the thin shirt. Telek lifted heavy pails of boiling water that had been reheated and had had kerosene and soap mixed into it with the dirt of their bodies and more kerosene added to make it deadly.

"It isn't what I'd do if it was warmer, but we have to finish. The sun will go down and freeze us all." Nelka started to pick up a bucket and Telek laid his hand on her arm.

"No."

He spoke so softly that Gretel barely heard, but Nelka stopped.

"Then you have to do it all, my hero."

Telek picked up the bucket and tossed the boiling water at the walls. It hit with a splash and went in the chinks between the wood.

"Get them, Nelka!" Hansel screamed. The lice were coming out of the walls and washing down to the floor. "Get the dirty things!"

Nelka, with skirts pulled up and her boots getting wet, ran into the puddles and dripped the rest of the kerosene onto the lice. They lay dead in pools of water and kerosene. The floor was soaked and the walls steamed.

Nelka took the broom and swept with such vigor that water and dead bugs and dirt flew in drops and splashes outside onto the mud.

"Wood, Telek. We have to dry it. And the snow is coming. We'll sleep here tonight."

Even the sun and the clouds mind her, Hansel thought, for as Nelka spoke, the clouds covered the sun and it began to feel colder.

"We'll steam for a while and then go to sleep like loaves laid on the stove."

"That was fun, Nelka." Gretel smiled and turned so that Nelka could braid her hair. Gretel lifted her arms and wanted to dance. She had forgotten what it was to be able to stand perfectly still and not have the crawling in her hair and on her body, not have to scratch until the skin bled.

Nelka took what was left of the kerosene and dabbed it on Gretel's wrists and neck and ankles. "Polish perfume." She grinned at Gretel, and Gretel blinked back the tears that the fumes of kerosene stung from her eyes.

Telek stacked up as much wood as Hansel and Gretel gathered in six days. They ate potatoes and bread and drank hot water with ground rye in it.

Telek pulled out a flask and Magda and Nelka took sips.

"Where do you get it, Telek?" Magda's cheeks were red. But Telek didn't say a word. Gretel knew it was vodka. Where would a ragged man like Telek get vodka? He didn't look like any of them. He wasn't afraid or angry. He just looked hard.

"Magda? Why do you have such a big stove?" Hansel asked.

"Because the baker's wife had to go and have twins and I got them out of her. He gave me his old stove when he brought a new one from the city."

"It's awfully big."

"Too big," Magda agreed.

They lay on the sleeping platform, Magda in the middle where it was warmest. Then Gretel and then Nelka. Hansel was on the other side of Magda and Telek slept on the floor.

In the middle of the night, Gretel woke and saw that Magda lay wide-eyed.

"Magda?" she whispered. "Priests don't have children do they?"

"Yes."

"Yes they do, or yes, I am right and they don't?" But she was so warm that she fell back asleep and didn't feel Hansel when he crawled over Magda and her and under the blankets next to Nelka.

"I love you, Nelka," he whispered. "I'm going to marry you."

She didn't say a word but gathered him in her arms and pressed her warmth against him. He lay next to her, the rhythmic kicking of the baby bumping against his backbone and keeping him awake until it blended with his own heart thumping in his chest, and Hansel knew no longer what was his flesh, what the baby's, and what Nelka's as he fell asleep.

"I told them that you needed it for a wound. Said you cut your leg chopping wood." Father Piotr was out of breath.

"I'll need a bottle every three weeks."

"The Germans must not want peroxide because I can still get it. But that may not last." He looked at the boy. "Cut his hair short first. That'll get rid of the curls."

"And the papers?"

"In a week. The children can't be seen until their baptismal certificates are done. Don't go to the village until then. The less you're in the village, the better."

When he'd gone, Magda called Hansel inside.

"Help me, boy."

She went to the corner of the hut and lifted a board in the floor. Under the floor were baskets of potatoes and onions and another basketful of odd metal instruments. Hansel sat on the table so Magda could reach him easily, and she cut off all his hair. Gretel picked up each curl as it fell and held them in her skirt. When he was shorn so closely that not a curl could show, Gretel took the hair to the stove and opened the heavy door. With a flick of her skirt, she threw the dark curls onto the coals where they lay for a moment and then vaporized, leaving threads of red until the threads disintegrated and became invisible.

"We're burning you up inch by inch." Gretel grinned at Hansel. "All the parts that are no good are going in the stove."

He put his hands over his penis and frowned, and Gretel giggled. "I'm joking, silly. Just your hair."

"I'll never get in the oven," the boy said.

"No one asked you to. Sit still, child." The witch had to use both bottles to get his hair the proper color. When she was done, it was a golden yellow, darker than Gretel's but believable next to the pallor of his face. Hansel's eyes looked even darker next to the hair. Unusual but possible.

"It looks really Polish, Hansel."

"I want to look like the soldiers. They have blond hair."

"What soldiers?" Magda held his shoulder as he tried to squirm down from the table.

"You know."

"Don't ever say you want to look like the Devil."

"They have guns."

"They're the Devil. They get out of bed and say, 'Where is someone to kill this morning?'"

"Nobody tells them what to do."

"Come outside, Hansel. We have to get wood." Gretel didn't want Hansel to make Magda angry. He had to stop.

"Don't go far, and if you see anyone, run back here."

And so began a stretch of days that lasted over a week. Each day it was the same. The children and Magda ate kasha for breakfast. There were wooden bowls for the food, but there were metal spoons. They drank hot water or shared Magda's hot drink of rye and acorns. Then they looked for wood. The stove was voracious.

At noon they ate cabbage soup and bread with beet marmalade on it. "It tastes like dirt," Hansel told Magda.

"There's no sugar in it, but when did you eat dirt?"

He had never eaten dirt, but he knew he was right. After lunch he sat on the snow and scraped until he had a clean patch of earth. He pinched up a lump of dirt and placed it on his tongue. It filled his mouth with the mold of long dead tree leaves and something else, something indescribable.

"I'm right," he shouted to Magda, running into the hut where she sat in the rocker. "Beet marmalade tastes like dirt."

Magda smiled but didn't move. Her bones hurt while the weather was so changeable.

"Once we are snowed in, I can move. Then in spring my bones will ache again until summer is here."

So the children played outside during the afternoon.

"I'm cold, Gretel. I want to go in."

"We have to stay outside, Hansel. That way, she'll forget we're even here."

"I hated the turnips last night," he said.

"You have to eat them."

"Nobody liked them. They were mushy."

"If Magda doesn't like them, then we have to like them a lot. That way she won't say we're eating all the good food and taking the best things away from her. We have to like all the bad food, Hansel. Then she won't mind feeding us."

When Gretel was ahead of him and couldn't hear, he whispered, "I hate mushy turnips."

They lived outside most of the time, running and moving to keep warm, eating everything allowed. The days went slowly. It wasn't like home. Home was before the ghetto. Before the cart and horse and the airplanes. Gretel could remember the piano, toys, and books, whole walls of them everywhere. Hansel could remember nothing.

"Not walls of them."

"Yes. Walls and walls of books from the floor to the ceiling."

He didn't believe it. In the ghetto there had been three books, and not toys exactly but sometimes there was a piece of chalk for a game or the cigarette cards.

Because his father had been a mechanic and went outside the barbed wire to work on the German trucks and cars, Hansel had the best collection of cigarette boxes of any boy in his building. The front of the box was always bright and clean and shiny. Cut apart, they made cards to play with or trade for something else.

Hansel frowned. He had left them under the blanket in the corner where they would be safe. Someday he might go back and get them. He knew the street. He knew the stairs. He tried to remember the name of the city.

No piano, Gretel thought, and her fingers twitched, remembering. Her mother's hands moving over the keys. The white and black of the keys so clean. Washing her hands before she practiced. The Germans had the piano now. They probably had all the pianos in the world.

It was hard to tell what day it was. Magda never went to the village. There were no calendars or clocks. The Germans didn't allow church on most Sundays. They slept in the dark and got up when it was light.

Days had gone by when the priest returned. With him was a man carrying a knapsack. Gretel saw them moving through the trees, and she drew Hansel behind her. The man was as ragged as the priest but younger and more frightened.

The two men went into the hut. Then Magda came outside. "Children?"

Hansel stared up into his sister's face, and Gretel felt the weight of taking care of him come down on her. She could hardly breathe.

The new man didn't look like a German. He was too thin. He looked too frightened.

She stepped out from behind the tree, and the three adults watched them walk toward the hut. The priest laughed.

"By God, the boy looks all right. A little odd with those dark eyes, but his skin's so pale. It may work."

The other man said nothing.

"It will work, and if not, then the wheel will go on."

It was something Magda said often. Gretel didn't know what she meant.

"Take their picture."

The new man spoke for the first time. "I have to get their heads just the right size. Then I cut them off and glue them over the other heads in the old photograph. Then I'll take another photograph of the composite picture. It won't be perfect, but if I age the picture a little—no one would notice without a good lens to study it."

"He's going to cut our heads off," Hansel whispered.

"No. He won't." Gretel wasn't sure.

"You can't cut my head off." Hansel tried to pull away from Gretel's hand and run.

The priest grinned. "We're not the Nazis. Just the head in the picture will be cut off."

Hansel was uncertain still, but the pictures of the children were taken. They stood separately and the man worked a long time to get the heads at a proper distance.

"It's done," the man said to the priest. "Give me the First Communion pictures tonight. The girl will be harder. I have to make her look younger. Maybe one picture will blur just a fraction. Maybe if she blinked."

He grabbed Gretel by the shoulder and stared at her eyes. "When I say *blink* you will blink very slowly. Do you understand?"

She nodded. He cried out the word and she closed her eyes and then opened them slowly while he took another picture.

And it was done. Seven more days of the light and dark coming and going, and the priest came back with a package.

Magda unwrapped the pictures. "That's a nice touch, using old frames." Magda stroked the wood gently. "Come look at what Christians you are, children."

Gretel and Hansel looked at the photographs that lay on the table. Hansel smiled. He looked wonderful. Below his face, which had a startled expression, was the body of a boy fatter than Hansel. He wore a black suit with short pants, clean white socks, and shiny shoes. There was a white flower in the lapel of the suit and a white ribbon with a bow was fastened around the sleeve of the suit on the child's left arm.

"My shoes are beautiful."

"Those aren't your shoes." Gretel was angry.

"Yes they are." Hansel was complacent. "I remember them."

Gretel stared at the picture of the girl. It was her but it wasn't her. The girl had blinked and her face was a tiny bit blurred. You couldn't say how old the face was, but the body—

"I was never like that." Gretel frowned.

"Yes, you were. I remember." Hansel picked up his picture and cradled it in his arms.

"You weren't born then." Gretel stared at the five-year-old girl in a white dress who carried a bouquet of white flowers and stared out with blurry eyes.

"I remember." Hansel smiled. "I want to hang it where I sleep."

The priest patted the boy on his head. "Now listen, children. These are your photographs of your First Communion. It is when you took the body of our Lord for the first time. Magda will explain all this to you."

He turned and grinned at Magda. "You have to teach them all of it. The prayers. How to behave at Communion. Confession."

"I don't remember those things."

"If you want to live, you had better remember, sister."

"You teach them."

"I can't come here every day. You must do it."

"They never allow services. Who will see them worshiping?"

The priest laughed. "Perhaps that is why God led these children here, sister. Perhaps it was to make you faithful at your devotions. Here—" He drew from his jacket a small book. "I brought you this. You can say morning prayers. Noon prayers. Prayers at night. The Lord's Prayer. The devotions. And—"

He put his hand back in his pocket and pulled out a string of wooden beads. "The rosary. They should know it. Say it every night until they can do it in their sleep."

"No."

"Teach them or die, sister. Teach them or kill everyone—the villagers—" He paused and then went on. "Nelka. All of us."

She took the beads reluctantly. "I'll teach them enough to answer the need. I'm not trying to make a priest and a nun."

"Perhaps they were sent to save you!"

The children said nothing. Hansel hung up his picture, and Gretel, after some thought, did the same. If people came in, both pictures should be there. She hung her picture on the wall but didn't like to look at it. The blurry eyes and the pale face over the well-fed body made her uneasy.

"It's like that fat girl ate me up," she told Magda.

Magda thought for a long while, rocking as usual, and then she spoke. "Let her eat you up, Gretel. There are worse wolves than that waiting with sharp teeth. Let the child have you."

Gretel hated it, but she knew Magda was right, so she forced herself to stare at the picture until she could no longer tell if it was her or not. She let the fat child devour the child she had been. After all, there were no pictures left of herself at that age or at any age. She had no pictures of her house, or her mother, or father, or the Stepmother.

The chair the fat girl stood beside, the lamp on the table with its shiny glass base, the carpet and the wall behind, and the physical fact of the child herself, this was what Gretel had for a past. She was uneasy, but she accepted it. Any picture was better than nothing.

The Mechanik

To live he had to find the motorcycle, but he could only think of his children, lost in the snow. The father, newly christened the Mechanik, moved steadily, concentrating on erasing his son and daughter from his mind. If he was caught, he must not think of them.

His feet began to sink in a bog of moss and mud, and he circled around it, moving slowly now, but steadily. The ooze of swamp had not frozen, and mist lay deep over the wet heart of the forest.

He saw a movement to his right and fell to the ground. Pushing his face into the snow-covered moss and leaves in his terror, he lay still. He caught no sound, and then, near him, the snort of breath released and a whickering.

He barely raised his head and saw the wild ponies in the trees. Four of them stood and stared at him, and only the jets of steam that their breath made in the cold air betrayed their presence.

"Too small for German horses," he muttered.

Their gray winter coats hung low under their legs, and he couldn't see their eyes for the shaggy hair that grew over their faces. The ponies didn't move until he stood and walked toward them, and then they disappeared into the trees and the white mist with only the squelch of hooves in the soft mud.

He stood resting, looking at the mist hanging in the air where the horses' breath had been, and smiled. The German horses. Huge and impossible to feed in the Russian winter. They had all been eaten by their masters. The Mechanik plodded through the woods. He chanted to himself, and it almost became a song as he walked on.

"The wrong horses, the wrong oil, the trains full of Jews they have to kill. No winter clothes. No oil for your tanks. No trains full of food. No trains full of oil. Just Jews. Jews. Jews. Jews. Jews, and your soldiers dying and dying."

He would have done a little dance, the words pleased him so much, but he had to concentrate on keeping the sun to his right as it began to fall in the sky. The road was south.

He had walked for most of the day and knew he must be close. Hearing a shout, he fell to the ground and waited. There was another shout, and it was in German, so he knew it was the killers.

"No dogs. Please. No dogs," he whispered. He crawled slowly toward the road bisecting the trees.

"Let's go," the voice shouted in German. "He's freezing his ass off back there."

It wasn't the first time the Mechanik was glad that he had learned German. Knowing German let you know when to speak and when to be silent and when to grovel in the dirt. Those who hadn't understood German hadn't jumped quickly enough, and died. He watched as two soldiers rode slowly back down the road on their motorcycles. Beyond them was an officer on another cycle.

Around four bends in the rutted road he caught up with them. The three motorcycles were clustered in the road. The Mechanik did not stop to see if his motorcycle was in the ditch near them. He moved more deeply into the forest and kept going alongside the road.

The children must be hiding nearby. Waiting for him.

He finally dared to draw closer to the road. He knew that he couldn't go much farther. His legs trembled, and without food he could never walk for another day.

"If I sleep, I die," he muttered. "If I walk many more hours with no food, I die. If they catch me, I die. If they don't catch me, I die. If I go back with no motorcycle, I die. If I steal a motorcycle from the Germans, I die."

He felt hysterical laughter rising up in his empty gut and fought it down. He couldn't even call to the children. They might be hiding two hundred feet away in the brush, but he couldn't call to them or the Germans would hear.

First he should make sure that the children were not dead. If a German had found them, he would have dragged them back to the officer. Then the beating to see if the children knew where the adults had gone. Then the shots to the head. The bodies would be on the road.

He walked through the trees and brush and began to move down the edge of the road, away from the Germans. He could move faster on the frozen mud.

The Germans wouldn't have bothered hiding the murdered children. They would have let the bodies fall with no thought of concealing the killings. Dead children were a good lesson for any Poles who came down the road. Little corpses kept the Poles docile until their turn came.

There were no bodies on the road, but he kept looking until he finally gave up and began walking back toward the Germans. He still stared ahead into every ditch looking for the boy's small form. The girl was older. They might have kept her for a while.

His face twitched at the thought. Not rape though. Not with an officer present. The soldiers would be shot on the spot if they had sex with a Jew. They probably wouldn't dare rape the girl with an officer leading the search, but the officer might rape her. He could send the soldiers off on the hunt and rape the girl before he killed her. The Mechanik's mind moved logically over these facts as he walked.

The voices shouted in German up ahead, and he moved into the trees. His whole body was hot and tense, and he hadn't scratched his lice since going into the forest the day before. It was amazing. It was as if the lice knew they had better not distract him or their host would die and be useless to them. Or his body didn't feel the crawling. That was a bad thing. It meant that death was standing next to you, waiting to step into your shoes.

The Mechanik smelled the cigarette before he saw the man. Twenty feet away the German soldier was smoking and holding a submachine gun in his hand. Not a German gun. It was a *pepecha*, the Russian PPD.

The Mechanik smiled. The killers were using any gun they could get now. Their own supplies were dwindling. They even had to use the guns of the despised subhumans. He stepped behind a tree and waited for the soldier to be called, to be summoned back to the road.

The soldier smoked and then there was a sound in the trees beyond them, the distinct crack of a twig, sharp and brief, then silence. The soldier threw down his cigarette and moved forward in a crouch. He held the *pepecha* in front and moved slowly.

The Mechanik's breath was fast in his throat. The children. One of them had stepped on a branch or rolled over on it. They were lying there in the leaves. Her blond hair like a scarf on the mud. His tiny face, so thin now, turned up curiously, looking for—

The ground was covered with wet snow, and the leaves were soggy. The Mechanik moved silently and not a leaf rustled. His feet were sinking in the damp soil and snow with no sound. An owl called nearby and the soldier jumped but did not turn. He stared into the forest, looking, waiting to kill again.

The German soldier suddenly sighed. It almost stopped the Mechanik. It was such a human thing, this soft, sad exhalation of air. The sound of a tired and homesick man who might be a normal man, sighing in his loneliness.

The Mechanik was so close he could smell the soap that the German had bathed with—the smell of oil from stolen Polish sausages and a whiff of the vodka he drank with his lunch to keep off the damp and cold.

A dark shadow, all bone and sinew, his clothes flapping around him as he leapt, the Mechanik jumped on the back of the German, closing his hands on the man's throat.

The soldier fell forward, taken by surprise and thrown off balance, and the hands of the Mechanik closed on his windpipe in a vise.

There was no choice. The Mechanik could only hold on, closing off any shout or cry of alarm with his hands, using the bony length of his body to hold down the man. Pressing in with his fingers as the soldier flopped under him, and thrashed, rose on all fours like a horse under the weight of the Mechanik until he grew dizzy and fell limply, convulsing a last time and lying still.

The Mechanik was afraid to loosen his hold, and he lay on top of the German with his hands clenched on the well-shaved throat until he thought he could go to sleep lying there.

His mind kept telling him that it was over, and finally he released his fingers. They were stiff from the effort, and he groaned. There wasn't time. The others would come looking for the soldier. The children.

"Children? Children?" he whispered.

They were too frightened to come out. They knew better than to come to someone who called. They were smart children. Jewish names would never draw them out.

Remembering their stepmother's idea, he called again.

"Hansel? Gretel?"

But there was nothing. Leaves and brush and more trees stretching endlessly. He had to get away from the dead soldier.

"It won't help them if I get killed," he whispered. "If I'm caught they might torture me. I might tell."

His mind rationalized as he stood staring back toward where the road was. He had to run, but he had to take what he could first. He moved back to the body of the soldier and jerked and dragged at the coat of the German until he got it off. The pants were good too. Woolen and thick. And the boots made him smile. Real boots. No holes at all. Well polished. He undressed the soldier and dragged the pants on, slipped into the coat which was too large and still held the warmth of the German's body, and after a second of hesitation, took the boots in one hand and the gun in the other.

He was breathing hard. There would be no motorcycle. He'd never be able to take it now. But he could take the gun. A *pepecha* and the cartridge belt was a prize. And the boots. Good boots saved your life in the winter.

The German lay on his back, legs naked, tongue stuck out between engorged lips, face darkening. The Mechanik lay down the gun and boots and grabbed the man by the shoulders.

"Help me, God," he whispered, and then he was angry. He had never believed in the God his father had talked of night and day. He had never believed, and there had been nothing since 1939 to make him believe.

The body was heavy, but he dragged it behind a tree and rolled it into a depression in the earth. Moving as quickly as he could, the Mechanik threw small pieces of dead wood onto the body and kicked leaves over the white skin of the man's legs. He wasn't covered well, but it might give the Mechanik an hour or two.

Collecting the gun and the boots, the cartridge belt over his chest, he picked up the hard leather pack the soldier had dropped to the ground and moved off through the woods. He had to find his wife.

The pack had some weight. He opened it, and the smell hit his face when the top flipped back. He kept moving as he turned over the contents.

Sausage—a good-size piece—and bread, and something that looked like a piece of beef wrapped up, cheese. A flask. A small canteen. And most miraculous of all, an apple.

He took the bread out and ate it slowly as he walked.

"I'll keep the rest for her," he whispered.

He finished the bread and then began tearing at the sausage with his teeth.

"I'll save the apple and the cheese for later." He crammed the food into his mouth. He was eating too fast, and he knew it. It could make him sick.

His need to live was like a murderer rising up in him, killing his good intentions. The apple he ate, core and all. Then the beef. Then the cheese. There was no sound from behind him. They weren't looking for the soldier yet.

He unscrewed the flask and poured the vodka down his throat, hardly tasting it. He gulped it all and then threw the flask into the leaves. The partisans might not like it that he hadn't shared the vodka.

"If I die, it doesn't do my wife any good." He felt the grease of the meat begin to travel through his gut. He knew it would give him the runs.

He walked on. The gun and ammunition would be enough booty

for the partisans to let him live. If not, he would kill the Russian and the others and take his wife and go.

He walked a little faster now. The vodka had stopped his legs from shaking. If only there had been coffee. He didn't know if the Germans still had real coffee. A cup of hot coffee would have given him the strength to walk for a week.

And maybe the children were moving in the same direction. Their bodies were not lying in the road. They were hiding. It was cold, but the girl was smart. She'd find a farm or a village. She'd find a way to get food.

"I never called out their names," he said aloud. "I never did." And that seemed like good luck to him. If you did not name a thing, then it did not exist. There were no Jewish children for the murderers to find in these woods.

He told himself this as he moved into the forest, deeper and deeper, farther from the road and the dead man. He kept saying it over and over as he walked and jogged onward, and only his eyes betrayed him and leaked bitter water onto his face as he fled.

The Village Piaski

"What's your name?"

"Hansel Cegielski."

"Where's your mother?"

"Germany. Working on a farm." Hansel picked up a stone and threw it at a rook who watched them from a fence post.

"Pay attention." Magda moved steadily down the narrow road. It was frozen hard so the mud didn't catch her feet like glue.

"Our father was killed in September of 1939. He wasn't a soldier. He was hit by a truck when he was walking on a road pushing a wheelbarrow." Gretel spoke earnestly as she shifted to her other hand the basket that held their First Communion pictures and the false papers that said she and Hansel had been born in Warsaw and were members of the Karaites.

"Why did they circumcise you, Hansel?" Magda stopped to catch her breath. She stared into the gray forest and shivered. Perhaps she shouldn't take the children to the village.

"Because the Karaites believe that boys should be cut."

"And when they tease you about it?"

"Jesus was cut too. So why shouldn't a Christian be the same?"

"You won't say that unless they're pushing you hard. Who told you that about Jesus?"

"The priest of the Karaites. They said it was true. I'm just like Jesus." He wasn't paying real attention. His mind was on the rooks that sat waiting for him to scare them off.

Magda walked on. The girl was wary. There'd be no problem with her, but the boy was impulsive and too young. He had been quiet when the children came to her three weeks ago. Now Hansel jumped and ran and talked all day.

It's the food, Magda thought. Kasha and potatoes and turnips and the occasional bit of salt pork, dried mushrooms, and berries and herb tea. Tenaciously fastened on life, his body recovered. If only she had a little farm, a few pigs. Then she could do without the ration cards.

Magda groaned as the cold crept up her legs and her hips began to ache. There was nothing for it. A guest in the house was God in the house. The old folk saying came to her.

"Will we have to talk to the Germans, Magda?" Gretel fingered the plait of hair which hung down over her shoulder. Magda had braided it with her swollen fingers and tied it with string.

"I can talk to them. I talked to them a lot. Look, Magda." Hansel stopped walking and drew himself rigidly to attention. He clicked his heels and threw his arm out. "Heil Hitler!" he screamed. He held the pose for a moment and then relaxed and grinned at Magda. "Sometimes we got bread when we saluted."

"They won't give you bread in the village if you do that. Too many mouths to feed. And if you act like a little Nazi, the village brats will beat you up."

"They won't beat me up. I can fight. And I can run." He ran down the road, around a curve and was gone. He slipped on the ice only once and with an acrobatic leap corrected his balance.

Magda sighed.

"He'll be all right, Magda. I'll watch him."

"He's too young. He'll kill us all." Magda walked on, but it had become serious now. Forcing her brother to behave like the Christian he had always pretended to be had been amusing, but it wasn't amusing anymore. It seemed an act of stupidity now. Trying to save two Jews.

Like dancing with death, but maybe that was appropriate at her age. And her grandmother would have helped the children. The Grandmother would have spit on the ground and said, "Fuck the Germans. They don't get their way every time."

Magda smiled at the thought. And the boy was almost like one of the Rom. How could she throw him away?

Gretel didn't ask if Magda was afraid. Everyone was afraid when they had to speak to the Germans. And if they didn't speak to them, there would be no ration cards. Magda couldn't feed them all winter on her card alone.

"Hansel? Come back here." Magda needed to collect the boy. She needed to walk into the village quietly, with no wild jumping and running and calling of attention. Two new children would be bad enough. Two new mouths to eat up what the Germans had portioned out for the village. No one would be happy to see them.

Hansel trotted back, trying to slide on the icy road and slipping, falling, getting up with a grin, his cheeks red from the cold and the running. "I'm coming, Magda."

The boy took the old woman's hand firmly and swung it as they walked on. She didn't pull away, and the warmth of his hand gradually warmed her own.

They smelled the village before they got there. It was the smell of smoke from wood fires, and mud churned up by feet and hooves and the hard round wheels of the carts.

"It's not the same," Magda murmured.

"What's not the same?" Gretel smoothed her coat gently. It was a safe coat. There was no darker patch on her chest where a yellow star had been sewn and then torn off. This coat had been stolen in Bialystok by—she almost stumbled on a rut in the road. Stolen by someone. She did not think his name. "What's not the same?" she asked again.

"When you live in the forest, you forget what people smell like when they live all together on one piece of mud. But it used to be—" She hesitated, thinking. "It used to be better. I would walk into the village and almost decide to live here."

"Why?" Hansel still held her hand, but he skipped and jumped occasionally and she felt his energy springing out as she walked more slowly.

"Food cooking. Bread baking. Hunter's stew and meat roasting. Pancakes sizzling in oil, and in the summer the smell of melons and peaches hung over the fields around the village like perfume. My God! What a lot we ate then!"

"What do you miss the most, Magda?" Gretel knew what she missed. Her mouth watered delicately as she remembered it.

"Good Polish soup. Full of everything the earth gives us. So thick you stick a spoon in it and it can't fall over. Soup with a little beer mixed in, and a glass of strong wine beside it."

"I miss oranges." Gretel could hardly say the word. Water filled her mouth at the memory of the sweetness.

"That's for city folk. Maybe at Christmas they'd bring a basket of them out here."

"I don't think oranges are all that good." Hansel pulled away from Magda and picked up a stone. He threw it, and it went wild and hit a tree limb with a sharp click. He blew on his fingers to warm them.

"You never had an orange. You were too little when we had them. Babies don't eat oranges." Gretel was sure of it.

"You never had oranges either." He ran behind Gretel and jerked her braid.

"I ate an orange every day." Gretel stopped. The memory was clear. He had white hair, and he came every morning. He crept in very quietly and gave Gretel an orange and he smelled of tobacco and he smiled as he held the waxy orange fruit out to her. He said that she would have an orange every morning of her life. He had been wrong. She had called him Zayde, a Yiddish word, even though Father frowned. Her Zayde. Grandfather.

"Gretel?" Magda stared at the girl.

Gretel opened her eyes. It had been so clear. The warm room with the table. His coming in and handing her the orange.

"Daydreamer, daydreamer," Hansel chanted. He leaped from side to side on the road, taking twenty steps for Magda's one.

"Hold my hand, Hansel. We're there." She was almost glad that the Nazis had shot all the dogs. The way they used to run at her whenever she went into the village, barking and snarling. She hadn't liked it any more than the Nazis. But the dogs were dead now.

Magda walked around the curve in the road, holding the boy firmly by the hand. Her face was still and had the blankness of one who lives alone, but her heart convulsed in her chest with quick jerks.

The road ran through the village of Piaski with streets even narrower and muddier going off it. There were only three buildings larger than the huts of the peasants: the school, the building for the village officials with the jail in the back rooms, and in the middle of the village, the church.

The Communists and the Nazis between them had burned all the other churches in the district, but not this one. The spire, tipped with a cross for a thousand years, still stood in the heart of the village, but the cross had been broken off by the Russians. Only a stick remained.

The Communists had used the church as a restaurant, and they made the women cook meals in front of the altar. A big stove was set up where God had lived and the roof broken open to let out the stovepipe. All the soldiers ate there, and sang their Russian songs and drank until they puked on the floor and lay in it.

The stove had been bad enough, and using the altar itself to cut meat and vegetables—setting pots of water on the wood that stained it and left rings and tore away the finish and wax—had upset everyone. Except for the old women of the village.

"Don't worry, children," they said. "The Russians are barbarians who don't know what clocks are. They don't know that every time we cut meat on the altar we think of God. It will be over someday and God will have been here all the time."

Magda had no use for the church, but it gave the people heart. The Communists couldn't take it away. The Communists vomited on the church but they couldn't drive it out of the heart of the Poles. The Nazis made her brother get a signed paper every time he had a service, but the people still went whenever they could.

"Stubborn bastards, us Poles," she muttered.

The poorer people lived on the edge of the village. A few hardened cabbage stalks still stood in the gardens, and a pig rooted in a pen near the road. They walked past the huts and came to the second largest building, unpainted, shutters hanging crazily with neglect, on their right.

"What's that?" Hansel asked.

"The school."

"School? I'm going there." He stopped skipping and stood stock-still.

"No." Magda laughed. "No school for Polish children."

He ran up the steps and scrubbed the dirty glass of the window. Magda watched the boy and was amazed that the glass was not broken. The windows of the church were all gone.

"Magda, come tell me."

She went up the stairs and peered into the school. It was empty. The desks were long gone. Chopped up for firewood, she supposed. Mud was turning to dust on the wooden floor.

"Who are they?" he demanded.

She raised her eyes to the wall where three pictures hung, dust-covered but still staring out over the bare boards of the floor. On the left was Lenin.

"Beady-eyed bastard," she whispered. "It's Lenin on the left. The one with all the hair is Stalin, on the right." A crucifix with Jesus on it hung between the two pictures.

"Jesus is hanging between two thieves like he always has," she muttered. She grinned and spit on the porch. "It doesn't matter. You won't be going in there."

"No school at all?"

"They have classes once a week and teach counting to one hundred and how to write your name. They teach you to recognize all the ranks of the German army and how to address our conquerors. That's all the school for Poles. And they do it outside. You stand in the mud like the pigs. I don't want you coming here for that. They won't care. They don't like education for Poles."

"I can count to a thousand and read a lot."

"You can't. You can only read a little." Gretel shifted the basket.

"I read as good as you." He glared at his sister.

"I can read Polish and some German and some French." She smiled. It had been so nice to sit with a book on her lap and let the hard cover of the book be a wall that shut out everything in the ghetto room where they lived with seven other people.

"You just brag. You're dumb, Gretel." He danced in front of them and made faces, but Gretel ignored him.

Magda shook her head. It was too complicated. A boy who needed to run. A girl in a poor village in eastern Poland who could read in three languages. She stopped walking as they got to the first house and stared at Gretel.

"He can run, but you aren't able to read anything but a little Polish. A little. The shop signs and a little from the Bible. You like to read cooking recipes best of all."

Gretel turned paler and nodded. Her face was almost as pale as the silver of her hair. "I read just a little. In Polish."

Magda nodded. The girl was possible. But the boy. Anything he saw that was strange to him, he asked about.

"Magda," Hansel called. "Magda, look at me. I can do this." He hopped on one foot and then hopped on the other, covering the ground almost as fast as he could run. "Look at me!"

"Come here." She sighed.

He came and grabbed her hand. She winced when he pulled her arthritic fingers too hard.

"Magda, I'm never going to stay inside when I grow up."

"You can be a farmer and work outdoors all day."

He thought about it and then shook his head. "No. I'm going to go all over the world and I'll never just stay in one house."

Magda smiled. He was dangerous, this child, but he was a child that her grandmother would have loved. She stopped smiling. There was no need to love these two. Just keep them quiet, get the ration cards, and be patient. It would be over someday. One hundred thousand Germans had surrendered at Stalingrad. The Russians were breaking the back of the Nazi army.

The three walked through mud torn up by carts, and the mud clung to their shoes making them rock with each step. A rooster shrieked in rage, most of his chickens slaughtered and their bones cracked and boiled until they gave up every last shred of nourishment.

Villagers who saw Magda turned away and didn't speak. Magda the Witch had found two children and had to register them. God knows what the day would hold.

Only Telek the water carrier followed them like a gray shadow, stopping to adjust his buckets, never looking directly at the three of them ahead of him, following behind. Magda was Nelka's aunt. Magda could help her when the baby came. Nelka would care if the Germans killed Magda. Telek followed and waited, letting his face relax into its usual blank stare.

Basha pulled back the rag of a curtain and watched Magda and the children walk past. "She's going to try and get ration cards for them."

"Who are they, do you suppose?" Her husband didn't really want to know.

"God knows. Magda isn't a talker."

"I'm surprised any of that family is alive."

"Hush." Basha bit her lip and crossed herself.

"She'll only stir them up registering two, strange children. She'll give them something to think about, and that's always a mistake."

"She can't feed them on her card. Eight hundred calories a day."

"On good days." Andrzej sighed and moved to the window. He limped heavily. Only his bad leg had kept him from being sent into Russia as a laborer when the Communists had taken the village. "And Jedrik, that fat bastard. Filthy collaborator. He could talk anytime about Magda's Gypsy blood. He'd do anything for a sack of potatoes."

"Her brother's the priest. Jedrik wouldn't dare tell about Magda's grandmother. She's Father Piotr's grandmother too. They'd kill him."

They stood silent for a minute and then Andrzej spoke. "I heard someone new is coming."

"Something to do with the farming?"

"Talk is, that an SS man is coming. With a woman. In a car."

"A car." That had to be bad. The Germans had stolen all the bicycles and used only them for transportation between the villages since the Russians had gone. Any Pole caught with a bicycle was shot. The trucks and cars had moved on with the war, leaving the dregs of the army to run the village. Only one lone truck brought the German mail and supplies for the Major.

"We aren't important," she said.

"No. But a car is coming. It was in Rastilkov yesterday."

"And now these children." She shivered. "And since October—" She didn't finish it.

"They'll kill us if they find out. Forget October. We have three children and three ration cards." He stared out the window. He didn't like to see Basha's face when she mentioned the dead baby, the baby who was buried in an unmarked grave in the woods, the baby whose ration card still gave them food each month because the death was unreported and undiscovered.

Neither spoke again. The street was quiet. Only Telek the water carrier moved slowly toward the center of the village with his two buckets swaying from the yoke across his shoulders.

———

Magda walked up the wooden steps to the building that held the mayor's office, although the mayor was dead, and the post office, although no letters came now, and the jail, although the Germans just shot anyone they arrested.

"Magda," Gretel whispered. "Maybe we should go back to the woods."

"When you're falling off a cliff, you can even grip a razor blade, child."

Magda opened the door and led them in.

Sugar

Hansel knew the Major immediately. He wasn't behind the desk but stood smoking a cigarette, staring out the window. He was wearing a tunic cinched tight with a leather belt, and the tunic wasn't very clean. He had mud on his boots like everyone in the village, and only his shoulder patches told his rank.

The man behind the desk was too thin to be German, and his eyes looked almost as anxious as Magda's did when he saw the old woman and the children.

"What do you want?"

"Heil Hitler." Magda lifted her arm. "My great-niece and -nephew have been sent to me."

The major stared at them, and Gretel made herself go very still. Then she turned slightly and smiled at him. She tried not to look at the patch that partly covered a scar of shiny, red skin. His left eye was blue, bright blue and damp with moisture. The Major wiped his eye quickly, pressing the moisture out, and stared at the children through his single red-rimmed eye.

"Where are the parents?"

"Their father died in 1939. Then their mother was sent into Germany as a farmworker. The children were brought to me." Magda said only what had to be said, with no embellishment.

"Who brought them?" The German threw his cigarette on the floor and crushed it into the scarred wood with only the toe of his boot. Hansel looked at the cigarette butt and wished he could pick it up. It was worth something, maybe a couple of potatoes.

"Someone put them on the supply truck from the city three weeks ago. Threw them in the back and the driver didn't even know." Magda stared at the floor.

Gretel knew it was her turn. "We climbed out when the truck stopped. We knew how to get to Aunt Magda's."

"And why did the truck stop?" He moved beside Gretel and lifted her plait of hair. Tugging gently, he watched her face.

Oh God, I didn't think of that question, Magda thought, but there was nothing for it. The child would either get them killed or not.

"The driver had to pee." Hansel grinned up at the Major.

"Papers." He lit another cigarette and moved back to the window. This fucking village. A mud hole in hell. Some days he didn't even appreciate that he had escaped the Russian front. It was hard to be grateful since it had taken an eye to get him out—and all the other men were still there.

Gretel set the basket on the desk and gently took out the First Communion pictures and the papers. The clerk behind the desk examined them, staring from the pictures to the children and back to the papers. The seals didn't look bad. The papers might actually be genuine.

Filthy alley rat, Magda thought. Sitting at this desk like he's someone. Dragged out of a Warsaw prison and working for the Germans.

"They seem all right. These are Polish children, Major Frankel."

The Nazi nodded. You could tell sometimes by the bones and the hair. The girl was quite a pure Aryan type.

"Give them ration cards." He smoked the cigarette and watched the old woman. Not an Aryan type. Dark eyes and short. Like a gnome. Twisted and subhuman. But her niece was perfect. Interesting.

"Was your father German, children?" He asked in German, and Gretel opened her mouth to answer. She closed it immediately, but he saw.

"Ah. You understand." It wasn't surprising. These lumpish villagers understood nothing, no matter how he screamed, but the girl was from the city. He smiled at her.

"What's your name?"

"Gretel, and he's Hansel."

His eyes widened, and he smiled. "I thought so. There's German blood in the family somewhere. We are the *Kulturtrager,* child." He spoke in rough Polish except for the one German word. "Tell me what that means."

"You are the bringers of culture," Gretel whispered.

He put his hand in his pocket and drew it out quickly. He stepped toward Gretel, and she moved slightly so she was between the Major and Hansel.

"And we rule by *zuckerbrot und peitsch.* Tell me what that means."

"By sweets and the whip," Gretel spoke slowly, like it was difficult for her to translate.

"Open your mouth and close your eyes."

Now he will shoot me in the mouth, Gretel thought, but she had to do it. If she ran he would shoot her in the back.

She let her eyelids drop and waited to feel the cold metal of the gun barrel against her tongue. Instead there was the rough touch of his hand and then sweetness filled her mouth.

She opened her eyes, and the tears rolled down her cheeks. Candy. She let the sweet lie on her tongue and tasted real sugar and peppermint for the first time in years.

"See her cry, Wiktor? A touch of nerves. It's that weakness that shows her Polish blood."

Gretel sucked the candy in silence. The man at the desk, Wiktor, stamped cards and threw them in the basket with the pictures and papers. "Go on, woman. Take them off."

Magda felt a touch of guilt for her anger at Wiktor. He might be a Warsaw jail rat, but he hadn't mentioned the card saying that the children were Karaites.

"Wait." The German was smiling. "I have an honor for you, girl. Because you have a German name, you can be the lucky child this week. Go to the store and tell them you will hand out the sugar."

Magda bowed and shuffled backward, taking Hansel with her. Gretel hesitated and then stepped toward the Major.

"Thank you." She stepped close to him and kissed the sleeve of his jacket with a soft brush of her chapped lips.

"You see, Wiktor? This one has a bit of civilization. She is almost mannered."

The three backed into the hallway and out the front door. Magda was panting. Hansel hadn't said a word, thank God, but Gretel—

"He noticed you too much. You have to stay out of his way."

"He liked it. He may give us more food."

It was true, but being liked was dangerous. Magda shook her head. "The store. We have to register your cards."

There were only two shops now. One store, with all the flour allotted the village, all the salt, all the bits of salt pork and beans locked in barrels, was in the middle of the village where there wasn't really a town square but a widening of the mud to allow a weekly market in summer.

Next to the store was the butcher shop where all meat was kept. Any meat not coming from the store, any pig or goat or cow not registered and numbered, was reason for death. A single slice of black market ham sent a bullet to your brain.

Gretel stopped by a post which stood in the middle of the mud circle in the heart of the village. Nailed to the post was a poster of heavy paper, clean and white, and she read it aloud:

" 'Any Polish woman who insults a German by word or action will be considered a whore and sent to whorehouses on the Russian front.' "

There was another piece of paper tacked on the back of the post. Gretel began to smile.

"Don't smile, child," Magda whispered.

"What is it?" Hansel whispered too.

" 'On October sixteenth two treacherous attacks on German soldiers were—' " Gretel hesitated.

" 'Perpetuated,' " Magda said.

" 'Attacks on German soldiers were perpetuated by two cowardly Polish criminals. Both Germans were injured, one severely.' "

Magda's mouth twisted like a wolf at the end of the hunt.

" 'As a consequence thereof, on October 19, three Polish criminals, who as members of the PZP and the PPR were hirelings of England

and Moscow were selected from a number of persons under death sentence by the court-martial of the Security Police, but previously designated for an act of mercy, and publicly executed. It is always intended to pardon the condemned. The population of the village Piaski is therefore called upon to do everything to prevent further attacks on Germans so no further executions will take place.

" 'Village Piaski, November 22, 1943.

" 'Major Frankel of the Security Police for the Security Service for the village Piaski.' "

"Lies!"

They all jumped at the deep voice. The man was big and square, his bones so large he didn't look thin. His eyes rolled and he turned and blew snot onto the mud with a fierce snort from his nostrils.

"They got drunk on some homemade vodka and knocked two of the Germans over in a joking sort of way. Just young fools. They took the Germans' cigarettes. Nobody would admit to doing it, so they killed three prisoners."

"Only three?" Gretel was impressed. They would have killed everyone in the building if it was in the ghetto.

"They only had three in the jail. It's getting harder to make grand gestures. Fucking *Shkopy*." The man blew his nose again onto the ground. "I can read snow like the Bible, and I tell you, it's going to be a blizzard, Magda. Go home."

He turned and stalked off.

"Who's he?" Hansel wanted to know everything.

"That's Feliks. He's been angry since they made his Jew run away."

Gretel stared at Magda, who sighed and told the story.

"He had a friend. A Jew. Jacobe was the only man in the village who could play chess with Feliks and make the game last longer than ten minutes. They played every week, sometimes all night. When they weren't playing chess, they sat and talked for hours. People said that when the end of the world came, Feliks and Jacobe wouldn't stop talking for it. Everything was quiet. We were waiting for the Germans. When we woke up, that first morning after the Russians had gone, Jacobe had run for it. Telek, the water carrier, saw him creeping into the woods at dawn. Jacobe was afraid of the Germans."

"He's in the woods?" Hansel asked.

"In Russia if he's lucky. Or dead. But Feliks has no one to play chess with now. He hardly speaks. He hates them for chasing off his Jew, his friend. Feliks had a brother, but his brother is gone. Feliks's real brother, the brother of his mind and spirit, was Jacobe, and Jacobe ran away."

"Where did Feliks's real brother go?" Gretel asked.

"Killed." Magda said no more, but the boy wouldn't leave it alone. "Why?"

"Because Feliks's brother wasn't perfect. So they killed him."

"What was wrong with him?"

"He was crazy. Not crazy exactly, just simple. Foolish. His mind didn't work right. The Germans talked to him, and saw he was simple, so they shot him. They shot all the crazy people."

"There was a crazy man—" Hansel stopped. He couldn't talk about the cantor who sung under the window. The three of them walked on in silence, Magda thinking of Feliks, and the children thinking of Feliks's brother.

The store was only a wooden hut with barrels behind the counter. Magda handed over the cards and waited. She hoped there were beans this week. A lump of fat. Her hands already had chilblains and so did the children, but there would be no fat for their hands this winter. The children had to eat all the fat. Bleeding fingers wouldn't kill them, but they were still growing and couldn't get too thin.

Gretel stood looking at the barrels. Magda, watching her, shook her head. The boy wouldn't grow so much, but the girl was at the age to sprout up. She would die if she didn't get enough food. Probably already stunted. She looked younger than she should, and her body would keep growing whether there was food or not. All the children in the village looked younger. And all the adults looked like old men and women.

"He said that the girl should hand out the sugar," Magda told the clerk. She didn't like it.

"Truly, Magda? Don't get me killed." He touched his neck nervously where an ulcer suppurated and rubbed his collar.

"Truly."

"Come on, girl."

He took a small jar and a spoon.

"Go with him, Gretel." Magda had to let her do it. The Major might ask.

Gretel followed the clerk outside, where there were children milling around the steps.

"No sugar until you're lined up."

The village children fell into a long line. Magda counted them. Fifteen. Twenty. Thirty-one. Only thirty-one left and almost no babies now. Women didn't get pregnant if they could help it, or if their men were in Siberia or dead or hiding in the woods.

Or the babies were dead. Most of them died from lack of milk. Polish women's tits were wrinkled sacks, empty like the cupboards in the houses. All the good food had been stolen away into Russia and was stolen now for the German soldiers at the Russian front.

The clerk stood Gretel on the top step and handed her the jar and spoon.

"One level spoonful for each child. In their mouth. Not in their hands. Put it in their hands and the little cockroaches sell it."

Gretel nodded. She scooped up one small spoonful of sugar, tapped it carefully against the inside of the jar to shake off the rounded top, and looked up.

"Begin," said the clerk. Magda didn't know his name. He was a Pole brought in to manage the food by the Germans. He had no ties to the village, so he had no one to be kind to, no one to save. He was called the Clerk. His name had disappeared with the war.

A child stepped forward and turned his face up to Gretel. He opened his mouth, and Gretel gently poured the sugar onto his tongue. She could see the saliva that had flowed as he waited, a pool in his mouth that caught the sugar. Another child stepped up, and Gretel poured a spoonful of sugar in his mouth. At the end, she held a jar with only a little sugar in it. She looked at the Clerk and he nodded. Gretel turned to Hansel and tipped half the sugar into his mouth. It was more than a spoonful. She watched his eyes grow round as the pure sweetness, so much fuller than the sweetness of saccharin with its metallic taste afterward, filled his mouth.

"More," he said.

She nodded. It was only fair. She had had the candy. She tipped the jar and he crunched the rest between his teeth and licked the edge of the jar to take off any crystals that clung.

She turned to give the jar to the Clerk, and saw the Major watching from the road. He stood in the mud, smoking, and smiled at her.

"He prowls the streets," the Clerk whispered to Magda. "He's guilty about leaving his men at the front. He can't sit by the stove and stay warm. He prowls."

Gretel did not smile back at the Major this time. He walked forward, and the village children were suddenly gone. Moving quickly, the soft mud hiding the sound of their wooden shoes and patched boots, they were just gone.

"She is a good girl. She gives generously and isn't greedy. So she gets a reward."

His fingers, smelling of tobacco, rough on her lips, pushed another candy into Gretel's mouth, and she nearly gagged.

"*Danke,*" she whispered, and in an hour the whole village knew that Magda had two brats staying with her and the Major was taking an interest in the girl, and the girl spoke German.

It was a mistake. All of it. But no one said it out loud. Magda had always been separate from the village. Perhaps any disaster would fall on her head alone, outside the circle of the houses. It was her mistake, and she could keep it out in the dark wetness of the forest with the wild ponies and the bison and the ancient hornbeam trees that blocked out the sun. It was hers and they didn't want it.

The Car

"Like being hit in the chest with a board," Magda muttered. Her feet, wrapped in layers of rags and socks inside her boots, were frozen stumps.

"Listen." Hansel looked at Magda and took Gretel's hand.

Magda finally heard it. Breaking the silence of the late afternoon was the mutter of a car.

"Hide." Magda waved her hands at the children like she was shooing chickens.

Before she could get out of the ditch and into the trees herself, the children were flattened out, not a trace of them in sight. Magda felt her numb feet breaking through the crust of ice in the bottom of the ditch and the muddy water rushing into the cracked soles of her boots. She barely had time to step behind an oak tree before the car rounded a bend in the road.

It was going slowly, and she listened to the engine sound with dread, leaning her cheek against the cold bark of the tree. Cars meant that something would be done to someone. It was a black Grosser Mercedes. The roof of the car still held the shine of layers of wax, and the mud splashed halfway up the sides didn't conceal all of the polished finish.

Two soldiers in front. Two in the backseat. The flash of black and silver. Worse and worse. An SS officer. And—Magda stared but couldn't see the other person clearly. Just a shape.

The car struggled slowly but steadily over the ruts. The motor never faltered. It went on down the road in a left-to-right motion, trying to avoid the deepest holes. Then it was gone and the sound turned into a low hum until the silence of the forest fell upon Magda and the children again.

"We have papers. Why do we hide, Magda?" Hansel knocked the snow off his chest.

"Cars mean people who cause trouble. If they don't see us, then we have no trouble."

"There was a woman." Gretel stared after the car. "And an SS." Gretel looked steadily at Magda. She didn't want to frighten Hansel. "Not like the Major. Not army, Magda."

The girl was sharp. But so was everyone else in Poland by now. SS. The skull worn proudly to show that they defied death and were not frightened by it. But to the Poles the SS were the Angels of Death, the winged skeleton who comes for your bones and drags them out of you while you squeal like a hog being butchered.

"The woman may be his wife. Perhaps it's just a trip to see the country." Magda looked at Gretel and saw the child was not fooled. Germans didn't leave the comforts of the city in the winter to visit a muddy Polish village where they had to eat black bread with saw-dust in it.

"I'm cold." Hansel shivered and clung to Gretel.

"Come on. Feliks was right. Snow's coming. A lot of it. I can smell it." Magda sniffed deeply and breathed in the almost metallic scent that had been growing stronger all day. Snow was good. It slowed them all down. Things were postponed during the hard snow. The war almost stopped.

And that was too bad in a way. The Russians had been killing the Germans, and now they would have to stop. Magda smiled when she thought of the springtime and the way that the Russians would rise up like animals shaking the snow off, killing again when the armies moved.

"The Russians," she said. "They're bastards and can't be trusted, but the Germans have made a mistake with the Russians."

"What do you mean?" Gretel carried the basket and the flour and tried to hold Hansel's hand too so he would walk faster and not fall behind.

"It's like a woodcutter who meets a wolf in the forest, and the man's too proud to run, so he grabs the wolf by the ears."

"Then what?"

"Nothing for a while. There they stand. The wolf waits and the woodcutter doesn't dare turn loose of his ears. But sooner or later the woodcutter tires and his hands slip. Then the wolf eats him up." Magda laughed. "Come on. I can't get sick. I want to live long enough to see the Germans turn loose of the Russians' ears." The first flurry of snow was covering their heads when they saw the hut ahead of them.

Major Frankel was sweating. He wiped his forehead with a gloved hand and cursed. There was a streak on the whiteness of the glove now. The SS cared about these things. It had been a miracle that he had found a pair of white gloves. Who the hell cared about white gloves?

"Wiktor. You Polish piece of shit!"

"Major!" Wiktor stood at attention behind the desk. He looked terrible.

"You Polish monkey! Straighten your desk." The Major always screamed at Wiktor in German. Wiktor's German was better than the Major's Polish, and Wiktor always responded in German. Sometimes Frankel wondered where a jailbird like Wiktor had learned such good German.

There was nothing on the desk except for two metal trays and two pens lined up neatly beside them. Not a piece of paper in sight. Wiktor moved the trays an inch or two and lined them up perfectly with the edge of the desk. He moved the pens an inch toward the trays.

"You asshole of the world."

The two men stared at each other until they heard the sound of a car engine.

Major Frankel forced himself to move down the hall to the outside door. Should he open it? Should he send Wiktor and remain in the office? Would the SS officer think he had nothing to do if he stood outside and greeted him? Should he be busy inside? "This fucking country."

Maybe it wouldn't go badly. This SS officer might be a comrade, a brother. He might even wear a ribbon worth having in his second buttonhole.

Major Frankel glanced down. It wasn't regulation. But the medal had been sent home after the winter of 1941–1942. There wasn't much use keeping the medal to get wrecked at the front, so he had sent it home to be framed and put on the wall. But he kept the ribbon. They all had. It was tied through his buttonhole where it always was. Dirty now and limp.

But noble, Frankel thought. Noble, goddamnit. Winter of '41–'42 at the eastern front had been so terrible, so huge, that only a token would do. It wasn't fitting to wear some hunk of metal with eagles and swastikas. Just a dirty piece of cloth to show you had been there for the dirtiest war ever survived, but every soldier knew what that ribbon meant. It meant you had fought the Russians through the worst winter of the century, and you were still standing. Wearing the ribbon tied through the buttonhole wasn't regulation, but it was the only decoration he'd ever wear.

Wiktor opened the outside door, and Major Frankel saluted. "Heil Hitler," he shouted.

The man was too high ranking. SS Oberführer. Almost a general. What was he doing here? With only a car and two soldiers?

"Heil Hitler." The Oberführer returned his salute.

"I am honored, Oberführer, that you—" the major stopped.

"Let me present Sister Rosa."

Frankel felt the sweat roll down his back under his shirt. Who the hell was she? Not a nun. But the brown cape and brown dress were odd. The Brown Sisters. He couldn't remember exactly what they were for, not nursing, something to do with the SS. He didn't know how to greet her, and his right leg began to tremble like a horse's leg when it sees a piece of paper fly across the riding ring and is getting ready to bolt.

"Heil Hitler," the woman screamed.

"Heil Hitler," he screamed back. Major Frankel stared at the Oberführer's chest and had to stop himself from smiling. Oak wreathes, swords on top of oak leaves, swastikas, glittering lines of medals. Every one a piece of crap. A bunch of damn medals for physical fitness. Athletic medals.

The SS man walked up the steps in front of the woman and felt a moment of disgust. It was obvious why the Major was in this dung heap of a village. He was a cripple. Hideous looking with that scarred face. And sweating like a pig, of course. The Major jumped for the office door too late. The SS man opened it and swept inside.

The Oberführer smiled again and turned to let the Major, who was almost walking on his heels, see the smile. Now the Major would sweat even more. And the insolence of it. Wearing his greasy little rag in his buttonhole like he was someone. After the war all these butchers and postal workers would leave the army, and it would be run by professionals.

I should have gotten the door, thought the Major. He was so hot he felt his eyeballs throbbing. I should have opened it. Maybe not. Maybe it was the soldierly thing to do. Men in the field. Everyone paying less attention to things like that. Comrades in arms. He looked around the office. Wiktor, ragged and almost green with fear, his nails black and the desktop scarred and unpolished. Some lint in the corner.

"I'm sorry for this office, Oberführer. It's impossible to keep clean."

"The world tells us that everything about our Reich is impossible, but the new German finds only possibility. Only possibility."

The Oberführer looked at Wiktor and waved his hand. "Go get three women. Quickly."

Wiktor ran from the room, and Frankel winced. By God, the bastard had jumped.

"I'm sure you're right, Oberführer. Any correction would be appreciated."

"You saw, of course, that the man did not salute and respond to my order. We'll take care of that. Just a detail, but details are the bricks that build success."

He's like a fucking training film, the Major thought. No one's talked that way since last winter.

The woman was still standing. Frankel didn't think that his grandmother would have worn such an ugly bonnet. He smiled at her, and she did not smile back.

"Sister Rosa will need accommodations. She's helping me with my efforts."

"Of course, Oberführer." Sucking his cock every night, Frankel thought. Sucking his ass if he wants. Ugly cunt. Won't smile at anybody but the SS.

"If you don't need me, Oberführer, I will take a walk and look at the village."

"Of course, Sister. Your eagerness to work is always commendable."

The woman left the room, her brown cape sweeping around her. Face like a mule's bottom, Frankel thought. It was starting to snow. Walking around. What the hell for? What sort of work?

A gabbling sound came from the hall, and three women were shoved into the office by Wiktor. One of them kept trying to put her body between the Major and the youngest woman.

"Ladies." The Oberführer smiled, and Major Frankel saw the fear in their eyes.

First it was stark fear, fear from the black and silver that the Poles must see in their nightmares now. But then Frankel saw another thing in their eyes. It was—

Almost a softening. Frankel glanced at the Oberführer and noticed for the first time how handsome he was. With his hat off, his wavy hair sprang up, dark and thick. Pale skin and dark eyes. If his hair had been blond he would have been a recruitment poster for the German army. Handsome cocksucker. Well, a lot of the SS were good-looking. They didn't take pimply humpbacks. Stalingrad was good enough for the ugly Germans.

The women stared and the Oberführer smiled.

"Ladies." He went closer and lifted his hand as if he would take theirs. The first woman seemed to think he was going to take her hand and kiss it. She flushed.

Instead his hand went to the woman's breast and he pinched her nipple between his thumb and middle finger. The woman gasped but did not move.

"Ladies. There has been some sort of mistake. And you will correct it. Yes?"

The Oberführer spoke in German, and Wiktor looked at Frankel.

"Do you wish Wiktor to translate, sir? I doubt these women know German." The Major prayed to God that Wiktor would translate precisely with no clever additions. The Oberführer might speak Polish himself, and Wiktor could be shot on the spot for incorrect translation. That would be damned inconvenient for getting all the paperwork done in the next months.

"Have him translate." The Oberführer smiled in a way that made the Major sure that he spoke Polish. He hoped Wiktor would be careful. Wiktor was a piece of trash, but he was a useful piece of trash.

Wiktor snapped his heels and translated slowly and correctly. The older woman looked like she might understand some of the German, but she waited until Wiktor had translated to respond.

"Yes, Oberführer," all three women said.

They had gotten his rank right. Frankel smiled. He had conducted some of the classes himself. The Poles could tell what rank a German was from twenty yards after his classes.

"Excellent." He was still clamped on the woman's nipple, and tears rolled down her face.

"Since you didn't come prepared, you will use your underclothes for cleaning rags. Strip."

Wiktor translated and the women dropped their coats on the floor. The youngest looked at Frankel for a moment, and then they all stripped naked.

"Now, ladies. Take your underclothes and make nice rags."

The sound of cloth tearing filled the room. The women used their teeth in their hurry.

"You see, Frankel. They are always willing, these slaves."

Frankel was staring at the body of the youngest woman. Not bad. Not too thin and great tits. Not worth being shot for, but nice. He thought of his wife and the guilt rose in him.

"Now you will get water and buckets and soap. You will clean all of this office. The walls, floor, furniture, ceiling. There will not be a speck of dirt. No dirt, ladies. I will send Sister Rosa to inspect. I think you should clean this office every evening, what do you think, Frankel?"

"Excellent, Oberführer. Thank you for the excellent idea. It is excellent."

One of Himmler's special boys. Frankel quashed those thoughts. Everyone had duties. Who was to say what was more important, but the arrogant bastard was flustering him. And what soldier would give a damn whether there was dust on a ceiling?

"And the other one—Wiktor?"

"Yes, Oberführer," Wiktor nearly screamed.

"You neglected to salute me properly when I spoke to you, Wiktor. So you will now demonstrate the salute to the Führer."

Wiktor stood so erect that his skinny back bowed like a green sapling. He flung his arm out and stood perfectly still, even his eyes fixed rigidly, gazing ahead. "Heil Hitler!"

"That is much better, Wiktor. Stand there until the ladies have finished their work."

The Oberführer sighed. As bad as the last village. He turned to stare out the window as the women went out to get buckets and water. All gray and drear. The snow coming down again. At least it might stop the Russians for a few months.

And then he saw her. A woman with hair so heavy, so darkly gold it was like the hair of a girl you would dream about. Moving gracefully through the mud. Cheekbones a little too Slavic, but pure-blooded. A mythic girl, fertile and ripe.

"Frankel, who's that pregnant girl?"

"That's Nelka. She's the bastard granddaughter of the priest."

"And her mother?"

"Gone. Don't know where. Dead maybe."

"Husband?"

"Taken into Russia, people say. Likely dead or in Siberia."

"The village may have possibilities, Major Frankel."

"You want to see Nelka, sir? I can send her to your quarters."

"There is time, Major. Now that the snow is falling, we have all the time in the world. We won't be able to get the car back to Warsaw until the roads are clear. Let's go to your quarters and have a drink. I brought some excellent brandy."

The two men left the room and nearly bumped into the three women who were coming naked up the steps. Their skin was blue from the cold, and they shivered as they lugged the full buckets of water. There was no one on the street, and the village was silent.

Wiktor stood at attention behind the desk and watched as the women crawled over the floor and took turns standing on the chair to scrub the ceiling. It went on for a long time, and Wiktor was in the way, but he didn't dare move so much as a centimeter. His arm grew so heavy that it was a lead weight held up by his shoulder, and then it went numb. He stood and watched the women and wondered how much worse it would get before it got any better.

The Burning

The Stepmother clung to her dream so she wouldn't wake up and be cold again, but the numbness in her legs made her move. She crawled over the other bodies gently, letting them cling to their own dreams as long as they could, and crouched at the entrance of the snow house for a moment, sniffing the air.

There was no sound, no smell of cigarette smoke, no barking dog. She had lived long enough in the woods now to smell almost as keenly as a wolf. Her hair was going white so fast that the Russian teased her and the others took it up. White Wolf, they called her.

She rose and walked stiffly to the creek, knelt, and could see the movement of water under the ice. She took off her glove and broke the ice with a blow. Putting her face down, she drank deeply, the water like a knife sliding down the throat and cutting the belly, and then she washed her face with her hand. It woke her up completely and she crouched, listening. Still no sound.

It might be possible to make a fire and have hot water with rye in it. She would have to wait until the Russian woke up. It was his decision.

She went back to the shelter, stepping carefully in her own footsteps. The boughs of trees over the pit in the earth had been covered with a new layer of snow in the night making it invisible except for her footsteps. Her husband had climbed out too and stood with his back to her. After he pissed he knelt and covered the yellow stain with snow.

A dog would still find it, but the principle was good. And there wasn't much you could do against the dogs except lure them away from the Germans and kill them. And the Germans had learned never to unleash the dogs until the quarry was in sight.

Her husband turned, and she liked the sight of him. He had gained some weight and lost the fragile, trembling, ghetto look. He smiled at her but didn't speak, another good principle when living in the forest.

She went to him and put her arms around him and they stood close for a moment. They hadn't made love in more than a year. In the ghetto they had shared the apartment with seven people. There was no privacy for even a minute. Others had coupled in the night, but they had not, both of them too shy, too private. And then hiding in the grease pit, they had the children next to them, and the terror, and the hunger. In the forest they had started to make love one night and he stopped.

"If you get pregnant it will kill you."

She knew he was right. They held each other at night, but he would not risk her dying for a baby. And so it had been for more than a year.

The Russian crawled out of the snow shelter, and Lydka followed. He was the youngest. Maybe fourteen, but he carried his weight and had gotten a MP34 Bergmann from a dead German. The boy was terribly proud of his pistol and cleaned it whenever they had grease.

The others followed, silent and crumpled, their eyes coming out of sleep as they stood and stretched, each man looking around as if no one else had been looking before them. It was a good group. Every person cautious. No one counting on the others to save them. Everyone was dedicated to saving themselves which made all of them safer as a unit.

The Russian's face was so pale that the scars of the branding stood out red and strange. She had gotten used to it. They were like medals. She knew that the Germans would pay someday for every time the hot iron had touched his flesh.

"We won't be back here for weeks now, so we can make a small fire. We'll drink something hot with the rest of the vodka to give us heat in our belly. We'll move fast getting there and getting out, but with any luck we'll eat well tonight."

All nine of them nodded. The days when they simply survived and hid were drawing to an end. The Russians had never stopped fighting except in the hardest blizzards of winter, and the front was moving closer.

As if he read her thoughts, the Russian went on.

"This is the winter when my comrades break them. We'll do what we can to destroy those who've collaborated with the Nazis. Our first job is to survive, and we can't survive unless we become as ruthless as the Nazis."

Her husband frowned. She knew he had no need to become ruthless. He wanted to get back to his clean machines and his immaculate ideas. She was glad that he didn't argue.

"Any collaborator in this part of Poland will be killed." The Russian watched as they all took the sticks out of their coats where they slept with them next to their skin to dry them.

"We'll give them no hole to hide in."

Everyone laughed then because Lydka had lowered his pants to get at two large limbs he had stuffed down his pants leg.

"You little bastard!" Starzec cried. "I thought you had a hard-on all night so I took pity and didn't kick it out of my back where it poked me. Took pity on you, you little rat!"

"A hard-on like a piece of ash tree! Your wife will be a lucky woman!"

She grinned with the men but wondered how he stood it all night.

"You're a strong boy to have pain so we have dry wood in the morning." She stepped up to him and pulled his pants together, buttoning the fly and belting him securely like a mother would. She pulled down his coat and patted his shoulder. "That was a good thing, little brother."

They made the fire and slurped hot rye drink with a splash of vodka in it. Dipping the bread in the liquid softened it and they all began to feel less insubstantial.

"Cover the fire with snow. You, Mechanik, brush out the tracks to the creek, and you and the boy follow behind and get rid of our tracks for the first half mile."

They set out, moving as quickly as possible. The new snow had drifted, but they were able to stay on the firmer tracks marked down for centuries by wood gatherers and animals, and it wasn't too bad. Sometimes there was a corduroy road of logs laid in a long ribbon, but most of those were gone now. The sky was gray and bright, like the sun was doing all it could to burn the clouds away. It gave them all heart.

The Russian stopped and lifted his nose and sniffed. Their noses ran with the cold, but they smelled it. Wood smoke. The Russian pointed, and they moved through the trees.

They were on the edge of a road, rutted and frozen. The top roofs of the village could be seen, squat and slanting. The snow covered them and was piled in drifts against the bales of straw stacked up to insulate the walls from the deathly cold.

"What village is this?" the Mechanik asked.

"Piaski." The Russian kept moving.

She felt her husband's hand on her shoulder, squeezing. It wasn't necessary for her to ask him what he was thinking. This place was close to where the children were left. Perhaps the children had been taken in by some villager. She glanced up at her husband. He was staring hungrily at the village smoke.

"A major and a couple of dozen soldiers were left here," said the Russian. "Not many but dangerous. The major was at the Russian front and he's no city policeman. We don't go near it. There's a man there who's our contact. You'll meet him today, God willing."

Everyone followed their leader through the trees except the woman and her husband, who hesitated a moment. He stared at the huddled warmth in the distance, and she stared at the fields looking for some marker so she could find this place again. She had grown up in the country, but all the villages looked alike to her in winter.

There. Two blasted lime trees. Shattered by lightning or by fire when the fields were cleared or shelled by the Russians or Germans. They stuck up like two fingers. She imprinted the memory of their silhouette on her mind and turned to go, taking his hand firmly in hers.

"We stay in the trees. It's harder going, but safer. Sometimes they hide sentries in the fields and wait to see what walks out of the woods." The Russian was moving at a trot now.

She felt her heart beat faster and her energy surged. She hoped it went well and no one died. She looked at the Mechanik. She hoped the collaborators had no children.

The farm was a large one. Her experienced eye compared it to her father's, and she was impressed. Many outbuildings for meat and storage. Two large barns, one of stone and one of wood. A distant hut near the river that must be the icehouse.

She closed her eyes and remembered going with the servant to get food in the summer. Digging in the sawdust for the kegs of meat laid on the ice. The smell of milk from the jugs, pans of milk clotting into cheese, butter mounded on plates and laid in the cold.

Her mouth watered and her eyes widened. She knew exactly where to go to find the food. She looked at the farmhouse and smiled. In the autumn the wealthier people had come to shoot with her father and brothers. Great days of tramping in the fields and feasting on wild boar and duck and goose. There was the huge veranda with hooks screwed into the ceiling to hang game.

None of the hatred of Jews then. Not for her family. Her father had paid the village church a generous sum every year so his Christian workers had reserved seats in their church, and an equal sum for the Jewish workers in the synagogue.

Her father hadn't attended services often. Twice a year perhaps. The Day of Atonement. And once again to pray for his parents. That was all. She remembered her mother lighting the candles and the perfect loaf of challah lying on the white cloth. Celebrating Passover every year.

She had left the farm. Studied at Lyon University like her husband, but they hadn't met at the university. It had been in Warsaw, and she had stayed in the city. A deep pang for the old countryside made her whole body twitch and she almost cried out loud.

"It won't be here tomorrow." The Russian slapped her on the back and she nearly fell.

"That must be the icehouse over there." She pointed to the low roof near the river. "Tell them not to burn it. It might be full of meat. Cheese."

"Good woman." He moved off, and she sat with her back to the farm. There was no point thinking about it.

They lay half asleep with Gregor keeping watch until it began to grow dark. Then there was a soft voice that brought all of them to life.

"Marilke sent us," the voice called softly.

"Then you are welcome," the Russian responded to the password, the name of a Jewess who had died a hero in the Bialystok ghetto, the password that had become common for those out in the cold in eastern Poland.

It was the group that had singled out this farm and needed them to help with it. They walked out from behind the trees, nine or ten of them, mainly Poles but a man who spoke Polish with a Lithuanian accent and another who looked almost Jewish. She didn't ask. It didn't matter, and it might be dangerous to single him out.

It was dark now. The animals were gathered in the barn. A woman had shooed the chickens into the poultry house. There were no children playing outside. Thank God for that.

"Now," said the Russian.

Both groups unwrapped their most precious possessions. The Mechanik caught his breath. They were lovely. Oily and properly cared for. Two Russian PPD. Submachine guns. The *pepecha* he had gotten from the German he'd killed, and another *pepecha* from the Lithuanian's group. The Mechanik could hardly wait for the sound of them. They said the rhythm was so perfect you could set a watch by it.

Everyone was smiling. There was the chance that this would leave a few of them dead. The *pepecha*s gave them the edge they needed.

The night was moonless and dark, like they had all fallen down the throat of a wolf. Finally, two whistles sounded faintly from behind the farmhouse. The *pepecha*s were trained on the front door and men waited at the back of the house.

"Now, woman. Scream. Shout for help. They'll open up for a female."

"Oh, my God! Help! Help! Help me, Pan Dlugosz!" she shouted, using the polite address.

The lights in the house went out so the man would not be silhou-etted, and the door opened. He came onto the veranda carrying a shotgun.

She smiled. Hearing the voice of a woman, he came out unpre-pared to shoot.

She screamed again, and he moved forward. Two other men came behind him.

There was a muffled shout from the stone barn as some farmhand was knocked in the head. It alerted the farmer, and he had turned to leap inside when the *pepecha*s began to fire.

The Mechanik's mind leapt with love for the machines. The sound filled his head, and he listened to the steady rhythm of it. It was true, they were steady—dependable—deadly.

The man with the shotgun fell and both the other men made it to the door but fell in the doorway. They could hear shouting from be-hind the house.

The Stepmother was running now, behind Lydka, the thump of boards under her feet and then stepping on the body of the dead farmer and almost falling inside.

A hallway with boots lined up. Rooms to each side. No one in the parlor. Probably not used much now. No one in the dining room. A movement under the table caught her eye. She dragged the cloth off and bent down, her pistol ready to kill.

"It's a woman. Maybe his wife. Tell the others."

The child killer. The woman with no pity. The one who was more clever than her husband and let the Nazis stay in the barn while she lured in partisans for hot bowls of soup. The woman who watched while partisans were tortured and then had to dig their own graves. The woman whose hot soup led to the deaths of seven children tracked to earth with their parents in the forest.

"Tell them I have her."

The only debate was about the farmworkers. Five of them. A skinny, sad lot. You could see that the largesse of this place hadn't ex-tended to them.

"We had to work for him," one of them sobbed. Falling to his knees he blubbered, "It wasn't our doing. We had to work for him or they'd kill our children. Don't shoot us."

The Russian and the Lithuanian whispered for a moment. Having witnesses wasn't a bad thing. They'd tell every peasant in the district that the partisans were as dangerous as the Nazis. It would mean more cooperation. More food.

"We'll let you live, but you have to work."

"Anything. We thank you."

"God hold your soul in his hand, Master."

"Bless you—"

"Shut up!" The Russian was getting restless. They had to get out. "Take them and get to work," he told Gregor and Lydka. "Fire everything but the house for the moment, but take what you can. We leave nothing but scorched earth for the Nazis. Not a blade of hay. Not a potato."

The house was ransacked and the clothes and food were packed in bags. The wooden barn was in flames, all the winter fodder on fire, a square candle of burning flame against the sky. They had to move faster. The flames blinded them to anyone coming out of the darkness. The sound was deafening when the men ran past the barn. The wind caught the fire and it created a sucking chimney that roared and occasionally exploded when a can of gasoline ignited.

The Lithuanian who led the other group had business to do. The woman was dragged upstairs and stripped. They spit on her and slapped her and she screamed.

"Bitch."

"Collaborating cunt."

"Nazi."

"Shkopy."

She howled and begged, but in her eyes the Mechanik could see that she knew it was over.

The Lithuanian began. "Elwira Dlugosz, I accuse you of collaborating with the enemies of your people, your church, and your country. I accuse you of causing the death of patriots."

He leaned toward the naked woman and smiled. "I accuse you of enjoying these things and bragging about them later. What do you have to say to this?"

She stood dazed from the slaps, her mouth bleeding. She knew it was hopeless.

"Throw her out," the Lithuanian said.

The Mechanik knew it had to be done. The collaborators caused too much death. But he turned and let the others do it. It had been their comrades who died.

He went down the stairs and outside, looking for his wife. The air was red now and thick with the smell of burning hay. He heard a thump and looked back at the house. Her body had been hanged and thrown outside the upstairs window. It hung kicking and flapping, her breasts and the fat on her thighs rippling until she was dead.

The house was already on fire, and the red light spread all around the hanging body, from the upstairs behind the window, and then all the downstairs sprang into flame.

"Beautiful, huh?" a Pole from the other group shouted over the sound of the fire, pausing to stare. "Like when you look in a woman's iron and see the lump of red coal."

The Mechanik nodded. It was beautiful. The whole house holding its shape but red and moving and alive inside. He watched for a minute and then turned away.

Everything was on fire now, and screams were coming from the stone barn. The loft had been fired, and the top was catching. The stored hay caught easily and would burn the roof off.

The screaming came from the partisans in the other group. Two of them were holding a man, and at first the Mechanik thought it was another farmworker, but it was one of their group.

He looked like a Jew, dark curly hair, something about his eyes. He was struggling silently.

"No, no. Let it go," they were shouting at him, but he broke loose and ran to the barn doors.

Throwing up the bolt, he opened them and plunged into the heavy smoke.

Horses. Neighing in panic. The thud of hooves against boards as they tried to break down their stalls. It was the last pride of the farmer.

"Don't," the Mechanik said, grabbing his wife's arm.

She shook her head. She wouldn't risk her life for the horses. The top would cave in at any second, but nevertheless—she cried out to think of the hot rafters falling on the backs of the horses. She had loved horses once.

Two horses came jostling and bolting out the door. The Jew had opened the stalls and was driving them out.

"They won't drive easy," she whispered. "Fire makes them crazy. They could kill him if he gets in the stalls to drive them. If there's a stallion, he'll die."

The Mechanik kept his hand on her with an iron grip. She mustn't try to help with this.

"Did you find food?" he asked, hoping to distract her, but she didn't answer and watched the flames now engulfing the roof of the barn. How many minutes did the man have?

Three more horses bolted out. The partisans were busy now. They chased the horses and caught those they could.

"The pillows," a man screamed. "Tie them on for saddles, brothers."

Another horse came out and then a stallion too wild with terror to get near. It galloped off toward the woods.

The man, staggering and coughing was at the door of the barn. Everyone cheered. He raised his head and grinned.

"Always in love with the damned horses," the Lithuanian shouted.

They could hear the terrified neighs, like women screaming, from the horses in the barn who were too crazy to run. He hadn't been able to drive them all out.

The Jew opened his mouth to shout back when from behind him came a horse with a chest like a wagon front. Before anyone could drag the Jew away, the roof began to fall in with tearing sounds, the wind catching the flames and making a roaring as a blizzard of sparks flew around them. The heat made everyone turn and run, and the last screams of the horses were cut off.

"He was already dead," the Mechanik said. "The horse killed him. He felt nothing."

"He got most of the horses out." She didn't look behind her. She hoped the Jew knew that he had saved the horses. If you had to be killed, she thought, it wasn't such a bad thing to be killed by a horse. It was a death unspoiled by any ideas at all.

She settled the weight on her back and lowered her head, letting the rhythm of walking take her over. They had a long way to go before they would be safe.

The Drawing

"Where did he hear about it?" Pawel asked.

There was silence. It didn't matter. The partisans, illegal radios, gossip. Who cared? The five men sat, the room lit dimly by the fire which they did not stir up.

"Hush." They strained forward and listened to the footsteps of the Major pass by.

"He can't sit by his warm stove like a normal man." Czeslaw was the oldest. He had seen too much of men like the Major.

"He left his friends to die in Russia. He can't rest." Bialy spit into the fire.

"At least he has friends left." Feliks had lost his brother, shot with the first executions.

"Katyn Forest," said Bialy, the name reminding him that the Major was one of the beasts who wanted to kill all the Poles. "Russians or Germans. Who gives a damn who did it?"

They all knew the story. Fifteen thousand Polish officers massacred after an honorable surrender. Lying in the forests of Katyn.

There was a soft knock on the door, and Telek slipped in and sat at the edge of the room. He was cold, but he didn't move close to the warmth.

The men waited. It was no use rushing Telek. He had always been different. His mother a suicide and his father running away. The boy sneaking out into the woods instead of going to school. Carrying water and selling berries and firewood for his living. They waited.

And Telek began slowly. "He is an SS Oberführer. He has no battle ribbons. Not a real soldier. He's been in the other villages between here and Bialystok. He and the woman are sorting them. They've gone to Bialowieza, but they'll be back."

"Sorting who?" Andrzej was impatient. He didn't want to be on the street after curfew.

"The children. He and the woman examine the children and sort them."

"Sort them how? Why would they want children?" Feliks was beginning to sweat.

"The children strip and are measured all over—head, body, legs, hips. They measure the width of the pelvis in the girls and the penis size in the boys."

"Degenerates." Czeslaw clenched his fists.

"Then they photograph them from all angles."

"Dirty pictures? Much good it will do them." Bialy turned and spit in the fireplace again.

"Go on, damn it. Finish it, Telek."

"They're looking for children who are blond and blue-eyed. They don't want thick lips, or ears that stick out, or cheekbones that are prominent. They don't want sloping shoulders. They don't want any flaws or scars or broken bones or birthmarks. The mothers are told it's a medical examination. They're told that sometimes the children need special treatment, but it's always the healthy, blond, blue-eyed ones that need it."

"And then?" Pawel thought of his three children. All blond. All perfect. A great feeling of coldness had entered the room, but no one got up to stir the fire or add another log.

"The mothers are given cards. A red card for a child who is physically perfect and blond, a white card for a child who is too Slavic or marked in any way."

"Enough." Feliks the chess player stood so suddenly that his chair tipped over with a bang. "Christ. Enough. They're sending the women away. Probably for their whorehouses or to be worked to death. But what do the devils want with the children? Babies aren't any good for work."

"I don't know." Telek sat in silence, his face reddened by the firelight. "We don't know what they're going to do with them. They send them into Germany."

The room was silent. No one could think very clearly for a few minutes.

"Be rational. They came here. The SS and the woman," Feliks began. The men nodded.

"And they didn't do anything. Just drank with the Major and terrorized three women."

The men nodded again.

"So maybe there's nothing they want here. We're a small village." Telek sighed. "They're coming back soon. After Bialowieza."

"There are children who are scarred, whose ears stick out."

"Children who look Slavic."

"We must do it ourselves first." Telek spoke almost in a whisper. "We must examine every child in the village and see which would be selected and which rejected."

"And then?"

It crept into their minds but no one dared to say it.

Andrzej finally groaned and stood up. He walked to the fire. He threw a log on, and sparks flew out onto the hearth. The room was brighter, and he turned and faced the others.

"We'll have to make sure that there are no perfect children in our village." He felt guilty saying it. His own were dark-haired, and the boy's ears stuck out. They were safe. He thanked God for Basha's brunette coloring.

"Why not just hide them?" Pawel was nearly in tears. "We could go into the woods."

Straightening his leg, Andrzej sighed. "And then you have to stay in the forest with tiny children for the rest of the winter."

There was silence. Everyone knew it was impossible. No child could live in the woods and survive the winter. You might as well hand them over to the Nazis.

"And who of us," Czeslaw asked, "will make sure they're imperfect?"

"Each man could care for his own children," Telek said.

"No." Pawel shook his head. "If someone has to hurt the children, it should be one person doing it. Then it would be—" He paused. "It would be on one soul only. It's too unnatural for a father to injure his child. No man should have to do it."

"It would save them," Telek said.

"What if you're wrong and we hurt the children for nothing."

"How many children are we talking about?" Bialy tried to remember all the children lined up to get their spoonful of sugar once a week.

"Thirty-one children in the village." Feliks squinted his eyes and thought. "At least seven are blond."

"Seven plus you have to count the two of Miron and Ania. Their eyes are blue."

"Tolek? And Jolanta's little girl? His ears stick out, and she coughs. It's T.B."

"So it's seven and maybe two more."

They all nodded in agreement.

"And the girl that Magda took in. The boy is brown-eyed, but the girl is perfect. We have to decide this fairly," said Bialy. "Pawel has a point. It's unnatural for a father to injure his own child. His wife might hate him forever, and the child—"

"We can do it by a drawing." Telek went to a broom that stood against the wall. Drawing his knife he cut six pieces of twig, five of them similar in length. Turning his back he cut one twig until it was only half the size of the others. He arranged them in his hand, sticking up out of his clenched fist, and turned toward the men.

"Six straws. You have to be in it too, Telek," Pawel's voice was shaking.

"Six straws."

Pawel leapt up and nearly tore a straw out of Telek's tightly clenched hand. "Is this a long one or a short one?" Telek said nothing. Pawel didn't know if his straw was long or short, but he moved away with a nervous laugh and waited.

Each man took a straw, and Telek's face hardened.

"You don't have children, Telek. It's better for you."

"Out in the woods all the time. You don't know the children like we do."

The men felt humble. They watched Telek as he opened his fist and showed them the short straw that was left. His forehead was beaded with sweat.

It's my fault that this has come to me, Telek thought. And they will dislike me more when I've done it. He knew the village would have no place for him when the war was over. The heart of the village would be closed to him. And Nelka. Would she forgive him for mutilating Gretel?

"But what will you do?" Pawel couldn't look into Telek's face.

"Do you think it has to be—" Bialy said, and then he fell silent.

"I'll think about it. It has to be soon because the SS Oberführer will be back in a few weeks. It can't look like we did it the day before he comes. It must look as natural as possible."

Telek threw the short straw into the fire. "Don't tell anyone yet. Don't frighten the children. I'll decide how to do it and then tell you."

They nodded. The fate of the children was in his hands.

"I'm sorry, Telek," Andrzej said.

Telek nodded. He wished he could stay, sit by the fire, and share the homemade vodka he knew they would pass around, be slapped on the shoulder and talk about where the Russian line was now. He glanced at them and saw the relief they felt that he was going. He nodded once and went outside, moving quickly down the street, looking ahead to avoid any soldier on duty.

"He doesn't drink much anyway," Czeslaw said as he sipped his vodka. The bite of the raw alcohol made his throat thick. "And he doesn't have children himself. It's better that he drew the straw. Telek has never been one of us."

They sat for an hour in silence and sipped the tiny glasses of vodka. None of them could bear going home to their wives yet. They heard the Major going down the street again, drunk now and talking aloud to his dead comrades in German, but they didn't move. No one wanted to go out into the darkness.

Gretel

"The children are playing too deeply in the forest. They disappear for hours."

Telek nodded, and without a word to Magda, turned and walked into the trees. He found their footprints moving not toward the road but straight into the forest. The children hadn't been running but had walked steadily and quietly between the giant trees.

The two had walked with the sun at their backs and had kept it there. He nodded approval. By following their own footprints and watching the sun, they could find the way back to the hut. But even if they didn't get lost, it wasn't safe. Too many strangers were wandering in the forest.

The two sets of footprints went on until they reached a clearing. At the edge of the clearing they had stopped and stood. The snow was pressed down in a spot there. He moved across the clearing and saw why they had stood still. The marks in the snow showed where two foxes had been playing. Probably male and female. The children had watched until they frightened the foxes off.

Or something else frightened them off. A crow cawed and then another one, irritated at his presence. They didn't fly off, so he relaxed and waited. Just silence.

He had walked on for a mile when he heard her singing. She was singing some sort of child's song. He tensed and then relaxed. Gretel was singing in Polish. A cautious child.

She was sitting on a huge fallen log, having carefully brushed off the snow and climbed up. She sat, the light turning her hair almost white, and the only color in the whole world was the blue of her eyes when she looked around at the forest. She seemed perfectly happy.

Telek watched for a minute, then stepped out from behind an oak tree. Gretel gasped but she didn't cry out. Hansel peered around the log.

"It isn't safe to be deep in the woods, children. You mustn't wander so far."

They knew him and relaxed, her face smiling that it was Telek. "We saw foxes, and a rabbit, and some animal was in the water. All dark and fat."

Hansel made a snowball and threw it at Telek.

"It was the beaver. They're building a dam near where you walked."

She smiled radiantly. "I keep count, Telek. I've seen owls and crows and deer. The deer walk in the snow and lift their legs like dancers. But more beautiful than dancers."

Telek climbed up on the fallen tree and sat beside her. He reached in his pocket and pulled out a piece of bread and a smaller piece of sausage. With his knife he cut the bread and sliced the sausage into thin pieces that he placed delicately in a single layer on each piece of bread. Hansel climbed up beside them. "Eat."

They ate slowly, and Telek finished long before the children. "What else have you seen?"

"I think a wolf. Or something." Hansel growled and slid off the log.

"What was it like?"

"It was dark and didn't come out from the trees."

"Did it move like this?" Telek jumped off the log and moved bent over in a smooth trot. "Or like this?" He lumbered slowly from side to side.

"Like you did first."

"A wolf."

"What other animals are there?"

"This isn't like any forest in all of Europe."

"Why not?"

"Bialowieza Forest has never been burned or logged. It has stood here since forever."

"No one owns it?"

"God owns it."

"But we take wood for Magda."

"Some wood is gathered, but no one has ever torn the forest apart. It is as it was all over Europe thousands and thousands of years ago."

Gretel breathed lightly. "And what other animals live here?"

"Animals that don't live anyplace in Europe anymore. There are cranes and storks and hazel-hens. Eight kinds of woodpeckers."

"Have you seen them all?"

"Yes. And there are elk and roe deer, lynx, wolf."

"Will the wolves kill you?"

"Not unless they're starving and you're helpless."

"What else is there?"

"The otters play in the spring. Sliding down the banks and leaping around near the river. And frogs and fish in the river." Telek looked around at the clearing. They reminded him of what it was to be a child and wander alone in the forest. After his mother killed herself, he had wandered until he felt like a wild creature himself. Men came and men went, but this forest was always here.

"Are the deer the biggest animals?" Hansel was busy piling up the snow in a wall.

"No. The wild ponies are heavier than the deer. And the wild boar is stronger. But the king of all of them is the biggest of all."

Gretel stared at him. "What is the king of all of them?"

"He's a shy king. You won't see the bison easily. And he's like a house he's so big."

"It's magic." She sighed deeply. "And think, Telek. They just live out here. They can walk around and are free and eat and play and have the whole forest to be their home."

"We have the forest too, child."

"But we don't have it the way they do, Telek."

He didn't answer, but he knew what she meant.

"If you promise not to wander so far again, I'll show you both something special."

"I love all of it." Gretel put her hand in Telek's.

"I know. But if you never again come so deep in the forest, I'll take you with me when I gather mushrooms in the spring. I'll show you"—he paused—"I'll show you everything by summer."

"Everything?"

"Yes."

"The bison and the wild boar and the frogs?" Hansel stared at Telek.

"Yes."

"All right. I'll wait for you to show me." Hansel dusted off his hands and jammed them in his pockets.

"Come on," Telek said. "Let's see what we find today."

He led them deeper into the trees through snow that was so soft he sometimes turned and picked up the girl, and the boy clung to his back. He could feel the faster beat of her heart through his coat. He had to hush the boy, but she was as silent as he.

They were closer now to where he had been going, and he slowed, dropping her onto the ground. He put his finger to his lips, but he didn't have to worry. She had no need for words. Her eyes were big with excitement and blue, like the sky had broken and fallen into her face.

The boy was excited too, but more wary, more cautious.

Telek sucked his index finger and raised it into the air. Nodding at the children to do the same, he watched as they raised their thin fingers, sticky with saliva.

Bending until his mouth was next to their ears he whispered so low that they could barely hear him, "Which way is the wind blowing?"

She shook her head. A city child.

"Which side of your finger is coldest?"

She thought and pointed to the pad of the finger. He nodded. "The wind is blowing in our faces. The animals behind us can smell us on the wind, but any animals in front can't smell us."

The boy's eyes were wide in surprise. "How do you know about the wind?"

Telek shook his head. He had never thought about it. He had known it all his life as if he had been born knowing it. He whispered again, "When you want to see the animals, you keep the wind in your face."

She nodded and he knew she wouldn't forget. He walked on very slowly now, straining to see through the trees. First it looked like more snow that was banked and piled, but he knew it was too gray to be snow. He pointed slowly and they stood, the man and the children, and waited.

Through the trees they came, pawing at the snow to uncover the moss and leaves, eating any low-growing twigs and chewing the bark. Gretel caught her breath but didn't move or speak. Telek took her hand, and they stood in the snow and did not even blink while the ponies came toward them.

They were smaller than domesticated ponies, and their heads were heavy, almost like the heads of donkeys. They were thickly built and moved surely in the snow.

Two mares were in front, the first with a belly swollen by foal. Their coats were dense and pale gray and hung almost to their hocks. The hair hung over their faces, and you couldn't see any glitter of eye. The younger mare came second and the little stallion, more watchful, pushing them on with a thrust of his head butting their flanks, protected their rear.

They didn't see the humans, and Telek waited for the moment when either they would see him, or he would make a movement and startle them so they wouldn't trample the children.

He looked down at Gretel without moving his head so the horses would not run. Her mouth was slightly open and her eyes dilated with joy. She clutched his hand so tightly that her nails pinched his skin.

Before he could raise a hand and end it, the stallion lifted his head and gave a sudden blow of steam through his nostrils. The mares lifted their heads too, and in one movement it seemed, they all three broke and ran toward the east in bounds that cleared the deeper drifts of snow.

Telek gripped Gretel's hand warningly and didn't move. He grabbed the boy's coat collar and pulled him close. Something had frightened the ponies. He saw nothing, but then he smelled it. Tobacco smoke.

"Not a word," he whispered, and he picked Hansel up and ran to a fallen tree covered with a drift of snow. Gretel followed on his heels.

He shoved the children under the tree and knocked snow over the footprints. They disappeared in a shower of powdery white.

Telek ran past where the horses had been toward the cigarette smoke. He saw the man in front of him. He was standing, smoking, and Telek stopped behind a tree and watched.

"Is it you, Telek?" the man called.

Telek moved out from behind the tree and saw the others. It was the Russian and his group.

"Yes. It's me. Looking for rabbits."

"What news of your village, Telek?"

"The SS man has come and gone."

"The same that was in the other villages?"

"Yes."

"He's coming back."

"Yes. We'll try to deal with it. The Lithuanian warned me about this."

The Russian nodded. Telek saw that he had two new members. The man was tall and could have been a Jew. The woman was small, but she wore a German uniform and had a pistol. Her hair was white in streaks. Telek nodded but didn't speak to them.

"Go in peace, Telek. Here." The Russian reached in his coat and offered a small flask. Telek took it, drank quickly, and gave it back to the Russian.

The partisans moved on, going away from the village, moving into the forest, looking for a place to sleep before the sun went down. Telek moved away between the trees, and he was gone when the woman looked over her shoulder for him.

Gretel lay perfectly still where he had put her. Hansel had climbed out and was behind a tree. Telek pulled the girl out of the snow and laughed.

"You did well. You lay as still as the rabbit when the fox is hunting. If the rabbit lies still, the fox never catches her. But if she runs—" Telek snapped his jaws twice.

"I wasn't still. I was going to help. I can fight too."

"When I say be still, you must be still."

"I want to help, Telek."

Telek grinned at the boy. He was foolhardy but brave.

Gretel shivered. "What was it, Telek?"

"A wild boar. I would have shown you, but they're hungry and angry in the winter. It was better that you stayed here."

"I want to see one." Hansel started forward, and Telek grabbed the boy and put him on his shoulders.

"Someday. I'll show you that and the mother pig with her piglets. But we'll climb a tree and sit like squirrels and let her come to us. Magda is worried, and I have to get you home."

He took Gretel's hand and began to lope through the snow, going around the drifts and avoiding the patches that covered the swampy places, the boy's weight light on his shoulders.

"You children must never come here alone, Gretel. Never again. There are bright lights over the swamps. People say it's witches trying to draw us into darkness. Listen, Hansel."

"I wouldn't be afraid. I want to see it all."

"Promise you won't come in the forest alone."

"I promise, Telek," Gretel said, squeezing his hand.

"I'll show you the forest, Hansel, but don't go beyond the creek again. Do you promise?"

"I promise," Hansel said.

"Yes," she said, promising for the second time.

The boy was too independent, but Telek was satisfied by Gretel's promise. She was not like other children. There was something in her that he could understand as he had never understood a child before. She felt about the woods as he did. Telek tightened his grip on her hand and moved faster toward the hut and Nelka.

In the Cage

Hansel looked at Gretel, who lay with eyes half open, breathing heavily on the sleeping platform. Her cheeks were bright red, and he could hear her breath rasping. It had been ten days since they had wandered off and been found by Telek.

Magda took a small bottle and poured a spoonful of dark syrup into a cup. She added hot water, and the smell of raspberries filled the room.

"When it cools a little, she must drink it. God help us. I have almost no herbs left. Everyone has been sick for the last three months." Magda went to the girl and felt her head.

"She's too hot."

Magda lay her head down on Gretel's chest and listened. The lungs were filling.

"It is a grippe of the lungs. Help me pile logs against the wall of the platform. Cover them with a pad of blankets. We have to make her sit up so the lungs will be easier."

Hansel lifted the largest logs he could and made a backrest. Then the blankets. The two of them pulled Gretel until she was sitting upright, her head lolling back onto the blanket.

"I don't feel good, Hansel. I don't like it. Let me eat snow, Magda. I'm hot."

"No, child. Open your mouth wide . . . wider."

She turned the girl's head toward the light coming through the waxed paper of the window.

"I have to swab it."

She began to cry. "Don't do it, Magda. Leave me alone."

Magda got the bottle of iodine and with a few firm twists wrapped the tip of a twig in clean cotton. Hansel stood clutching his own throat with his hands.

"You make people well, don't you, Magda?"

"Hold her shoulders, Hansel."

Hansel climbed on the platform and held Gretel down. He struggled against her determinedly.

Magda opened Gretel's mouth and put a piece of wood between her back teeth so the girl couldn't shut her mouth. The old woman dipped the cotton in the iodine and slowly painted the whole of the girl's throat with the stinking medicine. She painted it so deeply that Gretel gagged repeatedly. Then Magda would stop and wait. She didn't want the child to vomit and take the iodine off the membranes of her throat.

When they were done, Gretel lay limp. "I hate it," she whispered.

"You were a good girl," Magda said. "That will make your throat heal."

"It hurts." Tears ran down the child's face.

"I know." Magda gave Hansel a bowl. "Get a few icicles off the trees. Not from the roof, they have soot in them from the stovepipe. She can suck them and it will get some liquid into her."

Hansel ran outside, not stopping for his coat. The larger trees were too tall, but the saplings had lovely icicles hanging from some of the branches. Then he saw the pine trees ahead. The icicles were small and easy to suck, and when he broke them off, they smelled faintly of pine sap.

Hansel filled the bowl and ran back to the hut.

"Let me," he said. Sitting on the platform beside Gretel, he held the icicles to her lips.

"It's nice," she whispered.

Hansel sat beside her all day, getting fresh icicles from the pine trees and encouraging his sister to suck, but she was not getting better.

Magda shook her head. It was a bad grippe. She could hear the gurgle of liquid when she pressed her head to the girl's chest.

Magda didn't believe cupping would help much, Gretel was too far into the grippe now, but trying anything was better than doing nothing. It was growing dark. The fever had to break before night.

"Darkness sucks the life out," she muttered.

"What, Magda?" Hansel sat up from where he lay beside Gretel.

"Nothing, child. We're going to fool her body."

"How?"

"We'll make her body think about something besides the lungs. Take Gretel's shirt off and lay her flat on her stomach."

"It's my piano!" Gretel shouted weakly. She flung her arm out and it struck Hansel.

"Magda!"

Magda sprang to the platform and helped Hansel roll the girl over. Without the shirt her arms were almost fleshless, and Magda could see all the veins under the skin.

Magda sighed. Gretel ate all Magda had to give her, but it was a time when the girl should have been growing. Every piece of bread was burned off by her growth.

"Hold her, Hansel, while I prepare the cups."

Magda went to the floor and took out a basket that held her cups. Clear glass, they had a lip at the bottom. She took three of them and lit a candle.

"On my mother's milk I pray to you, Virgin. Make it break the fever."

Holding the glass with a cloth so she wouldn't burn her fingers, Magda heated the air in the cup until it was hot. Swiftly, she clapped it onto the white skin of the child's back, avoiding the backbone, which stood out like a fish's spine.

Gretel cried out and struggled, but Hansel held her down. With hands stiffened by arthritis but practiced in doing this, Magda heated two more cups and pressed them to the girl's back.

As the air in the cup cooled, it created a vacuum which sucked the circle of skin up in a puff of flesh into the cup. The skin turned bright red from the heat.

"See, child." She nodded at Hansel. "The cupping brings the blood to the surface. It distracts the body and makes it forget the lungs. The pain goes to her back, and then the lungs can fight harder and not just lie on the bed and give up."

Hansel watched the cups for about half an hour until Magda took them off by pressing down the flesh near the cup to break the suction and lifting the glass. They made a popping sound as they released the flesh, and there were three red circles on Gretel's back.

They rolled her over, and she struggled against them, turning and twisting.

"I want to go out!" she screamed. "I want to ride the pony!"

Magda knew that unless the fever broke, the girl would try to get up and leave the hut. She would fall off the platform. Tying her was too harsh. It was better if she could move some, but not fall to the floor. She needed to be on the warmth of the platform.

"Hold her down, Hansel. I won't be long."

Magda put on her coat and went out. If only it was still there. If only the children hadn't broken it up playing with it. She walked through the trees to a small clearing. It was downstream from the hut, and here she had once kept chickens. The last one had been eaten long ago. She hoped it was large enough for the girl. She hoped it was still unbroken.

Kicking through the snow, Magda searched the ground near the low shelter the chickens had used. Her boot hit something hard, and she dug the snow away with her hands.

Not very clean, but unbroken. Her eyes measured the wooden length of it. It would do.

It was frozen to the earth, but a few hard kicks freed it. She dragged it behind her to the hut and kicked it again before she took it inside. Most of the frozen mud had fallen off, and the wooden cage was wet with snow but unbroken.

Magda dragged the cage inside and put it near the stove. Hansel stared from the platform.

"Move her over if you can."

Hansel dragged the girl to one end of the platform, and Magda, with strength she didn't know she had, swept the blankets aside and lifted the chicken cage onto the wooden boards. She flipped open the top and laid blankets down until the bottom slats were covered and wouldn't hurt Gretel's back. The girl could roll and turn, but she couldn't fall off.

Hansel's eyes were wide, but he understood. "Just until the fever breaks, Magda."

"Yes. We can give her syrup and icicles if she'll take them. She'll just have to pee on the blankets." Although there had been no urine for hours now.

Hansel hauled and Magda pulled, and they dumped Gretel onto the blankets in the long cage. Magda closed the top and tied it firmly with a piece of rope.

"It looks cruel, Hansel, but it will keep her up here where it's warm. You go to sleep."

"I'll sit up too."

"No. If you want to help me, you'll sleep. I'll be tired tomorrow. By then her fever will have broken, and you can nurse her while I rest. But you have to be strong tomorrow. Sleep."

Hansel felt a wave of exhaustion come over him. Gretel had been sick for too long. He lay on the far corner of the platform and pulled the blanket over his head to shut out the sight of the cage. Sleep came on him like a hammer blow. The boy twitched once and then lay still.

Gretel muttered and sighed. She rolled and twisted, but she didn't try to stand. Her face bumped against the cage, but she was too weak now to hurt herself.

Magda went close to the cage and held out an icicle. "Suck on this, little dear."

The girl opened her eyes wide and stared into Magda's face. Gretel saw the cage for what it was, and began to moan in panic.

"It's just to keep you safe. You'll be sitting at the table again to-morrow."

Gretel's feverish brain tried to understand. The witch had trapped her in a cage.

"You're going to eat me. You're going to make me fat and eat me."

"No, no." Magda backed away. "No, child, I'm going to make you well."

"The witch is going to eat me."

Gretel slept during the worst of the night, her breathing quick and shallow, her face red. The girl's thin body twitched and she moaned, but she slept.

"The Hour of the Wolf has passed," Magda whispered. That was the worst time, the darkest moment before dawn when the souls of humans gave up and stopped hoping for the light.

She was nearly asleep when Gretel began to scream hoarsely. Magda stood beside the girl, gazing at her face, but Gretel didn't see anyone. Just a ragged scream going on and then another one, not stopping, the girl lost in her fever dreams.

Hansel was awake. He moaned as his sister screamed.

"The fever hasn't broken, child. Soon, I hope."

Hansel looked around the hut. His eyes were wild.

"Go outside and get an icicle off the roof, child. It doesn't matter about the soot."

"No! Don't open the door, Magda. Be quick, be quick." Hansel remembered now. He remembered what people in the ghetto did when a child was near death. He had seen it done. "Get some money."

"I don't have any money, boy. What do you want it for?"

"You must have a coin! Quick!"

Magda could hardly think. She couldn't bear the one child moaning and screaming and now the boy shouting at her. She moved to the wall and slid a board to one side. Taking out a leather sack smaller than her palm, she opened it and shook out two coins and a button.

The button was the one from Hansel's coat. Magda remembered tearing it off as payment for the charm. She remembered how the boy had looked, standing in the circle she drew in the dirt, weeping over his lost bread.

Hansel stood close and turned Magda until she faced Gretel.

"I am selling Magda my sister," Hansel said loudly. He took the coins from Magda's hand, leaving the button on her palm. "You now own her. She is not in my family anymore. She is sold to you. Her soul is safe in your family."

Then Hansel climbed on the platform and took up Gretel's ragged clothes. He took her coat and shoes and the rags she used for socks. Leaping down Hansel threw open the door of the stove.

"Gretel is gone. She isn't here with me anymore. She's dead," the boy shouted. With swift thrusts he put the clothes on the coals and they sprang up in flames. Looking wildly around the hut, Hansel saw the stick doll that Telek had made for Gretel. Hansel snatched it up and pushed it into the stove. It lay on the burning clothes, and he slammed the door of the oven.

"Gretel is dead," he screamed. Hansel reached to the neck of his shirt and tugged. "Help me, Magda," he cried. "Tear it!"

Magda was dazed, but she tore the cloth with a twist of her hands, and Hansel wailed.

Magda understood then. The dark spirits outside must be fooled into thinking that the girl was dead. Magda grabbed the hem of her dress and tore it upward. She touched the floor by the stove and made her hand ashy. Stepping forward she rubbed ash on Hansel's face and on her own.

The two of them stood close in the hut, the boy and the old woman, keening and shrieking as if Gretel were dead. Breathless at last, they stood there, the only sound the crackle of burning cloth; the smell of burning leather, like flesh, filled the hut.

"She's dead," Hansel said. He walked to the door, trembling, and flung it open.

"We've burned her clothes and her doll. Gretel is dead. There's only a girl here that belongs to Magda. Poor Gretel has died." Hansel shouted the words into the darkness.

He stood in the cold draft from the forest and the wind began to blow. Hansel shivered and stepped back as the blast of cold air entered the hut. Magda moaned, and the tears ran down her face, black with ash. For several minutes the wind howled and gusted in the forest around the hut, and the woman and the boy stood and let it clean out the smell of sickness. Then the wind died down, leaving only the bitter cold.

Hansel closed the door. It was not dawn, but the quality of the darkness was not so heavy.

"It's gone."

Magda nodded. The Angel of Death had been fooled. It was gone. She turned back to the small form of Gretel, the girl whose soul she had bought, lying in the cage. She was shiny, wet, gasping for breath, and Magda began to laugh.

"Help me get her out, Hansel. The fever has broken."

The two of them lifted Gretel out and washed her thin body gently. She shivered, but she was clean now. Magda wrapped her tightly in the blankets and kissed her forehead.

Then she turned to the exhausted boy and lifted him, she knew not from where the strength came, and sat in the rocking chair with Hansel curled in her lap.

Gretel lay on the platform and watched, half-asleep, as Magda began to hum.

The old woman hummed, the sound from deep in her chest, until Hansel, eyes nearly shut, was filled with the vibration, and it warmed him inside in all the deep parts where he had been frightened.

She hummed, her eyes slits, trancelike, and then began to sing. The key was minor, not a song but a chant. Magda was a Gypsy now, and she did what her grandmother had done with her. She looked far ahead and told Hansel who he was and who he would be.

"You are a beloved boy, a boy of laughter. You loved the park and the squirrels. You knew every street and crept through the wall once all by yourself. You will live and grow old."

The words stopped, and she hummed again for a long time until he was nearly asleep.

"You will be brave and it will be hard. You will be the big brother. You will be the older one. You will finally run after death itself. And when you are a man, you will find many cities and travel around and around the world. You will belong to a country where you can be free forever."

She hummed, and her rocking nearly stopped.

"You will have a wife, my gypsy boy. Children will call you father and grandfather."

She smiled and hummed more.

"You will never be rich, my child, you will be moving too fast to be burdened with all those things that the outsider, the *gadji*, want. You will be filled with the fire of the world."

Magda hummed and hummed, the notes strange and not like anything the boy had ever heard.

"I'll live with you, Magda," the boy whispered. "I'll take you everywhere."

Magda stopped rocking and sat very still.

"The wheel turns," she sang. "The red wheel with the blue sky above and the green grass underneath. It turns, my little boy."

"You will go with me around the world," Hansel whispered. "You and Gretel."

And then he fell into a dreamless sleep, not disturbed by the coughing of his sister that went on for hours as liquid came out of her lungs and freed her from drowning.

Magda hummed softly, sitting between the coughing child on the platform and the child in her arms. She hummed and stared at the yellowed oil paper of the window as it grew brighter when the sun rose. Then she sat silent for more than hour, not asleep but alert and quiet.

Finally, she groaned from the stiffness of sitting with the weight of the child on her lap. She stirred a little and his hand moved from under the blanket and clung to her blouse.

She looked down at him and smiled. The button from his coat was in her pocket. He had thrown away his luck, but then she had made a charm. The boy had paid her, and she had brought his luck back. She looked at Hansel and thought of what had come to her through the mist when she had sung to him. She shook her head and sighed.

"I will not go around the world with you, little gypsy love. Child of my heart, I will never see your children." The crisis of the night had passed, and she would sleep in the chair until the children awakened.

It had been Basha's idea, everyone said. Something in her fierce heart couldn't watch her children wasting away. When the smallest one died in the first icy days of October, Basha did not report it. She made Andrzej take the tiny corpse to the forest and bury it in secret. Then the food coupons for the child could still be used, and that meant seven hundred extra calories for the remaining two children, and now Basha and Andrzej had been hanged for the deception.

Nelka walked down the street. There were no children playing outside today. It was snowing lightly, but that usually didn't keep them inside. It was what hung in the heart of the village, the bodies of the man and the woman left swaying in the cold wind, not even a scarf over her face, that kept the children crouched by the stoves.

Nelka didn't look up at the bodies as she crossed the square. She didn't want to be in the village. Gretel's fever had broken ten days ago. Hansel hadn't gotten the grippe, so Nelka could go and stay with Magda. She couldn't bear the village now. Nelka stopped and groaned. She had been hungry for two days, ravenously, painfully, waking at night hungry.

She was beside the last house with fields in front of her when she heard it. She looked up, open-mouthed, and far above her head was a humming like a fly. The plane was barely visible, a small gray thing in the gray of the snow clouds, and then she saw the paper floating over the roofs of the village and blowing like larger flakes of snow.

Nelka bent and picked one up. She smoothed it with her cold fingers. She hadn't seen any paper since last summer. No one had paper except the Major. It was roughly printed in Polish.

POLISH PEOPLE!
GREETINGS FROM OUR BELOVED LEADER,
JOSEPH STALIN
AND THE SOVIET PEOPLE.
BE COURAGEOUS AND STRUGGLE UNDER THE YOKE OF THE FASCIST OPPRESSOR! YOUR SOVIET BROTHERS AND SISTERS ARE TOILING WITHOUT REST TO FREE OUR NEIGHBOR POLAND. THE SO-VIET TROOPS ARE VICTORIOUS AND DRIVING THE GERMANS OUT OF OUR BELOVED MOTHERLAND. WE WILL GREET YOU SOON AND FIGHT SHOULDER TO SHOULDER TO FREE YOUR TOWNS AND VIL-LAGES.
TAKE ARMS! WEAKEN THE GERMAN BEAST IN EVERY WAY AND PREPARE FOR OUR TRIUMPHANT ARMIES TO COME AND JOIN YOU!
THE BATTLE WILL BE TAKEN TO GERMAN SOIL, AND THEY WILL BE MADE TO SHED GERMAN BLOOD FOR EVERY RUSSIAN AND POLISH MAN AND WOMAN WHO HAVE DIED IN THIS GREATEST OF STRUGGLES.
JOIN US!

WE ARE BRINGING YOU LIBERTY!

Setting down her basket, Nelka ran back and forth picking up all the paper she could. It made the most wonderful paper to use in the outhouse.

It was too bad you couldn't write on it. No one was allowed to write now. You could be hanged for just writing a list or a letter to a cousin. But the Germans didn't mind if it was used to wipe your bottom, and it would be comforting sitting in the outhouse, reading the message.

Telek said the Nazis were a rabid dog in Poland's house that was biting and killing the family. Now a Russian black bear, lean from winter starvation, savage and wild, knocks on the door. The bear will kill the dog, but how do the Poles get rid of the bear?

She wished she had the courage to take two of the sheets and pin them to the flapping coats of the two hanging bodies, but it was a stupid idea. It wasn't worth death.

Nearly at Magda's, she had to urinate. She squatted and the urine came out in a fine stream and then gushed and cascaded out of her. Her water had broken. She felt the first long pain as she stood and pulled her coat around the swelling of her belly. She didn't wait until the pain was over. She turned into the trees and walked between the enormous trunks of the hornbeams and oaks, moving toward the warmth of the stove that glowed like a soul in the darkness of Magda's hut.

Telek knew it wasn't a good time to leave the village. Nelka had said the baby wouldn't come until after Christmas, but women couldn't carry their babies full term with so little food. The babies seemed to push out into the world already hungry, desperate to take their chance of getting more food in the cold air of the village than they did in their mother's womb.

Telek set his mouth in a grim line and loped steadily down the road. There were no trucks or troop to be seen. The Major had been sleeping when Telek slipped away from the village and circled around the one sentry who guarded the road. Telek passed close enough to the sentry to cut his throat, but that was for later. The soldier was only a boy. The young one had been sent lately from the Russian front. He was asleep, and his rifle sagged, the tip touching the frozen road.

It was tempting to hit him on the head and take the gun. The boy wouldn't have dared go back to the Major without a rifle. He would have ended up hiding in the woods, but Telek kept moving down the road. He would deal with the boy later. By spring, perhaps. He loped at a steady pace like a wolf. He could have gone on all day.

The Lithuanian saw Telek first. "He's here."

"That's all of us, then."

"We waited this long for one man?" The Stepmother frowned.

"He's worth waiting for," the Russian said.

The others laughed and watched as Telek came toward them. The man on sentry waved at Telek and he came through the drifted snow beside the road.

"We have everything. Another hour of walking and we reach the rail line." The Lithuanian said, shaking Telek's hand.

Telek looked at the group. Seventeen in all. The Russian had done well. They all wore the greatcoats of the German army. And the woman was still with them.

Telek squatted and took the flask they offered. He drank a deep sip of vodka and coughed. They waited while he ate bread and sausage.

"Let's move out." The Russian turned and looked at the Lithuanian. "Should we stick to the road and take a chance on meeting Germans?"

"There hasn't been anything for three weeks except the usual deliveries for the villages. I think it's safe, and we'll make better time on the road. The truck that brings supplies is every Thursday, between two and five on this part of the road."

"Their punctuality might kill them someday," a man muttered.

Everyone laughed, and Telek looked at the man. It was the new one. The one who looked like a Jew. It was amazing that he had lived so long, but the rifle in his hands was clean and glistening with oil. He wasn't a helpless city Jew.

They all loped down the road now, guns at the ready. Telek had no rifle, but he held his pistol in his hand and it made him feel comradely.

It was a beautiful gun. Not as powerful as some of the new German pistols, but Telek would never part with it. He had taken it off the body of a dead Polish officer who had been wounded and crawled in the woods to die when the Russians had invaded eastern Poland.

The gun was a VIS, the automatic pistol of the Polish army, made before the war. It had the Polish eagle on the slide, staring out fiercely, the wings strong and ready to soar, claws sharp to tear flesh and kill. Telek had promised the dead officer that his gun would have an honorable war.

Nelka wore an old shift of Magda's. It clung to her body, wet with sweat, and she sat on the stool precariously, gripping the edge of the table to keep her balance when the pain rose and the vise that clamped her belly tightened and pressed. Her belly was hard as iron and low, and Nelka groaned with the increasing waves of pain.

"Send Hansel out," Nelka said to Magda when the last pain ended. "Send them both out."

"The girl is only over the grippe for a few days. They have to stay warm."

Hansel knelt beside Nelka and held icicles to her lips. They were bright red from where Nelka had bitten them to keep from screaming.

Magda sat in the chair and waited. The girl was strong. The baby was turned right. She had made sure of that a week ago. It had not slipped wrongly, and the head was down. She rocked and hummed and waited.

Gretel lay on the platform as far into the corner as she could squeeze. She lay with her face to the rough boards of the wall and breathed with her mouth open. She'd seen a dog do it once, the pups coming out in thin sacks, the mother dog tearing the sack and eating it, licking the pups.

That was when she was somewhere else. A long time ago. The pups and the mother dog had disappeared the next day. She wondered what had happened to them. She remembered the dog grunting and moaning, panting with her mouth open and her sides heaving.

Hansel wiped Nelka's face with the melted water from the icicles. Nelka smiled at him.

"Will you help me take care of my baby, Hansel?"

The boy shook his head. "I hate it."

"Pant, girl," Magda said. "Pant. Like a dog."

Nelka tried to think only of the panting. When the contraction ended, she sat gasping.

"Why didn't Telek bring you?" Magda asked.

"He said he would be gone today."

The two women looked in each other's eyes for a second and then away.

"Probably gathering wood for someone."

"Yes," Nelka said. She closed her eyes and breathed deeply, waiting to fall into the next chasm of pain that was ahead of her.

The Russian was smiling all the time now. The tracks led due east, through the forests and over the swamps into the heart of his country. The trains ran east carrying guns and ammunition and troops to kill his people. They came out filled with German wounded, picking up any Poles who were strong enough to work as slaves in Germany.

"We must stop a train going east," the Russian said. "You're sure of the schedules?"

"They radioed the man in Bialystok that it's coming. Unless they change their timetables."

They walked down the tracks, the trees pressing so close to the line that branches had been cut or the trains could never have passed. It was late afternoon and the light was changing.

We'd better hurry, Telek thought.

They rounded a bend in the track, and everyone smiled. The Lithuanian didn't have to tell them. This was the place, a broad meadow in the heart of the thickest forest, an open space.

"Telek?" The Lithuanian called him. "You know the woods and how to use them. Put every man in position. Help them set up the guns."

Telek moved off, followed by the others. Only the woman hesitated. She looked back at the Russian and the Lithuanian and her husband who bent over a knapsack near the train tracks. When she turned, Telek caught her eye and she stared him down.

"You," he said to Lydka. "Get pine branches and make a wide broom. There won't be a footprint on this meadow when the train comes."

"But it's coming at night. They wouldn't see our footprints."

Telek stopped walking and turned to the boy. "What if there are lights on the train? What if a party of soldiers comes through on foot?"

Lydka nodded, his cheeks red with shame. "I know, Telek," he said. He ran off toward the forest, shambling in the snow as if he were truly his own nickname and a calf leaping in the field.

Telek looked around the bowl of the meadow. It was a good place. With this terrain, most of them might live to see the sun come up. He hadn't expected so much.

———

Nelka tried to sit on the stool and let gravity pull the baby out of her, but the pain was so heavy it pressed her to the floor. Gretel lay on the platform, not asleep but tired. Hansel had covered his head with the blankets and his hands were pressed over his ears to try and shut out the awful noise.

"Magda," Nelka cried. "How much longer? I didn't know it would be so terrible." She moaned as Magda's hands, strong now with the memory of all the babies she had brought into the world, kneaded her belly.

"Soon," Magda said.

"I want a daughter. They kill all our sons. Pray it's a girl," Nelka nearly shouted.

Magda only shook her head.

"Do you know what the baby is, Magda?" Hansel asked.

Magda smiled.

How can she know? the boy thought. But he knew Magda did.

"Ahhhhhh." The howl was squeezed out of Nelka's throat. She wasn't Nelka anymore. There was none of her left. The pain had eaten all of the girl she had been.

"Magda," she called, needing to confess it. "My husband may be alive in Siberia, and I'm in love with Telek."

Magda said no words of absolution or comfort. She only nodded.

———

The Russian unwrapped the packages. He breathed lightly and handled them with hands so gentle you would have thought he was touching a woman.

The Mechanik watched and waited. He was ecstatic, squatting

there beside the cold steel rails. He knew about machines, and what were bombs but a sort of machine?

The parts lay beside the track, and the Russian looked at the Mechanik. The Russian's eyes glittered and his mouth was slightly open.

The Mechanik picked up the parts and checked them with strong fingers. He wasn't as gentle as the Russian. It couldn't hurt anyone until—until he made it.

It was lovely to make things. He smiled to himself, and the others moved a little away.

There were only three parts. The container was a Soviet ammunition box. The explosive was cheddite manufactured by the ZWZ, those brave men, in Poland. The fuse, the thing that made the whole thing come alive, was a compression fuse, and he checked it carefully.

There was a vial of sulfuric acid and paper. He sniffed it and caught a faint whiff of the rotten smell of the acid. He opened the second vial of potassium chloride and rolled the paper to fit inside. It soaked up the solution, and he connected the paper to the vial of sulfuric acid.

Now came the more difficult part. He thought about the best way to do the job. Lying on his stomach to examine the steel rail, he left the bomb behind him and crawled six or seven feet, staring at the rail and the space under it.

Here. The earth had worn away a little. It would be faster to dig.

He rose and pointed. "Dig here," he said. "The hole has to be deeper than the box at first. Then I'll adjust it. And dig out as much of the rail around it for as many feet as you can. It'll make the rail move more when the train comes."

The Russian and the Lithuanian took turns chipping the frozen earth out from under the rail. It took them nearly an hour before the Mechanik was satisfied. Finally it was done.

The Mechanik smiled at them and his smile was as sweet as an angel's. "Move back to the woods. I'll try to make sure that if it goes off too soon it tears up the rail when it explodes."

And you with it, the two other men thought at the same time. They each shook his hand, and the Russian kissed the Mechanik on both cheeks like a brother.

The Mechanik was alone on the tracks. He placed the fuse on the bed of cheddite in the box and raised it to his eye level. It was perfect. Gently he lowered the lid, his eyes watching as it closed, the top finally going down the last half inch slowly, until he felt, rather than heard, the lid meeting the resistance of the fuse and closing.

Nothing happened. It was ready. He hummed to himself, picked up the box and carried it gently, as if it were a baby, the six feet to the perfect square hole. He put it in the hole and measured with his finger. The box had to fit tightly under the rail, and there was still space between the box's top and the rail when he put it in the hole. He had to make the hole shallower.

It took him a while to remove the box and pack the soil so the lid of the box fitted snugly under the rail. He couldn't force the box or it would blow up before the train came. He positioned it inch by inch in the hole, and the top touched the rail line now. It was done.

He was pleased with his work. Even if it did blow up early, the track would be broken and could be covered with snow to conceal the break. The train would derail anyway. He looked up and saw Lydka standing with his broom of pine boughs.

"I have to sweep up the footprints when you're done," the boy whispered.

The Mechanik kept on humming and nodded. He turned and walked toward the woods where the others waited. Lydka followed him backward, sweeping the Lithuanian's, the Russian's, the Mechanik's, and his own prints away in long careful strokes of the branches.

It was odd, the Mechanik thought. The song he had been humming. He hadn't heard it since he was a boy, but it was that song. The Mechanik laughed out loud, and the Russian waved his hand at him from the trees. The Mechanik waved back, and he laughed again. Strange the way his mind worked today. He had been humming the Kaddish exactly the way his father had. He had been humming the prayer for the souls of the dead.

It was the end now. Nelka screamed rhythmically as the pain became one long pain with no space in it to rest. Magda knelt beside her and worked. She massaged the skin with oil around Nelka's vagina where the baby's head was crowning.

"Good girl, good girl. You won't tear. It's a nice, slow, good baby."

Nelka's screams became deep grunts of effort ending with a shriek, and Hansel clutched his knees on the platform, tears running down his face. He hated the baby. It was killing Nelka. The dirty baby. He sobbed and his nose ran, mixing with the tears.

Gretel sat wide-eyed and watched, too amazed to be afraid. She watched and felt older and proud that she was present.

"Push," Magda said.

"I can't," Nelka screamed.

"Don't make her," Hansel shouted from the platform. "Don't hurt her, Magda."

"My God." Magda sighed. "Everyone's a midwife today. Push girl, when I say so. It's past my bedtime and dark outside. We all need our dinner."

Nelka felt the pain coming and she was terrified. It was going to kill her. She knew it would. She was dying, and no one could help.

———

The moon was dead and the stars gave no light through the clouds. Only the white snow of the meadow allowed them to see a little in the black night. They crouched, waiting, the cold numbing even their lice until the itching stopped and they were alone with their thoughts.

They heard it long before it got to the meadow. The silence of the forest was broken by a tiny hum that they thought was only their own nerves, and then a rhythmic hum, and then the real sound of a train. It was coming steadily, and the falling snow was too light to slow it.

Telek waited and felt his pistol inside his coat, warm against his heart. He'd get a rifle out of this if he lived.

The Russian was triumphant. It was coming from the west. The Germans on this train were going east to kill Russians. Fresh troops. Not the wounded and crippled of the last battle being hauled back to Germany.

The sound of the train was louder. The *chug-chug-chug-chug* came closer and the men gasped with the tension of it. Their breath went in and out as though some hand struck their chest.

Then the train was in the meadow. Coming fairly slowly. The engineers had to watch for trees fallen and lying across the tracks. Trains weren't able to move through Poland anymore with any sense of security.

The Mechanik strained his eyes to see in the dark. Surely it was over the bomb now. Past it. Oh God, help us, he thought, the bomb has failed, and just as he thought it, the air filled with noise. The train wrenched upward, and two cars came down crooked. The six cars were shuddering and moving, the locomotive still pulling, and then it happened. The two cars in the middle fell over and the whole thing stopped.

For a second there was only the hissing of steam, and then screams began in German.

"Wait, wait, wait," the Russian called softly. "Wait."

The German soldiers climbed out of the cars and milled near the train. The engineer was running down the tracks.

"Now," the Russian called.

They opened fire with the two *pepechas* and the rifles. Telek bared his teeth and waited. The Germans were too far away for his pistol. He would fire when they ran in to finish them off.

It didn't take long. A stove in one of the cars had ignited the walls, and the Germans were dark targets against the red flames. They were in shock and ran toward the woods where the Lithuanian and his men had been placed by Telek.

The Lithuanian had great control. He waited until the Germans believed they were safe, almost in the woods, and then they opened fire. Soldiers fell screaming and torn to pieces, their blood making black splotches on the white snow.

Telek ran toward the train. He climbed onto the first car and peered in. There were three men lying in the car, two unconscious. Telek shot all three and moved on to the next car.

There weren't as many soldiers as the Lithuanian had expected, and they found out why when they opened the last cars. The heavy doors slid apart, and the men laughed and pounded each other on the back. One car held a huge artillery gun on wheels. They'd have to get horses and a sled to pull it. It meant a long night and morning of work, but it was a real weapon.

And the other two cars had no soldiers either. Food. Warm clothes. Vodka. Oil for the machines. It was a treasure trove.

They counted their dead and wounded. The Lithuanian had lost two. None dead in the Russian's group, but Lydka had taken a bullet to his shoulder and was laughing and refusing to have anyone look at it. There was vodka enough to sterilize the knife and dig out the bullet.

Telek moved from dead German to dead German until he found the rifle he wanted. He took it out of the hands of the corpse and began collecting cartridge belts.

The night was warmer now, and the falling snow had turned to a slushy rain. It was coating the trees and ground and Telek knew it could turn to ice. They had to move fast and hide the food and clothes. And there was the artillery gun. It would be a long night.

As dawn lit the sky, the woman, soaked to the skin as they all were but not feeling it yet because of the hard work and the vodka, went to Telek. Her black hair heavily streaked with white lay plastered to her head.

She worked in silence beside him, loading boxes of food onto a sled, but Telek saw she wanted to speak.

"What is it?" he finally asked her.

"You are from Piaski?"

"Yes."

"Did two children come to Piaski? A boy seven, nearly eight, and a blond, older girl?"

Telek nodded. "A woman got false papers for them. They have ration cards and live with her. Outside the village in a hut."

The woman looked around quickly and then whispered, "Don't tell any of the others about the children. They're the Mechanik's, and he'd go and take them. They can't live with us. They'd die, or we'd get killed. They're better where they are."

Telek nodded again. She was right. The children were safe for the moment, and they would die if the Mechanik tried to have them in the woods. Telek knew the Russian. Nothing was going to endanger the safety of his group, and children were too unpredictable. Children got you killed. He wondered if the woman was their mother. Probably not. She would have said so.

The woman kept on working in the rain that was beginning to freeze now. In a little while she stopped and looked at Telek again.

"I'll tell the Mechanik later. When it's over. Tell the woman that we'll come and get them when the Russian front moves past the village."

Telek wasn't sure that he'd tell Magda anything. She might let the children know that their father was alive, and it was better not to raise hopes. Better they forget everything except living with Magda. He and the woman worked side by side as the sun rose.

———

Nelka heard Magda shouting at her, but her body was beyond her control. She lay and felt the pain, and her body convulsed on its own accord. She heard Gretel cry out, and Magda laugh, and then the hut was silent.

Nelka lay still.

"She's dead, she's dead," Hansel sobbed. He wanted to go down on the floor and kiss poor Nelka, but he couldn't do it.

"Wake up, you troublemaker." Magda's strong finger with its swollen joints cleaned the mouth of the baby lying on the floor, and then she lifted it and shook it gently. Its chest heaved and it choked and gasped. A strong wail came from its bloody face.

"It's alive!" Gretel felt like dancing and singing.

"Of course it's alive." Magda shook the baby again just to clean its lungs a little more, and then she laid it on Nelka's chest while she pulled out the afterbirth.

"I hate that baby." Hansel jumped off the platform and threw his arm around Nelka's neck.

"Do you want to cut the cord?" Magda asked Hansel.

He hesitated, but the knife was shiny and he was never allowed to play with Magda's things.

"Yes."

"Cut right where I tell you."

Hansel took the knife and sawed the cord where Magda held it doubled up in a loop. The birth had been much bigger and messier than either of the children had expected.

"What is it?" Nelka whispered.

"Look for yourself." Magda cut the cord closer to the baby's belly and tied it with a twist. Then she began wiping Nelka with cloths dipped in boiled water.

Nelka raised herself on her elbows and looked down at her child. She felt the tears in her eyes, hot and relentless. She couldn't stop them.

"Oh, Magda, I have a son."

The amazingness of it came over her, his perfect feet and toes, the rounds of tiny penis and scrotum, the hands moving, and the eyes staring up at the ceiling, so dark blue they looked black. A perfect maleness that had come out of her female self.

Nelka's heart felt like it was breaking. He was radiant and warm and alive and not even crying. And they would all try to kill him, all his whole life, because he was a man.

She sobbed over the boy, and Magda laughed.

"You can't stop them from being born men, my dear."

"I know. I just want him to be left alone. I love him so much."

"Too bad he isn't a girl." Magda grinned.

Nelka swept the baby up into her arms and held him tightly. "He's what I want, and they'll never hurt him. Never." She blew gently on his round head until the fine hair, damp from Magda's scrubbing, turned from brown to pale golden.

Magda touched the baby's cheek and said, "May I eat at your wedding, boy." But her voice was sad when she said it.

Gretel watched wide-eyed and listened to the cold slush of rain hitting the roof. It was the most beautiful thing she had ever seen and it was also the scariest. "Isn't it beautiful?"

Hansel shrugged. "It hurt Nelka."

Gretel climbed down and sat stroking Hansel. She began to hum the way that Magda did. The room was quiet except for the high, clear humming of the child.

Before they left the meadow, the Russian had them take the corpse of the highest-ranking German they could find and nail him to a tree with spikes from the rail line. His right arm they nailed through the hand to the sapling next to the tree with the index finger pointing westward. The sign hung around his neck said:

BERLIN—1000 KILOMETERS

Ice Storm

The light in the hut was intense, the oiled paper of the window golden with the brightness of dawn. Gretel crept off the sleeping platform and pulled on her boots and coat. She'd get water at the creek for Magda and then look for firewood. Nelka lay curled around her baby, and Magda and Hansel were deep in dreams, their eyelids twitching in the morning light.

It was two days since the baby had been born, and Gretel was doing a lot of chores so Magda could help Nelka. Gretel opened the door, and had to blink. The forest nearly blinded her. The cold rain had gone on for hours until the darkest point of the night. The sleet covering the forest had frozen into ice on everything she saw.

She walked toward the creek carrying the bucket. The snow was covered with a thick crust of ice that crackled under each footstep. Her foot sunk a few inches, but the snow was so frozen and her weight so slight that she walked over the deep snow as if she had on snowshoes.

Gretel stepped on the thicker ice of the creek and thumped the bucket hard on the ice in front of her. With two thumps the bucket broke through. She carried it to the hut where she set it gently inside the door. Then she went into the forest and crouched down to pee.

Standing up, she broke off a twig from a limb and stared at it. The black of the twig was enclosed in a thick layer of transparent ice. She sucked it and the hardness of the ice grew even smoother in the warmth of her mouth. Every branch, every twig, was coated in a thin layer of pure, clear ice. The entire world was diamond-coated. There was an occasional rainbow high up in the trees or on the snow, a patch of color, the sun caught in the ice as in a prism. The smell of snow was astringent, like breathing in chilled alcohol.

"I wonder if the ponies have ice in their hair," she said. She could get wood later. The others wouldn't wake up for another hour.

Gretel moved as fast as she could. She passed the wide bend in the creek where the beavers were building a dam. The top round of twigs and mud was coated with ice, and the beavers were nowhere in sight. A raven in a treetop watched the child but didn't call out.

The fallen tree where Telek had found her sitting before was blocking her path, and she paused to admire it. The bark was so coated in ice, climbing on it would be impossible. She moved around it and went on through the trees.

The ice on everything glittered, and it was magical, but it confused her. She knew that Telek had moved north when he showed her the ponies. She kept the sun on her right side and walked faster.

The child had gone about a half mile farther when she heard the sound. Stopping, Gretel listened. It was the crunching of the ice layer on the snow being broken by an animal.

Delicately she licked her finger and raised it into the air. The air was still. Her finger grew cold, but there was no part colder than the other.

Gretel frowned. She hoped that the ponies couldn't smell her. The crunching noise was closer now. She stood perfectly still and waited. She wanted the ponies to glitter and chink with sound when they moved. But she heard no clicking of ice.

"Dream ponies," she whispered.

The two men saw her before she saw them. Their ragged coats and pants were the color of the tree bark, but they didn't shine with ice. One of them had a rifle in his hand.

"Oh!" Gretel was startled and then disappointed. It wasn't the ponies, was her first thought. She forgot to be frightened until the man with the rifle ran straight at her.

She was lighter than the men and didn't sink so deeply in the snow, but they were faster. She felt a hand on her shoulder and heard the panting of the man as he hit her hard on the back, knocking her down.

She didn't scream. She rolled on the snow and tried to get up, but he was on top of her, his weight pushing her through the ice crust into the softer snow. He put his hand over her mouth and lay on her, perfectly still. The other man stood over them, holding his rifle cocked.

She knew that the two men weren't German. Their coats were ragged and old. They had beards. They didn't have any signs of any army, not Russian or German, and as the man lay across her she could smell him. He stank like men do when they haven't washed in a long time.

The man whispered in her ear in heavily accented Polish. "Alone?"

Gretel thought. If she said yes, it would be dangerous. But if she lied, he would find out soon and then might kill her for lying.

"Alone."

He rose to his knees and began to go through the pockets of her coat. He found a piece of bread she had left from the day before. Handing it to the man standing, he kept searching. He tore the coat off her, working with one hand while he held her mouth. He even felt the boots looking for any weapon, anything that might be useful.

When he was done he stood and held his hand out to receive half the piece of stale bread. The men stood over Gretel, and she did not dare move. It was silent except for the chewing and swallowing of the men.

The one holding the rifle looked around and then nodded toward a fallen log, the bark shining black with a coating of ice making it smooth and glittering. The other man lifted her with a wrench that hurt her arm, but she didn't make any sound. He dragged her to the fallen tree and slammed her against it. She nearly bounced off the trunk of the tree, but he pushed her back.

The one with the rifle raised the gun toward her head. Gretel watched the barrels coming closer, the perfect holes of steel, dark inside and shiny.

The rifle hesitated at her head and then the man jabbed it suddenly under her jaw. Gretel's head tilted back, the cold metal pushing into her throat.

The man who had thrown her down lifted her and pushed her backwards onto the curved tree trunk. With a twist of his hand he ripped off the long pants of Magda's that Nelka had taken in to keep her legs warm and then the cotton underpants. She felt the frozen bark on her bottom.

Her head tilted back against a broken limb, and she could see both of them. He shoved open her legs and grabbed her thin hips. There was a pause while he pulled at his pants, and then something shoved against her where she peed, where she was private. It shoved harder and she screamed out. He was inside her and she was in pain as he shoved in and out. She knew it was his penis. The Stepmother had warned her about strange men doing this.

Gretel's first scream turned into a whimper. Then the man finished and stood away. Her legs fell onto the frozen tree, and she felt something trickling out of her. She couldn't remember what the Stepmother had called this. She knew the word, but her mind couldn't find it.

The man pulled his pants together and buttoned his coat. The other man said something that Gretel didn't hear, and the first man laughed.

Then the other man grabbed her legs, giving the rifle to the man who had hurt her. He leaned close to her face, his breath stinking of onions, and shoved inside her. Gretel moaned. The first man put the rifle tip against the side of her head.

"Be good. We not kill," he said in the funny Polish.

But Gretel knew he was lying. They would kill her. She was dead now, and she knew it. Her own death filled her mind and everything else was driven out. Her mind became an empty hole with no memories, no words, just the gun and the bullet that was going to kill her. She didn't try to think anymore. There was nothing in her head but space and sunlight and the glitter of ice.

And then a lot of things seemed to happen at once, but very slowly—slowly—as if she was not in her own head watching.

The man with the rifle jerked it away from Gretel's head and turned. The man shoving inside her pulled back and opened his mouth, and Gretel knew that he was screaming—but she couldn't hear a thing. The whole world had gone silent.

The blast of the rifle broke through the silence of her shock. She knew she had been shot. Gretel lay with open eyes and waited to feel the pain, but the only pain was between her legs where she burned as if she were on fire.

The man who had been between her legs was gone, and so was the man with the rifle. Gretel stared up into the forest, and it was silent except for someone moaning a long way off. The girl was light-headed, and she couldn't remember where she was.

When she tried to think it was like being in a room and running into walls wherever she turned. She lay there for a long time, but her mind had become a single, light-filled room that kept her very still. After a while, she remembered Magda and then Hansel, and that seemed to be enough. And she began to remember things from the past, the distant past, but all the last months and hours were blank except for the names of Magda and Hansel.

She began to sing then.

> *"Flowers, flowers, they are in our garden.*
> *They smell sweet when the wind blows."*

The child half-lay on the tree and sang and never wondered where the men had gone. She heard another sound as she sang. It was the gasping of someone dying, but she didn't know what it meant, or where it came from, or why it was there in the glittering light of the forest.

When she had sung every song she knew, she hummed to herself. It was lovely. The bright sun. The flowers all around her. She was in the garden and it was warm. He opened the gate and came in, smiling at her. He raised his finger to his lips so her mother wouldn't know.

Gretel pressed her finger to her lips and smiled. It was their secret. She held out her hand into the air, and he leaned toward her. She watched while he put a perfect orange into her hand. He leaned forward and his white beard, smelling of sweet tobacco, tickled her cheek, and she accepted his kiss smiling. Her Zayde.

It was a good morning. Gretel smiled. She looked at the orange and raised it to her nose. Scratching the peel, she sniffed deeply. She hadn't had an orange in so long because—because—her eyes closed. She didn't know why. She opened her eyes and began to peel the invisible orange.

Behind the trees, many feet from the child, there was another moan. The woman's hair, black with heavy streaks of white was wet with red now. The blood poured out of the head wound. Her chest was sodden with red too, and her arm. The pistol lay in the snow beside her.

The Stepmother knew she had done it. She had shot the one man between the eyes, and the other was dead too, but she hadn't been quick enough. He had gotten off a round from the shotgun, and it had killed her. She lay staring up into the perishing glitter of the tree limbs and felt her heart pumping its blood out onto the snow.

The girl was alive. Her beautiful hair and the smile she had. Her lovely girl would live. It made the Stepmother happy, and she smiled, her lips opening slightly and moving against the snow.

Her mind was moving back and forth in time, randomly, and the joy she felt at saving the girl was confused with another child. A boy, younger than the girl. The Stepmother saw the boy toddle toward her, running over grass. She didn't remember that her own child had been killed during the first days of the war. She didn't see past the arms of the baby stretched out for balance. The two children, the lost and the saved, became one in her mind and both were alive.

Her last thought was of her husband, the Mechanik. Of his hands on her breasts. His lips. She groaned uneasily as she remembered him. Something was wrong. There was a mistake somewhere, and she struggled to find it.

Fighting to hold on to consciousness until the memory came, the Stepmother fought with her mind. And then she got it. She hadn't told him. She had come alone to see if his children were all right. She hadn't told him that they were alive. She thought of how she loved him. How good it felt to lie against him and see him smile with the left corner of his lips raising higher than the right.

She hadn't told him that his children lived.

The ice above her head began to sway. The wind was rising. A wet storm was coming across the swamps from the east. The trees began to move and the ice rattled and chinked.

The Stepmother lay and listened to the *clink, clink, clink* as the whole forest talked and the light grew brighter around her until the brightness faded and darkened and was gone forever.

Gretel had promised him. She had promised twice, but Telek knew the glitter of the ice-coated forest was too great a lure. He ran, following her footsteps in the crust of the snow. Then he stopped looking for her prints. He knew where she was going. Back to the wild ponies.

He couldn't hear her singing because the wind had sprung up and the ice-covered limbs rattled above his head. It wasn't safe being under the larger trees. The icicles could fall like knives.

Gretel sat on the fallen tree trunk. Her legs were blue with cold, and a red line of blood ran from her bottom and was frozen on the icy side of the tree. The bodies of two men huddled in the snow. Telek drew a deep breath and looked around. Except for the rattle of the ice-coated branches and the child's humming, it was silent.

He went to the child, taking his coat off. Her thighs were covered with blood.

"Oh Holy Mother, help us. Oh, Gretel," he whispered.

He wrapped the coat around her and she smiled at him. Her hands moved in some strange way in the air in front of her.

"Look, Telek! He gave me one. He hasn't come for so long!"

"Who, child?" Telek looked into her eyes. She was so happy.

"My grandfather, you know him. He comes every morning."

Telek stared at Gretel. "Tell me what happened—" he began, and then he stopped. He wrapped the coat around her tightly, leaving her sitting on the tree, and bent over the men. He didn't touch them. They were both dead. One shot in the head. A beautiful shot. The other was shot in the gut and had crawled a little way before he bled to death.

From the way they were lying, the shooter had been standing east. He moved softly through the trees, looking for footprints.

He found her behind a tree. It was the woman who had been with the Russian's group. Her hair was soaked in blood, but he could still see patches of black and white. He knew immediately what had happened. She had wanted to see if the children were safe.

Telek picked up the pistol and slipped it in his jacket. She had nothing useful in her pockets. There wasn't time to bury her now, and the ground was too frozen to dig. He'd take the child to Magda and come back and hide the bodies in the snow.

He glanced at the dead men. They were meat now. Lithuanians maybe? Escaped Russian prisoners? Polish bandits? Even Jews, but probably not. The Jews had been killed already. It didn't matter. They were wolves. No. Wolves were innocent of the possibility of evil.

Telek picked up Gretel and carried her. She smiled at him and sang songs that he didn't know. She offered him a piece of her invisible orange, and he gently declined.

"The flowers are beautiful, aren't they, Telek? I thought it'd never be summer. Can we go look for the bison now?"

"Soon we'll look for him." Telek felt the tears in his eyes and he blinked them back. She was alive. She was too young to get pregnant from this, he thought. Magda and Nelka would nurse her. The girl's mind was gone, but it might be better that way. Why should she remember?

The ice clinked above them all the way back to the hut, growing louder as the wind increased. Telek had to hurry. He had to come back and hide the three bodies.

"Please eat a piece of orange, Telek. It's so good."

Telek opened his mouth and she put an invisible segment of orange on his tongue.

"Thank you, dear one," he said. He had to hurry. It would snow again before midnight.

Hansel

Telek walked into the hut carrying Gretel. He laid the child on the sleeping platform, and whispered in Magda's ear for a moment. He stood looking back and forth from the sleeping baby in its nest of blankets to Gretel.

"It's a boy," Magda whispered, but she looked at Gretel as she spoke.

"Nelka?" He moved to the baby and leaned over the tiny child. Gently, Telek touched the cheek that was so soft his finger barely felt the flesh.

"The birth went well. Nelka is outside. She needed to walk a little."

Gretel lay very still and shivered, and she was singing but not paying any attention to Hansel who stood beside her. There was blood on her legs, and Hansel didn't want to look at it.

"What's wrong with her?" Hansel flushed with anger.

Telek slipped from the hut without answering Hansel.

"Go out and play." Magda was heating water on the stove.

"It's too cold. It's ice everywhere." Hansel stared at Gretel. He didn't want to cry, but she looked funny. She had stopped singing, and the blood was bright red against her skin.

"Go out." Magda turned on Hansel and her face was dark and angry.

He went outside banging the door to the hut and not caring. "Nelka," he called to her where she stood whispering with Telek. "Magda threw me out!"

Nelka didn't stop to hug him or talk but ran to the hut and went inside.

"I want in," he shouted. Hansel shivered and threw sticks against the side of the hut until Magda opened the door and shouted at him.

"Don't bother us. You can come in later."

The boy looked back to where Telek had been, but he had vanished. Hansel stuck his tongue out at the closed door. Just because Gretel had gone off and gotten hurt. Just because she was so dumb that she got lost and Telek had to go find her. Hansel scuffed his boot against a log and tried to be angry, but he kept thinking of the blood.

"*Raus, raus, raus,*" he shrieked, picking up a stick and brandishing it over his head. But how could you play soldier all alone? He was cold, and they didn't care.

"I won't be here when you open the door," he shouted, turning and running fast until he was through the trees and onto the road and had put a bend in the road between him and the hut.

He ran like a dog was after him, snarling and biting at his legs. He ran until he was out of breath. Then he stopped and walked on, waving his stick of a sword. The village wasn't far and it wasn't snowing. He'd find someone to play with and come home before Magda knew he was gone.

He smelled the wood smoke of the village before he saw the first roof. Hansel walked past the houses until he came to a pig rooting in the frozen mud.

"Pig, pig, pig," he crooned. He'd never been so close to a live pig before. Carefully he touched the side of the pig with his stick, and it grunted and leaped away. Hansel was so startled that he jumped backward, tripped, and fell on his bottom with a thump.

Getting up, he heard the laughter. It was two boys, one bigger than he by a head, the other the same size but with straight black hair to his shoulders.

"The pig knocked him on his ass," the black-haired boy said.

"No it didn't."

"You're scared of the pig." The older boy tapped Hansel on the shoulder.

"I'm not."

"Then go kiss it."

"You don't kiss pigs." Hansel picked up his stick.

"You're scared to get close to it."

"Kiss it. Kiss it. Kiss it," the black-haired boy chanted.

Hansel walked past the pig who was rooting again in the road. It stopped rooting, turned its head and fixed its small eyes on Hansel.

"He's scared! He's going to shit his pants he's so scared!"

"Run home to the witch, baby," the boy shouted. "Go back to the woods and hide."

Hansel stepped forward gingerly and kissed it on the back above the stringy tail.

"I did it! I'm not scared!'

"He kissed the pig's butt! He kissed the pig's butt!" Overcome with laughter, the two boys leaned against each other and pointed at Hansel. Three other boys had edged up and watched.

Hansel looked at the pig and then at the boys, and he felt the tears in his eyes. The hotness of rage flushed his cheeks, and he clenched his fists. "Shut up."

They howled with laughter, and Hansel flew at them. The force of his run knocked down the bigger boy. Falling on him, Hansel punched twice and then leapt up. Catching the smaller boy off guard, Hansel knocked him down, and they rolled over and over in the road.

"You dirty Nazi," Hansel screamed.

"I'm not a Nazi! I'm a girl!"

Hansel stopped punching and lay on the road. The girl sat on him and Hansel put his hands over his face so her punches bounced off. "Girls can be Nazis."

"No they can't." She punched twice more and then stood up.

"I've seen them," Hansel said.

"Where?"

He couldn't talk about the life before the woods. "I don't know."

"They're all men," she said.

"There was that woman in the brown coat," one of the boys said. "She was SS. Do you really live with the witch?"

"She's my great-aunt."

"Where's your mother?"

"I don't know."

"Where's your father?"

"He died in the war."

Silence greeted this information, and the children moved closer.

"I'm Halina. I live with my aunt and uncle. They killed my mommy and daddy too."

They were silent. Then one of the boys spoke. "Her parents were hanged—"

"Shut up," the bigger boy ordered, and the other child cut off his words as if he swallowed them. He gulped twice and no one looked at Halina.

Hansel could stand it no longer. And he didn't want to talk about the thing with her parents.

"Let's play," he said.

"Play what?" The children vibrated with interest.

"Soldier."

"All right. I'll be the general of the Poles, and you"—the bigger boy tapped Hansel on his shoulder—"have to be the Nazi. I'm Jerzy."

Jerzy chose first, and Hansel hesitated and then chose Halina.

"I'm the Generaloberst," Hansel said, "and you're the Oberst."

"I want to be a general too."

"There's only one general, but you're next to a general."

When they had chosen, Hansel had three on his side. The girl and two boys.

"I want to be the Oberst."

"Me too."

"You're the Hauptmann and you take command from the Oberst. And we have to have a regular soldier, so you're the Grenadier," Hansel told the youngest boy.

"I won't. I won't be a regular soldier."

"The Grenadiers get to do most of the fighting."

The Major who was standing on the porch of a house leaned against a post and watched. This boy was sharp. He had properly memorized all the ranks of the army as Polish children were ordered to do, and he was smart enough to know who did the real fighting.

"Good job, Generaloberst. Always respect your men."

The children shrank back and stared, but Hansel clicked to attention and saluted.

"Heil Hitler," he shouted.

The Major sprang to attention and returned the salute.

"Come here, boy." He reached in his pocket and took out a handful of peppermints. He counted out five into Hansel's hand. "One for the Hauptmann. One for the Oberst. One for the Grenadier, and two for the Generaloberst."

Hansel gave another salute and stood at attention.

"Dismissed, Generaloberst." The Major moved on down the street.

Hansel turned back to the other children and was surprised at their still faces.

"You saluted him." Jerzy spit on the snow. "He didn't make you. You just did it."

"Look what we got!" Hansel grinned and showed the candy.

"Dirty Nazi," Jerzy whispered. He hit Hansel's hand and knocked the candy onto the road.

Hansel picked up each piece. They were stupid. He had gotten five pieces of candy.

"We'll all eat it," he said. "Here."

Hansel laid the candy on a porch rail and carefully cracked it into smaller pieces, catching them in his hands. He turned and held out pieces. "Why throw it away?"

First the littlest boy and then Halina took candy and put it in their mouth. Their eyes grew round with the shock of the sugar and sharp flavor.

"Lovely," the girl sighed.

They all took the candy except for Jerzy.

"I don't want to play," the littlest boy said. "I don't want to be a Nazi."

"Me neither." Halina tied her scarf more tightly.

"We'd just beat you anyway," said Jerzy.

"I have to go. Magda will be mad." Hansel turned and moved a few steps down the road. The other boys ran back down the street playing tag and shouting.

"Don't go." Halina shook the hair out of her eyes. "We can get potatoes and roast them."

"All right." Hansel didn't want to go back yet. He'd show them. They'd miss him, and he was glad.

Halina's house was like the others in the village, raw boards and a sloping roof that nearly touched the ground. Bales of hay were piled around the sides for warmth.

"If my aunt asks what we're doing, you have to talk to her so I can get the potatoes."

The aunt sat near the fireplace with the daylight coming through the oiled paper onto her lap. She was sewing pieces of cloth over the holes in a pair of pants.

"Yes, children? Are you cold?"

"He's cold." Halina pushed Hansel toward her aunt. "I want a drink of water." She went to a curtain and pushed it aside. The pantry and buckets of water were behind the curtain.

"You are the boy who is staying with Magda?"

"My sister and I are staying with her. For now."

"For now." The woman looked at him and put down the sewing. She looked into Hansel's eyes and then stared toward the curtain. "Magda brought you to the village today?"

Hansel shook his head.

"You came alone?"

"She said I could," he lied.

The woman watched him until the flush spread up his neck to his cheeks.

"Halina! Get in here!"

The girl came out from behind the curtain.

"You don't play with this boy again. You never bring him in our house. Never."

"But we just—"

"Halina, you never talk to him. You leave him alone." The woman was standing now. She turned to Hansel and waved her hands at him. "Get out! Go away!"

"We were just playing."

"You should play in the woods. It's better that you not play in the village." The aunt reached out and pulled Halina to her. She held the girl's head tightly, looking down into her face. "You never play with him again." Halina's aunt leaned over, burrowing her face against the child's neck, kissing her cheek. "You smell like snow. Don't stay out late. I don't want you getting sick."

Hansel watched from the door.

"You, boy, you heard me. She can't play with you. Go back to the woods."

Hansel ran out and jumped off the porch. He began to walk very fast down the road. He didn't want to cry in the village where other children would see.

He heard footsteps behind him and slowed, looking over his shoulder. It was Halina.

"Don't run off. Come on."

"She hates me. She said I had to go back to the woods."

"I've got three potatoes."

"I don't care." Hansel wiped his nose on his sleeve.

"Let's go cook them. Just us." Halina took out one potato and showed it to Hansel. It was clean and didn't have any mold on it.

"How do we cook them?"

"You didn't cook potatoes in the city?"

"We cooked them on the stove."

Halina crept close to a woodpile on a porch and took an armload of dry sticks. She led Hansel out of the village, and in a field near two trees, Halina showed Hansel how to cook outside.

It took a long time. Halina had used up three matches before the bit of candle caught and the smaller wood lit. Then they had to wait until the fire burned down, and they could put the potatoes on the coals. The potatoes roasted slowly, and the children burned their fingers turning the charring lumps so they'd cook evenly.

Just when they were nearly done, Hansel heard Halina's aunt calling.

"Halina! Halina! Come home now. You'd better come right now."

"She'll be mad."

"She's not my mother. She can't boss me."

Hansel didn't say anything. Halina's aunt didn't go beyond the last house on the edge of the village, and her voice died away. Halina lowered her head again and the two of them watched the coals for another half hour until the potatoes were done.

Hansel was so hungry that he burned his mouth and had to suck air in to cool the potato. Halina giggled at him and blew on her potato until she could pick it up.

"Good," Hansel said. It was soft and mealy inside and black and tasty outside, the burnt part adding a nice crunch that potatoes cooked in pots didn't have.

"You don't have a house. Or toys or anything." Halina licked her fingers carefully.

"I have things."

"What?"

"I have a secret. It's important."

"Tell me."

"Can't."

"You don't have a secret. You don't know anything."

"I do. I'll tell you sometime. Really."

It was getting very cold. Hansel walked over the field to the road. The sun was a red eye watching them through the bars of the tree branches.

"Come play again. When the ice melts, we'll catch fish with a string and a pin and cook them in the woods. And we'll pick blackberries and raspberries."

The children sighed almost as if they breathed in unison. They stood fidgeting, and Halina suddenly broke away and ran down the road toward the village. She ran back just as suddenly and kissed him on his mouth, a cold, firm kiss. Then she ran down the road again as fast as she could.

Hansel stood watching until she had rounded a bend in the road and was gone. He turned and began trotting away from the smoke of the village. He thought about the aunt shouting at him. He thought about Halina and the pig and the candy, but mostly he thought about when the aunt had hugged Halina, how she had smiled down at her, and then later came out in the cold and looked for Halina.

It was dark when he got back to the hut, and Magda was angry.

"Where were you, Hansel?"

"I went to the village." His eyes kept sliding toward Gretel. She lay very still.

"You never go to the village unless I or Nelka take you," she said. "Never."

He nodded. But he wanted to tell Gretel about it, about what Halina's aunt had said.

Gretel lay wrapped in blankets on the platform. Hansel crept close to her and whispered so Magda wouldn't hear.

"Gretel, I went to the village and Halina's aunt told me to go away."

"The village must have a lot of flowers now."

"There weren't any flowers. Halina got potatoes. We cooked them out in the field."

Gretel smiled at him and hummed to herself.

Hansel reached out his hand and shook her shoulder a little.

"Listen. The aunt was mean. She shouted, and I hadn't done anything."

"You must have walked on her flowers. I did that once, and Grandfather picked me up and told me not to. Grandfather picked me up and said—" Gretel's mouth hung open, she frowned and then shook her head hard like she was trying to shake the words out of her mouth.

"We can't talk about that. We can't talk about before," he whispered.

"What's my name?" she asked him loudly.

"Gretel," he whispered. Hansel stared at her. His stomach felt terrible and the potato almost came up.

"My other name. I remember the orange. But I can't think what he called me."

"Your name has to be Gretel."

"I can't remember my name. It's gone."

Magda turned and saw the girl's face. "Now, dear one. It's all right. You're safe now."

"I want it," Gretel spoke loudly. "I want it."

"You're Gretel. That's your name." Hansel was crying. He wasn't crying because she couldn't remember her name. He was crying because he wasn't sure that he remembered it. It felt like they had been

in the forest forever. Her name—he didn't know what it was. Hansel
tried to think of his own name, and then he stopped and began to sob.
It could get you killed if you thought about things. He opened his
mouth wide and wailed.

"Magda, Magda," he sobbed. "What's wrong with her? She can't
talk like that. She can't be crazy. They kill crazy people."

Magda stroked Gretel's head and tried to take Hansel's hand.

"She's been hurt. Two men caught her and hurt her, Hansel. But
she'll get better."

"She can't remember—" Hansel sobbed louder. If Gretel forgot, he
wasn't sure if he'd remember. She was the one who knew things.

"Listen to me." Magda took his head with her hands and put her
face close to his. "Your sister is hurt. Her mind is not well. She can't
think right."

"Why?"

"Because men hurt her."

"When can she think right again?"

"Someday. But now we have to take care of her."

Gretel struggled out of the blanket and looked at Hansel.

"Poor Hansel, you mustn't cry. I know your name."

"What's my name?" he whispered. He knew she shouldn't say it,
but he couldn't think what his old name was. His heart hung on her
answer.

"Your name is Hansel." She smiled at him and out held her hand.
"I have an orange. He gave it to me. You can have a piece."

"You come back," he shouted at Gretel. "You have to come back!"
Gretel sat beside him, but he knew she was gone. He didn't have a big
sister to take care of him anymore, and it made his stomach turn over
again. He'd never lived without a big sister.

"You're the big brother now," Magda said. "She'll get better."

"When?" He felt everything slipping away from him, but Magda
didn't answer, and Gretel just sat smiling between them.

Telek

"Don't expose the baby's face. It's so cold, Telek. I can't stop thinking about Gretel. Five days, and she doesn't remember the rape or the shooting or any of it."

Telek had told them that a partisan had killed the rapists but not that the dead shooter was someone he had met before, someone who knew the children. Hansel and Gretel mustn't have more grief, or be distracted from their new identities. They could be told later.

"Maybe it's kinder that she doesn't remember." There were dark patches of ice under the snow, and Telek walked carefully with the light weight of the baby on his arm.

"It's too much. That SS officer and the woman. She keeps staring at the children. Giving them candy."

They walked, and Telek knew he had to tell her. "The woman is selecting children, Nelka."

"Why? Children can't go to Germany and work." She stopped walking.

Telek couldn't bear to look at her and stared off at the fields smothered with snow. "They are taking children. We don't know why, for adoption, for slaves maybe. If they select your baby, I'll take you both into the woods. They'll never get him."

Her chapped lips trembled. "Babies can't work. Why babies?"

Telek felt like a fox caught in steel jaws with no way out. He must mutilate the children, including Nelka's perfect blond child. What mother could love such a man? And if he didn't, the baby would be taken and probably die being transported to Germany in this winter cold.

He wanted to kiss her. He had never kissed her in all their living in the village. It might be his last chance in life to kiss Nelka, this woman he had loved at a distance for so long.

His mind told him to hold back, but his body moved as if it were not part of him. Holding the baby with one arm at his side so he could be close to her, Telek put his arm around Nelka, drew her to him, and kissed her. It was a deep kiss, long and yearning.

"Oh, Telek."

"They won't get him."

The child began to cry thinly. Nelka's breasts rippled with twinges of pain from chest to nipple as she heard the cries, but she ignored the sound and raised her face, taking joy in his mouth. She had wanted to kiss him for months, and now she took and prolonged a second kiss until they gasped for breath.

They pulled away from each other, panting, luxuriating in the rush of feeling. It was done. They had leaped into love, and the whole world, the dark trees and the fields, shimmered with bright light. They saw this and smiled at the same time.

"Hurry. He wants to eat," she said, and her voice trembled as she commanded him.

They walked on faster, and Telek thought about love and about her baby and about Hansel and Gretel. Hansel had brown eyes and curly hair, and Gretel's mind was gone. It was hard to win with the Germans. They wouldn't kidnap a crazy girl, perfect though she was, but the Germans killed crazy people. Crazy people weren't productive. They'd shot Feliks's brother. There were too many things he didn't want to think about. Her baby. The children he had to hurt. Hansel. Gretel.

He had to save Nelka's baby and the children. She had to love him, because he could never bear to live again as the man he had been for thirty-five years before she kissed him on the road.

The first houses of the village appeared. Nelka took the baby from Telek. The boy was screaming now for his nursing. Telek touched Nelka's cheek and went to get buckets. She would need water.

Feliks stood near the village well with his bucket while Telek drew water. "The SS and the Brown Sister are finishing in Bialowieza. They'll be here soon. What about the children?"

Telek moved under the wooden yoke and grunted as he lifted the weight of four buckets.

"You drew the straw. It has to be done."

"They should take care of their own children." Telek felt the jaws of the trap around him.

Jedrik, the only fat Pole left in the village, slunk past Telek, and Telek didn't look at him. Jedrik got food from the Major since he had pointed out the Mayor, and his wife, and the Jews.

And then there was Feliks. Walking miles to other villages. Taking a chance on getting caught and shot. Bringing information. Taking information to the partisans.

"Every Pole who isn't a devil is an angel," Telek muttered. There would be time to take care of the collaborators after the Nazis were driven out by the Russians.

He stopped and left a bucket on Nelka's doorstep. Tonight he would begin.

Telek walked up to Pawel as if he was trying to sell him some wood.

"Look at the wood on my back and listen."

Pawel nodded. He lifted the top pieces and felt them, as if to see how wet they were.

"Tonight you and your wife will go to see her sister. You'll leave the children in the house. If your wife has a brooch or anything of value, have her wear it."

"Everything we had went into Russia. They stole the clock off the wall."

"Be gone by dark. Leave the children."

"All three?" Pawel was so pale that blue shadows lay around his eyes and mouth.

"All three."

"Telek, don't—"

"It's this or have them kidnapped. And for God's sake, don't tell your wife." Telek hesitated, and then climbed the steps of the church. He dropped the wood on the porch and went inside where the man hung on the cross.

"Why don't you do something?" he said to the crucified man. There was no sound in the building except the sound of the wind through the broken windows. It would be a bad night.

Pawel and his wife had gone. The light of the fireplace burned steadily. Telek stood outside and watched. He heard the boy calling out occasionally, arguing with his sister. The baby was probably asleep.

It was no good standing in the cold. The Major was always busy after dinner drinking vodka and getting a little drunk. He wouldn't prowl the streets for another hour. Telek entered quickly. The boy turned, and Telek hit him hard with the stick. The girl stared as Telek moved over her and struck her on the head too. Their bodies lay limp on the floor.

He moved to the curtains and jerked them shut. The baby was asleep, no need to strike it.

Telek was sweating. His breath came in gasps. First he took the kerosene lantern and filled it carefully from a jar he carried in his coat. If anything was left, it had to look like an accident so the parents wouldn't be blamed.

He took a stick from his coat that was wrapped in rags. He lit the rags, and they sprang to life. He let the torch burn for several minutes until the boy's legs twitched. He didn't want to hit the child again. It was hard to hit lightly enough not to kill.

Telek took the torch and held it against the arm of the boy. He came awake with a shriek, and Telek hit him with the wood of the torch. There was a long burn on his arm. Telek lay the torch on the boy's shoulder and neck. The shirt took flame and Telek smothered it with his coat sleeve.

The girl was next. She was so still. He had hit her a little too hard. His hands were shaking.

Telek looked at her face, and he couldn't stand to scar it. Instead, he lit the fair hair, and let it burn. He put it out when she began moaning. There was a livid burn on her scalp. He touched her hand with the torch and burned it, watching the pale skin bubble into blisters.

The baby he couldn't stand to look at. He rolled it over, pulling the blankets off and the nightshirt up. He burned it once on the neck and back, and the baby shrieked and flung its arms and legs spasmodically out like the flopping of a wounded rabbit.

The rest went quickly. He took the kerosene lamp and spilled it all over the room. Grabbing up the howling baby and the two others in his arms, not caring if he hurt them, just wanting to get it over, get them out, Telek flung the torch which smoldered onto the kerosene.

He had to stand and wait while it lit and the room began to burn. He stood holding the moaning children, waiting for the flames, and when the room was an inferno and the fire moving to the thatch roof, Telek stepped to the door and went out into the cold darkness.

"Fire, fire!" he screamed hoarsely. "Fire!"

Men began to run from the houses. The thatch had caught and the house was a torch.

Pawel was at his side, taking the children from Telek.

The fire would be impossible to put out, but it wouldn't spread. They had lost everything, but now the Major wouldn't accuse Pawel and Marta of damaging the children on purpose. No one would deliberately lose their shelter in the coldest days of winter.

———

The Major stood and watched the house burn to the ground. Once the thatch caught, the village men gave up and moved back. The roof blazed and fell in with a soft whoosh and a great puff of sparks that rose in the still air for hundreds of feet.

"God damn Poles. Leaving their children alone with a kerosene lamp. Cows are better parents. It's a miracle that any of the children grow up with such fools caring for them."

Wiktor stood beside the Major, and his curiosity rose. Why hadn't the parents taken the children with them? But he said nothing. It was no business of his.

Three done. Only four more. Telek thought about it the next day. It was a problem. How badly mutilated did the children have to be?

He approached Patryk and his wife together. They were sensible and closemouthed. They had to know before he injured the child.

"Are you sure of this?" Patryk watched Telek's face closely.

"They're doing it now in Bialowieza. They have done it in other villages."

"He is very high up in the SS." Patryk looked at his wife. "We wondered at the time. A man that high coming here."

"It's something that Himmler cares about. He must promote those who do it so no one can interfere." Telek waited.

Patryk looked at his wife. "Should we trust Telek to do this?"

Zanna stared at Patryk. She turned it over in her mind. The men sat and waited.

"We'll do it ourselves if it has to be done. We can't live in the woods until spring. It's too harsh a winter. The boy could die."

"And she is pregnant again," Patryk said softly to Telek.

"What God wills," she said.

"You understand that it has to be done soon. And it must look like an accident."

Patryk was a strong man. He didn't wait. The accident happened while Patryk was gathering wood. "I was going down the road with a full load of wood, digging the cart out when I had to, when it happened," Patryk told the Major.

"What fool thing did you do?" The Major sighed. It was constant, the problems of trying to govern these people. They couldn't even drive a cart and horse.

"A deer leapt over the road and the horse bolted. The cart went into a tree and the axle smashed. My son is hurt."

"Next time you'll learn to keep a tighter grip on the horse. And the wagon?"

"The axle I can repair. Tomorrow we'll lift the cart out of the ditch and mend it."

Patryk went home. His wife was setting the child's leg, broken in two places, and the boy moaned in pain. There was a long gash on his face that would leave a thick-edged scar.

"Shall I get Magda?" his wife asked.

Patryk touched his son's head softly. "No. Clean his face and let it be."

"The Major may wonder why we didn't sew it up."

"We'll tell him we didn't think it needed it."

"Will he believe that? A cut this deep?"

"We're just Poles who don't have sense enough to hold on to our horses. He must look ugly!"

She and her husband sat beside the boy's bed, holding hands as the night grew colder. He was all they had left other than the new heart beating underneath her own, his two sisters lying under the frozen ground for two years.

———

Telek knew he should wait and space out the injuries, but he couldn't stand it. Three more. And Miron and Ania's two who weren't perfectly blond, but close enough to be chosen. He couldn't make up his mind about them. He knew his nerve would fail if he didn't hurry.

He took the first little girl and, tying a cloth over her eyes, her body drooping, half asleep from all the vodka sweetened with raspberry syrup her mother had fed her, her small mouth sticky and stinking of fruit and alcohol, laid her hand on the table. With a single blow of a butcher knife, Telek severed her index finger.

"Say it was an accident. She put her hand on the chopping block when he was cutting meat. They'll believe it, but wait a day. There mustn't be too many accidents on one day."

Telek ran from the house and had to force himself to walk. The child had screamed even with all the vodka. Now the parents had to make her believe that it had been an accident. The sound of her scream bounced in his head and he couldn't get rid of it. He walked to the well and pumped water onto his head. It was so cold that it began to freeze in his hair, but the pain of the icy water on his scalp drove the scream out. The whole village was silent again.

He walked to the edge of the village as if he was going to get firewood. The walk calmed him, and he began to warm up as he moved quickly. Then he began to enjoy the blankness of the fields and the occasional coughing cries of the ravens. When he realized that he was relaxing and taking pleasure in his aloneness in the white silence, he stopped short and jerked around. He went back toward the village almost at a run.

He thought as he moved, and he knew it wouldn't be easy. The next child was the son of Jasia, and Jasia would be a problem. Her four-year-old son looked exactly like his father, and his father had been kidnapped and taken to Russia. Jasia talked about her husband, but she knew that he was a dead man. If he lived through the trip in the boxcar, the frozen heart of Russia would never give him up.

Telek's mouth grew hard as he knocked on the door, and Jasia stared at him as he pushed inside. It took a while to convince her, and he talked so fast that he had to keep repeating things.

"Don't hurt his face, for God's sake, Telek. I can't live if you ruin his face. It's his father—when I look at him—"

Her father had been the Mayor. When the Mayor and his wife had been shot, Jasia had been allowed to live because she was the clerk who handled all the records of farm yields. The Germans needed her to make up lists for summer production. She had slipped through their net by making endless copies of farm records.

"I won't hurt his face," Telek promised. "Go draw water, Jasia. Stay away."

"No. Take him in the bedroom. I won't leave him."

The boy also stank of raspberries and vodka. Telek's stomach rolled over. He knew that he would never eat raspberries again. Perhaps never drink vodka, although God knows what that would leave to drink in Poland.

Telek broke the boy's arm with such a wrench that it dislocated the shoulder.

"I'll send Magda when I've done with the other one," he whispered to Jasia as he fled.

Telek entered the last house looking so fierce that the parents fled. He took the almost unconscious child, again the stench of fruit and vodka, and holding him tightly, he put the child's left hand on the stovetop. The smell of seared flesh filled the room. Telek looked at the hand calmly and lowered it again. It must be a bad burn. One that made the child almost a cripple for months. It must make him useless for whatever labor the Germans intended.

This time he ignored the child's screams. He left the house and it was done. They'd disliked him since his mother was left in poverty and then killed herself. No one in the village had liked him. The odd one. The boy who stayed in the forest and didn't speak much, and now they had a reason to fear him. He was a man who could torture children.

He staggered off the porch of the house and walked down the muddy road like a drunk. His hands hung loose at his sides like dead things.

"Nelka." He walked into her house with no knock. "Nelka."

She was making bread. The flour was gray with rough sprinkles of sawdust. She had mounded it carefully and was kneading it, making sure that not a single grain was lost.

"Telek? Don't wake the baby."

"I had to hurt them. I burned Pawel and Marta's house. The children were perfect. They had to be mutilated. I burned the girl's head. I hurt her."

"You hurt children? So they wouldn't be kidnapped? But why you? You have no children."

"I drew the straw. They didn't want to make their children hate them. Only Patryk took care of his boy. I had to scar the rest of them. My straw was short."

"So the SS man will leave them in the village?"

He nodded and looked into her eyes. He wanted to be dead.

"The cowards. And they let you be one of them. Part of the village council. They paid no attention to you before the war. And now when you go in the forest and bring news and do things that are dangerous— then they meet with you." Her cheeks were red.

"I drew the short straw."

Nelka glared at him, and he began to cry.

She stroked his face with her hands. "They were cowards, and you saved their children."

He was so grateful that he began to sob. He could tell her. He could tell her anything. She was wiser than he had understood. He had only seen her beauty, but she was also wise.

"They all stank of raspberries and vodka. They screamed."

"Oh, my darling." Nelka tried to move away so she could see his face, but he clutched her.

"I couldn't do Miron and Ania's two. They have dark hair, but their eyes are blue. I can't do any more. If their blue eyes get them kidnapped, their parents will have to save them."

"It wasn't fair, Telek. Every parent should have to protect their own."

"But there's more." He looked toward where the baby slept.

"But he's just born! He cries all night."

Telek stared at her, and knew he couldn't mutilate a newborn baby. It was too much.

"You promised to take us and hide in the woods."

He pulled Nelka to him and held her until she was still. The weather would kill the baby, but he could save her. He had waited too long for her, and she was all he'd wanted.

"I'll take you both into the forest, but you have to understand. It's cold. They bring dogs and sweep the woods looking for partisans."

"I'll carry him inside my clothes and keep him warm. I can feed him."

"The constant walking. No food. You'll lose your milk."

"You can kill ponies for food, or one of the bison."

"They're preserving this forest for Göring's special hunting grounds. If they found a carcass, they'd kill all the village."

"I won't have him look in the mirror and see all this evil marked on his face all his life."

Telek picked her up and carried her to the curtain that hid the bed next to the oven. He felt himself growing warm as he laid her on the bed. "I'll take you both into the forest. We'll survive."

Telek stripped and lay beside her. She rubbed her hands, covered with flour paste over his chest and back. She stroked him hungrily, and he moved swiftly over her, taking her clothes off with clumsy fingers.

She wanted him so badly, wanted the maleness of him, the hardness of his body against her so much, that she sobbed as she pushed against him. He held her and they both were lost in their passion, getting finally what she had wanted for months, Telek had wanted for years, and they rocked together in love that was done and then done again during the gray afternoon.

When the baby finally woke, Telek rose and took the child to Nelka. She nursed him there in the bed made damp with their sweat, Telek lying beside her, watching.

"Will you love us, Telek?"

"I always have."

"But will you love him?"

"He's my son now."

She nodded and lay nearly asleep, the only sound in the hut the wet sucking of the child.

Blood

It was an ugly room. Floorboards unpolished and darkened by years of mud. A bed next to the wall. Two chairs, neither comfortable. A pine table. There had been a rag of a rug, but the Oberführer had it taken away. He supposed the Russians had stolen any decent rugs, assuming that the village ever had a rug worth owning. Major Frankel said it was one of the better houses in the village because the floor was wooden rather than clay. It was barely sufficient.

But other things were proving more than sufficient. Sister Rosa had examined the woman's blood. It was a magnificent chance. Nelka's blood type and his matched. They were both O negative.

The door opened and Nelka came in. Following her was Sister Rosa, dressed as always in her long brown dress and dark bonnet, a gray cape sweeping the tops of her boots.

"I see that your baby was born." The SS man smiled at Nelka. She was pale, but the golden quality had not been disturbed by childbirth.

"Yes, Oberführer. He is not well. I think he may die before spring," Nelka lied.

"What a shame." The Oberführer nodded at Sister Rosa, who put her leather bag on the table and began to unpack it.

"The baby was early. It's weak." Nelka tried not to look at the woman. They had drawn blood from her, and now they had called her back to see the SS officer.

"I sympathize." The Oberführer gestured to Sister Rosa. She went to him, her small eyes lowered humbly, and carefully, with caressing movements of her thick fingers, she unbuttoned his tunic. It took a few minutes to do. The woman undid each button and then moved behind the man to take off the tunic. She put her hands over his shoulders almost in an embrace.

Nelka watched in silence and thought, They've done this before.

The stiff fabric of Sister Rosa's dress pressed for a second against the Oberführer's back. She felt the hot flush spreading up her neck and mottling her cheeks. She knew her nipples were hardening as she drew his tunic off. She moved in front of him and unbuttoned the shirt cuffs as he extended each hand to her. She unbuttoned the shirt-front with delicate movements.

Sister Rosa yearned to lay her hands on his white, white chest and stroke the silky hair that flowed in a line down to his navel and disappeared under his pants. She wanted to touch each of his dark nipples, press them flat and feel them harden under her fingers, but she resisted as she always resisted. He never allowed her to touch him. Never.

Nelka watched. How terrible can it be, she thought. I have made love with two men, my husband and Telek. This is only a man. I can go to Magda's and make a bath and scrub when he's done. Magda will make sure that I don't have a child from this, and besides, it's hard to get pregnant when you're nursing a baby.

Sister Rosa was panting slightly. She didn't know if the excitement was caused by the body of the Oberführer, muscled like a statue, or if she panted at the thought of what was to come. It was exciting that the man could do anything he wanted.

"Take your clothes off, Nelka." The Oberführer kept his pants and boots on.

"I am nursing the baby," she began. She wondered if the Brown Sister was going to stay.

"Obey." Sister Rosa moved toward her. She hated to move her eyes from the man. He was pale and beautiful, and Sister Rosa trembled. She would have taken the place of the Polish woman if he asked, but he never asked.

Nelka unbuttoned her coat and laid it on one of the chairs.

"Quickly now." Sister Rosa was checking something medical looking. Tubes. A needle.

Nelka took off her dress, and the two shifts, and the pads of cloth wrapped over her breasts, and the long pants and boots, and the socks and rags wrapping her feet. She stood in the warm room, and one of her breasts leaked a drop of milk. It fell and made a spot on the floor.

Sister Rosa moved to her and squeezed Nelka's breast. The milk shot out in a stream into the air. The SS Sister saw the man watching closely, smiling, and she squeezed again to please him. She held Nelka's breast and offered it to him like a fruit.

"She's thin, but with that much milk she's healthy." Sister Rosa took a stethoscope from her bag and listened to Nelka's chest, front and back. "No tuberculosis." The woman pulled Nelka's eyelids down. "Open your mouth."

Nelka obeyed. The Oberführer stood and watched.

"Her mouth is pink and fresh. No jaundice in the whites of her eyes. She's clean."

"She has a certain look, don't you think? I noticed it when we were first in this village."

"What do you want?" Nelka knew she shouldn't have asked. It didn't matter if she knew. They would do what they did.

"I will lie on the mattress," he said. "Set the chair over my body so she sits on the seat."

"Help me," said the Brown Sister. Her face was bright red. Nelka helped pull the mattress off the frame. It fell onto the floor.

"This will help get rid of the tiredness I've felt for the last few weeks." He lay down on the mattress on his back.

"Are you a nurse?" asked Nelka.

"I am a Brown Sister. Our duties are to assist the creation of the new world that is coming."

She talks like one of their posters, Nelka thought.

Sister Rosa picked up the chair and carefully placed it over the knees of the Oberführer.

"Sit on the chair."

Nelka sat carefully, one leg on either side of the man's body.

"Move forward on the chair, Nelka. I want to see you."

She obeyed him and slid her buttocks forward.

"Almost come off the chair. Spread your legs wide." He stared at

Nelka, her breasts full and leaking milk, her body tilted back. Her sex, surrounded by dark blond hair, was violet pink.

A strange rose, he thought.

There was fear in her eyes now, not much, but he saw it. He sighed.

"It would be better if she had no fear at all," he said, but he was lying when he said it.

There had been a woman once who had no fear. A Dutch woman. When he had taken all of her blood that he wanted, and the needle had been taken from his vein, he ordered that the needle stay in the woman's arm. The rest of the woman's blood ran out of the tube and made a puddle under the chair where she sat. Even when the puddle wet her feet, and she was dying, the fear never entered her eyes. Only a final glazing over before she fell off the chair. He'd shot her then.

Nelka looked in the man's eyes. They were going to kill her. And who would feed the baby? She watched the Oberführer's handsome face. More handsome than Telek. Almost as handsome as her husband had been.

He watched Nelka and wondered why it was that the fear made a difference. A fearless woman was no use to him. The blood of the Dutch woman hadn't given him any energy at all.

Sister Rosa put the rubber strap around Nelka's arm. She rubbed the crook in the girl's arm where the skin was soft. When the vein popped up she inserted the needle smoothly, and the blood began to rise. Quickly, Sister Rosa attached a tube to the needle.

Bending to the Oberführer, the woman did the same to his arm. Gently, with deft fingers, she attached the blood-filled tube from Nelka to the needle in the man's arm. The blood now dripped freely down the tube from Nelka to the Oberführer.

"You are really quite beautiful. I like it that you are a mother." He moved slightly to make his arm more comfortable. Sister Rosa sat quietly on the other chair and watched.

That was it, he decided. It was beauty. A woman with fear in her face achieved a desirableness, a radiance. Courage in a woman's eyes made her face hard, arrogant. Even a rather ordinary woman achieved a delicate beauty when she was afraid.

"Why do you want my blood?"

"Do not speak unless—" the Brown Sister began.

"I don't mind. The idea came to me from my days as an athlete. Sometimes transfusions were given to increase energy during the last Olympic games. Your blood will refresh me and serve a higher purpose. Go, Sister Rosa, and do what I ordered."

Sister Rosa, the graying spinster selected for service by the SS, nodded, put on her long cape and left the room. She was trembling a little, and she wanted to stay. She wanted to tell him that it would be her joy to stay. She wanted to say that she could watch his pleasure with the Polish woman, and his pleasure would give her the greatest happiness any woman had ever had. She wanted to tell him all this, but she didn't. She simply obeyed because he wanted it.

Leaving the other woman with him, naked and golden, connected by a cord of blood, Sister Rosa felt the pain of being sent away, and even that gave her such pleasure that she nearly cried out as she left the house and moved down the street, her cloak a dark shadow around her.

"You will help me stay strong, Nelka," the Oberführer was saying to the young woman.

Nelka was beginning to get dizzy. The shiny red line of blood swayed as she tried to move a little and get better balance.

"I won't take too much. Just enough for a beginning. You can do this again in two weeks. You are giving service to the Reich. The highest thing a Polish woman can aspire to is giving service to the German people. You are a chosen one."

Nelka said nothing, and they sat for what seemed a long time. Then he began to talk again.

"You are a chosen one, Nelka, and I am chosen also. But there is a difference. You are the giver. Your duty is to be drained of all you have to serve your masters."

He smiled, and Nelka couldn't look into his eyes. He is insane, she thought, but not like the insane people I've seen before. His penis had begun to swell and pushed against his pants.

"I am also chosen, but differently. I was selected by God to be the receiver. I am the Chalice." He liked the sound of the words and repeated them again. "I am the Chalice."

The forest, Nelka thought. I can go into the forest with the baby and Telek.

They sat, joined by a tube of blood, for twenty minutes. Then the door opened and Sister Rosa came in.

"It's locked in my room with a guard."

The Oberführer smiled. "Just a minute or two more, Nelka."

The woods, she thought. The woods. The forest that had never been burned, never been logged, the primal forest that man had never dared to harvest and prune and use. The wet moss. Snow that hid your tracks.

"Sister Rosa will take perfect care of your baby. It will be in Sister Rosa's room. You can go and sit with it. You will nurse it. It will sleep with Sister Rosa for the moment. Is he sick, Sister Rosa?"

"He seems healthy. Quite good-looking. Blond and with no marks."

"My baby?" Nelka tried to stand, and Sister Rosa slapped her gently to make her sit. "Where's my baby?"'

"Safe in my room. You can see him anytime you need to nurse."

"You have him?" Nelka stared at the woman. She was light-headed. "Why?"

"So you won't be tempted to run away from me, my darling." The Oberführer felt the power in his body. He was hot all over, and his arm stung from the needle. The girl's blood was good. "You're a lucky girl, Nelka. I could become quite fond of you."

Sister Rosa saw the girl sway. Stepping forward she grabbed Nelka roughly by the shoulder. It was terrible that he had called Nelka *darling*.

"Take the needles out."

Nelka dressed with the help of Sister Rosa.

"You may go to the baby. The soldier has orders to let you in. Sit with the baby as long as you like. You'll both be quite safe." The Oberführer lay on the mattress. Nelka saw that he still had an erection under his pants, but he didn't touch himself or seem to notice. Only Sister Rosa stared at the man's swollen penis pushing against the cloth.

"And, Nelka?" he said to her.

"Yes," she whispered.

"You must not tell anyone about this. If I hear that anyone knows, I will have to deal harshly with them. And with you. And with anything that is yours. Do you understand?"

"Yes." Nelka moved to the door. She had to see the baby.

"Here." Sister Rosa pressed something into Nelka's hand. It was a chocolate bar.

"Eat it. It will get rid of the light-headedness. Take this also. You need more food."

Sister Rosa handed over a sack. Nelka knew from the weight and the lumpiness that it held potatoes, perhaps a twist of salt.

She walked out onto the street with the food in her hands. The snow was falling again.

Nelka moved toward Sister Rosa's house. She had to see if her baby was safe. She walked slowly, each step an effort, but didn't stop to rest. His sweet little body. He might be wrapped too loosely. He might be hungry.

Nelka moved down the street looking for her baby. She had to see if it was true that he had been taken from her.

Wiktor stood in the dark and watched Nelka leave the house and walk unsteadily down the street. He twisted his hands together, and his forehead was crumpled into lines as he thought.

Being the clerk gave him a certain freedom and certain responsibility. He could come and go after dark simply by right of being the Major's clerk. He got more potatoes and bread and a glass of decent vodka when the Major was drunk enough not to care who drank with him.

He was responsible for all the paperwork. The Major had trouble caring much about the paper that flowed into the village and must flow back out or cause trouble with headquarters in Bialystok. Wiktor did the paperwork, but the responsibility that interested him the most was staying alive. No one in the village would help him with that. He was a dog to them. He was the Nazi Major's clerk, brought from a jail in Warsaw, but he was still a Pole.

"I'm as Polish as they are," he said, almost too loudly.

And that thought decided him. He moved toward the Major's house. The man would be awake and drinking as always. The Major would want to know all about what Wiktor had seen, standing in the dark. The Major wanted to know everything that happened in the village, and Wiktor told him what he chose to tell. He didn't tell it all, but some of it.

And this information was so amazing, so strange. Lying there under the naked woman and taking her blood. It was something peculiar. Even for the SS, it was peculiar. Wiktor was unsure of the exact laws governing the fraternization of Poles and German officers, but he knew that taking blood from a Pole would be a closeness that might interest the Major.

Wiktor grinned then for the first time. He liked keeping the Germans as uneasy as he could. It was a small thing, but he liked it when they had to think about things and worry. He walked up the steps to tell the Major, but he carefully rearranged his face into a look of docile stupidity before he knocked. He wouldn't smile even once when talking to the Major about this.

———

"He did what?" Telek stood over Nelka, who slumped in the chair.

"I feel drunk."

"What did he do to you? Where's the baby?" It will only take me a moment to go to the forest and get my gun, Telek thought. Just a quick run, and then I could come back and—

"He said he'd kill me if I told. He'll kill the baby."

"Tell me."

Nelka shut her eyes. She couldn't live alone with it.

"The baby is with Sister Rosa. I saw him. He's warm, and I fed him a little. I have to feed him there now."

"Why does he want the baby?" Telek thought of the boy's perfect blondness, and he shivered.

"So I won't run away. Then he can do it again."

Telek's throat constricted, but he forced the words out. "Do what?"

"He took blood. The woman connected me to him with needles

and a tube. He was transfused from me." She could barely say the word and slurred it slightly. "Transfused," she said, trying again.

"If he isn't wounded, why does he need blood?" Telek knew his voice sounded angry.

"He just did it. He said it gives him energy. She wanted to watch, but he made her go, and that's when she took my baby."

"Watch you giving him blood?"

Nelka nodded. She couldn't think very well, but she knew that she wouldn't tell Telek about having to take her clothes off. About how the Oberführer stared at her on the chair. About the man's erection under his pants.

"He bled you?" Telek didn't want to ask, but he had to. "He didn't make you— rape you?" he finished bluntly, and his voice was loud in the room which seemed so silent without the cry of the baby. Telek hadn't realized before how one tiny baby filled a room.

"He didn't touch me. Just the woman. Just the needles. But they have my baby. They're keeping him in her room."

"I'll take him. Tonight. We'll go in the forest."

Nelka shook her head. It was so heavy or her neck was so weak, she didn't know which. She laid her head down on the table and shut her eyes. "They have a guard. You'd get shot."

I'll kill him, Telek thought, and she read his thoughts without looking up from the table.

"If you kill him, they'll chase us. And they'll kill the village for reparation."

"Blood." Telek thought about it, and he was puzzled. He didn't like being puzzled by the Nazis. It wasn't safe when you didn't know what the Germans were going to do.

"He said he'd do it again when I recover. Maybe every few weeks." Nelka felt the tears, hot under her eyelids.

"I've heard about using women for blood. It was information passed on months ago, but they were using the blood for the wounded."

Nelka said nothing. She knew that the Oberführer was not really a logical man. There was not a reasonable explanation. It had to do with her nakedness and his excitement, but she wouldn't tell Telek that.

She wondered if the Oberführer would be more excited as he took more and more blood. She wondered if she'd have to die so he could come to orgasm.

Telek sat and put his hand on her head. He stroked the heavy knot of hair that caught the light from the window.

"He said he'd only do it sometimes, Telek. He doesn't touch me."

"I can kill him," Telek whispered to her.

"Only if you kill all the Germans. Every one. Or they'll kill the whole village."

"If he touches you, I'll kill him," Telek said.

"He can't have sex with me. I'm Polish." Nelka raised her head and smiled at Telek. "It's against their law for him to have sex with me. They'll be gone soon."

Telek sat and didn't move to kiss her. Nelka sighed. She was so tired. She wanted to be petted and rocked like a child but Telek was rigid with shame and anger. His woman was being used by another man, and Telek could do nothing. He couldn't even look her in the eyes.

Nelka wanted to lie down wrapped in blankets and slip under the darkness of sleep like slipping under dark water in summer, when they swam in the river after working all day in the fields. But Telek sat beside her, his face white with the pain of his helplessness.

"Come to bed, darling," she whispered, standing with effort and taking his hand. "Come to bed and let me love you."

Telek rose, still not looking in her eyes, and she moved against him and kissed his mouth until some of the rigidity of his jaw softened.

I can do it, she thought. I can make love to him, and I can give blood to the German, and I can wait and steal the baby away when the Russians come. I can do all of it. She was still thinking this as she led Telek to the bed.

Christmas Eve, 1943

"If the beaters can't find another one, I'll shoot them," the SS man said.

The Oberführer carried the beautiful gun on his shoulder, and the Major winced when he saw that it was not broken. Unbroken guns were how hunting accidents happened. Even the Major knew that, and he had never owned such a glorious, expensive gun in all his life.

"The gun is worth ten of the man," the Major whispered to Unterfeldwebel Rahn, the sergeant who followed at his elbow.

"How long will he keep us out here?"

The Major shrugged. Half the boys of the village were strung out in the woods. The man who should have been there, the one most likely to find a boar, Telek, was mysteriously absent.

"Probably trapping rabbits," Wiktor had offered, but the Major didn't believe it, and the boys of the village had flushed only one small sow who had squealed her way through the beaters.

"It's here someplace." The Oberführer stopped walking. "I can feel that he's near. This is a smart, old boar." Hunting in Poland was as bad as he had feared it would be. His father would have laughed at him, trying to kill a boar with a handful of children and the deformed Major.

"It's getting dark." The Major didn't want to meet a boar under these giant trees at night.

And then they heard it. A rumbling grunt, loud and unafraid. The hair rose on the back of the Sergeant's neck. It didn't sound like a pig.

It didn't sound like anything he'd ever heard, and the man crossed himself surreptitiously.

The Oberführer was smiling. "He'll rush us soon. Neither of you fire. It's my shot."

The Major drew his pistol. He'd disdained to carry a rifle, and now he was sorry. It was a bad thing, this hunting in the Bialowieza Forest. Göring had said it was to be the private preserve of the Nazi high command. They could be court-martialed for poaching.

"Shot because of a pig," he muttered.

"Silence." The SS man stood and waited, and the glossy stock of the gun wavered.

"You have to stand like a rock to hit a boar when it comes at you," the Sergeant whispered.

The silence lay all around them, broken only by the noise of the boys coming closer through the forest. Their calls had a minor key, like a lament, as the sound came to the three men.

Hansel, serving as a beater, was crying with exhaustion and frustration. The pig had slipped past him. It was going to be killed. He had tried to drive it back toward the creek, but the stupid beast kept moving toward the guns.

"I smell him." The Oberführer was smiling.

They stood in the snow and waited, and the boar was silent.

"There," the Sergeant shouted, and he forgot the orders of the Oberführer and fired his pistol toward the darkness under the trees to their left.

"He's mine," screamed the SS man, but he didn't fire. The darkness was too solid where the bushes grew densely under a lime tree. "He's mine."

The shadow moved and then shaped itself and came straight at the men. It was a boar, huge, and looked as large as a bull to the Major. The animal ran with his head up, the glitter of eye fastened on the men, watching them as he charged.

Suddenly a child ran at the boar screaming. A curly-haired boy waving his arms.

"Get out of the way," the Major shouted, but the boy ran at the boar and the animal hesitated.

The Oberführer fired, with the Major screaming at him to stop. The boar's tusks flashed yellow-white in the dusk, and he slashed at the Sergeant who leaped backward.

"He's mine! He's mine!" The Oberführer was swinging the gun wildly.

"Then shoot!" the Major screamed, but the boar was already past them and galloping off into deeper forest, away from the beaters and the guns.

The Oberführer fired again. "I've wounded him!"

The boy lay in the mud sobbing. It was obvious to the Major that the boy had tried to save the boar from the guns.

The Oberführer pointed his gun at the boy. "I would have killed the beast except for him."

"He's just a clumsy little bastard of a Pole. Your quarry is getting away, Oberführer."

The Major held his pistol and stared at the SS man. To kill the boy was indecent, but typical of a man who hadn't fought in a single battle. The Major wanted to taunt the SS who stood pointing the gun at the child's head, but he knew that would probably ensure the boy's death, and the whole village might riot if they brought back the body of a child.

Seeing the Major's face and his hand holding the pistol, the Oberführer raised the gun and fired through the trees in frustration. "I'm sure it's wounded. We can get torches and track him."

Hansel began to crawl slowly into the shadows. Seeing him move, the Oberführer turned and fired near the boy's head. Hansel crawled like a roach and his chest heaved.

"Look at what years of breeding mud children gets you." The Oberführer spit angrily.

The Major grinned at the Sergeant and knew they had the same thought. That was one mud child who had probably saved a boar's life.

The Major shook his head. "I'm not going in the forest at twilight after a wounded boar."

"You'll go if I order you." The Oberführer was shaking, and the boy had disappeared into the forest, running back toward the village.

"Blood," the Major said.

"What?" The Oberführer turned his pale face toward the other man. The Major stared back. "If it was wounded, there'll be blood."

"I told you both not to fire."

Sergeant Rahn shook his head. The beast had nearly torn their bellies open, and this man was worried that someone else would take credit for a kill. It was a terrible end to a long day. All he'd wanted when he accepted the Major's invitation was dinner and some brandy. A quiet evening to celebrate Christmas Eve so far from home.

"We look for blood." The Oberführer moved forward.

———

"I see it!" Gretel pointed toward the east. "Hello, first star."

"Now Christmas begins." Nelka led them toward the hut.

Inside, they had to stand near the wall because the table was in the middle of the room. Magda held the oplatek, the baked wafer, that tangible symbol of love. It was only made of the same rough flour with sawdust that everything was baked of, but Nelka had made a cross of dough surrounded by a circular indentation in the bread to decorate the top.

"We should wait for the boy," Magda muttered.

"He'll be back. We'll save his share." Nelka kissed Magda firmly. "He'll be all right."

Magda broke a piece off the flat wafer and put it in her mouth. Then she broke off more pieces and gave one to Telek, one to Nelka, and one to Gretel. One piece she put aside for Hansel. They chewed the hard bread solemnly, ceremoniously.

"Now the candle. Help me, Gretel."

Nelka set a candle on a rude shelf under the window. Telek took a twig and lit it from the stove. He gave it to Gretel, and the girl, with a waving pass of her hand, lit the candle.

"A sign of welcome for those lost in the woods, those crippled by war, all the prodigal children." Nelka held her hand to the candle and felt its warmth.

Magda took Nelka in her arms and kissed her on both cheeks. Nelka kissed Telek, and then everyone began to kiss everyone.

"I love you, Magda. Good health in the coming year!"

"I love you too, Nelka. Good health!"

"I love you."

"Good health."

"I love you, my sweetheart."

"I'm hungry," Gretel said.

The table was covered with an old piece of cloth and on it was the usual bowl of soup, another bowl of potatoes and turnips, wooden cups for herb tea, and a flask of vodka that was Telek's contribution.

Gretel lifted up the corner of the cloth and began to pull out the pieces of hay which made the cloth lie unevenly. "There's hay under the cloth, Nelka," Gretel whispered.

"There is hay because the Christ child lay on hay in his manger."

"Who's this for?" Gretel pointed at the bowl next to her, set carefully for a sixth person.

"What if a poor traveler knocks at the door?" Nelka smiled. "What if he was in rags, all cold and dirty and sad? And what if he cast off his rags and was Christ the babe in shining splendor? Or an angel wandering on the earth, with strong white wings stippled with gold?"

Gretel's eyes were wide. "Do angels eat, Nelka?"

"They do in my house." Magda took a large bite of potato. "Eat now."

"I saw an angel once," Gretel said, and she smiled at the gathered family.

No one spoke for a moment, and then Nelka asked, "Is Father Piotr coming, Magda?"

"No. He refused."

"Next Christmas, children, we will have—" Nelka rolled her eyes and thought. "Herring in sour cream, dark bread and vodka, smoked salmon, red-beet soup with mushrooms, dumplings with mushrooms, trout in brown gravy, parsley potatoes, three kinds of pierogi: one with dried mushrooms, one with cheese, and one full of sauerkraut."

"I want chicken," Gretel said.

"No meat. Christmas Eve is a fast day, you know that, darling." Magda had taught the children. They had to remember if the Germans asked them.

"Then we will have fruits and dumplings full of walnuts and triangle-shaped cookies and ginger cookies and Magda will make kutia with bulgur and honey and nuts and poppy seeds, the most perfect kutia in the world."

"Then we will all have krupnik," Magda said.

"What's that?" Hansel slammed the door behind him.

"Oh God, he's hurt!" Magda swept the child up and wiped his face.

"It was the pig. It bled but it got away. I saved it, Magda. It ran at me but I helped it so it won't die and the SS shot at me too."

"Dear God!" Magda sat the boy down at the table and gave him potatoes and bread. "He's right. He isn't hurt. Sweet Virgin! He shot at you?"

"He missed. He isn't a good shot." Hansel filled his mouth. "What's krupnik?"

"A liqueur made of sweet honey and heated until it lies on your tongue like a kiss." Telek spoke before he thought, and then he blushed.

Magda saw the blush and looked at Nelka. Magda had seen it coming, and it was good. Some would say that the girl's husband might come back from Siberia, or that he had been gone and possibly dead for too short a time, but a day during a war was like a month of real time. A month of war was a year, and Nelka needed someone to help her.

Magda stared into the red light from the oven's fuel box and shivered. She had gotten up from the table. Tradition said this would bring bad luck to the family.

"Magda?" Nelka watched her and touched the old woman's hand. "Are you tired?"

"I want music. What is Christmas Eve without music?"

"No Midnight Mass this year." Telek looked at Magda.

"You'd think we could just ring the church bell." Nelka bit her lip and they all sat silently.

"I always liked it when the music started." Magda thought of the sound as the church would fill with light and the tiny organ burst forth. "The Russians burned the organ."

"Enough of this." Nelka went to the stove where her surprise was keeping warm.

"We all can have a piece. It isn't like yours, Magda, but it has honey and nuts and pieces of dried fruit. And you can thank Telek, who got the ingredients for me, God knows where."

She carried the plate to the table and drew back the cloth. The smell of honey and spice filled Hansel's nose and he sneezed.

Nelka cut the flat pastry and climbed up onto the sleeping platform.

"Now listen to me, children, while your mouths are full of sweetness. Listen.

"Mary and Joseph were given the gift of a child. They were so poor that the babe was laid in a manger, and angels and shepherds and wise men came to see the beauty of the baby. An evil king wanted to kill the child, but angels warned Joseph in a dream, and he put Mary and the baby on a donkey and fled into Egypt so the evil king couldn't kill his son."

"Like the motorcycle," Hansel whispered.

"The baby was saved and lived to grow up. And he teaches us to be brave always and never lose hope. Never. Even when all the world wants to kill your innocent babe."

There was silence when her voice stopped, and Nelka sat thinking of her baby alone in the village, his father dead or in slave labor in Russia. She knew she would cry if she thought of him, so she shook her head hard and spoke more loudly than she intended.

"In the darkness of deep winter, when everything is cold and dead, the babe is born and God begins to walk in the world. He walks for the next four months among us, and then he will be killed, and rise from the dead because there is no death. Death will die in four months."

Nelka paused and looked at the little family at the table, oddly assorted and brought together by history. "God cannot see the darkness that man has created and not throw out light to combat it. He is walking in the world."

"Are you sure, Nelka?"

"Yes, Hansel."

Hansel looked at Nelka and he began to feel warm from the hot soup. Nelka said it would be so. He knew that she would never lie to him.

"Nelka, I have something for you for Christmas." Gretel rose from the table and went to Nelka. The child frowned and then wrung her hands, a gesture so adult that it upset Magda, and she wrung her own hands.

"I don't know where it is," Gretel said. "I had something, and now it's gone, Nelka." Gretel made the motions of peeling an orange. Her hands trembled in anxiety of remembering.

"Come sit by me, little girl," Nelka held out her hand toward the child, and Gretel climbed onto the platform and lay with her head in Nelka's lap.

"I will sing," she said, stroking Gretel's hair. And she sung all the beautiful old carols. One after another the songs came from the young woman who sat stroking the mad child.

"I think the angel has come," Magda muttered.

Nelka sang. Telek watched her and grieved that he couldn't kill all the Germans. Hansel imagined that he had her baby in his arms, and was handing it to Nelka, and she was kissing him, and saying that he was wonderful. Gretel lay and tried to remember another holiday when she had gotten presents, when the room had been bigger and the people had been other people.

Magda watched them all and made herself concentrate on the music of the carols filling the hut. She forced the darkness of the future time, which she saw coming, out of her mind, and for the rest of this one night, the witch allowed only the sweetness of love to fill her heart.

Hidden by the night, the boar dug into a pile of leaves and pine needles under a log which had fallen twenty years before and still lay slightly off the forest floor, supported by its roots. The spongy peat under the leaves gave off a dense odor that mixed with the musky smell of the animal. It lay silent, its dark eyes open and watchful. Across its back was a single line of red where the Sergeant's bullet had taken off a layer of skin and bristle. It was a slight wound and only oozed a little blood.

The animal grunted once and rolled to dig itself more deeply into the floor of the forest that stood all around. It lay on the matted, decaying matter, warm and alive, only the glitter of eye betraying its presence and watched the dark forest until the light began to change toward the waiting dawn of Christmas day. As the stars faded and dimmed, the boar finally lay its head down and slept, hidden by the darkness of shadow as the morning brightened.

Father Piotr

January began with more snow and storms so fierce that everyone stayed inside as much as they could. "Winter is howling because his back is broken," Magda muttered.

"I'm bored." Hansel frowned.

"Be patient, boy. Life is sometimes a great waiting."

The knock on the door made her jump. The door opened and Father Piotr came in.

"I hear you've become a drunk," she said.

He took off his coat and it dropped to the floor.

"My God, sit down." Magda took the kettle from the stove and poured the water over herbs. "It's the last of the peppermint. We might as well drink it."

Magda made a cup for Gretel and a cup for Hansel. The children took their tea and climbed onto the sleeping platform. They watched the priest slantwise, never letting him see them staring.

Father Piotr sat in a chair and did not touch the cup that Magda put on the table in front of him. He rubbed his hand repeatedly over his face.

"What's wrong with you? Getting drunk every Sunday just when the Germans give permission for Masses?"

"I am an evil man, Magda."

"You've always been cursed with ordinariness. You're just a human for all of it."

"I had women and they threw me out of Rome. Then the birth

of the girl in this village. I never had a church better than a peasant's hut."

"Still grieving over lost glory?"

"I don't care anymore. But now I'm ending this way."

"Brother, your weakness was never drink, but now you are drunk at every Mass." Magda suddenly understood. "They've ordered you to get drunk every Sunday. It makes you a buffoon and a weakling. The people will hate you. It could break their belief, but if you tell the people that the Nazis ordered it, the Nazis will kill you."

Pushing the cup aside, he put his head on the table and sighed deeply. "It is the idea of the new one, the SS, and yesterday was the worst of all. I can't stand it anymore."

"What happened?"

"They came to our houses before light with a truck. Feliks and Patryk and I. We had to dig the truck out of the snow when the road was too deep. I was nearly dead with it."

"We're too old for that sort of work, brother. And then?"

"We went to the rail line. There was a boxcar they wanted to use for wounded Germans. The Germans were laid around fires to keep them warm, waiting for the train, but first we had to free the boxcar."

"From ice?"

"No. From people."

Magda frowned and rocked slowly. Hansel heard the words as if he were dreaming them, and Gretel was nearly asleep.

"Magda?" Gretel spoke suddenly, and the priest jumped at her voice.

"Yes, child?"

"Will I dream my name?"

"What do you mean, Gretel?"

"I can't remember it, Magda. But when I dream, I'm that girl again. The one before the fat little girl in the picture."

"What does she mean?" Father Piotr whispered.

"You will remember your name when God wills, Gretel."

"But I want him to will it now." Gretel fell asleep and didn't hear Magda's answer.

"He is keeping you safe, child. Go to sleep."

They sat in silence for a time, and then Magda's brother began again.

"We were given axes and crowbars to force the doors open because of the ice. Inside there were people. Standing. Lying. Stepped on. Crushed against the walls. We had to use the axes to chop them out of the boxcar. They were frozen solid. Stuck together."

"Who were they?"

The priest nodded his head toward the children. Magda silently mouthed the word, *Jews*, and he nodded again and went on with the telling.

"Finally, there were only two left stuck to the walls. Two little ones. They made me chop them out. The ground was too frozen to bury them. And we couldn't have found enough dry wood to burn them. We threw them in a ditch and covered them with snow and rocks. Then we cleaned the boxcar as best we could and loaded the wounded soldiers. We heard the train coming as we got back on the truck."

Magda sat in silence and rocked gently. Her brother put his head down on the table again and for a while they sat. Then he spoke again, and he didn't lift his head so she couldn't see his face.

"There's more. I've hurt the girl."

"What girl?"

"Nelka. I couldn't stay away from her grandmother. She became pregnant, and I hoped people would think she'd gone to the city and gotten pregnant there."

"Villages are like families, brother. You can't fool them for long."

"I pretended it was nothing to do with me. She never married, and then she died. And my daughter died too. After her death, Nelka came to me. She told me that she knew everything. Her mother was barely in the ground. She just wanted to love me—to know me—to have me as family. I drove her off with platitudes. I lied and said that we weren't related. I'll never be able to speak of it to her. She thinks I have no feeling for her."

Magda stood and went behind him. She put her arms around his shoulders and pressed close to him. The magnificent golden head, now white-haired and aged, pressed back against her.

"Come and sit with me sometimes, brother. Our differences are not so large anymore. I don't curse your church much now, and you don't tell me how wicked I am."

He sat and sipped the tea, and Hansel thought of what the priest had said. He could picture the bodies frozen together. It was like in the ghetto, when the bodies piled up in the street froze and had to be torn apart to be carried away. Some of the tougher boys who lived alone on the streets had made walls of the bodies and thrown snowballs at each other from behind them.

"Come and sit with me, Piotr. The winter is waning. Then springtime."

He nodded, and Magda stood behind him for a long time, holding him and sighing deeply. Winter was going, but the sun was still covered by dense clouds and the hut was dim. She began to croon and hum, and the fire fell to coals in the stove.

"Come now, my little boy," Magda said to Hansel early one morning. She took his hand and led him through the giant trees. They walked for a long while beside the creek until it broadened and became a river, and still Magda walked, stopping only to pant for breath occasionally.

"Gretel will miss us, Magda. She won't know where we are."

"Gretel mustn't know about this. Telek and Nelka know, but no one else can know."

He nodded and took her hand. They walked on, both of them beginning to feel the cold all the way to their bones. They walked until Magda stopped and turned him to face her.

"Listen to me, Hansel. We followed the creek to the river. You know how to do that?"

"I can get to the river."

"Good. Then we turned directly into the sun and walked until we came to this rock. Now we turn south and walk until we come to what you must never tell anyone about." Magda stared into the boy's face. He must understand how serious it was, and he was so young. If only the girl hadn't lost her mind.

"You will never speak of this? Not to anyone for any reason. Not to Gretel."

"I won't tell, Magda. Not anybody."

"Good boy." She turned and moved south for about a hundred feet. Then she stopped and pointed. There was a small grove of saplings in front of them.

"I made this years and years ago, boy. When the villagers were angry with me and threatened to get me and kill me. When they were sure that I was a witch."

Hansel nodded. There were many reasons to kill people.

"So I made this." She knelt in the snow and began to brush it away.

"Magda! It's boards. What is it?"

"I never used it. The pigs stayed here when the Russians stole our food. Go down."

He dropped into the pit. It was just big enough for five or six people, and in the corner were rocks with sacks on them. He opened a sack and saw frozen potatoes and turnips. The sack next to it had bread, flat and hard. Two buckets sat on the dirt floor.

"One bucket to piss and shit in, one bucket to hold snow and let it melt so you have water to drink if you have to stay in the pit for very long. You can't eat snow. You have to melt it."

Hansel looked quickly at her face above him and then lowered his eyes. He shivered.

"Hansel, can you bring Gretel here and stay inside and be very quiet if you have to?"

"I can find it, Magda."

"And can you stay in this hole to be safe? Maybe for weeks?"

"You'd be here. Not just me and Gretel."

"But if you didn't have me. Can you do it?"

Hansel wanted to cry, but his chest was too tight for it to heave. "I can do it," he whispered.

Magda stared down at the boy. "All right. Now come out."

He climbed out and the two of them pulled the boards back into place.

"Look," she said.

Hidden between the thin trunks of three saplings that grew close was a small piece of pipe. It rose barely three inches above the snow.

"For air. It's dark inside, and it won't smell good when it thaws, but there is food and it's as safe as anything in Poland now."

Hansel nodded. He helped push snow over the boards. His face was very white and his eyes almost as dark as Magda's. It was smaller than the grease pit outside the ghetto walls.

"When, Magda?"

"Soon, I think." Magda looked in his eyes. She knew if she shut her eyelids she would feel the darkness coming down on her.

"I know things. I don't know why. Don't forget the way." She shivered and took his hand.

They walked back to the river and began to struggle through the snow which was now soaking their legs almost to Magda's hips.

Father Piotr arrived at the hut before noon, and only the girl sat on the platform, singing.

"Hello, Father Piotr."

"Hello, child." He stood and looked at her. She smiled at him the way children used to smile, her mind blocking out the war and all the dark days they were caught in.

He looked at the girl and began to cry. He coughed and blew his nose.

"What's wrong?" she asked, frowning.

"I am sad, child. I've become a slave, and God is gone. The winter is dark, and I'm tired of being cold." You fool, he thought. You childish old man.

Gretel's face brightened. She jumped off the platform and went to the floor where Magda kept her baskets. Kneeling, she lifted the boards and groped in a basket. Carefully she took out something and put it in a sack. She put the boards back and went to the stove. She lifted the iron top and took out a few red coals with the tongs, placing them in a small bucket. Then she pulled on her coat and opened the door.

"It's cold outside."

"Come on." She pulled him by the hand and he followed her.

They walked between the trees, and the child paused occasionally, looking around. She would shake her head and walk deeper into the woods. "Here," she said finally.

They were in a circle of tall trees. The snow was unmarked, and the only sound was the water of the creek smothered by ice. Gretel brushed a circle large enough for them to sit. She rounded the edges of the circle and then turned to him. "Sit down. It's nice now."

He felt such pity that he sat on the snow and watched the child. She was playing some game. He would sit awhile. It might quiet her. Then he could take her back to the hut.

Opening the sack, Gretel took out eight pieces of candle. All different sizes, most of them only stubs, and began to arrange them. "All in a straight row. None higher than the others. Not in a circle. Far enough apart so the flames don't touch," she chanted.

The child worked hard. It wasn't easy getting the odd-sized candles level, but she packed snow to hold them until they stood in a ragged line between her and the priest. "Now the shamash." She drew the last candle from the bag.

The priest winced at the foreign word. It was a dangerous word from her past, he knew.

Taking a twig, she lit it on the coals in the bucket and then lit the ninth candle. She used it to light the other eight. "Candles right to left, light them left to right," she chanted.

All the candles were lit, and she set the ninth candle beside the others in the snow.

"And what is this, girl?" He knew what it must be, but he wondered if she remembered.

"It makes the stars come out at night," she said, and then she shook her head. "The first star—" she whispered and shook her head again.

They sat in silence and watched the flames so golden against the whiteness around them.

"I know," Gretel said. "It means that God is here. God loves us. And all of it"—she made a sweeping gesture with her arm—"is a miracle."

The priest began to cry. His body was chilling, but the tears were warm on his skin.

"Don't cry. I made God be here for you, and now we're free."

"I'm not free, child. I'm a sinner. I need to confess, but it would take until summer." He began anyway. "I never took care of my daughter. I took no responsibility for her—for her mother. I haven't helped Nelka, and now she has a baby." He groaned and rocked back and forth in the snow. "I've never helped any of them. Oh God, help me. Let me not die so sinful."

Gretel remembered now. When the candles were lit it meant that they would live. It was lovely, and she began to sing one of the Christmas carols that Nelka had taught her.

The voice of the child reached to the tops of the trees and drowned out the mutter of the creek. The priest sat crying before the menorah, listening to a Christmas carol sung by a Jewish child driven into madness.

It was cold and he ached but suddenly he felt happy. The trees were solid and lifted to the sky where the sun tried to break through the clouds which moved quickly above them.

"I am happy," he said to the cold air. And he wished he could do something, some act that would prove his joy, allow it to shine forth to the world and make up for the past.

Magda and Hansel found them sitting beside the candles guttering in the snow, the old man and the girl, smiling into the bright air of high noon.

"You wife's gone a long time," Lydka said to him.

The Mechanik nodded absentmindedly. It had been a crazy idea. She suddenly wanted to go to the burnt-out farm and see if any of the horses or cattle had wandered back after the fire.

"We can't feed a horse," he'd told her.

"But the cows. They ran during the fire, but cows always come back. If one came back, I could drive it here. It'd be a feast."

It hadn't been like her to think about food so much. She always said that thinking about food was weakness. The next morning she was gone.

"Can't keep your woman under control?" the Russian joked. "Get a stick, Mechanik. A good beating is what she needs. I bet she finds a cow. I bet she finds three cows."

After two days, the Mechanik set out toward the farm. He was stronger now, but he only found the farm because of the standing walls of the stone barn and the chimney of the house. He sat in the woods and watched for an hour. She wasn't there. He waited until he was sure that no one guarded the place, and then went to the ruins and walked around them. There were no other footprints in the snow. The stone walls of the barn stood blackened with the sky over them.

He stood in the ruin of the barn and tried to think logically, but his heart was breaking. He tried to be quiet in his sobbing, but the sobs tore out of his body, and finally he cried out with each gasping sob so loudly that the ravens flew over the barn and called back to him in curiosity.

He waited until noon the next day, and then gave up and walked back to where the Russian and his men waited. With every step he hoped that she would be there, the Russian making fun of her for thinking she could find a cow. He groaned when he saw them step out of hiding. No dark head, smooth and round, streaked with silver. No small hands to take his when the others weren't looking. No sidelong look and smile to give him heart.

No one asked anything when he rejoined them. They all knew. Somewhere out there she'd been killed. The Russian made the decision.

"We have to move. We aren't safe anymore."

So they moved. They walked for days until they were close to another road on the other side of the river. They crossed the river by walking on the patches of ice. Sometimes the ice gave under their boots in the middle, but they reached the other side.

The Mechanik almost stayed behind, but the Russian persuaded him gently. "Go with us. If she's alive, you'll find her someday. After it's over."

"When it's over," the Mechanik said. He tried to have hope. She would have despised him if he became depressed and lost heart. So he thought of what he would do after the Russian army came. He pictured the map of Poland in his mind as they walked and sectioned it off neatly into parts where he would search for her and the children.

At night he talked to her in his head as he lay next to the others, trying to get warm, trying to go to sleep. First it was as if she was alive and lying beside him. He would tell her about the day and what they had done. Then he noticed that the talking to her had become like a prayer, so he stopped doing it and lay staring at the cold sky until he fell asleep. You only prayed to dead people. Or God. And he didn't believe in God and couldn't accept that she was dead. He was left lying on the frozen earth with the dark sky above and his heart unable to take comfort from anything.

"At least I don't believe in God," he told the Russian one morning.

"And if you did believe, Mechanik, what then?"

"Then I'd kill myself. Because if God is all-powerful and all-knowing, he must have no pity. He looks down and sees everything and doesn't bring the evil to an end. I wouldn't live if I thought a God could end the pain and didn't."

"And what good would your death do?"

"It would teach God a lesson." The Mechanik walked on and didn't care that the Russian laughed. He knew it was true, and he was glad that he didn't believe. It saved his life every day.

"We keep going east," the Russian said. "The Soviet army must be just ahead of us. We'll thread our way through the Germans, link with my people, and fight our way to Germany. You'll make a good Soviet, Mechanik. We don't give a damn about religion, and you don't believe in God anyway. We'll make a Communist of you."

When the Russian paused for breath, they heard the voices.

"Fix the damn thing! What use are you? This goddamn country."

The words were German. They dove into the woods. Using the trees for cover, they moved parallel to the road until they saw the truck. Two German soldiers had the hood up. Another soldier stood guard beside the truck holding a rifle, watching the woods. A man in civilian clothes paced on the road beside the truck. He was the one talking so loudly.

"I'll take the guard." The Mechanik pressed his rifle against the tree trunk to steady it.

"I'll get the one whose butt is hanging out of the engine. You—" The Russian pointed to two others. "Take the other guy near the hood, and you take the little jerk in the suit."

"No." The Mechanik whispered. "The man in the suit doesn't show a gun. Shoot the other three, and then we take the one in the suit and get information."

"Don't get killed trying to take the bastard," the Russian warned. "When I count three."

The guns fired and the crows flew up in a panic of fluttering wings and loud cries. Two of the soldiers dropped and lay still. The man who had been bending into the engine was hit in his buttocks and screamed. The Russian fired another bullet, but he still moaned.

The man in the suit broke into a run and kept slipping on the ice and giving little shrieks as he fought for balance.

The Russian was roaring with laughter. "Catch the bastard."

The Mechanik went to the moaning soldier and shot him in the head. The road was quiet except for the crows and the cries of the man in city shoes who ran up the road. They brought him back, searched him, and stood him before the Russian. The German's teeth chattered so hard the Mechanik wondered if he would crack them.

"I'm not a soldier. I'm a medical student. I'm not a soldier. I don't have a gun."

"You understand this, Mechanik?"

He nodded. "I'll translate."

The Russian looked at the truck. Two of his men were searching the flatbed, opening the containers. "Any food in those boxes? Any guns? What's our young dandy carrying in his truck?"

One of the men leaned over the metal barrel and reached inside. He pulled out a round thing and held it up. It dripped liquid.

"Blessed Virgin!" The Russian stepped back and crossed himself. "It's a fucking head!"

"There're more of them. Packed in liquid and bags of bones. Human bones."

"I'm not a soldier. They ordered me to do it," the German whispered.

"Ask him what the fuck this is," the Russian shouted. "Translate, damn it."

"It wasn't my idea. I'm a doctor." The young man scrabbled in his inside pocket and came out with a paper. The Mechanik read the paper out loud slowly in Polish.

"SUBJECT: Securing skulls of Jewish Bolshevik Commissars for the purpose of scientific research at the Reichsuniversitaet, Strassburg. The war in the east presents us with the opportunity of overcoming the deficiency of Jewish and Russian race skulls in our collection. By procuring the skulls of the Jewish/Bolshevik/Communists who represent the prototype of the repulsive but characteristic subhuman, we now have the chance to obtain a palpable, scientific document.

"Dr. Wolfric Rahn will be in charge of securing the material, can take measurements, photographs, and determine the background, age, and personal data of the prisoner.

"Following the subsequent induced death of the Jew/Russian, whose head should not be damaged, Dr. Berue will sever the head from the body and transport it in a hermetically sealed tin made for this purpose and filled with a preserving fluid. Skeletons should also be carefully harvested and cleaned of their flesh. They should be labeled and packed in separate bags."

The men stood silent until the Russian walked over to one of the dead soldiers and unbuttoned his pants. He urinated on the corpse and then buttoned his pants slowly. Then he lit a cigarette. It was one of the last ones from the farm. He had held it back for a special moment. He dragged deeply and passed it to the man next to him. They all stood and shared the cigarette, and looked at the truck and the tin boxes and the bags.

"Bury them," the Russian finally said. He turned to the young German who was shaking all over now. "Whose heads are in those boxes? Maybe my friends?"

He hit the German and the man dropped like a sack of potatoes. They buried the heads under snow and piled logs and brush on them. The bones they were going to leave in the bags, but the Russian shook his head.

"Bury their bones clean. Let the earth have them."

When they were done, they waited. The Russian was pacing, and his scarred neck and face were livid. They waited for him to say what to do next.

"Now." His voice was calm. "Strangle this bastard," he said, and the oldest of the Poles fell upon the young German, and knocked him back down on the road, and clenched his chapped, rough hands on the slender neck. The German managed to batter the Pole's face, but his throat broke and he flopped for a minute and then his tongue came out and he was dead.

"Take all their clothes off. We can use the coats and pants."

The Russian stood and looked at the naked bodies. "I want you to cut their heads off and put the bodies in a line with the heads at their feet."

It took an ax to sever the spinal cord. The Mechanik had helped undress them, but he didn't help with the cutting. They should move on. You couldn't revenge yourself on dead men.

The headless men lay in a row. The Russian stabbed the order from Himmler on the chest of one of the corpses with a German knife.

They walked on down the road, listening for more trucks. It was too bad they had to leave the truck, but there was no petrol to run it. Looking back, the Mechanik squinted his eyes. It was hard to tell what the dark splotches on the road were from a distance. He wondered who would find the bodies. He hoped it wasn't a child.

"And that's the difference between us—Poles and Russians and Jews—that's the difference between us and the Nazis," the Russian said that night as they all drank vodka a farmer had given them. "We have to get drunk after we do such things. Drunkenness is a good sign. It means you still have some feelings. That's why the Russians are drunks. They feel too damn much." He passed out before midnight and they covered him tenderly with blankets.

"It was a Nazi idea to murder people for their skulls," the oldest Pole said. His face sweated from the homemade vodka. "But it took a Russian to think of what we did on the road."

"It's one or the other for Poland," sighed one of the men.

"Don't think about it now. Think about it later." Lydka's face was red and his eyes were glazed from drink, but he spoke fiercely. "First kill the Germans. Then deal with the Russians."

They all slept deeply until noon the next day. They never spoke again of the truck and the thing they had done. The sun was shining, and they moved on down the road.

Eindeutschung

"It's time to take back the baby. A storm is coming. Our tracks will be hidden."

"Can you hide the whole village, Telek? You'll have to kill the guard, and the Major will retaliate. How many of this village will die so we can run free?"

"Your husband is dead in Russia, and that baby's all that's left! Think of him."

They sat and Nelka stared at him, and he stared back until she leaned forward and lay her lips on his. He didn't move, didn't respond, but Nelka kept her lips on his and then, catlike, began to lick his lips slowly with her tongue.

"He's going to bleed you dry."

"We can't have the death of the village on our heads. Why has the SS stayed so long?"

"I don't know, but I can guess."

"He wants my blood. That's why he stays."

"No. He's afraid of the Russians. They're in Poland now, and he has to leave with the Major. The car would never get through the mud in March."

Nelka stretched out and turned so the fire heated her back and the round of her buttocks. Looking up, she saw his eyes. "Telek?"

"They call it *Eindeutschung*—making things German. I've told you, Nelka. You have to believe me. They steal children that look German. They've stolen thousands, maybe twenty or thirty thousand. The underground says they give them new names, and tear up all the identification papers. They are culling out the Aryan-looking children before they put the rest of the Poles in camps and kill us—after we build their new cities."

"I was going to have the baptism before Easter."

"It might be better not to name him."

"That's an evil thing to say. His name will be Janek."

Telek felt like he was torturing another child watching Nelka's face. "The SS has a paper typed up that'll be posted in the square tomorrow. They're going to examine the children." He didn't care about the village. He would kill the soldier guarding Sister Rosa and the woman too if it came to it. They would run.

"We can't let Magda and Hansel and Gretel get killed."

"We'll warn them. They can hide in the pig hole in the forest."

"Make love to me," she whispered. "If you make love to me then it is two of us. There is just one of him when he takes my blood, but we are two."

"We are two and more than two," he whispered in her ear, and then he lifted her and carried her to the bed.

When the Major posted the command to bring the children to his office on the next day, Telek went to the hut and told Magda. Magda seldom prayed, but that night she prayed.

"Oh Queen of Poland, dark Virgin Mary of Czestochowa, hear my prayer," she whispered, kneeling near the oven where the warmth made her joints ache less, and the coals of the firebox shone through the slits, reddening her face as if it were washed with blood.

"Your son was taken into prison and beaten and tortured. You know what it is to love a child and watch men kill him. You had the strength to stand and let him know he was not alone when he was nailed to that tree. You didn't cower at home and cry but stood before him and watched his death. You are no weakling."

Magda paused and thought.

"These children are Jews—like you were—like your son was. If you'd been a Polish woman and pregnant with your son when this war started, you and he would have been shot and buried in the forest. Let the Germans pass over the two children. Let me take them to the village tomorrow and bring them home again. If Gretel acts crazy, they'll shoot her, but if she acts normal, they'll kidnap her. I'm an old, old woman. Take my soul and kill me instead of them."

She had done what she could. Magda got up slowly and felt all the pain in her hips and her knees and her wrists. She had little hope. Magda didn't believe her prayers rose very high.

"Next!" The soldier shouted although the women and children stood patiently in line.

Magda went inside the Major's office. Gretel was quiet today, not singing loudly and talking about oranges and such, but silence was no good. She had to be mad or they would take her. But not too mad.

"Papers." Wiktor examined Magda's papers and the communion certificates of the children. He looked up at the Brown Sister who stood beside the desk. The Oberführer sat in the corner and watched. The Major leaned against the wall and smoked.

"Strip. Both children. And step up on this stool, one at a time." Sister Rosa spoke fluent Polish that was heavily accented with German. She held a notebook and a pair of calipers.

"The girl is silly sometimes, sir and madam. She hasn't—" Magda tried to speak.

"We will decide." Sister Rosa looked almost as gray-faced as Magda. It had been a long winter going from one godforsaken village to another. But it was a job that had to be done. The children with Aryan blood deserved the chance to return to the German people. Sister Rosa looked at the boy who stood on the stool.

"Circumcised?" She spoke suddenly in German. "A Jew still left in Poland?"

She sounds like a raven, Hansel thought, and before Magda could answer, he began to talk.

"My mother was a Karaite. They believe that you have to be circumcised because Jesus was circumcised. So she had me cut."

"Ah. The Karaite story." The Oberführer sighed.

Wiktor almost smiled. His suspicions were correct. The Oberführer understood Polish.

"You'd think half of Poland had become Karaites just before the Germans arrived."

"I remember it," Hansel said.

Oh God, Magda thought, he's gone too far, and I can't help him.

"You remember? Tell me about it." The Oberführer leaned forward.

"They dressed me up, and I wore a long white robe and a crown."

"A crown?" Sister Rosa frowned.

"A crown because I was going to be like Jesus."

Magda breathed shallowly. Her chest was tight. Where did the child dream up such a story?

"Then what happened?" The Oberführer was watching Hansel, and Major Frankel stood leaning against the wall with no expression on his face at all.

"They made me lie down on this big table, like in the church, and a man had a knife, and they cut my penis and threw away some skin and then I was like Jesus."

"Did you bleed?" The SS man smiled.

"A whole lot."

"He cried. He screamed and screamed and screamed." Gretel smiled at the Oberführer.

"You remember this also?"

"He shrieked until I had to cover my ears. And then they gave him wine, and I drank wine, and everyone was happy."

Let her stop, Magda thought. Let her stop.

"What happened next?" The Oberführer moved closer and looked at the small penis.

"We went to the church and ate the bread. Just like on Sunday."

"He doesn't look like a Jew," Sister Rosa spoke in German so the old woman wouldn't understand. "His nose is almost perfectly Aryan, and his lips aren't simian and thick."

"His eyes." The Oberführer smiled, and now he spoke German also. "There is a touch of the Tartar who raped his great-grandmother in those eyes. I think we needn't worry about Jews in this area. This last summer was the end of Jews in Poland. They're gone."

Sister Rosa turned Hansel's head. She nodded. "Do you want the measurements done?"

"No. Send the little Karaite home. His eyes would have been all right three years ago, but the standards are constantly going up. In five more years, my brown eyes would disqualify me from being in the SS."

"A great loss for the Reich." Sister Rosa took a paper and wrote on it. She handed it to Magda and spoke brusquely in Polish.

"If he had been sick, we would have taken him to Germany for treatment. You're lucky that the Reich cares so for your children."

Magda nodded. She took the paper, and Gretel pulled off her last shift and stepped naked onto the stool. Hansel tried not to look at Gretel. He tried not to think about her being crazy. He reached for Magda's hand and held it tightly.

"Very nice." The Oberführer stepped forward and touched the child's pale nipple.

"A beautiful example of how the Aryan blood comes out even in the worst dung heap." Sister Rosa took calipers and measured the width between Gretel's pelvic bones.

"Not very wide, but possibility for breeding potential."

She measured all of Gretel's face, the length of her nose, the width from cheekbone to cheekbone. "We'll take pictures of this one. She's quite perfect."

Gretel stood still, but when Sister Rosa turned her and began running her thumb down Gretel's spine, the child suddenly screamed. She didn't move but the scream tore out of her lips.

Sister Rosa jumped. Major Frankel cursed.

Then Gretel began to sing. She sang of the flowers and of love and of standing under the lime trees in spring.

Gretel smiled and held out her hand, the palm up, fingers cupped. Sister Rosa stared.

"Her mind is disturbed sometimes since the rape," Magda whispered.

"She was raped?" The Oberführer made no pretense of not understanding Polish now.

"Two men. They ran off, and the child came home bloody. Sometimes she isn't right. But she is good for fetching wood. She's harmless." Magda waited.

The Brown Sister took Gretel by the arm and led her off the stool and to the desk. She laid the girl across the desk and spread her legs. Gretel still sang.

"The hymen is not intact. She could well have been raped. She's quite perfect, but her mind is no good anymore. These Polish children don't have the strength of German children. They break easily." The Brown Sister shook her head and wrote in her notebook.

"I will mark by her name that she must be sterilized at thirteen."

"She's a good worker." Magda waited. This was what being in Hell was, she thought.

"Sterilization can be done, but it's wasteful to let her live." The SS man shook his head.

"Why not let her live?" The Major spoke for the first time. The child reminded him of his sister at the same age when they swam secretly. The same skin. The same hair.

The Oberführer shook his head. The mentally defective must be destroyed. The new world would be absolutely perfect when everyone had been sorted and the deficient culled.

The Major watched the SS man's face. The child stood again on the stool and hummed to herself. The Major saw that it was useless to object. The Oberführer would have the girl shot.

"Oberführer." The Major spoke quickly in German before the order to shoot the girl could be given. "The child is related to the woman Nelka, isn't that so?"

The SS man hesitated. He didn't know where the Major was going with this.

"I mean, Nelka is her cousin or aunt or something."

"That's correct," Wiktor said. "You are right—Major," he finished awkwardly.

"Well then." The Major paused and lit another cigarette from the butt end of his old one.

Magda was panting. Her heart fibrillated in her chest.

"Nelka has been useful to the Brown Sister, I believe. She

spends time helping Sister Rosa? Sister Rosa is concerned for the baby?"

"The baby stays with Sister Rosa."

"Of course"—Major Frankel blew the smoke out with a harsh sigh—"none of us want more contact with these Polish subhumans than we have to have for the sake of the war."

"Of course."

"Not only because of the illegality of contact, but because it would be disgusting." Major Frankel looked at Gretel. She did look like his sister around the eyes and in the way she smiled. He turned his good eye and looked the SS man in the face. "I wonder if it's wise to upset Nelka. Nelka is one of the few women in the village presentable enough to serve Sister Rosa, and killing this girl might drive the peasants into the forest."

Magda thought she would faint if the rattle of German didn't stop.

The Oberführer looked out the window as if he barely heard. He couldn't tell if the man knew of the transfusions or if he was really concerned about Sister Rosa having a proper servant. The Major probably knew nothing, but taking blood from a Pole could be used against an SS officer in some quarters. And there was that information that Jedrik had hinted at last night. Jedrik's information might complicate things.

"If she's useful, she can live. The children are not in need of medical treatment. We'll leave them in the village." The Oberführer handed Magda two white cards.

They went outside, and Magda didn't look at the other parents. Telek said that all the children who might have been chosen had been made imperfect. Except for Nelka's baby, and it was so small. How would they keep it alive all the way to Germany?

"Go home, Magda." Nelka tied Magda's scarf firmly under the old woman's chin.

"He was going to kill her—then the Major talked—" Magda whispered so Hansel couldn't hear, but he clung to her side and heard the words. He breathed heavily through his mouth, a hoarse sound in the cold air. "I'll stay until they look at the baby." Magda nodded, but her lips trembled.

"Go." Nelka gave Magda a light push, and some hardness in the girl's face made Magda turn and go. Nelka didn't need the presence of a great-aunt called a witch by half the village or kinship with a mad child and a circumcised boy.

They walked as fast as Magda could go. The road was growing soft with the slush that replaced the icy snow of January. Thank you, Mary, she thought, for letting them stay with me. Magda stopped walking and closed her eyes, praying a last time. Sweet Mary, she prayed silently, don't let them take Nelka's baby away. Let God come to earth if he has to and kill the SS man.

Hansel had stopped skipping and was watching Magda. "Are there any Jews left in any of the villages, Magda?" His neck itched. He knew it was the lice. He hadn't had a bath for weeks.

"The Germans have eaten the Gypsies of Poland for breakfast, child, and then they ate the Jews for lunch, but soon it will be supper."

"What will they eat then?"

"All the rest of the Poles, my boy."

Hansel ran toward the hut. "Magda, can I put a piece of bread on the boards for the birds?"

"No, child. The bread is for us now."

"You said you'd always give the birds bread. You'd rather be hungry than scared."

"I was foolish. Now I'm wiser."

They went in the hut and closed the door. The sleet began again and fell straight down like a curtain, closing off the hut from the forest with strings of gray.

"Not a single child in the village worth saving so far. All of them ugly and round-faced or mutilated by carelessness. It's odd that the children all had accidents. Could they have known?"

Forgetting that he never spoke unless spoken to, forgetting that being involved in this line of thinking could get him killed, forgetting all the survival skills he had learned in the jails of Warsaw and then used when he was selected by the Nazis for work—forgetting everything, Wiktor spoke.

"It's often like this at the end of winter. There are more accidents when it's cold."

Wiktor stared down at the desk and cursed himself silently. All his creeping and crawling and his silences and his work. He had taken a chance on throwing it all away for peasants in a mud village who weren't even his kin. But they were Poles, and Wiktor was still a Pole. The Nazis couldn't change that. Wiktor looked up, but the Oberführer turned away when Nelka knocked.

"Put the basket down."

They forgot Wiktor, and he sat feeling the sweat slide like oil down his spine.

Unwrapping the baby on the desk, Sister Rosa displayed its legs and arms, its smooth stomach and the perfect bobble of its uncircumcised penis. As the Oberführer watched, the penis lifted slightly and a strong stream of urine jetted up.

"A sign of health," Sister Rosa said firmly. "And look at the limbs. The straightness. The eyes are blue, I can testify to that, and the hair is the palest blond. See the ears? They lie flat the way the ears of an Aryan should. You agree that he should receive the red card?"

The Oberführer sighed. "There is another matter. I will question the mother, Sister Rosa."

"Of course, Oberführer."

The Oberführer saw Sister Rosa's slyness, and rage began to make his neck feel hot. The bitch. Rosa had been present when Jedrik had blurted out the village gossip. So now it had to be brought out. If he didn't question Nelka, Sister Rosa would be suspicious. She might even report him when they got back to Berlin.

"Nelka, I was told that you have a heritage not as pure as I assumed."

Jedrik must have told, Nelka thought. No one in the village bears me bad will, but Jedrik will do anything for a sack of potatoes and some salt.

"Perhaps you have an ancestor who was a Gypsy? Is this true?"

"I don't understand." Nelka stared at the baby.

"If you are of pure Polish blood, and if your husband was untainted by Jew or Gypsy blood, this baby is perfect for assimilation into the

German people. He will be taken to Germany to live as a free man in the new world that we are building. If he is part Gypsy, then we are merciful, of course. You and the child would be sent to a camp until you can be relocated."

She had heard of the camps. No one returned from the camps.

"But if the baby is sent to Germany. I can go with it?"

"That is unfortunately impossible."

If she said that her blood was part Gypsy, she could stay with the baby. They would be in a camp, but they might live. The Russians were close. If they could live just a month—two months.

"In Germany—" She stopped. There was hardly any air in the room.

"Your child would become a true German. You should be proud." Sister Rosa smiled.

Nelka thought. She could go to the camps. They could live there until the Russians came and freed them. She opened her mouth to say that she had Gypsy blood in her veins when she remembered. Father Piotr was her grandfather. Magda was her great-aunt. The trains. The cold, damp spring in a camp. Neither could survive it. If she admitted her Gypsy blood, it followed that Magda and Piotr had Gypsy blood, and Hansel and Gretel, her cousins.

"Death," she whispered. Nelka bent her head. She would have to be separated from the baby and take a chance on searching for him in Germany. She couldn't doom her family.

"There is no Gypsy blood in me," she whispered. "My child is pure-blooded."

The Oberführer smiled. "I knew it. The rumors were simple jealousy because your child is the only perfect one." He stared defiantly at Sister Rosa.

Sister Rosa tucked her notebook and the calipers in the baby's basket. She took a red card, wrote the baby's identification on it, handed it to Nelka, and left the room. The baby was hers now. She carried the only perfect Aryan child in the village of Piaski.

"I am relieved that the rumors are false," the Oberführer was saying. He stared at Nelka. She would understand. It was their secret. He had her blood inside him now, and if that blood was tainted, he would have been very angry. More than angry. He would have been murderous. He smiled as he thought of it, the joy of unleashing such a feeling.

The Major wondered why he hadn't been told this rumor of Gypsy ancestors. Wiktor should have heard something, but what a magnificent joke it would be if Nelka were part Gypsy! What a disaster for the arrogant bastard, an Oberführer who'd avoided every major battle in the war.

Nelka went outside and walked down the steps into the sleet. She didn't even put her scarf over her head but let the frozen rain wet her hair and face unchecked.

"I didn't think she had Gypsy blood. You can always tell. It would have been tragic." The Oberführer shook his head.

Major Frankel almost laughed. He knew exactly how tragic it would have been.

"Of course, I would have shot her immediately. And the child. I'm glad it wasn't necessary. Such a mess in the office. Bloodstains are hard to remove. Depressing for you and your clerk."

"Blood is impossible to remove. It can be the hardest stain to get out."

The Oberführer stared at the Major for a second, but the other man's face was bland and faintly bored. With a nod, the Oberführer left the office, and Major Frankel lit another cigarette. He looked quickly at Wiktor, but the man had enough sense to be staring down at the papers on the desk as if he heard and understood nothing.

The Major sucked the smoke deeply into his lungs. There were parts of this war that would never bear remembering. He sighed, the smoke expelled from him in a diffuse cloud. For a moment he actually wished he was in the trenches again at the Russian front.

They had walked for three days when it began, groups of men and trucks, a thin trickle fleeing Poland. Then the trickle of Germans began to grow. At first the partisans were afraid. They stayed deep in the woods, away from the road, but after a while they crept closer to watch.

The trucks stopped only to refuel. The German soldiers walked with great exhaustion, but they moved as fast as they could. They didn't even step behind the trees to piss but pissed on the road openly. And that was wise. If they stepped into the trees, they were easy prey for the partisans. A lone man would not be missed in this great exodus out of eastern Poland.

The men and machines turned into a thick snake that was never broken. Even at night they passed. The only sound in the forest was the tramp of feet, the engines of the machines, and the curses when guns were stuck and had to be abandoned or loaded on trucks.

And the constant stuttering of guns came from the distance. The partisans hardly heard the noise after a few days. If it had stopped, they would have been startled.

The airplanes were flying overhead now too. They passed in waves, too high for the Germans to bring down with their guns. The planes were Russian this time, and they moved west, toward Germany. The Russian grinned whenever he heard their drone above the trees.

But sometimes the planes, as if the pilots couldn't stand watching the snake of German soldiers and equipment moving unscathed below them, dove and strafed the road, scattering men and machines and delaying progress. After the strafing, the dead had to be picked up and buried. The trucks that burned were pulled off the road, so the retreat could go on. The partisans watched from the safety of the forest, and the Russian sometimes had to shove his fist in his mouth so he wouldn't shout out loud with joy at watching the men who had branded and starved him lose their war.

The partisans had to move through the trees, the roads being full of Germans now, so they went more slowly, but the weather was changing. The snow had melted, and that meant they didn't have to push through drifts, but all of them wore a layer of mud to their hips. The mud was like glue catching their boots, and when they found rocky areas, it was a great relief. As they moved east, the rocks were fewer and the ground was more swampy.

"It's hard for us, but think what it is for them." The Russian moved relentlessly now, not letting them rest for more than a few minutes.

It was March, and they were beginning to see tanks as well as trucks. Most of the motorcycles were abandoned by the road because the mud was so churned up that they were more trouble to ride than it was worth.

The partisan group sat beside a field and watched tank after tank cross it. The tanks came in a regular pattern, a swooping curve that avoided the worst of the low, swampy places. Beyond the field was smoke from a village, but the crows had moved deeper into the forest. Except for the noise of the tanks, it was silent.

They had fought the tanks as best they could. Every village had soup tureens, and when they were upended and covered with dirt, they looked like carelessly laid mines. Starzec, the oldest man of them all, had thought of the idea, and it delayed the tanks so they could pick off the men as they climbed out to check the mounded mud. Many Germans had been killed that way.

———

They had worked all one morning laying pots in the dirt, until suddenly the Mechanik stopped walking and turned his face up to the sky, listening. It was beautiful. The most beautiful sound he had ever heard.

They all stood, draped with arms around one another's shoulders, and were silent. The booming was steady and definite. It was gunfire, but not the stuttering they had heard for weeks. This was the steady beat of heavy artillery. It throbbed in the distance like the thunder of a coming storm, and they all smiled. It was the sound of a mighty force coming toward them. The full weight of Mother Russia was moving over the land.

"My brothers. We're going to drive the rats out and kill them and then go home and be heroes and make our women happy." The Russian began to sing a song in Russian, and the Poles sang in Polish, and the Mechanik, for the first time in his adult life, began to sing a song in Yiddish that his father had hummed when he sat with his grandchild in the garden and fed her oranges.

They sang softly, the rhythm of the artillery serving as a drumbeat to the songs, until they saw the first tank coming through the woods into the meadow. A man rode on top peering ahead. Another tank was behind and several men clung to the top of it.

They waited, and heard the man on the first tank scream out a warning. The tank sputtered and churned to a halt. There was a lot of shouting in German that the partisans couldn't hear clearly, but they didn't have to hear it. The Germans thought the mounds of dirt over the pots was a minefield.

"They'll have to go back a mile to find any other field. And that one leads to a swamp."

"They'll take to the road."

"They're too heavy. They'll sink in the mud by afternoon. The mud will be impossible."

The tanks had disappeared, and a group of about twenty men trotted into the meadow. They began to approach the buried pots cautiously.

"They're going to clear a path." The Russian was almost dancing for joy. "Let's get rid of this bunch."

With one accord, the partisans raised their rifles and began to pick off the Nazis. The meadow was littered with their bodies.

"They'll think a mine got them. This field is going to stay empty for a while." The Mechanik was pleased. Since his wife had disappeared, he had taken more joy in seeing the Germans die.

The men grinned. They all shook hands and one of the younger village men who had helped collect the pots stood before the Russian and saluted as if the Russian were a Polish army officer.

"My parents are slaves in Germany. I'm not afraid of dying. Let me go with you."

"What do you call yourself, boy?" The Russian looked the peasant over. He had a rifle in his hand and the lump of a pistol under his coat.

"Dobry. I can fight."

The Russian laughed and slapped the boy on the back. He had guns. He was strong. "Fight with us then. Until we drive them to Berlin and kill them."

They moved off around the field, heading toward the sound of the artillery in the distance. It wasn't much that they'd done, and they knew it, but every German slowed down, every tank abandoned in a field or bogged in the swamps, was a small victory.

"When we get to Germany," Dobry asked Starzec, "will we find our people, do you think? The ones they took to work?"

Starzec shrugged. He didn't have the heart to tell the boy how unlikely it was that the Germans would let a Polish slave have food when the Germans were hungry. He didn't want to discourage this orphan.

"What God wills is what happens. Pray for the Poles in Germany and Russia, boy."

Dobry nodded out of respect for the older man. After all, Starzec had had the idea that stopped the tanks. But he didn't pray. He had prayed for three years, and there was no good that had come of the prayers. As if hearing his thoughts, Starzec spoke again.

"We prayed that the Russians be driven out, and the Germans did it. Now we've prayed that the Nazis be destroyed. Look at the Nazi bastards on the road. They're beaten. While we're killing the last of them and driving them out, we can pray for those Poles kidnapped and stolen from us."

Dobry thought about it. It was true. The Russians had been beaten back into Russia, and the Nazis were now fleeing Poland. He shook his head stubbornly.

"It didn't happen fast enough. Half of Poland died before God helped us."

"God's time isn't our time." Starzec sighed.

"God shouldn't have let this killing happen. God should have stopped it."

Starzec gestured at the trees and the forest around them. "Do you see God? Where is he, you fool?"

Dobry flushed and shook his head. "I don't know."

"God didn't come down and kill us. I don't see God shooting children and priests. None of us met God beating up Jews and shoving them into railroad cars. This is men doing the murdering. Talk to men about their evil, kill the evil men, but pray to God. You can't expect God to come down and do our living for us. We have to do that ourselves."

Starzec turned his back on the boy and walked on, feeling the pains in his knees and back and ignoring them. He had a long walk before this war would be over and he safely back in his bed in Warsaw—in what would be left of Warsaw when the Nazis and the Russians had burned and looted it—but he didn't like to think about that.

The young peasant stood staring after the older man, and he was so flushed that his eyes watered. He brushed away the tears and trotted behind Starzec, and his mind, almost against his will, began to form prayers for his father and mother, for all the Poles taken from their country, kidnapped and beaten and starved and perhaps worked to death or dead already in the camps. He prayed, and the prayers developed a sort of rhythm as he walked, and his mind grew quiet as they moved steadily eastward toward the thunder of death.

They had no trouble finding food. There were trucks, abandoned and pushed off the road into the trees, that had food in them. There were dead Germans left behind in the race to stay in front of the Russian troops and get out of Poland.

"They know if my countrymen catch them, there'll be no pity." The Russian smiled. "The Russians have suffered like no one else. They won't let a German live."

The older Pole shook his head. "Let's not debate who has suffered most. Anyone alive hasn't suffered that much, or they'd be dead," he said. "The real sufferers can't brag about their suffering anymore."

The guns were near now, and there weren't many Germans left on the road. It was desolate and silent, only the machines torn apart and cannibalized so other machines could be fixed, the bodies abandoned, the guns sunk in the mud, a reminder that the German army had struggled past.

That night they found boxes in the snow, the ropes of the parachute and the silk cloth still attached. Inside were treasures they hadn't seen since before the war.

The Mechanik used the can opener taped to the side of a can, and when it opened with a glitter of tin, the men stood silent. Their mouths watered as they smelled it.

"Canned meat!"

They dug in with their fingers and smeared the meat paste on the hard bread. There were guns and ammunition and vodka and, most amazing of all, a little medical kit with aspirin and bandages and salve for wounds, a needle and some gut, and a vial marked MORPHINE.

"Good Russian bread," the Russian cried as he held the bread in his mouth. It was too hard for his teeth, but he held it and thought it tasted better than the Polish bread.

The guns were silent now except for an occasional boom. They walked over fields that were covered with holes from the shells.

It was late afternoon on the eleventh of March when they saw up ahead, on the other side of a field, coming over the top of a rise in the ground, men walking. They didn't walk fast, but there was a relentless quality to the movement that made the Mechanik shiver. He looked at the face of the older Pole and saw that he was shaken too.

It wasn't men so much as it was a wave of humans. Most weren't in uniform. They were a flood of ragged, gray men who just walked and didn't stop. The tide of men covered the hill behind them.

"Move back to the road," the Russian said. His face glowed. "I'll call out in Russian first, and get the attention of some of the men. You can hide until they see I'm a Russian."

First a truck passed them and then a small vehicle. "It's a Jeep," the Mechanik said in awe.

"What's that?" The Russian watched the odd, open car, painted dark green, move off through the mud.

"The Americans have them. I saw a picture once. In Bialystok."

"How did the Russians get it?"

"The Americans must have sent them."

They watched as tanks and trucks and more Jeeps began to fill the road. They were muddy, but they had a modern look that pleased the Mechanik. Other engineers had been busy while he lay hiding in the ghetto. His hands itched to open the hoods on the trucks and see what they had been inventing since he had been trapped in the irrational world of war. When the road was nearly covered, the Russian made a gesture with his hand, and all of them melted back into the woods.

"Pray," Starzec said as he lay behind a log. "They are killing everyone in their path."

The men heard the Russian calling out in his own language. He called for a long time, and then other voices shouted answers. None of the partisans understood the language.

"Come out," the Russian began screaming in Polish. "Come out. My brothers are here."

The Russian was standing in the road. Men were kissing him on the cheeks and on the lips. They were grabbing him and laughing.

"Come on," he said, shouting at them. "We're going with these comrades. They're going back to our part of the forest to clean the Nazis out of the villages. We can show them the way."

The Mechanik began to smile. They were going back to where the children had been left. Back to that village near the road where he had last seen them in November.

"I'm coming, my darlings," he whispered. "And you, my wife. I'll find you. I'm coming." They could be where he had left the motorcycle in two weeks, maybe in ten days. Then he would go to each village and ask. Someone must have taken the children in. She was such a beautiful girl. His son was so quick and alert.

It was March 11, 1944, and they weren't partisans anymore. They were part of the gray locust hoard of the Russian army, fighting in the open, cleaning out the enemy. The partisans walked down the road with the Russians, and even the Poles were smiling. This foreign army was walking on Polish soil, but perhaps they would be content to return to Russia when the Germans were dead and beaten. Perhaps freedom was coming soon.

There was so little left to steal or use in Poland. Half the Poles must be dead, the flower of the men killed. Surely there was nothing about Poland for anyone to covet now. The government in exile in London said that the British and the Americans promised freedom for Poland when the war was over. They had heard it on the illegal radios in Bialystok for a year now. Freedom would come. The world had promised it to them.

"I'm not supposed to play with you." Halina dropped her head and stared at the floor of the porch.

"Why?" Hansel stood in the shadow of the porch, staring up at Halina.

"My aunt said. And anyway, you don't have anything to play with. You don't even have a house where we can play."

"We could play at Magda's. She doesn't care."

"My aunt won't let me go to Magda's. She's a witch."

"No she isn't."

Halina went down the stairs and stood close to Hansel. She took his hand and swung it. "If I went to Magda's, she'd find out. We can't play in the village. Everybody will tell."

Hansel stood and thought. He looked at Halina, and she smiled.

"I could get potatoes. We could go out in the fields, but it's cold."

Hansel shook his head. "Come on. I know where we can play. It's a secret. You can't tell."

"Where is it?"

"You can't tell."

They ran up the road and were nearly at the bend when the aunt came out on the porch.

"Halina! Get back here. I told you not to play with that boy. Halina!"

She watched them disappear around the curve of the road, heading toward the woods. She'd find out later about this. The girl couldn't play with the strangers. Her parents were dead already. The boy wasn't safe. He could get all of them killed.

Both children were breathing hard by the time they got to the river and found the rock and turned south. Hansel ran to the saplings and pulled the brush off that covered the boards.

"See? It's a hidey-hole. There's food and everything. Nobody will know we're here."

"We can play house." Halina clapped her hands. "It can be our special place."

"Just us. And you can't tell, Halina. You can't tell no matter what."

"I won't tell. My aunt will just think we played in the woods. I'll never tell, Hansel."

Hand in hand they climbed into the hole, arranging the boxes like tables and chairs.

"We need candles. It's dark."

"We can only use one, Halina."

"You light it."

Hansel set a candle on the box and lit it with one of the matches Magda had wrapped in oilcloth. The glow filled the dark hole, and both children sighed in pleasure.

"You're the papa and I'm the mama."

Hansel leaned over and kissed Halina on the cheek. "We can play till it gets dark."

Halina was busy arranging potatoes on the box. "And we can fix dinner for the children."

"Yes. I just came in from work and you are going to make dinner for us, but you have to not tell. Never. About this place."

"I won't. Besides, who'd care anyway?"

Confession

Telek walked to the village, doubled over with a mound of firewood. Unable to lift his head, he stared at the mud and walked steadily on, making up his mind.

The baby was going to be taken into Germany by the Nazis. Telek couldn't believe the SS man would give up Nelka either, and if she disappeared into Germany—but he couldn't think about that. That was a bone he wouldn't gnaw until it was thrown at him.

He would kill the Brown Sister and the guard, and take the child, but he wouldn't tell Nelka that he was going to do it. He'd kill the two of them, and go straight to her house with the baby in his arms. She'd have to run, and the village could take care of itself.

Telek threw the wood down and began to stack it. By tomorrow he would never see this wood again, but he must act as if it was an ordinary day. He hummed while he neatly built the pile.

Nelka went to get water and saw Telek at the well. He turned to her and smiled, and he was different. His face was smooth and his eyes were not narrowed and anxious. Telek tossed his bucket over the edge, watching the rope uncoil and follow the bucket into the darkness, and Nelka heard it hit the water and sink with a gurgle.

"You're different today, Telek."

"Because I love you."

"You're going to do it. You're going to get the whole village killed."

He set the bucket on the cement lip of the well, and he looked so relaxed that she shivered.

"I do it for love of you. The child is my son now."

"It isn't just love, Telek. The village made your life hard since you were born. They always made you the outsider. Because of your mother. Because you went off in the woods alone. And since you saved their children, they flinch when you walk by. The children run when they see you. The village never accepted you and now they can't. You'll leave here anyway. You can't stay."

"Would you stay if I left?"

"If there is no place here for you, there is no place here for me. But we can't go with blood on our heads. We could follow the Germans and steal the baby after they leave the village."

"Once they have it, it will disappear. There is too much going on, too many soldiers, too many armies on the move."

"But killing them and running will kill the whole village. Go confess this, Telek. Save your soul before it's too late. Talk to the priest. Tell him you are going to kill everyone. I ask you to do it. For me." She walked away and disappeared down the mud lane that led to her house.

Telek turned and threw the second bucket down the well with such rage that it hit the side and nearly cracked. What was the point in confessing sins that were uncommitted?

Father Piotr was behind a curtain stained along the edges from his fingers pulling the cloth back and forth. It blocked the rest of the room from his bed where he sat and waited.

"When was your last confession, my son?" Father Piotr wanted this to be finished. Most of the villagers didn't confess anymore. It was forbidden as the Mass was forbidden.

"Maybe three years ago."

Father Piotr sighed. He hoped that Telek wasn't too scrupulous. It might take a long time.

"And what do you have to confess?"

"I came because Nelka asked me to do it."

A flash of anger came over Father Piotr. He didn't want Nelka to love this man, a common water carrier, but he asked automatically, "You have been lying with Nelka?"

"I've always done anything she asked. She never had a wish that I didn't take care of. I'll always take care of her." Telek brushed his hair out of his face nervously. This man was the priest, but he was Nelka's grandfather, and it made the confession difficult.

"Telek, you know that if we're discovered—you have to be quick."

"I'm going to kill the Brown Sister and the soldier who guards her room. I'll take the baby, get Nelka, and hide in the forest. I won't let the Oberführer take the baby with him, or Nelka."

"It is wrong to kill," the priest said automatically, but his heart had lifted. He was smiling. His anger at this man was gone. His granddaughter. The flesh of his flesh. And his great-grandson. They would live. He knew that Telek could survive in the woods. Telek would never let them die, but his priestly training made him speak almost automatically. "This is a noble thing to attempt, the saving of a child and its mother, but deliberate murder is a sin."

Kill the Germans, Father Piotr wanted to say. Kill them, and save Nelka and the baby.

"I could do it tonight, or tomorrow night. The SS and the Major always sit on Saturday night and drink. The soldiers get a ration of vodka. If I don't do this, the baby will disappear into Germany. God knows if we could ever find him there."

There was silence in the room except for the heavy breathing of the priest who panted as if he had run a race. He finally made his decision and spoke.

"I understand your desires, my son. I only ask this one thing. Do nothing until tomorrow night. Come back tomorrow morning and we will talk again. Do you repent the sins you have committed since your last confession?"

"Yes, Father." Telek didn't know if he did or not. He wasn't sure what was a sin and what wasn't since the war began.

"Then I absolve you of your sins. Say the rosary once. Before tomorrow morning. Pray to God to forgive you."

"And what about the other thing? What about the baby? I'm going to do it, Father."

"A planned murder will lie heavy on your soul. Do nothing to-night."

"And then?"

"Give me the night to think."

Telek hesitated. The Oberführer wasn't leaving tomorrow. He was sure of it. There were no movements of Russians in the area yet. "I'll wait a day, Father, and I'll say the rosary while I clean my guns and pack my knapsack."

Telek left the house, and Father Piotr sat fingering the cloth. This younger man's imperfect confession had brought it all back. "I must be losing my mind." The priest laughed.

The smell of the fields. Her scent. Hair the color of wheat and her eyes looking at him. Moist summer and the heat on his back as he lay on her. Cuckoos calling, and the far-off falling of water over rock.

The love had lost him any chance for advancement, and it had cost him the respect of the village. They came to him still, but they never loved him the way he wanted to be loved. He had not paid the price the people demanded in order to gain their love, and he had been a fail-ure. A man with no courage when they shot the Mayor and the Jews of the village.

"My soul is such a little one," he whispered. "It is so worthless." He sat for a long time until it began to get dark. Then he got up.

The Babe

"If we survive the next week, we might survive the war." Feliks stood holding his shovel, watching the plume of smoke rise into the tree branches. "The fucking Nazis are hiding the evidence from the Russian cameras. They're on the run."

Telek knew how hard this was for Feliks. The bodies of the village Jews, and the Mayor, and Feliks's brother reeked of the meaty stench of death and mildew and rot from leather and cloth. It was late afternoon, and the fires smoked fitfully. Feliks poured kerosene in a jar and threw it on the flames. They blazed up as Patryk dragged another of the corpses out of the trench. While the men dug, they had only one thought. When the bodies were dug up and burned, the ashes spread, and the evidence gone, would they be next?

Telek watched the day disappear and knew he had another job before he could sleep. He couldn't kill Sister Rosa and her guard and run into the forest leaving Magda sitting in her hut. The Major would take his revenge on the old woman because of Nelka. He had to tell her to take the children and hide in the pigsty when he killed the Germans.

It was obvious that the Germans would be leaving soon. A truck had passed through two days ago, and the Major had commandeered it. The Russians, like a deadly flood of gray water, were pouring over the forests and washing the rats out of their holes.

"Fill in the ditch." The Major stared at the men. He should shoot them so they wouldn't tell about those killed in the first taking of the village, but there was only him and sixteen soldiers. If he shot these men, the rest might riot. The people knew the Russians were coming.

He could see it in the way they met his eye now in the street, and why should he kill these peasants? He had followed Berlin's orders. Sometimes he thought everyone at High Command had gone mad. They should have pulled back weeks ago to defend Germany's border.

"Drink with me tonight, Telek." Feliks shoveled slowly but steadily. His brother was ash, and he wanted to get drunk. If he'd known the Nazis killed simpletons, he could have hidden him.

"I'm too tired. I need to rest. When will they pull out, Feliks?"

"When the trucks come from deeper in the forest, from Bialowieza. Soon."

Telek kept shoveling. He knew that he would have to wait until tomorrow night to take the baby back. Tonight he would tell Magda to go into the forest by dawn. The old woman moved slowly, but if he told her to go at dawn, they'd be hidden and safe by noon. The smoke blew in his face, and he knew that he breathed in the ashes of the dead. He kept shoveling and didn't raise his head until the ditch was filled.

"I will take the children and hide tomorrow, Telek." Magda coughed and held on to the table so she wouldn't fall. The grippe had come suddenly. Telek stared at her for a few minutes. Her cheeks were red with fever. Magda couldn't survive long in the forest with the grippe.

"I'll have to kill the soldier and the German woman. There will be revenge on the village." Magda nodded. There was nothing else to be done now, and then it was best to hide until the Germans retreated and the main force of the Russians had passed over them. By the time Telek killed the woman and the guard tomorrow night, Magda would be hidden with Hansel and Gretel in the hidey-hole.

Back in the village, Telek stripped naked in the darkness of night and washed with pails of water and lye soap that burned his skin, expunging the stink of death before he touched Nelka.

Hansel had listened, eavesdropping outside the hut, breathing through his mouth so he wouldn't make any noise. Telek would get killed, and maybe Nelka would get killed too. He shoved his fist in his mouth so he wouldn't cry out. Someone had to do something for Nelka and Telek. Someone had to help them.

Night came later now. It was still the same cold and chill as it grew dark, but the earth had the smell of mud during the day and the water from melted snow flowed over the land and filled the rivers until it was as if the whole earth wept. The curfew in the village was tighter. Everyone lay quietly in their houses and waited for what was coming.

Father Piotr thought about going to the church and praying. He wanted to kneel down and ask forgiveness for all his sins, but it seemed hypocritical. He picked up the poker from the fire and shifted it in his hand. Then he laid it down in its usual place and sighed. He went to the curtain in front of the kitchen and pulled it back.

There were three knives. The carving knife was worn so thin it might break. The second knife was small, for paring vegetables. The third knife was his newest, a gift from the butcher when he said his confession before Christmas. Father Piotr put the knife in the pocket of his coat and slipped a small jar of homemade vodka in his other pocket. He looked at the clock, and impulsively took it off the hook where it hung. The Russians would steal it. They liked clocks. He threw it on the floor and stamped it to trash with his boot. Then he went out, closing the door carefully.

"I should have waited another hour," he muttered, but he was afraid to wait. He might fall asleep. He might be too tired. He might lose his nerve.

The woods were so dark that Hansel fell into the ditch twice when he wandered off the road. It had been hard keeping awake until Magda finally fell into a deep sleep, her breath rasping like she was breathing underwater. Her face was flushed, and Hansel knew she was sick.

If he was caught on the street after curfew, the soldiers would shoot him. Hansel shook his head. He could slip behind the houses. The shadows were dark, and he didn't care if he got caught. He had to tell Father Piotr. Father Piotr was Magda's brother. He was the priest. Priests were supposed to help people. Hansel ran faster toward the silent village.

———

Hansel stood at the bottom of the steps. He was panting, but he gasped it out. "You have to help them. Help them. They're going to die, Nelka, Telek—"

Father Piotr raised his arm like he would strike the child. "Go home. Go back to Magda. Tell her to go into the woods. Run. Don't let the sentry on the road see you. Get back to the hut and take Magda and Gretel to the secret place in the forest. Take them now. Run!"

Something in his eyes made Hansel turn and race back toward the forest. He slipped behind a house and then suddenly stopped. He couldn't bear not seeing what was going to happen. Hansel turned back and crept from house to house in the dark of a moonless night.

———

Father Piotr didn't see the small shape of the boy come up behind him. He walked down the street, not bothering to stay in the shadows himself. The soldiers knew that he visited the sick at night. He moved, lurching, almost as if he were drunk. He was glad the dogs had been shot. If the dogs had barked at him as he walked down the street, he might have lost his nerve.

Hansel followed Father Piotr and nearly called out, but now it all seemed very scary and serious. The boy followed, creeping, his mouth dry, watching for the sentries.

The house where the Brown Sister slept was near the far end of the village. It had a wooden porch that lay in shadows, and Father Piotr saw the soldier. He had been there since eight when the guard began for the night. At dawn he would be relieved.

Father Piotr smiled at the young soldier who didn't stand when he saw it was the priest.

"You're breaking the curfew, old man," he said in bad Polish.

The soldier had only been shaving a few years. He was the boy whose arm was injured at the Russian front. The arm had healed, and he picked up enough Polish to be useful, so the Major kept him.

"Jolanta's child is dying. Please let me go on," Father Piotr whispered.

"No one is allowed on the street. Major's orders. She'll have to die without you."

The priest sank down on the step as if exhausted. Thank God the boy spoke so quietly.

"Let an old man rest, my son." He fumbled in his pocket and brought out the jar. "A sip of this will give me strength to get home." He offered the jar to the boy.

"Against the rules to drink on guard duty." The boy smiled, took the jar, and drank deeply. As the jar tipped up, Father Piotr took out the knife and hid it beside his knee.

Hansel, lying flat in the shadow of a house, saw the flash of metal. His legs began to shake, but he couldn't stop watching.

When the sentry tipped the jar a second time, Father Piotr reached up with a stabbing slash, the full weight of his shoulder turned into the blow, and cut the pale throat that curved outward slightly and bobbed with the swallowing. The soldier made a bubbling noise, and the jar fell onto the mud beside the steps. That was the only noise except for the splash of blood on the wood.

Father Piotr held the boy so he wouldn't fall while his blood pumped out, his hand over the young man's mouth to hush the gurgling. The priest was soaked with the hot liquid, and the stench was all around them. The soldier was limp, the blood seeped slowly, and Father Piotr still held him.

I have to move, he thought, but he stayed very still with the boy in his arms, feeling the blood soak into his coat and wet his skin. He forgot to say a prayer over the dead body.

After what seemed to Hansel a long time, the priest stood and, as quietly as he could, let the soldier's body bump down a step so he could be propped against the post that held the handrail at the bottom. If anyone saw the guard from down the street, he might think the boy was asleep.

Father Piotr climbed the stairs. The house had not been repaired before the Brown Sister moved in, and the policeman who had lived there before the Germans killed him never had a strong bolt. No one would rob the police.

If they put on a new bolt, she'll scream before I can get in, the priest thought, but his shoulder crashing against the door ripped the bolt off at the screws where the wood was rotten. He was inside.

The woman struggled out of the dress she had been taking off, and that gave Father Piotr the second he needed. As she flung off the brown cloth, her arms up in the air, mouth open in surprise, he stepped to her and slashed at her throat.

It caught the chin and part of her throat. She fell backward onto the bed, and Father Piotr fell on top of her. A choking scream came out of her mouth, but he dug the knife into her throat and twisted it with the ferocious strength of his own terror. The woman's scream became a gurgle as she thrashed against him. The baby began to cry from its box in the corner, and the woman battered his back with her hands while he turned the knife against the gristle of her neck.

She finally lay limp, and he staggered back from the bed, leaving the knife in her neck. Her eyes followed him as he moved to the wall and leaned against it gasping, and her eyes stayed open after she died. Whimpering, he moved to a corner of the room to avoid her stare. The baby cried louder, and Father Piotr heard steps outside. The door, flopping loose, pushed open slowly, and Nelka was there.

"My God! My God!"

"Take the baby," he croaked. "Get Telek. Run."

She moved to the baby and picked him up. Clutching him to her, she stared at Father Piotr.

"Come with us," she said.

He shook his head.

"But they'll kill you." They stood in the house, the smell of blood around them, the sound of the hungry baby growing louder. "You have to run too."

"If they catch the murderer, they won't follow you until morning. They may not find me here for hours."

"If you go home and clean yourself, they won't suspect you. Who'd suspect you?" She was sobbing. "Telek wanted to run. I said they'd kill all the village if the baby disappeared. The SS would kill them all. You want them to find you here?"

"They have to kill someone for this." He was terribly tired. This beautiful girl. This beautiful child.

"Take the babe and find Telek. Run." She moved to embrace him, but he couldn't bear for the sticky blood to mark her and threw his arms out to keep her away.

She gave him a last look, turned, and moved swiftly out the door. She pulled open her coat and blouse and pushed the baby's mouth onto her nipple as she moved. His wails turned to sucking as she disappeared down the porch steps.

Father Piotr didn't like to stay in the room with the dead woman. He went outside and sat on the porch at the top of the stairs and waited. A man would come at four to relieve the sentry. The priest wished he had the rest of the vodka. He stared out into the darkness, sitting above the crumpled body of the soldier.

Still hidden, in the shadows, Hansel knew he had to move. Nelka had taken the baby and gone, and he had to go back to Magda. He had to tell her.

The child crept up the stairs, trying not to look at the soldier's body. "Father Piotr?"

The priest didn't recognize Hansel at first.

"It's me. Hansel."

Father Piotr stared at the child.

"I'm going to tell Magda. They'll be mad now. The Major and the Nazis."

"Tell Magda." Father Piotr ran his hand over his face, leaving streaks of blood on the pale skin. Hansel shivered. Father Piotr rallied for a moment and remembered his sister.

"Oh God! Run, boy. Tell Magda that I am a dead man. Tell her to hide in the woods. Tell her to take both of you with her. They'll find me and want to kill her because she is my kin. Run!"

"You should run too." Hansel moved forward and took the old man's cold hand, trying not think that the wetness was blood. "You can come with us."

"There isn't time to speak of this. It's done. Now run, boy! Don't look back, and don't get caught. Tell Magda and go into the forest. There's time to hide. Run!"

Hansel dropped the man's hand and turned. He ran behind the house, into the shadows, and didn't stop running until he came to the bend in the road. Then he slowed, breathless and aching, creeping into the trees to avoid the sentry. Magda was so sick. He had to wake her up. He had to get her and Gretel out of the hut. Hansel began to run again, ignoring the pain in his side.

———

The whole village lay in silence, not even an owl breaking the peace. The sentries stayed near the Major's offices and were nearly asleep. Father Piotr was the only fully awake person in the village, and he was like a man awake but dreaming.

I didn't ever tell her how much I love her, the priest was thinking. His mind was confused for a moment. Did he mean the woman? The beautiful woman in the field of wheat ? The only one he had ever loved? Surely he had told her.

"I told her I loved her, and it was true," he muttered. But he hadn't told Nelka.

He knew he was going to be cast into the outer darkness when he died. He had murdered in cold blood and had never told Nelka that he loved her. It was the final, crushing sin.

At first he thought it was his heart he heard as he sat crying, but it was deeper than heartbeats and slower in rhythm. It was the booming of massive artillery. The Russian line was moving, and of all the villagers, he was the first to hear the guns as they came closer.

At three in the morning, the Major saw the priest sitting on the steps. The Major called out to him, and when the man didn't move or speak, the Major walked up the steps past the bloody body of the young soldier who was so obviously dead that the Major didn't even roll him off the steps and examine him. The door hung ajar, and it swung open slowly. He saw the knife in the woman's throat, the empty box where the baby had slept, and knew what had happened. He left the priest sitting. He had seen men in that condition at the Russian front. The man wouldn't run.

The Brown Sister had been a cruel bitch, but a German bitch nevertheless. She had to be avenged, but it was the soldier's corpse that made the Major angry. To endure Russian bullets and blizzards and die on a porch for nothing, butchered like a hog. It was too unfair. Going back down the street, the Major called softly, and the soldier posted at his office ran toward him.

"Take the priest. He's killed the boy and Sister Rosa. Wake the others. Get Wiktor, but don't wake the Oberführer and don't tell him about this yet. Let him sleep. This is our concern."

He went inside and sat at the desk. It created terrible complications. The Oberführer would want to kill the whole village, but there were only sixteen—no, fifteen, he corrected himself—fifteen soldiers. The fucking Poles. They had guns hidden. He knew it. "I won't have my men killed in this dung heap," he muttered. Germany was going to need them.

And his orders were clear. No bodies were to be left for the Russians to find. He had just disposed of all the old corpses. They were to leave nothing to photograph.

The Major spit on the floor. It was insanity. They should stop this and pull back into Germany. Make a line and hold it. All this delay while soldiers dug up bodies and made bonfires. And they said the trains still carried Jews eastward when they should have filled every train with supplies to help the army's retreat. Madness.

Wiktor came in, wearing no coat in his haste. "Heil Hitler." He saluted correctly.

"The priest killed Sister Rosa. And Corporal Elend."

Wiktor sucked his breath in. It was bad. He wanted to run, but he didn't dare move.

"Both dead, and the priest sitting on the steps. Covered in blood." The Major massaged his face with his hands. The trucks were coming. They didn't have enough time. "Take three soldiers and find that girl, Nelka. It was her baby."

Wiktor nodded. If only the girl was cowering somewhere with the brat. The Oberführer would get to take them as planned, or kill them. They'd die either way, and it might save the rest of the village. It might save him. He left running.

"He won't find her," the Major muttered. "She has Telek. They're in the woods by now."

And there wasn't time to burn the priest's body. The trucks could come by noon. The Oberführer might insist on some semblance of a trial. The man kept acting as if this collapsing world was all some great plan that worked normally. The reality was that the Poles wanted to kill every German on the earth. The Russians had broken through the German lines and were moving down on them. A hundred thousand Germans had been sent to Siberia, and millions had died, and the Oberführer was spending his time measuring babies' noses and having transfusions of blood. The Major groaned and spit on the floor.

He opened the drawer of the desk and took out a flask of brandy. He sipped it slowly. There was the problem of the priest. That he could take care of by dawn. The woman and baby were gone. He was sure of it. He sipped and stared out at the darkness. Dawn was hours away. Anything might happen before dawn.

The guns were shelling all the time now. The Russian and the Mechanik and the others stayed in front, looking for stray units of Germans, usable guns and trucks, clearing abandoned tanks from the road, checking each village for German soldiers. The Russian troops killed every German they found. Wounded Germans, Germans barely breathing, Germans with hands up and guns thrown down, the Russians killed them all. Like shooting rats.

For days now they had backtracked. Soon they would be at the village called Piaski. The Russian said that was the village closest to where he had left the children in November. Someone would have seen them. She was a smart girl. She would have found the village.

"Mechanik! Get your ass up here!"

They had found another tank. He had to try and start it so it wouldn't block the road when the main force of men and equipment needed to pass. He climbed up on the cold metal and hoped that no one was inside. He hated working on the machine with a dead body beside him.

"What's the date?" he asked the Russian.

"It's about the fifteenth of March, Mechanik. Maybe the sixteenth."

"How long until we get to that village? Piaski?"

"Maybe by the twenty-first. Maybe sooner if you get the damn tank off the road."

The Mechanik opened the lid of the tank and looked in. No corpses. It was a good sign.

The Oberführer had woken up. He heard the sound of voices, dressed quickly, and went outside. The trucks must have come already. He hoped so. He'd been in this village too long.

"What's happening?" he asked a soldier running past. "Are the trucks here?"

"The Major could tell you, sir. I've been ordered to his office."

The Oberführer sighed. The man was lying. The soldier knew what was happening, but he was too loyal to the Major to answer a simple question. Those men who had been at the Russian front would all have to be killed someday. Their loyalty to the Führer and the larger plan had been compromised by the stress of battle. Their usefulness was over.

When he walked in the office, the first thing the SS man saw was the priest.

"The priest has murdered a soldier, Oberführer. The boy who served so bravely at the Russian front. He also killed Sister Rosa."

The Oberführer stared at the priest. "Why—" he began, and then he knew. The man was the great-grandfather of the chosen baby. That made him Nelka's grandfather.

"Where's Nelka? The baby?"

"Gone, Oberführer. The man Telek is also gone."

"Kill the priest. Have the village present, and then kill every third person. Nelka had other family? An old woman? Two children who lived with her? They're related somehow. You'll have to send soldiers to get them. None of the family can live now. We'll kill all of them."

The Major breathed hard. His hands trembled. The bastard with his orders. He'd never fought a single battle. "There are problems with that, Oberführer. My orders are to leave no bodies. We just dug up those that were shot when the village was taken and burned them. There isn't time to burn all those people before the trucks get here, and the trucks can't wait."

"Shoot them in the forest. It's deep enough to hide anything."

"If we begin shooting women and children now, we might not see Germany again."

"Are you telling me that a German woman and a German soldier were murdered in cold blood, and there will be no reparations?"

"I have only fifteen soldiers. There are fifty men who are able in this village, and women who would fight if we start shooting children."

"They have nothing to fight with."

"God knows what they have. I don't want to find out. I'll kill the priest. He's the murderer. He admits it. That's justice."

"I demand that you kill at least a third of this village."

"And what do we do with the bodies? Take them all the way to Germany with us?" The Major was standing now. The priest sat slumped and leaning against the wall. One eye was swollen shut and his mouth was bloody.

"You will follow my orders or be court-martialed when we return to Germany."

"And Nelka?" The Major had never intended to let the Oberführer know that he knew about Nelka and the blood. He had never intended to say anything, but he was angry. "As head of this village, I hear many things, Oberführer. I heard that you used the woman, Nelka, for your own purposes. Something to do with transfusions, I believe."

The Oberführer felt the anger rising and twisting in him. Who had told? Not Sister Rosa. She would never go against his will. It had to be the bitch, Nelka.

"I also seem to remember that someone reported something about Nelka's ancestors. It was rumored that Nelka's great-grandmother was a Gypsy. That makes Nelka a subhuman."

"It was a jealous rumor. She is of pure blood."

"In some circles—at home—the rumor might be believed. It's too bad, really." The Major didn't smile, but he let his voice relax into amusement. "That would make you one of them now."

The SS man took a step forward and the Major put his hand lightly over the pistol at his side as if resting it there.

The rumors of Gypsy blood could have been right, the Oberführer thought, and it would end his career. Nelka had known all along. The bitch hadn't told him. She sat on her chair and watched him being contaminated. His hatred of her made him begin to pant. He stepped to the priest and kicked him twice, as hard as he could, but it didn't help. The rage was so great it made him sweat.

He needed to kill the Major and all the soldiers. The Major could have told all of them about the blood. He had to kill them, and he knew it was impossible. If he killed one soldier, the others would kill him. They had that loyalty to each other that the Russian front had bred. All he could do was hope that they died in the fighting of the next months.

He had planned so carefully for how he would live after the war if they lost. "I am the Chalice," he whispered. The great truths had been poured into him, the selected one. He held the knowledge, and if the war was lost, he would be able to teach the next generation. But he must be pure. He must be the purest of the pure, and Nelka had ruined that. And Nelka must have told the old woman. The children would know. The boy was always hanging on to Nelka.

"You can at least round up the old woman and those brats that live with her."

The Major hesitated. If it satisfied the Oberführer, it might be possible. Then the man would let him get on with the job of retreating and saving as many of his men as he could.

"We'll execute the priest. When the trucks get here, we'll collect the old woman and the two children. They can go with us until we get to a place where they can be disposed of."

"How are you going to kill the priest?"

The Major looked at the old man. He had murdered the boy.

"I'll shoot him myself."

"It's almost dawn. What's the date, Major?"

"The twentieth," the Major said and then remembered that he'd been up all night and it was a new day. "The twenty-first," he corrected himself. "It's the twenty-first of March."

Telek carried most of the food and blankets and a heavy canvas cloth they could use for shelter. That and his guns and ammunition weighed him down, but he moved quickly. Nelka wore all her warm clothes and carried the baby and a light pack with the flour and bread she had in her kitchen when she got back to the house carrying the baby.

"We have to go to Magda's first," she said.

"I told Magda to take the children and go into the forest at dawn, after I got back from burning the bodies. They may not find the bodies until the guard changes at four. They won't think of Magda in the confusion. They may not think of her at all."

"You're sure she'll leave at dawn?"

"I told her to. Magda and the children will be all right, but we could get caught if we try to double around and get to the hut. They guard that end of the road at night."

"As soon as we can, we'll go get them."

"When the Germans are gone. Feliks thought it would be in the next few days. Walk faster. We have to get to the swamp so our tracks can't be seen."

"Did you make your confession to Father Piotr, Telek?"

His silence told her.

"Oh God. He saved you from killing them."

Telek took small steps so she could easily walk where he put his feet and avoid the pools of water that were growing deeper around them. The spongy peat gave under his feet. He knew where they were going, and it would be shelter for a few days. Then they would move on.

"He saved the baby," she said.

Telek couldn't talk about it. He had wanted to kill the woman and the soldier for Nelka. He flushed in his shame that an old man had done it for him. They walked in silence for an hour and then rested for a few minutes on a sandy spit in the bog.

"The guns are closer." Nelka adjusted the baby and shifted the sack on her back.

"They won't come through this part of the forest. They'll stay on the roads. Trucks and tanks can't come over this ground."

Nelka looked up and gasped. It was like a bonfire in front of them, but there was no roar of fire. It jumped and moved and leapt in the air and then died down to appear again farther on. The dank layer of water vapor in the air was lit by blue, orange, and gold light swirling in front of them.

"Swamp fire." Telek put his arm around her shoulders.

"They say it's witches leading you into the bogs where you'll never get out."

"There are no witches, darling."

Nelka shuddered and made the sign of the cross in the air. They stood close until the fiery light died out and left them again in the swirling fog. "We'll go and find Magda in a few days?"

"When it's safe. I don't want to lead them to her."

In a few more hours they would be on a larger island of sand where they could rest. The Germans wouldn't follow them so deep into the swamp of the forest. Not with the Russian guns so close. They moved on slowly now, the water sometimes as deep as Nelka's knees.

"We don't have to leave until noon, child. Let me sleep."

Hansel had tried three times to get Magda up. She was too weak, and didn't understand what he kept telling her, and then she would fall back into a feverish sleep. He thought of taking Gretel to the hidey-hole and coming back for Magda, but Gretel might wander off and get lost.

Hansel groaned and rubbed his eyes. He wouldn't leave Magda. He'd never leave her. Finally, just before dawn, Magda woke. She had feverish memories of what the boy had said during the night, and then she heard it. Guns. Big ones. The front was moving toward them.

Telek said it was time to hide in the sty. She had told him she would be gone with the children by dawn. She sighed. There was still work to be done. She knew the Russians. They'd steal everything. And if they stole her baskets of medical tools, how would she support herself?

"Magda? We have to go. Quick. I told you."

"I'm trying, boy. It isn't a good morning." She coughed deeply.

"They must have Father Piotr now. Nelka and the baby are already gone."

Magda heard him distantly. It was such a lot of work to get her boots on.

"Telek will bring her, and the baby." Magda sighed deeply and sat down in the chair. They would need water. The bucket was empty.

"Magda." Hansel was crying. "We have to run. They'll get us."

It was barely light outside when she opened the door. Magda sniffed the air. They had burned the bodies of the dead. Dug them up and burned them. No peace even after death. The ground around the creek was soft and the mud covered her boots to her ankles. She pulled her feet out of the black earth with an effort and smiled. The land was running water. Weeping like a child. Everything moist and muddy and the night fog lying heavy.

Hansel kept talking to her, but she didn't understand most of it. The war was slipping past them, and perhaps they could have some peace. Telek said if they left by noon it would be safe. The boy must have been dreaming. Her brother would never kill. That wasn't his sort of sin.

Magda dipped her bucket into the creek and lifted it half full. They wouldn't need more than that. They'd be gone by noon. Her head spun with the fever. The boy's voice was very far away. She had to concentrate. It was a long walk into the woods.

The sound of the guns told every man and woman in Piaski what was happening, but they couldn't rejoice. The Germans weren't gone yet, and who knew what the Russians would be like.

"The women will have to hide in the woods for a week or two," Patryk told his wife. "The Russians will be like wolves."

She nodded. They sat in silence thinking of what to take with them.

"Raus! Raus! Raus!" The German order chilled them, and Patryk shuddered. They both stood and moved to the door. He picked up the boy and carried him. The boy could walk, but Patryk carried him anyway. With the child in his arms, he turned toward Zanna. She touched his forehead and made the sign of the cross on his skin. Then she made a cross on the boy's head.

Patryk pushed aside the heavy hair that hadn't been braided yet for the day and made the same sign on her forehead. Then they went outside.

"Raus! Raus!" the soldiers screamed.

"They're excited—" Patryk began and then stopped. He didn't want to frighten the boy.

It was the morning of March twenty-first. The Mechanik moved at a trot. It had to be close. He was beginning to recognize landmarks in the fields.

"How far to Piaski?" he asked the Russian.

"You'll see it today. What's there for you, brother?"

"Something, I hope."

"God willing you find your woman, brother."

The Russian could be right. What if she had gone looking for the children? It was something she might have done. Perhaps she had to stay and take care of them. With any luck they would find no Germans and have no battles. His mind couldn't hold that much hopefulness.

———

Everyone in the village gathered in the square. Not a child cried or made noise. They waited, watched by the soldiers who carried their guns at the ready and the machine guns mounted on the trucks.

The door of the Major's office opened and he came out. Behind him were two soldiers with a man between them. They almost had to carry him. His feet dragged the way men moved when they had been tortured and couldn't walk. It was Father Piotr, beaten so badly that only one eye was open. His mouth and coat were crusted with blood. A gasp shook the people like a light wind.

"This man," the Major said, "has been arrested for the murder of a German soldier and the murder of Sister Rosa, the Brown Sister, a German national, a woman. He confessed to this crime. Tell the people, priest."

Father Piotr opened his mouth. He hung between the two soldiers who grunted as they held up his limp weight. He wanted to tell the people how sinful he was. How sorry he felt that he'd failed them all these years. How they shouldn't worry about him. He wasn't important anymore.

It was hard to speak. His teeth were loose, and his tongue swollen. He opened and shut his mouth, but no sound came.

"Are you guilty of these crimes?" the Major shouted.

Father Piotr nodded. Those and others. The women. The drinking when he was younger. The throwing away of all his chances. Hating this village. Sneering at the uneducated peasants. Not taking care of his mother. Not telling Nelka that he loved her and the babe. All of it.

The soldiers turned loose of the priest. He fell to the mud as if already dead and lay with his mouth open. Stepping close, the Major put the gun to the back of the man's head.

"For the boy," he muttered as he pulled the trigger. The priest's body jerked twice and lay still. It was a better death than he had given the woman and the boy, the Major thought.

"Put his body in the shed behind my office. He goes on the truck with us."

"The woman, Nelka, and her child have fled the village," the Oberführer shouted at the villagers' blank faces. "We know the woman was involved in this crime. Do any of you have any knowledge of where she has fled?"

It was asinine, thought the Mayor. No one would ever say if they knew. The village square was silent except for the sound of the artillery in the distance. The Major's head was beginning to ache and the sun was barely up. The people all shook their heads.

"Since he confessed to the murder, only the priest will die." The Major didn't look at the SS officer. "But be warned. Today every person will stay in their house. Any person seen on the street, and this includes children, will be shot. You will go inside your houses and stay."

The Major knew it wouldn't satisfy the SS man, but that was too damn bad. They couldn't leave a pile of dead women and children for the Russians to photograph.

The trucks came at seven o'clock. The Major was pleased to see Unterfeldwebel Rahn driving a truck. At least there was one man he could trust. Everything was loaded in an hour. The Major made sure that all the files and papers and every single note and memo were packed and put on a truck. They had to get back to defend Germany. The people at home were sitting with the Russian guns moving down on them.

Two soldiers brought out the priest's body and carried it to the back of a truck that stood apart from the others. The Major looked in and saw ten or fifteen people crouched under the canvas top. Women and children. A few men. Jews he supposed. He was surprised. He thought all the Jews had been killed.

"Where are these people going?"

Unterfeldwebel Rahn shrugged. "We're taking them to the railroad line. They're the last. Orders are that we bring them with us."

"Put the priest's body in," the Major said to his men.

"He's dead. What's the point of putting him on a train?" Sergeant Rahn kicked at Father Piotr's corpse with his boot.

"I'm ordered to leave no bodies. There isn't time to burn it."

"So throw him in the woods."

"No. You throw him on the train. Orders direct from Berlin. We leave no corpses. None."

"Yes, sir."

The soldiers tossed Father Piotr's body in the back of the truck. The Major was exhausted, but he would do his duty as a soldier until he died. The Sergeant, who had been on the unlucky pig hunt, met his eye and nodded. At least one man understood the problems.

"Major? Do you know where the woman, Magda, lives?" The Oberführer had not shaven, and the Major was pleased to see that his shirt was dirty at the neck.

"Somewhere in the woods, off the road."

The Oberführer turned and walked to the nearest house. He opened the door and went in.

"You, woman!" He gestured to Zanna, who sat at the table with her son.

"Heil Hitler," she whispered. Patryk stood up and put his hand on her shoulder.

"You'll ride in the truck and show the driver where the Gypsy, Magda, lives."

Tears began to run down Zanna's face. Magda had delivered her children and tried to save her two daughters, the angels, when they were so sick and died.

"There's no need for tears." The Oberführer smiled. "We're merciful even though decent Germans have been killed by the trash allowed to live in this village. We are merciful. You show us the house, and then you can walk home." He smiled again and drew his pistol.

"I'll go with you," Patryk said. "The woman isn't well."

"No. Your wife can do this."

Patryk swayed slightly, and the Oberführer watched him with interest. The man had almost jumped him. Even though the peasant faced a loaded pistol. The Oberführer admired the spirit and wondered if he should shoot the man.

"Be sensible. You have a family to think of." The Oberführer smiled at the peasant, and backed to the door. He gestured to Zanna, who caught her breath in a sob and followed him. She didn't look back at Patryk and the boy.

"I never played with that boy," her son said suddenly.

The Oberführer stared at the child.

"The witch's nephew. But Halina did. They played off in the forest sometimes."

The soldiers put Zanna next to the driver in the truck carrying the priest's body. They waited for long minutes, and then a second truck fell in behind them with the Oberführer and six soldiers. The black Mercedes had been set on fire right in the shed where it had been stored. The fire burned quickly with a muffled explosion when the gas tank caught. It never would have gotten through the mud all the way to Germany, but they wouldn't leave it for the Russians to take back to Moscow.

"Take the Oberführer and this woman where she directs," the Major ordered Sergeant Rahn. "We'll rendezvous on the road two miles from the village where the crossroad is. Be quick."

Major Frankel waved the two trucks on. His headache was less intense now. The Oberführer had something to keep him busy and out of the way. The people were quiet, the trucks nearly ready. Soon they would be gone. He knew that even men with one eye would find battles to fight in Germany before the year was up. He welcomed the clean terror of battle after the years of sitting in the mud of this village. He felt like he was going to a lover.

The sun was up now, and Hansel kept wringing his hands as he tried to make Magda move more quickly. She was dressed and he hoped it wasn't too late. The fire had died out in the firebox. Only coals were left. The oven door stood ajar. The sleeping platform was stripped of blankets. The wooden bowls were gone from the table. The pegs on the wall were empty.

Hansel looked around at the bare hut. "Hurry, Magda. Please. Just come on."

And then Magda stopped what she was doing with the basket. She turned and stared at Hansel, and he heard it too. Voices. Speaking in German.

Magda thought she would faint. Her heart beat so unsteadily, she had to gasp for air. Looking out the partly cracked door, Magda saw them coming through the trees. German soldiers, the SS officer with them. It was only a little after eight, but they had come already.

She looked at the floorboards where she had hidden her food, but she had taken the boards up. They lay loose on the floor. There wasn't time for the children to crawl down and then replace all the boards perfectly. She looked desperately around the hut. Hansel had not been dreaming. Her mind moved in jerks and she couldn't think what to do. She stared at Hansel, who wrung his hands over and over.

The boy suddenly leaped toward the oven. He opened the door and stared at Magda.

"It can hold both of you. Quick, my darlings, do what I say. Inside. Both of you. Curl up."

"It's hot." Gretel frowned.

"It's hot, but you can do this." Magda took off her coat and put it on the oven's floor.

"Get in, lie still and for God's sake, whatever you hear, don't make a noise."

"But you, Magda? Where will you hide?"

"Hush, my little boy. Obey me."

"I won't go without you."

Magda slapped his cheek so gently, it was like a kiss. "Obey me, boy."

Gretel climbed inside. The boy followed her, giving a single dry sob, and they curled up in tight balls.

"Don't move an inch, Hansel. If the door latches shut, you can't open it from inside."

"It's hot. I can't breathe—" Gretel began.

"Silence." Magda's voice was harsh.

Hansel wanted to put his hand over Gretel's mouth, but he couldn't reach her. The metal was hot, and he tried to keep his back from pressing on it. The fire was out, but the metal still burned his back. He bit his lip hard so he wouldn't scream.

The door banged open.

"Take her," the Oberführer shouted. The soldiers grabbed Magda. One of them went to the boards lifted from the floor. He lay on his belly and looked under the hut.

"Where are the children?" The Oberführer spoke such thickly accented Polish, and his voice was so choked with rage, that Magda couldn't understand at first.

"Their mother came a week ago. She took them with her. She's trying to stay in front of the Russians." Magda looked him in the eye as she spoke. The lie was her death sentence, she knew it, but it didn't matter anymore. The truth or a lie, they'd both kill her.

"You witch! You knew what your brother was planning, didn't you?" The Oberführer slapped Magda. One of the soldiers threw a board and it hit the oven with a hard clang. Magda stared. The oven door had latched shut.

Magda collapsed on the floor as if she were too weak to stand. She crawled toward the oven.

"Get the woman. Put her in the truck."

Magda reached the oven and pulled herself up on it. As the soldier grabbed her shoulder, she slipped the latch up and pulled. The door came free as the soldiers dragged her outside.

"Search the woods."

The SS man was screaming at the soldiers, but he didn't panic Rahn, the stolid Unterfeldwebel. Sergeant Rahn stood and thought. They had to meet the others. If the caravan of trucks from the village left them behind, they were only a handful of soldiers on the road with two trucks, a bunch of Jews, and a dead priest. They'd be easy targets.

"We can't risk it." He spoke very respectfully but firmly. "The children are gone. If they're in the woods, we could hunt for days and not find them."

"Do what I said!" The SS man didn't shout, but he moved as if he'd hit the soldier.

"The Russians could be here in hours, sir. If they catch an SS officer—" Sergeant Rahn waited. The man was a fool. He hadn't even shot the boar when he had the best gun in the forest.

The Oberführer paused. The soldier was right. The Russians wouldn't let him die quickly if they caught him. He'd be sent back to Moscow and then on to Siberia. He couldn't starve to death in Siberia. He was destined to carry the truth on for the next generation.

"Torch the hut. Throw the old woman in the truck. There is one more chance. The child Halina may know where the children are."

He watched while one of the soldiers stepped to the side of the hut and emptied a tin of kerosene on the bale of straw piled to keep the cold out. He threw a match on it and it exploded into flame. The sun-warmed wood of the boards caught, and the man lifted a burning stick from the wood piled next to the straw and threw it on the roof. The soldiers watched for a minute while the roof began to catch. They ran back to the road, dragging Magda between two of them.

Zanna stood beside the truck. She couldn't bear to look at Magda. She crossed herself with a slight gesture hoping that the soldiers wouldn't see. "God forgive me," she whispered.

The Oberführer stared at the woods. The smoke rose in a plume. They had the woman. If Halina couldn't lead them to the children, they would probably die on the road anyway. Maybe he would even see them walking with their mother. He could watch for them. Nelka and the baby had slipped through his fingers, but he had more important things to think about.

He had to survive the war. Some men who understood the principles, the philosophy, had to survive so the next generation could be taught. Even if these incompetent fools lost the war, the ideas would live. He suddenly remembered the peasant woman standing beside the truck.

"The woman who showed us the hut," he said to the Sergeant in German. "Take her in the woods and kill her."

Sergeant Rahn was flustered for the first time that day. "The Major said we were to leave no bodies, sir. We'll have to put her body in the truck."

Color began to climb up the Oberführer's neck. The flush spread to his cheeks. It was probably better if this war was lost. The German people weren't ready for glory. They still did not obey instantly with the joy that the new world order demanded. The Sergeant was German, but he wasn't much better than the Poles. He stepped forward and slapped the Sergeant so hard it made him stagger. When the man regained his balance, the SS man slapped him again.

"Take her in the woods. Shoot her. Then we'll go. Those are my orders. If I wanted her body in the truck, I would have said so. You have disobeyed my order. I will have you court-martialed when we are in Germany." He drew his pistol. The rage he had felt at Nelka in the office came back to him, and he nearly shot the Sergeant.

The Unterfeldwebel saw the look in the officer's eyes, and he saluted smartly.

"Heil Hitler, Oberführer. It will be done."

He turned and grabbed the woman's arm. Zanna didn't resist, but she began to pray under her breath. She didn't understand German, but this couldn't be good to be taken into the woods.

The Sergeant dragged her through the towering trees until they were out of sight of the truck. Sergeant Rahn's face was grim. He had only said to the Oberführer what the Major had said. The orders had come from Berlin. No bodies left for the Russians to find.

"The Major was a hero on the Russian front," the Sergeant muttered. "That SS bastard never fought in his life. Fucking athletic medals. He might just fall off the truck before we get back to Germany. God knows, he won't help with the fighting when we get there."

Zanna stared at him in terror. They stopped finally, both of them out of breath. He turned to the woman and took his pistol from the holster. Zanna didn't cry but fell on her knees before him. She thought of the child inside her, the new one she carried. She tried to raise her skirt and expose the round of flesh that was beginning to show. She said nothing but struggled with her coat and skirt and kept gesturing to her belly.

He ignored her and pointed the gun. Unterfeldwebel Rahn fired twice. The bullets went into the earth beside her knee. She froze in terror and stared up at him. He pushed her down on her side and put his finger to his lips. Then he holstered his gun, turned, and ran back to the truck.

Zanna lay on the forest floor until she heard the truck engines start and move off. She began to crawl when the noise grew faint. She struggled to a bush and lay under it until she could control her breathing. Then she staggered to her feet and ran in a clumsy lope toward the village. She turned her head and tried to see the hut. There was only a line of smoke in the sky and the smell of burning wood.

She didn't understand why he hadn't killed her. She would never understand until she died, but she would pray for him forever, she vowed. Even though he was a Nazi. He had spared her and the child, so she would pray for him.

The Sergeant saluted the SS man again. "It's done, sir."

"One bullet is all a Pole is worth, Sergeant. Never forget that."

"Yes, sir." The man stood at attention while the SS man smiled at him for the first time. If the woman screamed or cried out, the Oberführer would shoot him for disobeying.

The Oberführer climbed into the cab of the truck, and the Sergeant got into the driver's side. Sergeant Rahn glanced at the SS man beside him. His chest was full of medals.

The Sergeant touched the rag of ribbon in his second buttonhole. It was all he needed. He felt warm when he thought that he had obeyed the Major. The Major was a soldier. If the SS bastard insisted on questioning the child in the village, it could be done quickly. Then they'd move to their rendezvous. It was the twenty-first of March. They were heading west now, away from the cold, godforsaken east. Germany was waiting for them.

Hansel heard the flames before he smelled the smoke. It covered the noise of the voices, and that was frightening. There was no way to tell if anyone was watching the hut burn.

What if they're waiting to see if anyone crawls out? Like they did in the ghetto. Setting fires and then waiting for people to jump out of windows. But his back was in such pain from the metal, he had to move his legs spasmodically, and the door of the oven flew open.

He crawled out. The pain of his burned skin made him gasp, whimpering, as he backed into the room. "Gretel," he whispered. "Come on."

"The witch was going to cook us, Hansel."

The girl's pupils were dilated and she panted through her mouth. Hansel took her hand. "Magda didn't want to hurt us."

The side of the hut was burning, and the roof was beginning to roar with the flames eating at the wooden shingles. "Not the door," he whispered, and the words were lost in the sound of shingles catching fire. He pulled Gretel over and pushed her down under the floor.

"Quick. Crawl out the back. Maybe they won't see us."

She dropped below the floor. Hansel was sobbing now and he wrung his hands over and over as she moved slowly out of his way so he could crawl under too. His chin was bloody from where he had bitten his lip. Finally she was out of the way, and he crawled beneath the floor. They scuttled toward the side farthest from the burning straw, and together they pushed more straw away so they could see out.

Hansel saw no soldiers, but they could be hiding in the trees to trick them. He heard the fire roaring louder. It didn't matter about the soldiers. They had to get out from under the hut.

"Quick, Gretel."

They crawled through the mud until they could stand, and then they ran, staggering, toward the woods. Hansel waited for the shouted order to halt, for the bullets that would knock him down, but nothing happened. They ran until they got to the creek, running between the trees, and then they stopped and listened. They heard the trucks moving off on the road. They stood until the sound died out, and then only the calls of ravens in the trees above them broke the silence. The roar of the hut burning behind them was faint and then died away.

Hansel stood and listened to the beaks of the birds clacking in protest at their presence. He looked at the water and waited, but they were alone.

"Magda," he whispered. He knew they should go into the forest and hide, but his legs wouldn't move. He fell down on the ground on his back and felt the wet mud seep through his shirt and cool the burning of his skin.

"It's almost spring, Hansel. Magda said her bones won't ache when it gets warm. My leg hurts where it was hot in the oven. Poor Magda. She was so hungry. She wanted to cook us."

Gretel lifted her skirt and stroked the cold, wet mud onto the red patch of skin.

"Oh, Magda," Hansel whispered again. He stared up at the branches of the trees and saw that the straight lines of the twigs had new swellings on them. Soon the buds would turn red against the black of the bark.

"Magda," he said a last time and then shut his eyes and lay still for nearly an hour until he fell asleep right on the muddy ground, Gretel singing softly beside him, while the ravens clacked their hard beaks overhead and the creek's cold water poured over the rocks.

It was late afternoon on the twenty-first of March, and the sun was almost setting. The Mechanik had run the last mile toward the village, and the Russian and Lydka and several soldiers had run with him, catching his excitement like a fever. The people of the village were quiet, talking softly, when the ragged soldiers trotted breathless down the street.

"We are partisans and friends, people of Piaski," the Russian called to them. "The Russian people extend their hands in friendship and ask your help in killing the Nazis and driving them from Poland. We come in friendship."

The Mechanik turned to the first woman he saw. "Two children? Last November? A girl eleven and a boy seven? They were both small. The girl is blond."

The woman stared at him. He looked like a scarecrow. Ragged coat. Long beard. His eyes glittering like coal.

"A woman," he began again. "My age with white streaks in her hair. She would have come here not long ago. Have you seen her?"

"I never saw the woman, but there were two children. Magda took them in."

"Where is this Magda?" He didn't smile. He couldn't hope. Not yet.

The woman looked at the ground.

"Where?" He was begging her.

"Her hut was in the woods. A mile from the village. Back the way you came. Turn into the woods by the big rock and the bend in the road."

He turned and began to run east toward the pounding of the guns that never stopped now but made a steady sound like the beating of an insane drummer.

"They won't be there," she called after him. "They killed the priest and went to get Magda. You won't find them. They killed them. We saw the smoke when they burned the hut."

She didn't shout too loudly. Maybe the children were still there. Maybe she was wrong. Maybe the Nazis had pity and only took the old woman. The man was too far away now anyway, running like a crazy person.

The Mechanik saw the bend in the road. He turned when he got to the large boulder beside the ditch and loped into the woods. He stared around, looking for the hut and smelled it before he saw it. Burnt wood. The pungent stink of smoke.

The blackened circle of ash was barely warm now. The lump of the huge stove, a stove surely too large for the size of this hut, lay on its side in the ash. The Mechanik walked to the circle and stood in the middle, ignoring the smell and the dust from the ash that covered his boots. He stared out at the enormous trees encircling where the hut had been. The forest was silent.

He opened his mouth to call, but stopped. The children would be afraid to come out if he called their Jewish names. His wife had named them, given them names that were safe, and the children had probably answered to those names since November.

"Hansel? Gretel? Hansel? Greteeeeel?"

The Mechanik shouted until his throat was torn and he was hoarse and then he knelt in the ash and lifted the soft stuff in his hands and poured it on his head. He rubbed the gray powder on his face until he was blackened. He had lost them. By a few hours, he had lost them. His wife must be dead, and his children dead too. He was an afternoon too late.

The Oven

Magda gasped in pain. She knew that a rib had been broken when they knocked her down. She was cold without her coat. The young woman beside Magda had circles around her eyes so dark it was as if her eyes had been put in her head with a sooty finger.

"I'm Rachele."

"Magda."

Magda turned her head and looked at the soldier sitting on the narrow bench that ran along the inside of the truck. His pot of a helmet hid his face until he turned. His unlined face and young eyes saw Magda staring, and he kicked out with his boot. The kick glanced off her leg, and she gasped in pain. The rib was going to cause her trouble. She hoped it wouldn't keep her from working. They said the camps were for work.

Magda didn't want to ask Rachele, but she suddenly had to know.

"Jew?" she whispered.

Rachele couldn't hear the old woman's whisper over the roar of the truck's engine, but she saw the lips form the word. She nodded.

Magda looked down and saw a body shoved under the narrow seat. It was strange they had bothered to take a dead man with them. She stared at the body, and her mind suddenly cleared. It was the patch on the back that she had sewn with her own hands. She recognized the gray tweed against the black of the coat. Magda tried to crawl to the body, but the woman held her back.

"He was the priest," Magda said. "Did they kill the priest?"

Rachele nodded. "He killed some German woman and a soldier."

Magda couldn't speak for a while. Then she thought of Nelka and the baby. If her brother was killed, and they came to get her and the children—

"Did they kill a young woman? Blond? She had a baby? A man with her too?"

"They asked if anyone knew where a woman was. They said she was related to the priest. They said her baby had disappeared too."

Magda began to be happy. Her brother had killed the Brown Sister and the guard who held the baby. Nelka and the baby had fled. If Nelka fled, Telek must have fled too. It puzzled her that her brother had done the murders. It was something she thought Telek would have done. Nelka and the baby could go to the hidey-hole and stay until the Germans were gone. Hansel would take Gretel there when they escaped the oven and the hut. She knew they would crawl out.

Piotr and me. Both of us so old that death has been sitting on our noses for years. All they could do is kill him and send me off to a camp, but our young ones are alive in the forest.

Magda wanted to tell Rachele what she knew, she wanted to have someone rejoice with her, but the woman sat with her eyes shut. The other people in the truck were strained and dirty, some of them had bruises and dried blood on their faces like they had been beaten.

Their look of despair, their helplessness, moved Magda. She thought of all the Poles who had died. All the Jews who disappeared, all the Gypsies, the priests, the mayors, the Polish army officers slaughtered. She thought of the stream of men and women sent into Germany and Russia. The kidnapped children. Her tears began, and she was angry with herself. She needed to be strong, but she couldn't stop the tears.

"End it," she whispered to God, not praying but demanding. "Come and end this world."

But Magda thought of Hansel struggling toward the hidey-hole. She thought of him leading Gretel on, and she couldn't wish that the world would end. She pictured Nelka holding her baby and fleeing with Telek, hiding in the earth and comforting Hansel and Gretel. As long as those young ones walked on the earth, she wanted it to exist for them.

"All right," she whispered. "For the children. Let the wheel keep turning for their sake."

She shut her eyes and sat silent for nearly an hour as the truck lurched on the muddy roads. It was moving more slowly now, and she heard voices from the cab of the truck. The motor coughed and they came to a stop.

"Because of Hansel you can let the world live," she whispered. "But if they kill him, I say that you must come down with all your angels and end it. I charge you with this."

The tailgate of the truck dropped.

"Raus! Raus! Raus!"

One of the bearded Jews lifted Magda as easily as a log of wood and set her on the ground. Her legs buckled, and Rachele put her arm around Magda. She had to get to wherever it was they were going. If she could just live for a month or two in the camp, the Russians would free them.

The sound of a train grew louder down the tracks. She hoped they could sit down soon. If she could rest in the train, drink a little water, then she could face the camp with some energy. The pain of her rib stabbed her with every step, but she ignored it. It was time to gather her strength for survival. Perhaps she would fool them all yet.

They were being driven by shouts and prods. Magda had to force herself not to look back. She didn't want to see what they did with her brother's body. The doors of the cattle car rolled open. Magda shook her head. The bodies of the prisoners were packed so tightly that it was impossible to fit in more people, but the soldiers began hitting them with clubs and screaming.

She didn't climb into the boxcar but was pushed from behind until she was up and wedged in tightly. Rachele was beside her, the two of them smashed together. The door crashed shut, and a man screamed as it closed on his foot. The door bounced on his flesh and bone, and then slammed. Magda heard the bolt shoved down and knew they were locked inside.

"But we can't even breathe," she whispered.

Magda thought of her notion of sitting in the train and sipping water, and she knew that nothing was going to be like what she had imagined. For a moment she was terrified and nearly began to scream. They were going to be killed.

"Where are they taking us?" a woman called out.

"Birkenau. The new camp," someone said. "Everyone goes to Birkenau since last year. History will remember us."

History is the bookkeeping of murderers, Magda thought, but she didn't say it aloud.

Magda stood, held up by the bodies around her. It wasn't cold because so many of them were packed together. Her mouth was very dry, and she wished it would rain so that some of the water might run into the boxcar, but it was clear and dry outside as the train moved on toward the west.

The worst of it was that she had to urinate. She held it as long as she could, and then she had to release the urine and let it run down her legs. The humiliation of it bothered her.

"Stop fussing, old fool," she muttered. "What's a little healthy urine in this place."

The sounds inside the boxcar didn't penetrate to the world outside, the mechanical chugging of the train covering up the cries. Only a single vixen in a field stopped trotting and turned her head as the train passed. Her hackles were raised, the fur roughened over her shoulders, and she bared her teeth warningly, ears pricked forward, ready for flight.

When the doors opened, Magda hadn't realized they had stopped. She felt the rush of air, cold but not fresh. It was air with a tinge of smoke and another smell in it, sweetish and cloying, that she couldn't identify. She was swept out of the car by the surge of people, and her legs were so swollen, her joints so stiff, she couldn't have walked except for a man who took her around the waist and half carried her.

"Come on, Grandmother," he said in a perfectly calm voice. His beard was filthy and matted. His face was ravaged as Magda knew her own was, but he nodded at her, and Magda found the strength to walk a little.

They were driven like pigs. Blows from sticks. Dogs lunging and barking. Driven so fast that she only got a glimpse of a series of large redbrick buildings. Steep roofs. Dormer windows. Neat walks. All the mud was shoveled off the walks, and huge piles of firewood, hundreds of yards long, were stacked against the brick side of the building.

"They have factories at the camp," she said to the man.

He said nothing but kept his grip on her, and they moved at a trot now. Magda knew that even with his help, she couldn't go much farther. But they kept on. He spoke to her occasionally.

"Little Grandmother, you are doing well."

"I chopped my own wood and drew my own water," she tried to say. Her mouth couldn't form the words properly, and it came out a garbled noise.

"Good. Good, Grandmother."

Then she fell when a soldier hit the man holding her with a stick. He was driven to one side, and she, managing to pull herself erect, was driven to the other.

"Line up!" The people were whipped into rows of five and walked past waiting SS men. The male prisoners were on one side, the women on the other.

Looking at Magda and the young woman next to her who held a baby, the SS man screamed, "To the left, bitches! Left!"

The young woman hesitated. She stared down wildly at her baby.

"He's dead," she cried out. "My baby is dead." She tried to go to the right with a man who held his hands out to her from the men's lines.

"He's dead," she screamed as the SS soldier ran toward her.

"Jew bitch!" The soldier lifted his stick and hit her such a blow that she dropped to the platform, blood streaming down her head. He kept hitting her until Magda knew she was dead, but Magda was in a line, and she moved on until the young woman, and her baby, and the man beating her, disappeared. A woman next to Magda, almost as old as she, put her arm around Magda.

"The woman told the truth. The baby was dead. I begged her to put it down in the train. We'll walk together, Bubbeh," she said to Magda.

Magda was barely conscious. The woman had called her grandmother. She knew that was what she had said. She had heard the Yiddish word before from the Jews in the village.

"I'm not a grandmother," Magda said, but the words were still just a gargle of sound.

The older men and all the young boys were walking with the women now. Magda couldn't understand this place. There were wooden barracks and barbed wire everywhere. It was much larger than she had thought it would be. It was a city.

The concrete steps under their feet led down, down until they entered through a door and went into a room underground. The soldiers stood on each side. They shouted and screamed, and the people around Magda tried to move faster down the stairs to avoid the whips and clubs. The woman helping Magda stumbled and nearly fell. The jarring cleared Magda's head a little, and she saw they could spread out some in the room.

She took a deep breath and frowned. There was a smell she couldn't place. She breathed again. Something burning. Something sweet like pork. Against the wall was a bench with numbered hooks above it. Magda wanted to sit, but the soldiers kept shouting.

"They want us to undress, Bubbeh," the woman said.

Magda stared at her. "But—"

The woman smiled, and something in her smile made Magda wonder if this woman was insane. It was such a calm smile.

"Here, Grandmother." She unbuttoned Magda's skirt and blouse, and Magda stood like a child and let her do it. All around them the people were taking off their clothes. "We're going to shower."

The woman undressed herself as quickly as she had undressed Magda. She hung all the clothes neatly and then took Magda's shoes and tied the laces together and hung them up on another hook. She tied her shoes up and hung them with Magda's. The room was filled with naked people, and they stood quietly now, some of them trying to cover their genitals, most standing with no modesty, stunned and not knowing what to do.

"I hope the water is hot," Magda said to the woman, who again smiled her gentle smile. Magda was relieved that her voice was clear enough to understand. She would recover from the train and work. If you could work, the Nazis would let you live.

"Remember the number on our hook," Magda said. "We'll have to dress quickly if they don't give us uniforms."

The woman put her arm around Magda's shoulders. Then the shouting began again. They were herded into another room.

"Look! Water taps. We can drink. And nozzles to shower."

The woman tightened her arm around the older woman's shoulders. Magda tried to support herself, but her feet stumbled over each other.

"I need a drink," she said, but the woman was staring back at the door where they had entered, and she tightened her grip even more. The door closed with a great crash of the heavy steel, and Magda heard the bolt slam down. Then she heard something above their heads. Voices.

"What are they saying?" she asked.

"I think they said 'Give them something to chew on.' I'm not sure."

Magda heard the sound of truck engines outside. They were revved up until the roar filled the room. She heard a rattling sound in the metal pillar next to where they stood. Pellets poured into the pillar from above and struck the perforated metal sides like gravel, and then she couldn't breathe. The air was full of something that burned her skin and lungs. She kept opening her mouth and taking air in, but the air wasn't air anymore.

The room was full of screaming. Magda was on the floor and others climbed on top of her, trying to get to the fresh air left at the ceiling. The shrieking and howling was muffled outside by the engines of the transport trucks which revved to drown out the sound of the people being gassed.

Pictures flew into Magda's mind. The giant hornbeam trees. A cup of water from the creek, trembling under her lips. Faces flipped through her mind like a book of pictures being thumbed. Brother. Sister. Grandmother. Mother, and the face of a child. A boy. Curly hair dyed blond. Black eyes. The flickering vision of life stopped with the boy, and his dark eyes stared into her own as she lay trampled and gasping, and then she was dead.

The mass of naked bodies became a mound that trembled only occasionally. Arms stretched out, fingers reaching for nothing, legs akimbo, heads thrown back, tongues out and eyes staring, the shivering mass lay still, and the room was silent. For a few minutes they lay there, and then the SS doctor, watching from his peephole, gave the signal to turn on the ventilators that pumped the gas from the room. The air cleared, but the men who came in, pulling at the mass of tangled corpses, wore masks. There were pockets between the bodies that still held gas.

Magda's body was under many others. A man leaned over her, pulled open her mouth and stared inside. There were almost no teeth, and no gold. He cut her hair with a slash of the dull razor and put the white locks in a bag. He turned to the man next to the old woman and smiled. Two teeth were gold. The camp worker knocked them out with two blows and looped a strap of leather around the man's wrist. This gassed Jew was too bald to bother cutting his fringe of hair.

The worker dragged the body with some difficulty to the elevator and went back at a run for Magda. She was as light as a child. He threw her on top and the elevator moved up.

The upper room was trembling with the noise of the flames. The fires that burned night and day were stoked with such violence, the ovens had become living creatures that roared and rumbled. The heat was so oppressive that the soot-stained workers felt battered by it.

A camp inmate threw Magda's body off the top of the pile of corpses packed into the elevator and it fell onto a metal stretcher. Working as fast as he could, he dragged off a man, almost as fleshy as a normal person, and threw him on top of the old woman.

The orders had been explicit. The best load for rapid burning was one fat body that burned well, one starved that couldn't burn much, and a child. It had been worked out and was proven to be the most efficient.

The camp inmate didn't stop to wipe off the sweat that ran into his eyes. He tugged at the bodies. There weren't many children anymore. Most were dead already, he guessed. He wondered if there were any children left in the world, but he stopped his mind from the thought. Thoughts were a luxury that led to death.

Not finding a child, he threw a small woman onto the stretcher and another worker grabbed the end of it. At a run, they took it and set it on rollers in front of the oven door. Five ovens in a line. Three compartments in each red mouth.

The oven door cranked upward like a metal curtain. Another inmate, as thin as the corpses he burned, shoved coke under the grate. The two workers pushed the metal stretcher into the roar of the oven, the flames so hot that their eyes dried from the wall of heat.

The stretcher lay on the grate, and in a smooth movement, one worker pushed a metal fork against the bodies. His partner pulled out the stretcher with a hard jerk, and the fork dug into the flesh, keeping the bodies inside the oven, letting them fall onto the grate.

The door rattled down. There was no time to rest. The men ran with the stretcher to the elevator and began to pull out more bodies. Some days it seemed the whole world was in line downstairs, waiting to come up on the elevators.

The short white hair left on Magda's head lit around her face and burned first. It was a puff of light for a second, and then the skin began to burn. It took only twenty minutes for her shoulders and torso and legs and her pitiful, twisted feet to turn to ash. The heat was so great that even the bones turned to ash and only an occasional tiny lump showed that the ash had been a person.

It was a while before the ash was raked from beneath the grate. Magda's ashes were raked out and mingled with the ashes of hundreds of others. And she had one last journey before the wheel of her life in this world stopped completely.

Her ashes were dumped with the ashes of thousands of others into a truck and covered so they wouldn't blow out. The truck drove off, one in a long line of trucks, to the banks of the river Vistula. There the workers shoveled and dumped the ashes on the water, but unlike a casting of bread onto water, no sins were forgiven by this act.

Magda, that which had been Magda, swirled into the air and fell lightly, drifting with the breeze which occasionally had a hint in it of the coming spring. The white ash fell on the surface of the river and lay for a moment, and then was gradually moistened by the water and slipped under the surface and washed down to be caught and moved in strong sweeps of current, icy with the runoff of snow, to disappear.

The men threw the shovels in the trucks. It was late in the day, but that did not mean that the work was over. There was no end to the work of the furnaces. The ovens had to be fed day and night or grow cold and useless. Any break in the burning was inefficient.

The trucks turned back toward the long brick buildings and the setting sun reflected in an orange glitter on the dormer windows as they drew close. The chimneys cast their smoke up into the sky, and the workers, inmates of Birkenau, saw none of it anymore.

They sat hunched on the floor of the truck and knew that they must not see it because if they saw this thing and thought about it, it would begin to eat at them. The furnaces would work their way inside them and char them from the inside out. Then they would weaken and be thrown into the fire by their fellow workers who had not looked at the chimneys.

But above the buildings, had they only dared to look, the air was disturbed, beaten, torn apart. The waves of heat lifted into the sky, and some said it was the natural dispersing of the heat from the ovens. The waves of hot air moved over the camp night and day, and one man in the truck weakened when they were nearly back at the buildings. He looked up.

He saw the dark smoke and the columns of vibrating heat in the sky, and the thought came to him that the moving air was the souls of all the people. There were so many of them going back to God, so quickly, that the air rippled, the smoke tossed by the heat of their souls rising.

The man shut his eyes. He knew that this single thought had made him fuel for the ovens. But he was too weakened, and he gave up and allowed himself to think of life before, the sweet face of his wife turned toward the child, a meal on the table, and then he looked up again at the chimneys and thought he could already see his own soul above the roof, rising in the hot air. He knew that he was a dead man, but he smiled and just sat smiling as the truck stopped, and all the others climbed out and began to run toward the fires.

Leaving

"Magda will worry. We have to go back to the hut."

"The hut's gone. They took Magda."

Gretel shook her head. "She'll be back soon."

Hansel stood and listened. A raven's call rattled over his head, and the creek gurgled. His back hurt, and the red marks on Gretel's legs must hurt too, but she didn't seem to notice it.

"You have to shut up, Gretel. You can't make any noise unless I say you can. Come on."

She took his hand, and he led her back toward the hut. When they drew close, the smell of burning was heavy in the air. Hansel crept from tree to tree. Then he could see the place where the hut had been. There was a circle of burned wood, no flames now, but the pieces of charred wood glowed red and the circle smoked. The huge iron stove was the only thing left. It lay on its side where it had fallen when the floor under it had burned through.

Magda had told him that he'd have to be the older one. He had to think now for both of them. He looked back. Gretel had stayed behind a tree and was invisible.

"Gretel, you can come out now."

"I didn't make any sound. We have to go home to Magda now."

"The stove is all that's left."

"That's not Magda's hut."

"They burned it. They took Magda. We hid in the oven." He was shouting.

"I was in the oven. She wanted to cook us. Why did Magda do that?"

"You're talking crazy. Gretel, please don't be—" Hansel sat down and moaned.

"Don't be sad. We'll go home and Magda will have soup. We can't sit here."

Gretel was right. They couldn't sit there. The soldiers might come looking for them. He glanced back toward the creek. The food was at the hidey-hole, and Telek and Nelka would come looking for them soon. There was nothing here that they could use, but he pulled the brush away from a fallen log and uncovered a basket. He took out a small bottle, pulled the cork, and sniffed. It was empty, but it still smelled of raspberry syrup. He sniffed deeply, remembering Magda using the syrup for Gretel when she was sick. Then he put the cork back in and slid the bottle carefully into the pocket of his coat.

"Come on, Gretel. Promise that you'll do what I say."

Gretel stopped walking and stood thinking. She had promised something once, but she couldn't remember what the promise had been. "I promise I'll do what you say. Really." This time she'd do it right. She had done it wrong before.

Hansel led her along the creek through heavy mud. They took their shoes off and waded part of the way, gasping at the icy water, their feet almost blue when he let her step back onto the mud of the bank. It would hide their scent if they brought dogs. Then the river, the rock, turn south, and he found it. The hidey-hole.

"There's bread and potatoes inside."

Gretel waited expectantly while Hansel stared at the brush covering the boards.

The three soldiers slipped from tree to tree. It hadn't been difficult. The village girl's directions were correct, and the two children hadn't been able to hide all their footprints on the mud banks of the creek. It would have been harder if the snow hadn't melted.

Behind them, the Oberführer walked without deigning to hide. Halina trotted beside him, smothering her sobs with her hand pushed against her mouth. The soldiers stopped and gestured ahead toward the two saplings that stood apart from the larger trees. Jerking the girl's arm, the Oberführer gestured and raised his eyebrows. Halina, a single sob wrenched out of her throat, nodded. The Oberführer dropped her hand and pushed her against a tree. He took out his pistol and gestured the soldiers forward.

Two of the men tiptoed to the pile of brush. One of them removed the branches gently, almost tenderly, while the second soldier sought a grip on the boards. There was a moment's pause. The first man took a grenade from his belt, pulled the pin, and nodded.

The boards flew up, the grenade was lobbed into the dark hole, and both men ran to hide behind trees. Even the Oberführer stepped behind a tree and waited. Only Halina, frozen against the bark of an oak, watched as the ground moved and a shower of boards and earth rose into the air. The child slipped to the forest floor in a faint.

Hansel lay with his hand over Gretel's mouth about two hundred feet away. They lay concealed by leaves under a rotten tree, but he saw the explosion. Gretel tried to raise her head, but he pressed her down.

She lay still, and Hansel watched as the men moved off into the woods toward the road. The SS man cursed the soldiers, and he slapped one of them. Halina lay limp on the ground.

Hansel thought of going to Halina and telling her that he was all right, but he couldn't trust anyone now. He made Gretel lie under the tree until Halina woke and ran away toward the village so quietly that he almost missed her going.

"Where's Magda, Hansel?"

"We'll find her soon," he lied. He wished she would stop asking him about things.

He turned and began to walk away from the village toward the east. They'd take the road in the other direction. They'd never been on that road. Everyone would expect them to go to places they knew. No one would think they'd go to a new place. They'd have to find a farm. Farms had barns and haystacks. You could hide in those and be warm.

His stomach was beginning to ache. He hadn't eaten since breakfast and they had no food. The panic rose in the boy and he moaned with each step.

"Hansel?"

He shut his mouth. He was the older one now. He took Gretel's hand. They'd been hungry before, and then they had found food. That's how it was sometimes. He walked faster, looking for any line of smoke rising in the sky that would show him where a farm was.

They had been walking a couple of hours, and he heard the voices of the men before he saw them. Hansel pulled Gretel off the road and into the trees where they lay flat on the pine needles. He raised his head just a little so he could see.

A group of men carrying guns moved at a fast trot down the road. They weren't Germans, but they carried guns, and the boy lay still and watched. The men ran in a tight bunch, a moving clot of gray cloth and guns and beards.

He tucked his head down and waited for them to pass. The men were heading toward the village. He didn't see his father, fists clenched, in the middle of the group.

"We have to go find Magda and the children." They had hidden in the swamp for three days, and Nelka was restless and worried.

Telek shook his head. They couldn't travel safely with the baby. It could cry at any moment. It was hard to silence a baby without smothering it.

"Then I'll go alone. I have to find Magda." Nelka began walking back in the direction of the hut. He knew she meant it.

"The baby could give us away. I'll go and tell you what I find. You have a baby, woman. Think of him." Telek moved as fast as he could through the sandy swamp. Ignoring his fears she followed, and he didn't modify his pace until he heard Nelka panting.

When he got close to the hut, he circled the area like a noose drawing gradually tighter. He smelled it in the air, but she hadn't noticed.

"Sit and nurse him. I'll see if it's safe." He gathered pine boughs and threw them in a pile where she would not be seen for the fallen trees. Nelka settled down on the boughs and he knew she was glad to rest. He moved carefully toward the hut, and when he got to the clearing, he stopped and stared.

The circle of burned earth did not surprise Telek. Being in the woods for days had made him sensitive to the smell of smoke and burning things. He had smelled it long before he saw it. He looked at the blackened dirt and the ash and the stove lying on its side.

Telek looped through the trees until he was sure that they hadn't posted any soldier to guard the place. Then he squatted, still not going near the ashes, and thought. He was still thinking what to do when Nelka walked through the trees. She ignored him and went straight to the circle of burned ash. Her face was so white it was blue around her mouth, and she held the baby so tightly that it began to shriek.

"Telek," she called to him, "we should have taken them with us."

"Magda would have wanted us to run. She loved you."

"We have to find out. They may know where she is. She could be in the village jail."

"If we go in the village, any Germans left there will kill us."

"Maybe she's at the hidey-hole. You warned her to leave early. It's my fault. Father Piotr killed to save my baby."

"He did it because of me. He didn't want me to get killed or have the sin. He did it to save me." The humiliation of it, having the old man kill when it was Telek's job, his joy, to murder and save the baby for Nelka, the humiliation brought tears to Telek's eyes.

"He did it for me," she said. "And we didn't save Magda."

Nelka began to walk fast, and he saw that she was going toward the hidey-hole.

"For God's sake, don't just walk in and get killed. They may know about it."

"I'm coming," Nelka whispered. "I'm coming, Magda."

They found torn up trees and dirt and footprints of men in boots. Nelka lay on the ground and sobbed, lifting the dirt to her face and pressing it against her face. Telek looked for the smaller footprints of children, but the pine needles and leaves of the forest hid the prints.

Nelka finally sat up and wiped her face. "Maybe they're in the village."

Telek didn't believe it. If Magda and the children had been taken to the village, why would the soldiers have come here? Unless it was to catch Nelka and the baby. And him. There could be traps set on the path to the village, waiting soldiers. But he had to do it or Nelka would do it alone.

They slept in the clump of trees and walked to the village the next day. When they got near, Telek made Nelka hide with him in the bushes near the well and watch. It was quiet. There was not a single soldier in sight. They sat and waited for nearly an hour.

Feliks walked toward the well, shouting over his shoulder: "You stupid shit! What's the point of it?"

"The point is Poland." Jedrik trailed after Feliks.

"Since when are you such a patriot? I didn't see you helping the partisans."

"We have to get rid of all the trash and make Poland pure."

"Poland's been raped for six years. She isn't a virgin, you asshole. Not after the Russians and the Nazis."

"We will cleanse her." Jedrik hesitated and then turned to look back toward the houses. He talked to himself in a mutter, and Feliks ignored the man and threw his bucket down the well. Jedrik moved on and Feliks was alone now. Telek waited until Feliks had drawn his water, and when he turned to go back to his house, Telek called out.

"Feliks?"

The man turned with no surprise. "It's you, Telek."

"Father Piotr? What did they do to him?"

"Shot him. Threw his body in a truck and took it with them. They wrapped the dead soldier and the SS bitch in blankets and put them in another truck. They're gone. All of them."

"Do you know where Magda is?"

"They burned her out and took her and the two little ones with them."

Nelka sobbed so hard that she had to put the baby on the ground or she would drop him.

"You're sure?"

"Yes. Then a man came. With some Russians and partisans. He was looking for the children. A relative, I guess. He went to the hut and found nothing."

"Where did they take them?" Telek knew the answer.

"The rail line. You know the rest." Feliks nodded at Telek. The radio from London had warned them about the camps. The partisans had known for over a year. "You'd better keep moving, Telek. The Major and his boys are gone, but the Nazis are all over the roads. If they're looking for you two, they'll look here first."

Telek nodded. Nelka was crying with her mouth open and her nose watering, mixing with the tears. He had seen her cry like that when she was a child, when her mother had died.

He sat and held her and wiped her face with the edge of his coat.

"It wasn't your fault."

"We have to go where the train takes them."

Telek said nothing. He knew about the camps. He had seen a few children pushed through tiny openings in the boxcars and thrown out into the snow. No one threw their children from a train in winter unless what lay ahead was worse.

"My love." He rocked her and stroked her hair. "My love."

"We have to try, Telek."

"They were dead as soon as they got to the camp, Nelka. They kill them quick. She was too old to work, and they were too young. They're with God now."

She sobbed in his arms, and the baby slept beside them. Dredging up a memory from some church lesson, he went on. "Their souls are warmed in God's hand and opening like flowers."

He was embarrassed at his own words, but they seemed to help Nelka. She stopped crying and grew quieter.

"God will have to—" Telek stroked her hair with a suddenly awkward hand. "He'll have to laugh when Magda walks into Heaven leading that mischievous boy, Hansel, and—" He couldn't bear to say Gretel's name.

Nelka nodded again and lay still against his chest.

Telek held her and tried not to think of Gretel. The way she had looked at the wild ponies with her mouth open in joy. The way she had offered him a piece of her magical orange. He shut his eyes and held Nelka tighter. It was over. He had no one in the village. Nelka and the baby had no one either. It was just the three of them.

"We're leaving this place."

"Where can we go?" She lifted her swollen face and he smiled at her.

"Away from here. Away from Poland."

"Leave Poland?" Her eyes widened.

"I won't spend the rest of my life killing Russians."

"But they promised. After the Germans are beaten, Poland will be free."

"Promises are easy to make."

He looked at the baby sleeping in a patch of sun.

"I don't want to teach him how to slit a throat, and there's no family for either of us here."

"If we have to go, I want to be where it's warm. Where there isn't any war."

"We'll find it. If we have to cross oceans, we'll find it."

"I don't think there is a place like that."

He turned her head up and put his face close to hers. Moving his chapped lips against the salty moisture from Nelka's tears that wet her mouth, he spoke slowly.

"I will find it for you."

He kissed her deeply and then drew back and saw her face with her eyes shut and the skin flushed and the beautiful lips open, and he kissed her again and again for a long time. They sat like that until the baby woke and began to cry, and Nelka nursed him. Then the three of them, Telek with his arm around Nelka, who carried their son, walked down the road toward the west.

———

"When the others come from Bialowieza, we march on." The Russian was so restless that he had hardly slept for three nights in the village even though they were given food and beds. Three days in a village while the war was moving on. It was hard to obey other men's orders again.

The Mechanik sat on the steps beside the Russian and said nothing. The sun was warm, but he didn't feel it.

"We'll join the main force again and march on to Berlin." The Russian laughed. "Let the bastards see what it's like fighting on their own soil."

He was so excited that he began to pace back and forth in front of the village store.

"I have to look for my children."

"Listen, friend—" The Russian cuffed the Mechanik lightly on the shoulder. "You know what they say the camps are. It's death in hours when you get there. Your children are gone, Mechanik." It was a hard thing to say, but the man had to recover from this. "Going to the camps is a waste of time. We're in the front line. We'll be in Berlin before the men who're coming up from the south. And what of the woman? What of your wife?"

"They haven't seen her here. She must be dead or she would have come back."

"You don't know that. Maybe she had to lie low or join some other group. Think about it. You know her. If she's alive, she won't stop until she gets to Berlin and the Nazis are beaten."

There was truth in this. The Mechanik had thought about what she would do. She would fight on and try to find him after the war was over.

"If you want to find her, you have to keep marching on to the end of the war. That's where she'll be. Let the children go. Pray for their souls, my friend, but let them go and keep fighting."

The Russian knew that it was hard for the Jew to sit and think. But they needed to move on. He wanted this man beside him. The Mechanik knew machines, and soon they would be able to ride. Soon they would be firing their own rockets and setting off real bombs.

"You're a Comrade now. You have to fight with us," he said over his shoulder.

The Russian was still pacing when he saw a man watching them from across the square. He was fattish and one of his hands was behind his back. The other hand held a wooden club. There was something about the man that made the Russian pause.

"What's your name, friend?" the Russian asked as the man walked past him.

"Jedrik." He held the club in front of his body and walked toward the Mechanik.

"What do you want?"

Jedrik walked past the Russian without replying, and it happened too quickly for the Russian to draw his pistol or take his rifle off his back.

"They say you're a Jew," Jedrik said.

"I'm a Jew. I've fought in the woods since November with the partisans."

"The Russians are bringing Communist Jews to rule Poland."

The Mechanik realized his mistake. He shouldn't have said he was a Jew. He had thought it was safe now. Jedrik pulled his hand out from behind his back. He held an ancient pistol.

"That gun hasn't been fired since the last war." The Mechanik almost laughed, but his hair began to rise on the back of his neck.

"Shoot my Comrade, and I kill you." The Russian didn't draw his pistol. He didn't want to panic the man. Jedrik moved his eyes back and forth from the Russian to the Mechanik, and the old pistol swayed back and forth from one man to the other.

"Don't move, Russian. I have no argument with you."

"You have no argument with me either," said the Mechanik. But he knew that it wouldn't matter to this man.

"The Nazis never would have fought us except for you Jews." Jedrik was pale and his hand trembled. "You were why they hate us. We let you live here in our land, and millions of Poles died because of you. They only came here because of all the Jews they wanted to kill."

"I'm a Pole too. Besides, they wanted our land." The Mechanik thought of his pistol, but it was buttoned under his coat.

"You're an asshole, Jedrik." The Russian laughed, but his laugh was tight. "They didn't give a damn about the Jews or Poland. The Germans wanted Russia. You were just in the way. Poland's always in the way of all the armies trying to kill Russians. The Jews were the excuse they used, but next time they'll have another reason to run over Poland."

Jedrik shook his head.

"Kill the Jew and you die." The Russian stared past Jedrik down the street. There were a few villagers who watched in the distance, but none of the Russian soldiers were on the street. He wondered if he could get his pistol out and shoot the bastard after Jedrik killed the Jew.

The Mechanik knew that this Jedrik was going to shoot him, and then the Russian would try to draw his pistol. If the peasant was a good shot, then the Russian would die too. The Mechanik stood slowly, his hands out at his sides so Jedrik wouldn't panic and shoot.

"We have all suffered. My wife is dead, I think. My children are dead."

"Dirty Jew. You should all be dead."

Jedrik talked on, and the Mechanik moved forward a little, incremental shuffles that took him closer, as if he needed to get closer to hear better.

"The Jews get rich off us peasants, and then they join the Russians. You're a Communist, Jew. And the Communists should die too. All of them. All the Russians will be killed like rats."

Jedrik had spittle at the corner of his mouth. The Mechanik nodded as if he agreed. He tried to look humble, and he moved forward a fraction as the man rambled on with his talk.

"Jews killed children. All of you did. You killed children and ate them."

The Russian saw the Mechanik moving forward, and he waited for Jedrik to panic and shoot, but the man kept talking. He wanted to say it all.

"You bled Poland dry and then you lived fat in the cities. I'm going to kill you, Jew, and then I'll kill the Communist who brought you here."

The Mechanik thought of all the poor Jews of this village who had been shot and buried in the woods. He didn't contradict Jedrik. He nodded humbly, hoping the man would keep talking.

He knew he couldn't get much nearer, or the peasant would shoot. He knew it was going to kill him, but if he could knock the man down, the Russian would have time to draw his gun. Sliding his eyes toward the Russian, the Mechanik spoke softly.

"Goodbye, friend. You saved us in the forest. Thank you."

The peasant opened his mouth to speak again, and the Mechanik jumped forward. He leapt over the six feet of ground and heard the explosion of the pistol as his body hit Jedrik's. The Mechanik screamed, but he held Jedrik's arm down as they both fell backward onto the dirt of the street. Jedrik got in one blow with the club, and then it fell from his hand.

"Jew! Jew!" Jedrik screamed.

The Mechanik felt like a hand had knocked the wind out of his chest. He knew he was shot, but he lay on Jedrik and held his pistol hand down. The gun went off again, and the Mechanik felt his eyes dimming. He was fainting, and everything began to darken at the edges of his vision. He saw stars over the face of the screaming peasant, but he couldn't hear him anymore.

The Russian, cursing steadily, dragged his pistol out of the holster and tried to put it to Jedrik's head. The two men were struggling so in the dirt that the Russian had to shuffle around them, almost dancing in the dust of the street.

"You stupid shit!" The Russian took his chance for a clean shot, put the gun almost against the peasant's head and fired. Jedrik's head popped like a broken squash and opened. He shuddered and twisted, his words gurgling in his throat, and then he lay still. The Mechanik lay on top of him.

"Oh God! Oh Jesus!" The Russian had to pull the Mechanik's hands from Jedrik. He rolled the unconscious man over and saw the blood on his chest.

He knelt and opened the Mechanik's coat and shirt. A single shot had passed into his chest, but it was on the right side. The Russian put his ear to the wounded chest. The man was breathing well. It had missed his lungs. No great spouting of blood gushed out. He rolled his friend onto his side, pulled his shirt up roughly, and laughed at what he saw.

"It went right through. You're in luck, Comrade."

The pain of being rolled over brought the Mechanik to consciousness, and he groaned. He opened his eyes, and stared at the dirt of the street. It took a moment for him to remember where he was. To remember what had happened.

The Russian rolled him gently onto his back and grinned down into his dark eyes.

"The peasant? He shot you?" the Mechanik asked.

"You took the bullet for me, Comrade."

"I'm shot?"

"Shot like a dog. But it missed your lungs and heart. You have a nice hole going through you. With luck, you'll heal, but you won't go to Berlin this winter."

"I'm shot." He lay in the dirt and thought about it.

"You're no good for marching now, Comrade, but you can come to Berlin after we've done the dirty work." The Russian called out to the peasants who were creeping closer. "You people! Come help me with this hero. He saved my life. That bastard, Jedrik, would have killed us both if this Jew hadn't jumped him."

"I'm shot." The Mechanik whispered it again.

The Russian grinned down at his friend. "The fucking Pole wanted to kill us all."

"There are Nazis in every country," the Mechanik said, but then he had to stop. The pain was making him light-headed.

"You get well, and I'll beat the Germans for you."

"You saved our life in the forest," the Mechanik whispered as darkness closed in on him.

"So now we're even. Don't worry. Every other German I kill, I'll kill him for you."

The Russian leaned over and took the Mechanik's face in his hands and kissed him loudly on each cheek, but the other man was unconscious again and didn't know he had been kissed.

"Every other one for you, my friend."

The Mechanik moaned a little in his unconsciousness, and the Russian grinned. There wasn't a lot of blood. The man might live if the wound didn't get infected. He just might live.

Swans

The children were hidden in the brush beside the road, watching the trucks move past them through the mud. The German soldiers in the trucks weren't clean like the Germans in the ghetto. They were dirty and slumped. Guns boomed in the distance day and night.

Gretel started to stand up, and he pulled her down.

"The trucks won't hurt us, Hansel."

"They're Germans. We have to hide. You promised to do what I said."

It was twilight when he saw the plume of smoke. It was hard to see, because it was nearly the same color as the sky, but Hansel saw it. He led Gretel over the fields in the middle of trees, and by the time they were close to the buildings, it was dark.

"Crawl," he told Gretel, and the two of them crawled under a broken board into the barn.

There was only a single cow, old and standing with her head down. Gretel climbed the ladder to the loft and called out, "There's hay, Hansel. We can sleep here, but I'm hungry."

They piled hay up behind a stack of straw, where it wouldn't be seen easily, and made a bed. The two of them, exhausted and cold, lay close together and pulled more hay on top. It was warmer lying between the stack of hay and the wall of the barn, and Hansel thought they wouldn't freeze. I'll get food tomorrow, he thought. He tried to think how he'd do that, but he fell asleep before he could figure it out.

They had hidden in the barn for two weeks. Gretel had been quiet and slept for hours during the day. At night Hansel crept out and dug through the straw in the ditch to gather half-rotten potatoes. He even stole two eggs he found in a nest outside the chicken house. When the farmer came to throw hay down for the cow, the children hid behind the piled-up straw.

One silent morning, Gretel, seduced by the sun, stood in the blaze of dawn looking out the loft window. Hansel woke when his sister began to sing. And then the woman screamed.

"Ladislaw! There's a girl in the loft. I can see her." The woman grabbed a pitchfork and ran toward the barn.

"Wait till I get my gun," he called, but she ran into the barn and was climbing up to the loft.

Gretel stood at the window, smiling. Hansel sat in the hay, his face twisted, his hair with its dark inch of roots and golden top like some odd cap on his head.

The woman stared at them. "How long have you been here?"

"Only a few days," Hansel lied.

"The girl looks Polish," the farmer gasped, out of breath from running.

"Well, the boy doesn't. Look at that hair! Get them out of here. If any Germans pass through, they'll kill your own child and us too. You know what these children are!"

She went down the ladder, throwing the pitchfork with such anger it nearly hit the cow.

"I want to leave now." Gretel was nearly crying. "I want to go back to Magda, Hansel."

"She's not that bad," the farmer said to Hansel. "The Nazis killed our son. Our daughter has the coughing disease. My wife is afraid she'll die. She's afraid all the time."

Hansel nodded, but he thought the woman was bad anyway.

"I'll give you some potatoes. Stay in the trees. Stay away from soldiers." He looked at Gretel. She was a beautiful little thing. He wished that his wife would take her in. The man slipped a loaf of bread in the sack even though he knew his wife would hate him for it.

After the children were gone, his wife cleaned the loft until no trace was left of them.

"We're not going to get killed now," she muttered. "Not after the last five years."

The children crept across the open fields, and Hansel didn't breathe easily until they were in the forest again. He knew where they were going.

The winter had lasted so long. It was April, the farmer had said, and the forest had changed while they were in the loft of the barn. The children had never been in a forest when it bloomed and buzzed with bees and the water flickered with the color of dragonfly wings.

The bud scales on the giant hornbeams had loosened and the leaves pushed out. The limbs above their heads, coated with ice and snow for so long, were now feathery with new leaves. The forest was beginning to fill out its canopy, and there was a pinkish-green roof over the children's heads.

Hansel walked as fast as he could. It was dangerous, going back to where Magda's hut had been, but he couldn't think of what else to do. The roads were full of soldiers. The men walking to the west never seemed to diminish, and the boy knew it wasn't safe to travel on the roads. He hated the sight of the soldiers and wanted to hide from all of them.

His hands shook all the time now, and he couldn't stop it. He wanted to sleep, even in the morning after he had woken up from sleeping all night. The forest was filled with new life, and he saw it, but it gave him no pleasure.

"Listen," Gretel said, smiling. "It's woodpeckers. They wake me up every morning."

Hansel heard the birds chirping above their heads, and at night the croaking of frogs startled him awake dozens of times. He couldn't hear if anyone was creeping toward them. He couldn't tell if soldiers were coming to kill them when the woods were so noisy.

"I hate it. I liked it better when it wasn't all birds and frogs."

But Gretel loved it. She remembered things that Magda had told her about the spring. She saw mushrooms, but Hansel wouldn't let her eat any of them.

"You're crazy! Magda said you couldn't tell the good ones until you're grown up."

Gretel didn't eat the mushrooms, but she found wild strawberries, and they feasted on the tart berries until their chins ran red with the juice. She found mint which she knew from the smell of Magda's teas, and they chewed on it while they walked.

"Where are we going?" They had walked for three days, and the food was almost gone.

"We're going back to where the hut was."

Gretel didn't really care if it took a long time to get there. It was lovely being in the woods. The forest ran with streams of water in the swollen creeks. Under the giant trees were deep layers of moss like velvet beds. Hansel let Gretel wander as they walked, and he didn't care if it slowed them down. He was so tired. She would explore and look at the plants and suck cool water off the moss, and he would lie and stare up at the leaves coming out, more and more of them every day. He had to force himself to stand up and move on.

Hansel knew they were close to the hut, close to where the pigsty was hidden. He got up early, before it was light, and made Gretel walk fast now. He couldn't find the pigsty unless he found the hut. They had to stop wandering. It was gray dawn and the birds were calling so loudly that it made his head hurt. He hated the noise.

"Here," he said. It was the curve in the road. The big rock. He turned into the woods. He wouldn't go to the hut. He couldn't bear to see the ashes.

"Don't sing, Gretel."

"I'll be quiet."

He looked at her and nearly cried. It wasn't fair. She was the big one. She should help him. He knew it was right ahead of him, but Hansel didn't recognize the cluster of trees. They were in bloom, and the tender fragrance of wild cherry blossoms filled his nose as he drew closer.

There was only the mound of earth and splintered wood from the grenade. No Nelka kissing him. Telek didn't rush out and throw him up in the air. No one was there.

"The sky is all flowers." Gretel reached up and pulled a cherry twig to her face.

Hansel sat sobbing and shoved his fingers into his mouth as if they were bread. Magda had baked the bread that got blown up by the soldiers. She had pushed it into a pan with her hands. He sobbed and sucked his fingers, and Gretel stood above the hole in the forest floor, smiling.

"We have to get clean," he told Gretel.

It was warmer now all the time. The chilblains on his hands had healed, but the lice were making him itch until his wrists and sides were scratched and bloody.

"We can make a fire and kill them."

"Somebody could see a fire. We have to drown them."

They sat beside the creek and took all their clothes off. She pounded her clothes on rocks, and Hansel pounded his clothes on the rocks too. When they were tired, they spread the clothes in the creek with rocks on top to weight them. He and Gretel lay in shallow water, and he saw little fish nibbling at his toes in the sun-shot water.

"Put your head back in the water and let it soak. They'll all drown," he said. The water was so icy it made his head ache.

After a long time, they dragged out their clothes. Hansel lay in the sun and fell asleep, but Gretel spread the clothes over bushes where the sun could reach them. In an hour, they were almost dry. Hansel woke up, and pulled on his pants. He didn't itch as much. It was lovely. He waited until Gretel had dressed and then he took her hand. Standing on tiptoe, he reached up till she leaned her face down and let him kiss her on both cheeks the way that Nelka did.

"I don't itch so bad."

She nodded. "Let's explore."

They walked hand in hand through the towering lime, hornbeam, and oak, the occasional smell of lilac growing wild and the pungent whiff of chamomile coming to them as their feet crushed the herb, not knowing what it was. They both heard it at the same time. It was a wild cackling ahead of them. Hansel knew they were nearly at the river.

A shallow bend in the river, the sand and gravel dredged over the rocks for thousands of years had made a little lake, but the children couldn't see the water. The whole surface of the shallows was covered with white birds, wings flapping, necks bending and preening, beaks opening and shutting in a great, constant cackling.

"They're swans," Gretel whispered. "Don't move." She put her index finger in her mouth and held it up into the air. "Animals won't know you're there when the wind blows in your face." Gretel frowned. Someone had told her that. Her finger was coolest on the side toward the swans, and she smiled. "They can't smell us. Let's watch."

"I wonder if we could catch one," Hansel said. "We could eat it."

"You can't eat them."

"Why not? They look like that goose in the village."

"Because swans are special. There were swans in my fairy-tale book."

It made him angry. He wanted to catch one and eat it. There was only one potato left, and Gretel didn't even care. She didn't care that it was so hard to steal food or just to find it and feed themselves. Gretel would let him starve and not care at all.

Hansel ran toward the swans, his fists clenched. The birds saw the movement and gabbled furiously, flapping their wings and flurrying in the water. Then they began to rise and fly, first one group, then another, then the whole mass of them, two hundred birds, a cloud over the river, flying up, turning in the sky, and going on south.

"You shouldn't have done that."

Gretel was sitting on the moss and Hansel didn't look at her. He didn't care if she cried. Hansel stood looking at the shallows, covered with white down, feathers floating in the air from the violence of the swans' lifting into flight.

"We have to leave the forest, Gretel. There isn't much noise now from the guns. We'll go back the way we came before we were in the forest."

"Which way did we come?" She was puzzled.

"I don't remember anything before the ghetto. So we have to go back to that. We were in the city and lived in the ghetto, and then we went in the woods, and then Magda." His voice fell as he spoke, and Magda's name was almost a whisper.

They ate the last potato and walked farther into the forest. Hansel wrapped the little bottle that still had the smell of raspberry clinging to its insides in a rag and put it gently in his pocket. The children walked through the woods that were ripening as it grew warmer and humming with bees and the scent of the flowers that preceded the fruit. As they walked on, the forest thinned and was less damp. Hansel watched uneasily as the light grew brighter, and he could see farther and farther ahead as the trees grew smaller. If he could see ahead, then anyone could see him.

At last fields spread in front of the children. Hansel pulled Gretel back by the hand, looking at the fields outlined by trees, the road with no shelter where they could hide. They stood in the last piece of forest, the last safe place, and he shivered. It was hard to walk out into the bright, unfiltered sunshine.

"Come on," he said loudly. "We're going out of the forest now."

"I haven't seen the bison." She thought about this while they walked. It was nearly summer, and she hadn't seen the bison. It made her sad, and she didn't speak again for hours. Even the warmth of the sun didn't cheer her. Behind her, farther away with each step, was something large, and dark, and beautiful that she had not found.

They couldn't go many miles each day. Hansel was too tired all the time now. They stopped and slept and rested a lot.

"We have to steal some food," he told her. "But they could kill us if we steal."

"Then I'll just ask them for it." Gretel smiled.

Hansel knew she had no fear because she was crazy. Everybody was afraid except crazy people. He had seen people like that in the ghetto, and they were the only happy people. Hansel sat and tried to remember the apartment. It had been years ago when they lived there, he guessed.

But Gretel did ask for food. She walked up to farms and went to the houses outside villages. She smoothed her hair and smiled and knocked on the doors and asked for food. It wasn't begging exactly. She just asked for bread as if she had been sent by a neighbor to borrow it.

And the people looked at the blond, radiant child, so thin you'd think the light would just shine right through her, and they gave her bread. Sometimes a person slammed the door shut and told her to go away, but mostly they gave her bread. Women offered to let the girl sleep inside for the night, but Gretel shook her head. It was warm now, and she loved being outside.

They ate and wandered, and Hansel knew he needed to find the city, but he couldn't remember the name of it, and he was afraid to ask at any of the farms. They just kept moving.

They had gone twenty or thirty miles when they came to a river. It wasn't a big river, only a tributary of the larger one, and it looked shallow, but neither of the children dared to try to wade it. They couldn't swim.

"We'll walk along the bank and maybe we'll find a bridge," Hansel said.

They walked past two bends in the river, and Gretel saw it first. There was a long field, rising to a hill, and over the hill came something large and white. Hansel was lying on his side, nearly asleep, and she called to him.

"Look, Hansel! It's a huge swan."

Hansel sat up and stared at the tank coming toward the river. There were more tanks coming after it. He knew they should run, but his legs were so heavy. He was too afraid to move. He sat and panted like a fox cornered by hounds.

Gretel watched the tanks coming, the white one, camouflaged for winter snow, leading, and six others behind. It was a swan, and it was coming right toward her.

The noise of the tanks was deafening as they came close. Hansel saw that there were men riding on top of the tanks. They laughed when they saw the children, and the white tank slowed. A man on the tank called down to Gretel, but she shook her head. It wasn't Polish.

Hansel knew it must be Russian because it didn't sound like German either. Some of the tanks had rags of red flags flying on the top. One of the men pointed across the river and gestured.

"*Tak,*" Gretel shouted in Polish. "Yes!"

The soldiers on the white tank laughed. One of them jumped down and tossed first Gretel and then Hansel onto the tank. The children sat, held firmly by the men, and the white tank moved on with a jolting rhythm.

"The swan is taking us across the river," Gretel screamed over the noise of the engine.

"It's a tank," he screamed back. "It's not a swan."

The tank moved into the water and when they had crossed the river and gone up into the next field, it slowed and the soldiers lowered the children to the ground.

"Goodbye, dear swan," Gretel called as the tanks moved away.

She thought it was a swan, and Hansel didn't care. They were over the river.

They lay in the fields that night. It was clear and there was no sound of guns, only the owls and the squeak of bats and the cicadas that were beginning their shrill calling.

"See the stars," Gretel said. "I know what they are."

"What are they?" Hansel was half asleep and glad it wasn't raining.

"All those stars in that big streak that goes over the whole sky? You see them? Those are all the Jews who've died. All of them died and went up in the air, and the stars are the stars that they wore on their coats. The stars on the coats come off when their souls float up and the stars live up in the sky forever."

Hansel stared at the mass of light in the Milky Way and shivered. "That's awful."

"No it isn't. It's lovely. They'll be there forever."

They were nearly asleep when he spoke again.

"It wasn't a swan."

But Gretel just smiled and looked up at the stars until her eyes shut and she fell asleep.

The Wheat Field

It was safer to move by day now, but at night the planes came and sometimes they tossed down bombs that left holes in the road. Hansel tried to think of everything.

Don't walk on the road at night.

Don't get close to the soldiers.

Don't get so tired you fall asleep out in a field where you can be seen.

As they walked in the Polish countryside, the skeletons of burned-out tanks and trucks lay scattered like the toys of the devil. There were dead bodies, and Hansel didn't look at them. The summer heat rotted the corpses so fast that the children could not take anything from them. The food left in the dead soldiers' packs smelled of their rotting flesh, and made them feel sick.

Gretel hated the dead horses. She turned her head when they came on one, legs stuck out, belly swollen with gas, in a field or washed up on the gravel bar of a river.

Hansel wasn't sure what he was doing now. He still thought of the city sometimes, but he couldn't hold the idea in his head. Mostly he looked for food and watched out for the airplanes and for stray soldiers who might be hiding in the fields. Sometimes he was angry with Gretel and screamed at her. She was supposed to help, and he couldn't always make her do what she had to do. Some days he just ignored her and didn't try to make her be quiet and hide when he did.

It was July, and the fields were full of food. Hansel looked for a field of chickpeas with tangled brush near it. The brush nearly always had berries they could eat, and the chickpeas made his stomach ache, but they filled him up.

Gretel was happy wandering, singing and telling stories she remembered from her old books. Hansel was too tired to tell her to shut up, and he kept walking even though he didn't think much more about where they were going. He still had the little bottle in his pocket. It didn't smell of raspberries now, and it was all that was left of the time in the hut and of Magda.

At night he fought with his sister. Gretel liked sleeping in open places, and Hansel knew it wasn't safe. He tried to make her crawl into brushy thickets, but she refused. He even threatened to leave her. She just laughed and walked away into the middle of a field where she lay down and stared up at the sky as it turned from dark blue to blackish blue to black. Gretel loved to lie and look up at the stars.

So Hansel, afraid to sleep apart, slept with her in the middle of the fields of growing things. They would lie and watch the sky and the waxing and waning of the moon as the summer passed.

The shooting stars disturbed Gretel. She was afraid that a Jew had fallen out of the sky, and she would begin to cry. Hansel didn't know what to say at first, but he thought of something that made her hush.

"They aren't falling. They're going down to meet other people that are going up."

Gretel liked that, and she stopped crying for the falling stars. Hansel wondered if he would be met by a star when he died. He thought he'd die soon. He wanted to lie down and sleep all day and all night and never have to wake up.

Finally, it was August, and the planes flew over less often at night, but the drone of the engines above the earth still woke Hansel. He would look for the machines moving between the earth and the stars, but they flew on, and he would go back to sleep.

And then they found a field that Gretel loved so much she refused to walk past it.

"Look," she shouted. "Look what I've found."

The thing stood on the edge of a field that was planted in wheat. The smoke from a village was over a distant hill, so Hansel let her stay in the field. There were no workers in sight.

"Look!"

He saw it, but he didn't know what it was. A wooden thing on legs.

"It's got hay in it. It's a box to feed the cows."

"No. It's not for cows. It's a grand piano."

She stroked the swollen keys, locked solid by months of rain and snow. Some were missing, and the lid of the piano was gone where the farmer had torn it off.

Gretel stood in front of it, and her mind began to remember a little. She almost fainted with the way she felt, standing in front of the mutilated piano. She placed her fingers on the swollen keys and began to play a song that sounded only in her head. Someone had taught her to play the song. In a house. A woman. A sweet smell. The woman put her hands on Gretel's hands.

Gretel leaned against the piano for nearly an hour, playing the same song over and over on the keys that didn't move. The gutted box of the instrument stood rotting. Hansel crawled under it and slept in the shade during the noon heat, but Gretel kept playing and playing the song. It disturbed her. She wanted to cry or laugh. She moaned a little but kept stroking the keys.

Gretel refused to leave the field. When she touched the piano, she was afraid, but she couldn't leave it. The music she heard in her head had stirred her up. "I'm sleeping here."

"It's too open. Let's sleep near the creek."

"I like the field."

"You could get water easier near the creek."

"No."

"You like the piano," he accused her. She would make stupid decisions just because of something like a rotten old piano. He stared out at the field. "And those flowers. You want to sleep on the flowers."

She nodded. The wheat was beginning to turn darker gold, and the poppies sprinkled in the gold were red and beautiful as the wind made them sway.

"They're like houses where fairies could live." She touched the red petals of a poppy softly.

The flowers looked like drops of blood to Hansel, but he didn't argue. They lay down by the piano, and both fell into an exhausted sleep.

Neither stirred as seven men slipped from the direction of the creek and walked into the wheat field, spreading out and lying down like the children but not sleeping, their guns, oiled and clean, beside them. They lay in the field waiting for hours.

The sun turned the gray light pink and golden. It was dawn. Hansel sat up and stayed perfectly still, thinking. Something was different. Something was not the way it ought to be in the morning, but he couldn't think what it was. He just sat and didn't move.

Then he realized what was different. The birds, the crows, and all the songbirds were not flying over the field. Few birds darted over the wheat catching insects. It was silent the way morning shouldn't be silent.

Hansel was listening so hard that his jaw clenched. And then Gretel woke up. She stretched and started to stand.

"Get down," Hansel whispered and reached out for her leg to stop her.

"It's morning. I'm thirsty."

"Shut up, Gretel." Hansel was straining to hear.

She pulled her leg away and stood up, lifting her arms over her head in a stretch. Hansel opened his mouth to call her, but the sound of his words were lost in the crash of gunfire. Hansel stood up and saw the men.

They were in the middle of the wheat and were firing at men in German uniforms who had just come out of the trees near the creek on the far side of the field. The Germans fell to the ground and returned fire.

Hansel opened his mouth and began to scream. Gretel stood stunned, looking at the men, her hands open in front of her, fingers wide apart, as if she could push the bullets away. Hansel didn't care anymore. He stopped screaming and began to walk toward the men with the guns. He was too tired. He had just woken up, but he was so tired that he knew he was probably dead. It didn't matter.

"Stop it. Stop it. Make it stop." The boy was running now toward the men with guns. He ran jerkily, screaming again at them, and soon he would reach the space between the men in the field and the men near the creek.

Gretel saw the movement of his body and turned. He was running toward the guns. He was going to die.

Something in her mind gave way and the memories came in like a wall of water, all at once, the thoughts filling every empty place in her head. She remembered. The war. The guns. Magda. Her father. The Stepmother. She had to take care of Hansel. The forest. The motorcycle. Telek. The ghetto. The tinkling of ice. Nelka. Hansel.

Gretel began to run as soon as the thoughts began, and she ran the way animals run. She bounded after her brother and caught up with him in a few leaps. She didn't try to call him, but fell on him and knocked him down and held him against her. He struggled and then went limp, and she was afraid he'd been shot and was dead. She ran her hands over him, felt no hot warmth of spilled blood, and then held him tight.

Hansel turned in her arms and clung to Gretel. He held her, pressing his face against her, and so they lay, each child taking the other and holding fast.

She opened her mouth, but her mind was so full of memories, she couldn't speak. Hansel lay totally still, clutching her, and she pressed her head to his and let her mind run free.

The hut. There had been a barn. And buckets, and she couldn't ever look out the window. Swans. She had seen thousands of them, and one of them carried her over the water. No. Something carried them. The oven. Magda.

Gretel shut her eyes. She lay and remembered and didn't know where she was or why she had forgotten for so long. She held Hansel, and when the guns stopped she lay and hummed to him. She hummed like Magda had hummed, softly, deep in her throat.

The memories kept coming while she was humming. She let them flow through her mind, and then she stopped humming suddenly. She wanted her name. Her real name. She wanted to have it. She lay still and tried to fish the name out of the water of memory that flooded her mind, but it was no use. She could only remember Gretel, the name that the Stepmother had given her when they were abandoned in the dark forest.

The girl held her brother more tightly and fought with her mind.

She couldn't get at her name or her brother's name either. Other memories were coming to her, although her mind still stuttered and was confused. Something had happened in the forest, when everything was made of ice—she remembered being very cold and looking up at rainbows in the ice. Something had happened, but she could not think what it was. That and the two names were gone.

The men, paying no attention to the children, but taking their guns, checking to see if one of their party was truly dead or only wounded, ran after the fleeing German remnant who had gone back over the creek. They left the field, calling to each other in excitement. Only one of theirs dead, and they had killed a dozen.

Gretel hummed, and in a while a single crow flew over the field in curiosity. The corpse of a man lay on his back, pressing down the wheat in the shape of an X. His red blood had spattered and was drying brown on the gold of the grain. The crow soared above the man and flew on.

The children lay together in the field, and finally Hansel turned his face up to her.

"I'm dead."

"No, you're not. I felt you. There's no blood on you."

Hansel pulled back and looked at her.

"Gretel?"

"I remember. I'd forgotten, but I remember nearly all of it now."

Gretel frowned. The names would not come to her. She remembered Telek finding her and carrying her back to Magda. She remembered the hut on fire. Gretel shut her eyes for a moment and then opened them and looked at her brother.

Hansel stared into her eyes, and saw that she had come back into the world. She was with him again. He sighed deeply and put his face back against her shoulder.

"I'm tired, Gretel."

"Me too. Where's the forest, Hansel?"

"The forest was a long time ago."

She lay there and thought. "We have to go back."

"To the forest?"

"No. To the city. We have to look for Father. And our stepmother.

There aren't so many soldiers now. The tanks are nearly gone. We have to find the city."

"I can't remember the name."

"Of the city?"

He nodded his head.

"It's Bialystok, silly. We went there when the Germans came, and that's where we were with Father last, remember? Father put us in big tires and we rode out of the ghetto on the back of the trucks. Then there was the pit with all the grease, before the forest."

Hansel shut his eyes and felt himself relax. He wasn't dead. She knew the name of the city. He began to smile and felt the sun on his body. He didn't think he'd ever get tired of the warmth.

"Gretel, what was my name? Before the forest?"

She was silent and tears came into her eyes. His name was as lost to her as her own, and she couldn't bear telling that truth to her brother.

"We have to call each other Hansel and Gretel. The Stepmother said. You know that."

He nodded his head. The Stepmother had said. Gretel didn't want to say his name because it still wasn't safe. Someday it would be different, and she could tell him. He fell asleep and slept deeply for the first time in months.

Bread

For three weeks they walked. Now that the Germans were gone, it was a little easier. People fed them, and they could walk openly on the roads. Gretel asked directions and begged food, and there was something in her insistence that made people point the way. A man once walked a mile with the children and showed them a dirt road that would keep them away from the stream of Russians moving toward the city.

"They captured the city at the end of July," the man said. He looked at the beautiful girl child. "But don't trust the Russians. Stay away from them."

"We're going to find our father and stepmother."

The man watched the children walk away toward the north and the city. Everyone was looking for someone. And most of them would be disappointed. He shook his head and turned back to his fields. He wondered who would steal his crops this autumn. Probably the Russians. He was too cynical, his wife said, but the world wouldn't care about Poland when war was over.

The road outside the city was full of trucks and tanks. The Russians poured into the city and onward toward the west.

"They don't look like soldiers," Gretel said.

"They beat the Germans. How are we going to find Father?" Hansel waved at the ragged soldiers who sometimes waved back.

"We'll go to the house in the ghetto and wait for him."

Hansel remembered being in the apartment with a lot of people and the cantor singing under the window. But that was all. He didn't remember anything much before the forest. There was just the forest and Gretel and Magda and Nelka and Telek and him.

A Russian soldier tried to speak to the children in broken Polish. He finally gave up and simply said, "Bialystok?"

Gretel nodded.

The soldier waved at a passing truck and when it stopped, he picked up the children and put them in the back. "Bialystok," he shouted at the driver. The Russian soldiers in the back grinned at Hansel and Gretel, and Hansel grinned back until his face was sore.

"They smell bad," Gretel whispered.

"They have to chase the Nazis. There isn't time to wash."

Gretel watched the buildings which were larger and larger and closer together as they drove into the city. She knew it was Bialystok, but everything had changed.

"It's big." Hansel shivered.

"I don't see anything I know."

The truck rattled over a damaged bridge, the railing shell-pocked and broken.

"Bialy Lake," she shouted. "We have to get out. I can get home from the park."

The men laughed when she tried to climb out, and they shouted to the driver, who stopped. Hansel and Gretel were lifted and dropped down on the far side of the bridge. They walked and walked, and she finally sat down on a patch of dirt and thought.

"This is the Bialy Lake. It has to be the park, but it doesn't look like the park anymore. They cut so many trees. And the buildings—"

Hansel looked at the buildings of the city beyond the dirt area. He shivered. Half of them were blackened and empty, burned out and roofless. The others had no windows and stood abandoned.

"Where are we?"

"I don't know. Shut up, Hansel."

But he didn't shut up. He walked down a street with Gretel trailing after him, and he began to ask people questions. Tugging at a woman's sleeve, he would demand, "Where are all the people who used to be here? Where did all the people live that the Nazis made live here?"

Hansel didn't dare say the word *Jew*. He asked in dozens of ways but he was afraid to say that word to anyone. An old woman stopped and stared at the child whose hair was half dirty blond and half brown. She shook her head.

"Where is the ghetto?"

"Burned, boy. Burned and gone. All of it."

"Where are the people?"

She shrugged and turned away.

"The city isn't like it was." Gretel sighed and sat down on a curb in the busy marketplace.

"What was it like?" Hansel put his head on her shoulder and watched the people bartering for vegetables and even an occasional lump of butter.

"There was a man with a monkey."

"What does a monkey look like?"

"It was little and brown and furry, and it took the coins out of your hand and tipped his hat at you."

"I want a monkey," Hansel said. "I want my own monkey."

"And you could get on the trolley and ride out to the woods. And the horses were lovely that pulled it. And the market on Piaskes where you could buy—"

Hansel stood up tiredly. They had to find the ghetto. He walked to a man who was carrying an old tire in his arms. Tugging at the man's shirt, Hansel asked again.

"Where are the people who lived here? When the Germans came? Where was the ghetto?"

The man turned, and Hansel looked up at him. For a moment they both stared at each other without moving. His hair was longer, more shaggy than when Hansel had seen him last, but the dark eyes and long eyelashes were the same, the handsome face was only a little dirty.

"Run, Gretel! It's him! Run!"

She saw the man and leapt up. The two children ran between the crowds of peasants, stepping on food laid out on blankets, uncaring about the shouts and curses that followed them.

The man was close behind them. He had thrown down the tire and was loping after them. The man was dressed as a Polish peasant but he had the face of the Oberführer.

Hansel didn't look over his shoulder. In the mass of people crowded into the square, he and Gretel managed to lose the man at first. They ran down a long street and stopped, panting, their hearts banging.

"Run! He's coming!"

The Oberführer had turned into the street with long strides and came after them. Hansel couldn't look back again. They ran and darted down one street and then another. Once they turned into an alley with no way out, and Gretel helped him climb through a little hole in the fence to get to the next street.

"Stop, Hansel."

He stopped and looked back at his sister. The Nazi was not in sight.

"This is it. This is where the ghetto was."

It was even worse than the rest of the city. The chimneys were torn from the building in front of her. To their right was a line of bombed buildings, the bricks blackened by fire.

"The cobblestone pavement," she muttered, looking down. It led to the alley where you turned. "The third floor, second door on the left. That was our apartment."

"We have to keep going," he begged. It was getting late. The sky was darkening. It was going to be night soon. The Oberführer might find them if they stood on the street.

They had run into the desolated section of the city until there were no people around them. Only the blasted buildings stood, their shadows falling on the two children.

"It was the Oberführer."

"Yes." She shivered.

"He'll kill us. He killed—" Hansel stopped. He didn't want to think about whether the Oberführer had killed anyone else. It was a big city. They would never meet him again with so many people.

"We'll sleep here, Gretel. Tomorrow we'll ask where the people went."

"There aren't any people left. I don't know if these are the right cobblestones. The buildings all look different now."

"Come on."

They climbed over rubble and went into the front of a house. It had been divided into apartments, but all the doors were gone, and the glass was broken out. The children walked up the stairs that still stood.

"Don't get close to the edge," she told him. The railing had been broken off and lay in pieces at the bottom.

They walked up to the next floor, and Gretel looked for a bed or a blanket to lie on. One room had an iron bed, but the springs and mattress were gone. Another room was full of feathers from a mattress that was ripped open, the cloth rotting and spotted with mildew.

Hansel picked up handfuls of the goose down and threw it in the air. It clung to his hair and shirt, and he laughed. There were photographs on the floor. A boy holding his dog. People sitting on a blanket outside wearing bathing suits for swimming.

"Look." Gretel showed him the photograph. "They were having a picnic."

"The Germans let them?"

"It must have been before the Germans." Gretel laid the picture down and covered it with feathers. "Come on."

They went up until they came to a stair that led onto the roof. It was a hot night. The air barely stirred. Leaning over the parapet, Gretel looked out at the gutted buildings standing close together, and she didn't see a single person. "Let's sleep outside."

Hansel nodded. He didn't like being inside anymore. It made him think about the hut and the stove. And Magda. He closed his hand over the bottle in his pocket.

They took some sacks out of a room downstairs and carried them up to the roof. The sacks were rough, but both children were too tired to care. Gretel fell asleep immediately, but Hansel twisted and turned. Finally he got up and crept down the stairs. He took Magda's bottle from his pocket and looked for something to use to tie it. Finding a piece of string, he tied it on to the bottle. Then the boy set the bottle on a broken piece of wood and put the string across the stair. He looked at his work for a moment and climbed back up to the roof.

Hansel fell asleep then, curled up close to his sister, both of them sweating lightly from the heat rising off the roof, until dawn when the breeze cooled them and they lay limp and dreaming.

———

It was still dark, but a gray sort of darkness, when the sound of glass splintering woke Hansel. He didn't stop to think but grabbed Gretel and shook her.

"Run," he whispered. "It's the Oberführer."

Groggy with sleep, Gretel stood, but his terror seized her and brought her to full alertness. They looked around, and Hansel took her hand.

"The roofs. We can jump."

Running to gain momentum, the children jumped off the edge and landed with a hollow thud on the next roof. It hadn't been a bad jump, only a few feet. The silhouette of a man came into the doorway leading onto the roof behind them.

Hansel had landed running. There must be a door, some way to get down. But the door was heavy and slumped on its hinges, blocking the stairs.

Gretel looked behind and saw the Oberführer's pale face looking across the gap in the buildings. "Why does he chase us? The war's over." She sobbed.

Hansel didn't care why. He took her hand and they ran across the roof, running around holes. The light was paler now, but it was still hard to see clearly. They jumped three more times until they came to an edge that was too far from the building next to it.

Hansel measured the distance with his eyes. Then he looked back. The Oberführer was moving more slowly now, but he kept coming over the roofs toward them. His beautiful pale face shone in the gray darkness. Gretel was close to tears.

"I want Telek."

"We have to jump, Gretel. He can't do it. He's too heavy."

"He'll catch us. We'll fall."

"No we won't."

The boy stared across the gap in the buildings. He'd never jumped so far before.

"That roof is all burned. We'll break through and fall. We'll die."

"No we won't." He was screaming. "Hold my hand. We'll run and jump. Quick."

The Oberführer began to run when he saw they were going to jump again.

Holding hands, the boy and girl ran toward the edge and simultaneously leapt into space. Light-boned and starved, their bodies hung in the air, and the Oberführer stopped to watch. They disappeared from view, and the man ran to look.

Both children lay on the edge of the roof opposite. He looked at the distance and the holes in the roof and cursed. "Fucking Gypsies!"

Gretel was sobbing. Hansel had cut his leg where it had gone through the shingle of a burned place on the roof. He stood up, ignoring the blood trickling down his leg.

"Come on." He trotted toward the far edge of the building, and he was ready to jump again, to jump hundreds of buildings, to fly if he had to, but he saw the old metal steps used as a fire escape clinging perilously to the side of the building. Hansel climbed onto it, and Gretel followed, still crying, but moving fast behind Hansel.

They climbed down for what seemed a long time, and finally had to drop six feet when the ladder ended above the alley. Hansel waited for Gretel, and they hugged.

"We have to get back where people are."

She nodded, and they walked toward the street.

Rising out of the dawn light, at the mouth of the alley, the Oberführer stood and waited for the children. He blocked their exit, and there were only tall buildings on each of the other three sides. Hansel looked back at the ladder, but it was too high for them to reach.

The man was on them. He picked up Hansel and slapped him, holding the boy with outstretched arms. "Nelka told you about the blood. You dirty Gypsies are going to use it against me. Trash. Mud people. Filthy Gypsies!"

The Oberführer was screaming, and he ignored Gretel who was beating against his side. The SS man reached in his pocket. Hansel saw a flash of metal and kicked out wildly.

He pointed the knife blade at Hansel's throat, and the boy froze.

Staring at the child, the man twisted his mouth and spit full in Hansel's face.

"Fucking Gypsy bastard!"

Hansel stared back, and then his rage came up in him. "I'm a Jew! I'm a Jew!" And he spit in the Oberführer's face twice, hard.

Gretel was battering the man with her fists, and Hansel kept screaming, "I'm a Jew," as the Oberführer tried to hold him still enough to get the knife to the boy's throat.

And then there were men behind them on the street, and the voice that penetrated the screaming was lazy sounding, almost amused.

"Put 'I'm a Jew' down. Now."

The Oberführer turned, still holding the struggling boy. The Russian soldier in the street cocked his pistol.

"Put him down."

The SS man dropped Hansel in the mud of the alley, and Gretel fell on him, covering him like a hen covering a chick. Hansel threw her off and stood up, enraged, screaming.

"I'm a Jew, and he's the Oberführer. He stole Nelka's baby, and he's a German."

The Russian soldier was joined by several others. They stood and watched and grinned. Afraid to speak, the Oberführer stood silent.

"How do you know he's German, boy?"

"He was in the village. He's bad." Gretel stood up and pointed at the Oberführer. "He wore the black and silver uniform. He's SS."

"Ask him to talk. Just ask him." Hansel stared at the Nazi. The boy knew why the man was silent. "He talks like the Germans do. You'll see."

"Speak, man."

The Oberführer opened his mouth and closed it again. Then he gave it up and began to curse in German.

The soldiers laughed until Hansel laughed too.

"Well, I'm-a-Jew, you've caught yourself a real, live Nazi."

A truck came down the street, and the Russian whistled it over. The Oberführer was loaded into the back, joining other men already caught, and the Russian grinned at the children.

"He's going to be a birthday present for Papa Stalin, kids."

"I want you to kill him," Hansel said. "He and that woman took Nelka's baby, and they took Magda away." His voice trembled and his face still burned from the slaps.

"Papa Stalin is smart, boy. He's thrifty. The German will go to Siberia and we'll get some work out of him first. They don't come back from Siberia."

The Oberführer rose up in the truck and leaned toward the children, shaking his fists. "I'll never die. You can't kill me."

The Russian soldiers slammed the metal gate of the truck shut in the man's face and slapped the side to tell the driver to move on.

"Don't worry, boy. He's gone."

Hansel watched the truck drive out of sight, and he called after the soldiers, using the word openly for the first time when he asked directions.

"Where are the Jews? Where can we find Jews?"

The soldiers looked at one another. The leader sighed and took a few steps toward Hansel.

"Try the refugee center. It's where the old age home was. Ask. Everybody knows it."

They walked for blocks until they came to streets where people were moving about. Already the bricks from bombed buildings were being cleaned and loaded into wheelbarrows.

"The old age home? The old age home?"

Hansel shouted it over and over, and the two children followed all the pointing fingers until a man nodded at a building with a banner on the front.

REFUGEES—SOUP KITCHEN

Holding Gretel's hand, he ran up the steps. There were men inside sitting at tables, and people stood around the tables, twenty deep, talking.

"Come on," Hansel said. Dropping on all fours, he crawled between the legs of the people and under the huge tables. Gretel followed, and they came out on the other side. He didn't care about the men at the tables now. Hansel was following his nose which was twitching from the smells in the building. It was the hot yeasty smell of bread baking, oil spattering in a pan, and some other smell he barely remembered.

"They're cooking meat," Gretel whispered.

Hansel walked faster now. He followed the rich scent that thickened the air, and he turned into a large room, pulling Gretel with him. The room had tables and chairs set up in rows. Women walked to and from the kitchen, which was behind the room, putting out plates, and spoons, and bowls on a long table next to the wall.

"Look! Oh, Hansel! Look!"

He looked. Stoves with shining pots almost as large as he was. Soup cooking. Meat roasting. Best of all, metal racks reaching nearly to the ceiling. Racks full of bread baked before dawn in the ovens.

Hansel stared and felt the saliva run down his chin. He wiped it away and reached his hand out to steal a loaf of bread. There were too many people in the room. He would be beaten and driven off. And that's when he saw it.

"Gretel, the breadcrumbs. They won't care about the crumbs."

He remembered now. The breadcrumbs he had thrown on the ground in the forest. The night. The owl calling. There were breadcrumbs on this floor, but a lot of them. A long path of crumbs leading to the back of the kitchen. Women carrying racks of bread walked past the children and more crumbs fell onto the floor.

"Magda said I threw away our luck. I tore up the bread and threw it on the ground."

"It was me," Gretel said. "I stepped on the line in the dirt. I stepped out of the circle the first day. When we found Magda. It was bad luck."

He was crying now. He moved away from his sister and crouched on the floor, sweeping the crumbs up and putting them in his pockets, trying to get every one. He followed the trail of flakes from the dozens and dozens of loaves of bread brought out of the ovens, and he was determined to pick up all the bread, all the luck that he had dropped and thrown away. He crawled across the floor, white-faced, intent, not missing a crumb.

Along the back wall was a line of ovens. Men stood with flat wooden paddles, and occasionally they opened the doors and shoveled out the loaves of bread cooked golden by the fires. Two men turned to stare at the boy and the blond girl who followed him.

One of the men, thin and dark-bearded, a round scar on the right side of his chest, let his paddle fall from his hand, and the crash of wood on the floor made Gretel jump. Hansel looked up and saw the man fall to his knees beside the oven.

The boy's face puckered. He frowned and clenched his fists. Then slowly he got up and walked over the crumbs into the arms of the man.

"You left us," Hansel said. "You went away."

The man sobbed and he held the boy out so he could look into his face. He ran his fingers over the poor, dyed hair and the pale skin. He touched the dark circles under the boy's eyes and the bruise on one cheek.

Gretel couldn't move. She stood and watched her father sobbing and Hansel standing rigid in his arms. She looked at the two of them, but she didn't move, didn't speak.

The Mechanik was able to stand then. He looked at the girl. His eyes were so tear-filled that her face blurred, and her hair became a pale light around her head and shoulders. Keeping his hand locked on Hansel's shoulder, he moved to her.

"Father?"

He nodded and pulled her to him.

"It was cold," she said. "She tried to cook us, and I never saw the bison." Gretel was shaking all over, and her mind was chaotic again as she tried to take it in. It was her father.

"She hasn't got it right," Hansel began, but he clung to his father and couldn't talk.

"You were gone, and Stepmother was gone and we've looked for you for so long." Gretel's body wouldn't stop shaking.

He nodded. "They told me you were taken to the camps. They said you were dead."

"I couldn't find the house where we lived. The cobblestones were gone."

"I knew you'd come to the city if you were alive. I knew you'd think of it." He stood with his children and the joy nearly made his heart stop beating.

"I remember so much, but sometimes it goes away." Her face twisted, and she stared into his eyes. And then she began to smile. The beard made his face like the face of her grandfather. The man who gave her oranges.

"I will help you remember," her father said.

"I can't remember either."

"What can't you remember, my son?"

"The Stepmother told me that I'm Hansel. But who was I before? Gretel got better, but she wouldn't say our names."

Gretel tried to remember her real name. She had dreamed about it so many times, since the wheat field, but she couldn't pull the name out of her dreams and speak it. The name had stayed gone, as if it were hiding from her. And her brother's name was gone too.

The man looked down at the faces of his children. So thin. So much older looking in the ravaged tightness of their skin. They looked back at him, heads tilted up and eyes shining, their lips half open, both of them waiting to hear their names.

He spoke each name slowly, quietly, the crowd of workers that had gathered around the three catching up the sounds and echoing the names in whispers. He spoke their names over and over, and watched these gifts brought out of darkness, these bits of flesh, this blood of his blood and bone of his bone, his children, begin to smile as they became, once again, themselves.

The Witch

It is finished. The tale is told truthfully, and truth is no heavier, no more beautiful than lies. Yet there is something that makes me love the truth, and that love made me wander and worry until the truth was given to you, like a gift. For this in the end is what we have. The love of something.

Wild ponies. A kiss salted by tears. The scent of raspberry syrup in a bottle. Oranges. Two lost children who come to your house in the dark forest.

There is much to love, and that love is what we are left with. When the bombs stop dropping, and the camps fall back to the earth and decay, and we are done killing each other, that is what we must hold. We can never let the world take our memories of love away, and if there are no memories, we must invent love all over again.

The wheel turns. Blue above, green below, we wander a long way, but love is what the cup of our soul contains when we leave the world and the flesh. This we will drink forever. I know. I am Magda. I am the witch.

A PENGUIN READERS GUIDE TO

THE TRUE STORY OF HANSEL AND GRETEL

Louise Murphy

AN INTRODUCTION TO
The True Story of Hansel and Gretel

"The story has been told over and over by liars and it must be retold."

In the winter of 1943, on the outskirts of a dark forest, two Jewish children flee the Nazis with their father and stepmother. In a moment of desperation, the children are given the aliases Hansel and Gretel and sent alone into the woods to hide. Gretel leads her younger brother in search of food and protection, while Hansel leaves a trail of breadcrumbs behind so that their father might find them again. So begins *The True Story of Hansel and Gretel,* which takes us along on their journey into a forest more ancient than man. In a landscape populated by exotic beasts, refugees, and revolutionaries, the two children embark upon a new life as Christian orphans, protected by a woman who is called Magda the witch and whose tiny hut is heated by an enormous baker's oven.

In this extraordinary novel by Louise Murphy, a fairy tale is reimagined and a war story retold. It is the story of individuals striving to survive and a village trying to outlast a war. Magda the witch lives on the edge of Piaski, in a region of Eastern Poland that has been overrun first by Russians and now by Germans. Her family is an assortment of outsiders: her brother Piotr a fallen priest, her great-niece Nelka a beauty in love with an enigmatic woodsman, her dead grandmother a Gypsy and an abortionist. The villagers are terrorized by a small but vicious Nazi presence and weary at the end of a war that has brought them many conquerors and few saviors. Murphy unflinchingly presents the war as a landscape of horrors, the village humiliated under the yoke of ruthless SS officers and by the necessities of survival under unbearable circumstances.

We also follow the trials of Hansel and Gretel's father, who endures a brutal winter of revolutionary action and personal transformation, all the while preoccupied with the fear that his children may not survive and the hope that he will find them again. This unique novel gives voice to figures that have before now been underrepresented in the writing of World War II: the voices of Jews who hid in the forests, of men and women who participated in resistance movements, and of Polish civilians. These characters struggle with their relationship with God, with their disgust for a humanity in crisis, and with the desire to define a new and more just world.

Yet Murphy manages to maintain the fairy-tale foundation of her story, returning again and again to the elements of an old story to infuse meaning into a newer one. The Bialowieza Forest, the oldest in Europe, is a place of mysterious and untouched beauty, and its lessons for the children and for humanity permeate the book. Murphy juxtaposes horror with lyricism, reality with magic. The primal nature of war is met by the primal power of story—and the belief that love can rescue humans from their worst capabilities. Hansel and Gretel are on a quest to reclaim their identities, and the witch and the forest—the world of the fairy tale—show them the way.

In prose both luminous and enlightening, Murphy explores the power of memory, the necessity of love in times of great trauma, and the redemption that can come about through the refusal to erase one's own past. This is the tale of two brave children who never give up, of women who refuse to be defined by convention, and of the bitter cost of survival. Over the course of the winter, Hansel and Gretel will come of age. Their mother dead, their father and stepmother in hiding, by necessity forced to alter their own identities, they become survivors.

A Conversation with
Louise Murphy

1. The True Story of Hansel and Gretel *is in part the retelling of a classic fairy tale. How long have you had an interest in fairy tales and in the story of Hansel and Gretel in particular?*

As a child, I did not like most fairy tales, particularly this one. The deep unconscious meanings in those stories triggered my nightmares. In college I took a folklore course that fascinated me as we traced and studied the folk motifs that are found in every culture.

2. The original fairy tale is actually quite frightening; is that one reason why you chose it as a frame for this harrowing tale?

This is the fairy tale that scared me the most when I was a child. It mirrors my worst adult fears about what the abandonment and blind violence of war does to children all over the world.

3. You seem to try to redeem certain characters, particularly women, from the traditional stereotyping they receive in fairy tales and elsewhere. The stepmother and the witch, two types often vilified, are portrayed very positively. Were you conscious of this as a feminist project? And are these stereotypes the kinds of lies that you have Magda refer to at the start?

Stereotypes are always lies. It was the idea of "the witch" that began my struggle to understand Magda and then all the other characters. Our culture denigrates older women, yet they are often the ones who protect and nurture everyone in the family. As many "blended" families demonstrate, there are loving stepparents in every culture. I don't like stereotypes of any group of people.

4. This story takes place in a particular region of Eastern Poland. How did you learn about the history of the area, and what kind of research did you do for the book? How did you balance research and storytelling?

I have no personal memories of World War II. It is all history for me, so I was lucky to have the Holocaust Library in San Francisco and the University of California library nearby with its huge collection of books. I read for three years and took hundreds of pages of notes to understand the area and the people, the timetable of the war and the daily details of life in a Polish village during World War II. Ultimately, it is the characters that matter to me. They take over the novel and drive the plot, but research gives the novelist ideas, and the setting of any story becomes part of its power.

5. The Bialowieza Forest is one of the last patches of primeval growth in Europe. It seems like the perfect setting for a fairy tale, a place where stories might both emerge and endure, almost outside of time. How did you find out about this forest, and have you ever actually been there?

I have never visited the forest. I learned of it while watching television! It was a program on the Bialowieza Forest, and it was like watching a film about a country in your dreams. I saw the program several years before I began the book, and vaguely thought it would be a wonderful place to set the Magda story, if I ever wrote it.

6. This region was also home to many of Hitler's concentration camps. Many people identify the Holocaust with Germany and have less information about the events that took place in Poland. Is this a reason why you chose to set the story in Poland rather than in Germany?

Poland was called "the anvil of the devil" during the war. The German master plan was to kill all the Jews, Gypsies, dissidents, and leaders in Poland, then starve off the old and the very young, leaving a work force to build cities for the new German world order. Children who looked Aryan must be kidnapped and "saved," because the Germans did not have enough population for their grandiose scheme. At the end of the building, all the remaining Polish workers would be killed in the camps. Setting a novel in this place allowed me to show the horrors of war against children and civilians and put my characters in situations where they had to make hard decisions daily.

7. You certainly do not flinch from depicting acts of true horror, and characters like the Oberführer seem to typify the Nazi as an incarnation of evil. With other characters, including some of the Polish citizens and Major Frankel in particular, you step away from such absolute characteristics and tread more in the realm of psychological ambiguity. Guilty though these characters are, you make them human beings. Was this difficult, especially when writing about such an iconic and horrific event?

I honestly do not understand the psychotic desire to control, torture, and kill that the Oberführer represents, and he was the most difficult character to portray. I experimented with humanizing him, but it was like saying that "after all, Hitler loved his dogs." No humanizing can explain and forgive such evil. Men like the Oberführer appear when historical events give them permission to use this dark side of the human imagination. Major Frankel is a very different type. He is a man in a dirty war who began as a patriot. He is every soldier, a normal man caught up in the dehumanizing actions that war demands.

8. Did you ever get just plain depressed by the actions some of the characters take (or are forced to take), and did you ever feel the urge to make parts of the book less graphic and therefore less painful? How difficult was it to envision a happy ending?

The research was so chilling that sometimes I would leave the library and take a walk in the sun, but writing the story, I could create a rescuer like Magda. I could save the children from death, which made a happy ending tempered by tragedy. When I finished the writing, I realized that I had not killed a single child in the novel. You hear of children dying, but do not see it. This was unconscious on my part and quite unrealistic since Poland lost over twenty percent of her children. I procrastinated writing Magda's death scene for weeks. As soon as I accepted that I couldn't bear to kill Magda, I sat down and wrote the chapter. It was terrible to kill a character I loved so much even though she is only a part of my imagination.

9. Though the novel is called The True Story of Hansel and Gretel, *it is also the story of the father and stepmother, of Magda and her brother, and of the entire village of Piaski. How did you incorporate so many different voices into one narrative? Were any of these characters based on real people?*

None of the characters were based on people I know. When I write a novel, I seem to create characters who are people I would like to meet, people I hope exist, people I hope to become myself someday, or people that frighten me. If my life requires it, I want Magda's courage, Father Piotr's self-knowledge, the Major's strength, Nelka and Telek's passion, and Hansel's capacity for survival.

10. How important was it to you, as the author, to let there be satisfaction for certain characters, and justice for others? Did you feel a responsibility to lend a kind of moral balance to a situation that was distinctly unjust?

Like most people who read about the Holocaust and the circumstances of any people occupied and at war, I long for justice. The story of Father Piotr and his final actions is a very complicated effort to show a man yearning for justice for himself and his family. I punish the Oberführer at the end, but I hope the lingering fear is present in the reader that this man will return, as evil always returns to haunt us. The responsibility of the artist is to try and find the truth, regardless of whether it is comfortable or not, but the moral balance is ultimately on the side of good people who manage to save children by courageous action.

11. The ultimate goal of the story seems to be to pass on hope, and to praise the value of love; this is certainly how Magda, as the narrator, frames the tale. How difficult was it to keep the idea of love meaningful while also writing so unflinchingly about evil?

I never really thought in terms of what abstract ideas I was presenting or not presenting while writing. Most novel writers become so involved in creating the characters and the plot, we leave the analysis to others. After the novel is done, we see things we did that weren't consciously conceived, and good readers tell us things we didn't see while we wrote. It is after the novel is completed that we find out what we, in our deepest heart, believe about life, and that is our own truth we give the world in our art. I believe there are as many truths about life as there are artists.

12. You dedicate this novel to your son. What are your thoughts about passing on memories and knowledge about the Holocaust to younger generations? Is this topic one that you plan to keep to in future writing, or do you feel that now you will move on?

Watching my son and a daughter become adults, I have been impressed with how much harder their decisions are than when I was growing up. The fluidity of values, the availability of drugs, the commonplace occurrence of divorce, and the movement of people every few years to find work has changed our world. I hope, perhaps too optimistically, that by showing the darkness of the Holocaust to our young adults, we will teach them to reject racism and war.

I was born in 1943, perhaps the darkest year the world has ever seen. Because I was born in the United States, I survived, but felt compelled to understand the time of my own birth. For all of my reading and work, I will never "understand" the Holocaust. It is too huge, too terrible to categorize or comprehend, but this novel is the best I can do to present the period that so deeply disturbs me. I doubt that I will write about this again.

QUESTIONS FOR DISCUSSION

1. Murphy begins and ends her fairy tale with the words of the wise witch Magda, who is the children's savior. She's an outsider from the village of Piaski, with Gypsy heritage, but she's also a relative to many characters: an aunt, a sister, and a surrogate mother to the children. How is she a traditional witch? What abilities mark her as such? How does she display her unconventional morals when considering the affairs of others? Why does Murphy make her a kind of narrator?

2. The primeval forest of Bialowieza is itself a character in this novel. It's a place that is harsh and wild but that offers protection to the children, to Magda, and to the Partisans as they work to oust the Germans. How does the forest enhance the fairy-tale sensibility? Does the forest have a personality; and if so, how would you describe it?

3. The forest is filled with wild beasts: the wild ponies, the elusive bison, the mad boar. Think back to some of the encounters characters have with these animals. How do wild animals function as symbols in the story? How do they connect characters? Do they serve as indicators of change at certain crucial moments in the plot?

4. Nelka and Telek are the romantic center of the novel. Each is forced to undertake harrowing actions in order to protect their families and the villagers. Telek in particular is forced to inflict harm in order to prevent an even greater wrong. What do these sacrifices bring them? How do you think they are able to endure these horrors and still imagine a future for themselves as lovers?

5. The stepmother is not a traditional fairy-tale stepmother; she is portrayed very positively, as an independent woman and a brave guardian of Hansel and Gretel's father. She does, however, make some excruciating decisions for the Mechanik and his children, decisions that have major consequences for them all. Consider different points in the story when she is forced to make painful choices; do you agree with those choices? Could she have acted differently? Do you think her fate—she is, after all, the stepmother— is a necessity of the fairy-tale genre?

6. At the start of novel, the children are given new names by the stepmother; they will struggle after a while to remember their original ones. Other characters receive new names too: the father becomes the Mechanik, the stepmother the White Wolf. The father notes that "His name had disappeared with the war"; what does this loss of names symbolize? Why do so many of the Partisans go by aliases? Why do you think Murphy chose not to reveal everyone's "real" names?

7. Memory is a key theme, especially for Gretel. At the start of the novel, she is already complaining that time in the ghetto has marred her memories of life before the war. By the end, those memories become key to her emotional well-being. What does it mean for her to lose and/or retain memories of a home before the trauma? How does memory serve the children during their quest to stay alive and find their father? Do you think Murphy implies there is a symbolic or real relationship between people and memory?

8. In many ways, this novel details a fairy-tale world, one with magical animals, the true love of Nelka and Telek, and a woman known as a witch. A traumatized Gretel spends part of the novel in the realm of madness, and for her it ultimately becomes important that she leave behind her immersion in fantasy and face reality. Hansel, too, has to give up playing war and lead his sister in a very real struggle for survival. Do you think that Murphy is suggesting that too much belief in fantasy can be an obstacle to maturity or to finding resolution? Or do you think that she shows how belief—in fairy tales, magic, and beauty—can help us overcome trials? Will Gretel continue to be an unusual child, or do you imagine her as more ordinary—more normal—as we leave her at the end of the book?

9. Both religion and magic infuse this story. There are scenes of Father Piotr's agony over his fallen priesthood, Hansel's folk cure for Gretel when she has the grippe, and Gretel holding a personal Shabbas. Often traditional church-centered worship and a more female-oriented magic or paganism have been in conflict in Europe and America; here it seems that a more immediate experience of evil erodes that conflict, at least for some of the central characters. How does this story allow church and magic to coexist? What does this say about the nature of spirituality for some of the characters?

10. On the other hand, the Partisans are distinctly antireligious; they dream of a godless communism to supplant the bloody passions of a world they view as too irrational. The father became an assimilated, nonreligious Jew, and throughout the book he struggles with his own inability to believe in God. At the same time he is trying with all his might to believe, against all logic, that his children will survive. How did the ending resolve this conflict in him, or did it? And what is Murphy suggesting about the place of religion in an ethical society, whether it be postwar revolutionary communist, or family-based? What place do you

think religion will—or should—have for the main characters in their new lives?

11. The village of Piaski is populated by many types of people: there are ordinary Polish citizens, collaborators, and secret revolutionaries, alongside Nazis and their imported workers. Though there are, as one character notes, "so many reasons to hate the war," many of the villagers seem to be trying to simply endure the world of devastation that is closing in on their small town in the hopes that the war will end before they have to make greater sacrifices. Who in the town did you sympathize with? Try to recall villagers you would characterize as collaborators. Were their actions understandable to you? What about Hansel's childish admiration for the Nazis? What might you have done in a similar situation?

12. The end of the novel brings satisfaction for some, but doesn't avoid the real consequences of the war on the lives of these characters; all of them face futures that are radically altered from anything they have known before. Which characters do you think achieved redemption? Who got what they deserved? What do you think the future will be like for Hansel and Gretel? For the people of Piaski?

———————

For more information about or to order other Penguin Readers Guides, please e-mail the Penguin Marketing Department at reading@us.penguingroup.com or write to us at:

Penguin Books Marketing Dept.
Readers Guides
375 Hudson Street
New York, NY 10014-3657

Please allow 4–6 weeks for delivery.
To access Penguin Readers Guides online, visit the Penguin Group (USA) Web site at www.penguin.com